THE

grown ups

Also by Robin Antalek

THE
grown ups

ROBIN ANTALEK

wm

WILLIAM MORROW
An Imprint of HarperCollins*Publishers*

Grateful acknowledgement is made for permission to reprint the following:

The lines from "(The Floating Poem, Unnumbered)" of "Twenty-One Love Poems." Copyright © 2013 by The Adrienne Rich Literary Trust. Copyright © 1978 by W. W. Norton & Company, Inc., from *Later Poems: Selected and New, 1971–2012* by Adrienne Rich. Used by permission of W. W. Norton & Company, Inc.

P.S.™ is a trademark of HarperCollins Publishers.

HarperCollins books may be purchased for educational, business, or sales promotional use. For information please e-mail the Special Markets Department at SPsales@harpercollins.com.

FIRST EDITION

Designed by Diahann Sturge

Library of Congress Cataloging-in-Publication Data has been applied for.

ISBN 978-0-06-230247-2

15 16 17 18 19 OV/RRD   10 9 8 7 6 5 4 3 2 1

For Mary Elizabeth and Mary Julia

O the evening deep in the darkling hamlets of childhood.
The pond beneath the willows
Fills with the tainted sighs of sadness.

—Georg Trakl, "The Nearness of Death"

ONE

Happy Birthday, Suzie Epstein
Sam—1997

I t was the summer all the children in the neighborhood caught a virus.

One by one they were felled for a week that involved buckets next to beds and cool towels to swab foreheads and mouths. Their mothers speculated on the origin, placing silent blame on Suzie Epstein's fifteenth birthday party, where Sarah Epstein, derailed by an argument with her estranged husband that took place in the front driveway of their home during the party, left twenty or so unattended teenagers to open all the cans of soda in the cooler and cut the cake, sharing forks and drinks and saliva with abandon. The bug spread so fast that Suzie Epstein's party had taken on the mythic proportions of a bacchanalia, the gossip chain now fueled by exhausted women whose nostrils were lined with the sour smell of their children's vomit.

In the evenings, when stomachs had quieted before the next bout began, women gathered on front stoops. If you looked down the street at dusk you would see an uneven trail of red dots, like a runway lit by a madman. Mothers, solitary and weary smokers, afraid to spread the germs to one another's homes, called from porch to porch to check on the wellness of the children contained within. *How's Frankie? Ruthie? Bella? Peter? Did Mindy get it too? Has the fever broken yet? Do you need extra buckets? I'll leave some on your porch.*

They drifted off to sleep to the disembodied voices of their mothers floating through the open bedroom windows as they lay twisted in pastel sheets, now slightly damp from their fevers, their stomachs hollow and their ribs aching.

By that first crack of daylight, as most of their fathers left for the train station, newspapers landed on doorsteps next to a pile of cigarette butts and often a lone empty glass, where the ghost of foam stuck to the rim. Milk soured in boxes and the deliveries were reduced from two days to one because no one felt well enough to drink milk, let alone dunk a cookie. It would be weeks before real food had any appeal: vacations got canceled; sleepaway camp and swim lessons and summer jobs were missed. In the glare of late July, as most of them recovered slowly, they left their houses in the mornings stepping onto unusually quiet streets, squinting into the sun, their arms, legs, and chests pale as December.

Sam was among the last to get sick, which surprised him because Suzie Epstein had been first, probably adding to the rumor of guilt. In truth, Suzie and Sam had missed the birthday cake and the cola. From where they were sitting in the basement, in the room where Mr. Epstein had been living before he moved out, they could hear their friends singing "Happy Birthday," unaware or uncaring that Suzie wasn't present. Thigh touching thigh, they sat on the floor, their backs against the bed, as Suzie showed Sam the box of photographs that she had found hidden in the closet way on the top shelf, covered with woolen ski sweaters patterned with snowflakes. The photographs were stored in a dented Buster

Brown shoebox, the lid ripped at the corners, mended with ample amounts of Scotch tape.

Suzie placed the box gently on Sam's lap. Due to the proximity of her bare brown thighs against his own, he was grateful for the extra coverage. "Here," Suzie sighed as Sam lifted the lid. As if she knew too well what he was about to see. The sound escaping from her lips would be something Sam forever associated with anticipation and disappointment.

Clara Stevens, Mindy's mother, was the first face Sam recognized. She was on the bench by the little kids' swings in Westside Park, laughing into the camera. It looked like a totally normal picture except that her skirt had gathered at the top of her thighs so a triangle of her underpants was slightly exposed.

Esther Newman, Ruthie and Celia's mother, was next. Her photo showed her in the Epsteins' pool, her floral bikini top bright, her arms blurry, splashing water at the photographer. Sam lifted each photo slowly, curious which mother he would encounter next and a little afraid to see his own mother included in Mr. Epstein's bizarre collection. The photos certainly weren't worthy of the *Playboy* magazines Johnny Ross and Sam had discovered in Johnny's basement, where Dr. Ross had hid them behind the nonworking toilet. But he did wonder what Dr. Ross would think of his own bikini-wearing wife sitting with her legs crossed at the ankles on the edge of the Epsteins' diving board.

The exceptions to the photographs were Mrs. Chang, who was older than their mothers and had adopted Peter when he was five; Mrs. Spade, Bella's mother, who had been in and out of the hospital for as long as Sam could remember; Mrs. Epstein, whom Sam didn't expect to see; and his own mother. Every other mother in the neighborhood was there.

Sam fanned the photos out in his hand, as if Suzie and he

were about to play a round of cards, before he dropped them back into the box. Suzie replaced the lid and took the box from his lap and went back over to the closet. She climbed on the chair and raised her arms above her head, and when she did her T-shirt lifted too and Sam could see the underside of her bathing suit top, where her breasts swelled away from her narrow torso.

When Suzie was done she sat back down next to him. Sam turned his head, about to ask her what she thought the box of photographs meant, and her face collided with his. Her mouth missed his that initial attempt, then their teeth hit painfully, and then somehow their lips were firmly pressed together. Sam couldn't say who opened his or her mouth first, but as soon as he felt Suzie's tongue against his, Sam's entire body was hot all over. His hands were down at his sides, as were Suzie's, and so they leaned awkwardly toward each other, connected only by their lips and then their tongues. Sam didn't even know how long it lasted. Longer than when Bella Spade and he had been locked in Peter Chang's closet during a game of Seven Minutes in Heaven and longer than the kisses he'd received from Mindy, Ruthie, and Celia during games of Spin the Bottle.

He didn't know how much longer they would have gone on kissing had they not heard Mr. Epstein's tires squeal against the drive as he backed out of the driveway, signifying that before long Mrs. Epstein's attention would once again be focused on the birthday party and, specifically, Suzie's absence from it.

When Suzie pulled back, Sam thought she would be embarrassed. Instead she smiled at him, her chin tucked to her chest. He noticed for the first time that she had a constellation of freckles on her left cheek that formed the letter S.

"Happy birthday," Sam sputtered, suddenly unable to think

of anything to say. He had known Suzie so long they had swum naked in each other's kiddie pools when they were toddlers.

"Thanks," Suzie whispered, her lips puffy and shiny from their saliva.

As it turned out, they could have stayed in the basement with their mouths attached for all the attention Mrs. Epstein paid them. Sam had come up before Suzie and saw Mrs. Epstein do nothing more than glance at the destroyed birthday cake before she slipped through the sliding glass doors and disappeared into the kitchen. He doubted she even noticed the clouds of yellow and blue frosting from the food fight floating in the pool like phosphorescent lily pads. She didn't bother to close the heavy glass doors all the way behind her, even though when Mr. Epstein lived there he could be heard shouting at Suzie and her brothers to close the door behind them, that he was tired of air-conditioning the outdoors. Sam watched Mrs. Epstein take a bottle of vodka from the cabinet over the refrigerator and pour herself a juice-glassful that she tossed back in one angry shot. When she was done she gagged a little, dropping the glass into the sink and holding the back of her hand against her mouth.

After that Mrs. Epstein moved further into the deep, dark coolness of the Epstein family home and she never emerged again, even as Suzie was opening her presents.

✦ ✦ ✦

The second time Mr. Epstein caused a scene in the driveway of the Epstein family home, the neighborhood was still under siege by the virus and was unusually quiet for the middle of a summer day. Later their mothers wondered aloud how Mrs.

Epstein could be so caught off guard, as the German motor of Mr. Epstein's diesel Mercedes-Benz heralded his arrival, enough to cause them to stop their various activities—hanging the laundry, changing the bed linens, deciding what, if anything, was needed for dinner—so that they all tensed and wondered whether they should call and see if Sarah Epstein needed them. But they didn't. Sam didn't know if it had anything to do with the existence of the photographs, but even his mother stayed inside that day while Mr. Epstein, from the driveway, his Mercedes still running, called his wife a drunk and threatened to report her to the police for child neglect if she didn't let him in the house to get his things.

When Mrs. Epstein had had enough she called the police, a fact she told Mr. Epstein from the front door, but then Mr. Epstein punched his fist through the screen door. Mrs. Epstein was faster. She slammed the inner door before he could unlatch the screen door. Everyone could hear him cursing that she had broken his fingers. When the police arrived Mr. Epstein was still standing on the front lawn, shouting and holding his throbbing digits. The police had to threaten to club him to get him to leave.

Sam was still sick then, too weak to get out of bed and look out the window. The shouting, though, woke him from a fever dream. The ice chips in the glass his mother had left on his nightstand had melted. Before he fell back asleep Sam wondered if Suzie was home, if she was still sick, if she was sitting in the basement looking through the pictures and thinking they were what her father had come to collect. One thing was for sure: he wasn't there for Suzie and her brothers.

The For Sale sign on the Epsteins' front lawn was the first thing Sam saw when he emerged from the house after being sick. There was a freshly planted pot of flowers on the front stoop, the screen door had been mended, and all evidence of a family with children living there had been erased.

Sam rode his bike to the town pool; apparently the Epsteins' pool was off-limits now. Mostly everyone had gotten better before him, and he was relieved to see Suzie Epstein among the group, in the same bikini she'd had on the day of her birthday party. Seeing her, Sam experienced warmth spreading through his body all over again.

Sam failed at making eye contact, and he wasn't sure if Suzie wanted their friends to know about them, or even if there was a *them*. He had zero experience with this kind of thing. Eventually, Suzie left with Bella Spade and Ruthie Newman, taking the long way around the pool and avoiding Sam altogether. If that was what she wanted, who was Sam to stop her?

They always hung out in Peter Chang's basement because Mrs. Chang took a sleeping pill and went to bed at ten o'clock every single night, and nothing ever woke her, not even a dozen kids in her basement. That night it started out with just Peter, Sam, Johnny Ross, and Frankie Cole. They had nearly exhausted their vomit stories from the past few weeks when Stephen Winters arrived with a six-pack of beer he had swiped from his parents' anniversary party a few weeks back and had kept hidden in the old fort they had built in the woods summers ago. The boys each popped the tab on the still-warm beer and brought it to their mouths quickly before the foam erupted. It tasted like the vomit they had just been bragging about, but they drank it. They were arguing about the last can when Mindy Stevens, Bella Spade, and Ruthie Newman arrived, at which point it was decided that they would let the girls drink the remaining beer.

"Where's Suzie?" Johnny asked.

Bella shrugged. "She had to babysit her brothers or something."

Sam wasn't sure if Bella was looking at him when she said that or if he was drunk and reading something into nothing; either way, he busied himself with the channel changer, trying to find something to watch on the fuzzy old black and white TV.

"Turn that the fuck off, Turner," Stephen called. "Grab that bottle off the table and get your ass over here." He pointed at the wine bottle they used for Spin the Bottle.

Sam picked it up and tossed it at Stephen. The girls swayed as a group to get out of the way and then they laughed, splitting apart like bowling pins that had been hit and settling into comfortable positions on the floor. "Come on, Sam, I saved you a place," Ruthie Newman said, patting the floor by her and giggling.

Sam walked over and sat down next to Ruthie. He felt more buzzed than he thought was normal after drinking a single beer. But he still wasn't eating very much and his mother had remarked that morning when he walked through the kitchen without a T-shirt on that he looked too skinny.

Sam leaned back against the wall and was about to close his eyes when Bella Spade said, "I have a surprise." She shoved her hand in the back pocket of her denim cutoffs and pulled out a twisted piece of tinfoil. She opened it carefully and held out her palm so they could see she had a joint in her hand.

"Seriously?" Peter Chang was on his feet looking for matches before Bella could respond.

Bella nodded. "My mother gets it from a doctor. It helps her feel better."

Frankie looked over at Bella with a newfound respect. "Your mother has a dealer?"

"It's not like that," Bella said, starting to look upset. Ruthie patted her on the leg, and then Peter produced an orange Bic lighter from between the couch cushions.

The first time they took deep drags and coughed and then after that Bella told them what she had seen her mother do and they were quick studies, all of them holding in their smoke until it looked like their cheeks and eyeballs were about to burst. The buzz came quickly, a soft, floating feeling that was better than the beer. They started to play Spin the Bottle, but as soon as Peter began kissing Ruthie, Johnny went for Mindy and Stephen groped for Bella. Frankie was still pulling on the joint, his eyes half closed, and Sam wandered out of the Changs' basement without saying goodbye.

He rode his bike through the dark, winding neighborhood streets until he was in front of the Epsteins' For Sale sign. Across the street the lights in his own home were flickering from the living room, which meant his parents were up watching television. He rolled his bike into a thicket of bushes at the edge of the Epsteins' driveway. He didn't want his mother, who often ended her night with a cigarette on the front porch, looking across the street at his bike.

Around back by the pool area Sam stood on his toes and peered over the stockade fence. Suzie was in the pool with her clothes on, floating around on an orange raft. "Hey," he whispered.

Suzie lifted herself up on her elbows and peered in his direction. She didn't look surprised. "Are you coming in?"

"Can I?"

Suzie rolled her eyes and Sam opened the gate, closing it carefully behind him. "My mom is out," she said.

"Oh."

"My brothers are watching a movie." She put her fingers to her lips and smiled. "You coming in?" She dipped her fingers in the water and flicked them at Sam.

Sam hesitated, still feeling very buzzed. "Why don't you come out?"

Suzie paddled to the stairs. When she got out the back of her T-shirt and shorts were wet and stuck to her body. She made a face and Sam said, "I guess it didn't make a difference."

She shrugged. "It was so warm I didn't even realize it, you know?" There were shadows in her cheeks and under her eyes that Sam had never noticed before.

"Were you sick a long time?"

"I guess. More than a week. My brothers got it too." She came up close to him and grabbed his hand. "How about you?"

Her hand felt like the skeleton of a bird in his. Sam held it lightly, carefully. "I just got over it."

She nodded. "I don't think I started it then. 'Cause, well. You know."

Sam's heart was thudding in his ears. "Yeah," he offered, "it wasn't you."

"Are you drunk?"

"I had a beer at Peter's."

"Did you smoke it?"

"What?"

Suzie hit him on the shoulder. "Come on. Bella's my best friend."

"Oh, yeah. Well, yeah." He coughed. "Bella's nice."

"Yeah, she's really nice. Why do you think she's my best friend?" Suzie smirked.

"So you liked it? Her mom gets some really strong stuff."

"Oh, have you? Before, I mean?"

"What do you think?"

Sam shrugged and Suzie laughed without making a sound.

"Come on." She tugged on his hand and before he knew it they were inside her house stumbling down the carpeted stairs to the basement.

He knew where they were going before they got there, and he knew she would get the box out. This time she set it down on the rumpled bedspread and plopped down beside it in her damp shorts and shirt. Sam had the thought that someone would know they had been down there if they saw the stains left behind by her wet clothes, but then Suzie grabbed his hand again and pulled him onto the bed, the box between them.

"Go ahead," she urged. She leaned back against the wall, her eyes half closed, a dreamy look on her face. "Go ahead and open it."

The photographs were in the same order as they had been the first time Sam saw them. He searched for something more in the mothers' faces, but he couldn't see anything. "What do you think these are from?"

Suzie exhaled. "I think my father was fucking them and my mother found out."

At Suzie's use of the word *fuck* Sam felt a twinge in his belly. He swallowed hard but it felt like something was caught in his throat. "I don't know, Suze" he said, returning the photographs to the box. He had been in the Rosses' kitchen earlier that evening and Mrs. Ross had given him a Coke. He thought of Mr. Epstein, who worked on Wall Street and made a lot of money. More money, he had heard his father comment to his mother, than probably anyone in the neighborhood.

Sam heard the box drop to the floor and felt Suzie's hand on his shoulder. She pushed him back and straddled his left leg, her upper body pressed against his so hard he could feel her breasts, and then their mouths were together again. Sam wondered if she thought his chest felt skinny. He brought his arms around her like he had done this every day of his life. Even though they had only been here once before, it already seemed easier.

Suzie's wet T-shirt stuck to Sam's hands. He searched for a dry place to put them but there was none. He hesitated, but there was no objection from Suzie as his hands found their way under her shirt to her bra strap. His breath caught in his throat as he fumbled with the clasp.

And then all of a sudden Suzie stopped kissing him and rolled off to the side.

"I'm sorry," Sam said quickly. His voice sounded funny to his ears, rough, like he had been coughing.

Suzie said nothing, and it took Sam a moment to realize she was pulling her shirt above her head and tossing it on the floor. He rolled over on his side and hoisted himself up on his elbow and looked down at Suzie Epstein's white bra. Her stomach quivered as Sam lowered a hand slowly onto the fabric covering her breast. Sam was grateful for the little bit of distance between their bodies, because the zipper of his jeans was strained tightly and he didn't know what to do about it. Suzie sighed as he tentatively moved his fingers over the top of her bra and touched her breast, drawing out the small, hard nipple.

All of a sudden there came a thump from above followed by a scuffle, what sounded like possibly a piece of furniture being knocked over, and then Suzie's brothers loudly shouting her name. Sam stopped moving.

Suzie's eyelids fluttered open. "No," she groaned. "Damnit." She sat up and looked for her shirt. Sam rolled onto his back and swept the floor with his hand, hitting the box before finding the shirt. He handed it to her and watched as she jumped off the end of the bed and pulled it over her head. "Don't move," she commanded. "I'll be right back."

"But . . ."

"Seriously, stay." She turned and ran out of the room. Sam stayed on his back for a moment, remembering the feel of Suzie Epstein's hard nipple in his fingers, before he slowly rolled off the bed.

Whatever was happening upstairs wasn't getting any better. Sam heard several more thumps followed by screaming. He shook his head to clear the images of Suzie on the bed. Sam was standing there so long dreaming of Suzie that he didn't realize someone had turned into the Epsteins' driveway. He heard the car door close, keys hit the pavement, mumbling, cursing, and then the retrieval of keys as they jangled together.

His only choices were to leave through the Epsteins' driveway and reveal himself or go deeper into the woods to the fort. Without thinking, he put the box away and straightened the bedspread where wet marks crept across the folds of the cloth. He took the pillows and rearranged them so they covered the darker areas before he ran up the cellar stairs and out of the Epsteins' house.

Sam's bike was where he left it and his house was dark. He thought of going back to Peter Chang's to spend the night, as he had planned, but he didn't move. He imagined what Suzie would look like when she came back downstairs and saw that Sam was gone. But he didn't know what else to do.

When Sam arrived home the next day his father was sitting at the kitchen table staring at the rooster clock on the wall. Sam knew his father hated the rooster clock. "It isn't even ironic,

Elizabeth," he had said after Sam's mother insisted on hanging it above the table.

Sam was sore from sleeping on the floor of the fort and hungry. He stood at the open refrigerator forever, but when his father didn't even reprimand him he finally said, "What's up, Dad?"

"Your mother is out."

"Okay," Sam said, slowly grabbing a piece of cheese and shutting the door. "Is she shopping? 'Cause there isn't any food."

"Huh?"

Sam rubbed his stomach. "No food." He pointed at the refrigerator.

His dad blinked at him and then looked back at the rooster. Sam's older brother, Michael, was at a science camp at Johns Hopkins for brilliant kids who would one day save the world. Michael had been gone since the beginning of the summer and sometimes Sam felt like their father was just waiting for him to get home.

Sam went to his room and fell back against the bed. He couldn't stop thinking about how mad Suzie Epstein probably was about finding him gone. He curled up on his side, his mouth tasting like crud from the cheese. He thought about getting up and taking a shower and brushing his teeth and going to the pool. Then he heard a car door slam. His mother, he hoped, back from the store. Sam peered out his bedroom window, which faced the street.

His mother was sitting in the car, staring at the house. The engine was off and the driver's side door was open, yet her hands were still on the steering wheel. She checked something in the rearview mirror, and that was when Sam saw that Mrs. Epstein was out in her front yard, pulling weeds from around the mailbox and planting flowers. Suzie was standing in the driveway in shorts and a bikini top, leaning against her bike and talking to her mother. A towel was wrapped around her handlebars.

Slowly, Sam's mother got out of the car. She took several steps toward the end of the driveway and called out, "How are you, Sarah?"

Mrs. Epstein glanced up, a clump of dirt in her hand. Suzie looked at Sam's mother and then stared hard at her feet, long and thin in black flip-flops.

Sam's mother waited a few minutes, and when neither Mrs. Epstein nor Suzie responded, she turned away. She moved toward the door of her house, Sam's house, like a heavy person who has to stop to catch her breath between steps. It took Sam a few minutes to realize that wherever his mother had been that morning, there hadn't been groceries involved.

At the pool Sam inhaled two hot dogs and an order of fries and listened to Peter Chang and Johnny Ross talk about the munchies. They claimed to have had the munchies so bad the night before that they had eaten three frozen pizzas after Bella, Ruthie, and Mindy had left. They elbowed each other in the ribs and talked about how they had been feeling the love from the girls, and Sam's fingers twitched thinking of his hand on Suzie's bra.

When the girls arrived at the pool Suzie was with them. Sam was in the deep end, hanging out underneath the diving board. She jumped in and swam the length of the pool underwater, grabbing his foot before she surfaced.

"Hey," she said when she came up for air.

"Hey." Sam paused. "So you know, I'm not some kind of jerk who just leaves."

"You're forgiven." Suzie smiled. "Seriously. It was probably good you left."

"Oh, oh. Great." Sam wondered if she meant she wanted him to leave or that he had done the right thing. His stomach clenched.

He had no idea all of this was so complicated. He waited, unsure of what to say next.

Suzie smiled again. "Great? So, you weren't having a good time?"

"Of course, yes. Yes I was. I don't want you to get in trouble."

"I was thinking . . ."

"About?"

"Well, you. Us. And how we need to maybe make a plan?"

"A plan?" It dawned on Sam that maybe Suzie was talking about a date. "Like going out?"

Suzie sighed. "How about you meet me in the fort tonight? Around ten?"

"The fort," Sam answered slowly. He didn't want to tell her he'd been in the fort the night before because he was scared to walk through her driveway. As he was about to answer, Suzie dove back underwater and swam quickly toward the girls.

✦ ✦ ✦

Neither of his parents was home for dinner and both cars were gone. Usually when they went out his mother left a meal in the fridge or money for pizza, but those things hadn't happened tonight. So Sam went over to Peter Chang's, where Mrs. Chang was just taking a sheet of Tater Tots out of the oven. Mrs. Chang liked to feed all of them and always welcomed them at mealtimes. She was afraid that Peter was lonely, since he was an only child.

The three of them polished off cheeseburgers and the Tater Tots, and then Sam and Peter went down to the basement. Johnny Ross came over with a half bottle of vodka. They shared the remains until it was gone, and Sam recalled seeing Mrs. Epstein wince after she drank that juice-glassful.

At quarter to ten Sam told Peter and Johnny he had to be home early and headed to the fort. He swept the leaves out with his hands and kicked himself that he hadn't thought to bring a blanket or something soft. He ran his fingers over the initials he and his friends had carved into the sides with a pocketknife and tried hard to remember what it felt like to be ten. S.T., P.C., F.C., S.W., and J.R. Sam recalled how they hadn't let the girls carve their initials because they hadn't done any of the work. It felt like a lifetime ago.

Suzie arrived with a tightly rolled joint, another one from Bella's mom's stash. She was wearing a black top that tied around her neck, leaving her back bare. Sam's mouth was dry at the thought that if he undid that knot, Suzie Epstein would be naked from the waist up.

They smoked half the joint, maybe less, before Suzie climbed into his lap and they were kissing and touching like the night before. When Sam shifted position because of the situation in his pants, Suzie batted her hand against him and Sam groaned out loud and was immediately embarrassed. "I need to catch my breath, Suzie, okay?" he said.

Suzie rolled off of Sam, sat up, and leaned against the opposite wall of the fort with her legs stretched out in front of her. Her hair was wild, a tangle of black curls, and her skin looked red from where he had kissed her. "Just so you know," she said, "I don't need to stop."

Sam laughed. He guessed it was easier in some ways to be a girl. "Well, I do."

"I'm aware." She smiled again and picked up the joint and the matches off the floor. "Want to smoke the rest?" She didn't wait for his response to light the joint and take the first hit.

They passed it back and forth until it was a tiny nub burning their fingers. Sam closed his eyes; the pot had calmed him down.

"So I guess I was wrong. You don't need the pictures to get excited, huh?"

"What? Your father's pictures?"

"I figured that's what guys need, right? Isn't that why they make those magazines with all those girls spreading their legs?"

"Suzie, come on." Sam thought of the magazines he and Johnny Ross had found. He thought the smiles on the faces of the naked women had been creepy, especially the ones who had their hands down between their legs. He didn't want to think of Suzie like that.

"Okay." Suzie's voice sounded small and sad. Sam opened his eyes. She was staring at him in the dark, her face unreadable. "Would you just hold me?" she asked. "I think I just want a hug."

Sam nodded and she crawled across the small space between them. Sam opened his arms and she curled up in the hollow, her head on his chest. He held her hard.

Two weeks before school started the Epsteins sold their house. Suzie and Sam were in the basement on the bed when she told him. Suzie was naked from the waist up and Sam was still distracted by the sight and feel and taste of her breasts even though they had been his for the better part of the afternoon, ever since Mrs. Epstein had taken the boys to Playland. His bathing trunks were stuck to his leg; he would have to jump in the pool to wash up before he went home.

Sam's chest was heaving still from the exertion of the afternoon when Suzie told him she was moving to somewhere in Massachusetts.

"I don't understand," Sam said. Massachusetts might as well have been the moon from where he lived in Rye.

"You knew this wouldn't last forever."

"What? Us?" Sam was confused. He had been beginning to think this might be what it felt like to be in love. He'd been picturing them going through high school together.

"We've had fun." Suzie ran a finger up his inner thigh. "More fun than I thought we would."

"When are you leaving?"

"Well, my father is coming to get us in a few days."

"Your father?"

Suzie sat up against the headboard. "I think he and my mom are going to try again."

"What?" Sam shook his head.

"My father is going to take me and my brothers on a vacation to Cape Cod while my mother supervises the movers. Then she's going to meet us out there and I guess we'll see how it goes."

"Wow. I thought he hated her." Sam swallowed hard. "I thought she hated him too. I guess you never know, huh?"

"Yeah, I guess."

Sam looked over at Suzie's breasts and wondered how long it would be before he would see them again. He pushed his face between them and inhaled. Suzie put her hand on the back of his head and cradled it before Sam lifted it off her chest and placed his mouth over one perfect brown nipple and then the other. When he pulled away he said, "I don't want to say goodbye." But he wasn't sure if he was talking more about Suzie or her breasts.

The entire neighborhood heard Mr. Epstein's Mercedes rumble through the streets. Sam was sitting on his front porch watching the activity at the Epsteins' and waiting for his last chance to see Suzie. Bella, Ruthie, and Mindy had occupied her entire morning with breakfast and a long, tearful goodbye on the front lawn.

This Mercedes was a newer model: candy apple red, with a

sunroof. If men bought sports cars to signify their single status, Sam wasn't sure what this car said about Mr. Epstein's current bid to take back his family. When Mr. Epstein got out of the car he very carefully avoided looking anywhere, even across the street at Sam's house. He walked with his head down, waved at the gaggle of crying girls, and opened his front door as if he had never left.

When Bella, Ruthie, and Mindy finally departed, Suzie stood in her front yard and looked across at Sam. She stared a really long time, neither smiling nor frowning, and so Sam stood up, unsure of whether she had seen him. Then she waved and held up her finger, disappearing into her house. When she emerged she walked purposefully down the driveway and across the street.

"You have to promise me something," she said as she stood on the top step of the porch, bouncing lightly on the balls of her feet. She was slightly breathless.

"What?"

"You won't open this until I'm gone." She handed Sam a square white envelope. "Please."

Sam was touched that she had written him a letter. He felt stupid for not doing the same. He probably should have gotten her something too, maybe a necklace or bracelet. "I don't have anything for you . . . give me your address so I can send you something."

When Suzie smiled she looked like her mother after Mr. Epstein had first moved out: weary, and tired of carrying around so many secrets. "It's okay. Just promise me. Okay?"

Sam took the envelope. "Sure. But you have to tell me one thing."

"What?"

"Why did you choose me?"

Suzie blinked. "Because you had as much to lose as I did." She threw herself against Sam, her arms tightly wrapped around his neck, kissed him somewhere between his ear and his neck, and then let go. "Goodbye, Sam Turner."

"Goodbye, Suzie Epstein." Sam was confused. Suzie always seemed so confident, and he felt foolish for never quite knowing what was expected. If he asked now what she meant, did it really matter?

Suzie turned and skittered down the steps and across the grass to her house. She didn't look back. Sam watched as the Epsteins loaded up the trunk and Suzie and her brothers jockeyed for the front seat, Suzie ultimately ended up sitting in the back with the youngest of her two brothers. Mrs. Epstein came running out of the house with a cooler. She handed it in the window to Mr. Epstein and lingered on his side a moment longer. As she walked backward Mr. Epstein tooted the horn and opened the sunroof. Suzie and her brothers stuck out their hands and waved to Mrs. Epstein.

Sam stared at the envelope. He had never been good at waiting for anything. He ripped open the seal quickly and the contents— photographs, not a letter—spilled onto the floor. As he bent over to pick them up he caught sight of the bikes carrying Peter Chang, Johnny Ross, Frankie Cole, and Stephen Winters as they rounded the corner, their tires squeaking against the hot pavement as they pedaled to catch up with Mr. Epstein's Mercedes.

Sam stood slowly, so it took him longer than it should have to realize that what he was holding in his hand were pictures of his mother smiling widely into the lens of Mr. Epstein's camera. He looked up just as Suzie, her body half out the sunroof of the Mercedes, began tossing more photos onto the street.

Peter Chang was pedaling his bike hands-free, waving his

arms as he yelled "Suzie, hey, Suzie Q, see you later!" The others bobbed and weaved behind the car, sliding first to the left, then right. Sam imagined Mr. Epstein cursing them as Johnny Ross, always the fastest among them, slapped a hand against the trunk of the Mercedes.

From deep inside the house Sam heard his mother calling his name. All morning she had been up and down the attic stairs, bringing down luggage for a trip he hadn't known she was taking until this very moment. As Suzie Epstein moved farther away, shaking the last of the photos from the shoebox, the neighborhood mothers fluttered in the breeze, suspended for one long, graceful moment in the air, until they fell to the pavement like the paper in a ticker tape parade.

TWO

How to Walk on Ice
Suzie—1998

S uzie was tired of the boys who talked and said nothing. When she had first arrived at the new high school in Brookline, the boys surrounded her while the girls ignored her. The boys spoke over one another, telling jokes to impress her, yet laughed prematurely, obliterating the punch lines. They boasted with tales of athletic accomplishments in sports while moving clumsily, knocking into Suzie and one another, as if their bodies were not their own. They were a force of nature, these boys, and so she put her head down and pushed forward until finally they stopped trying to get her attention.

She was lonely. And she ached for Bella as if an essential part of her anatomy had gone missing. The ache came up on her suddenly, it was like she'd forgotten how to breathe, especially when her thoughts inevitably drifted to Sam. She had never told Bella about Sam. So she couldn't ask about him, or even ask what happened after she left. At first she was certain that Sam must hate her for what she did to him, and then, as time went on, she felt stupid for thinking that any of her old friends still thought about her. They had called and sent letters that Suzie left unanswered. The reputation her parents had created, the very public arguments, the photographs, the making up, had forever tainted Suzie in some way. So if this had been her parents' clean start—why not let it be hers as well?

At her mother's urging, Suzie got her license as soon as she was able. Instead of the road trips she and Bella used to dream about taking one day, she drove her brothers to soccer practices, dentist appointments, and Hebrew school. She picked up takeout food and library books. She used up tanks of gas circling the roads that led to their suburb until her eyes hurt and her fingers grew numb and cramped on the steering wheel. She would have been in touch with Bella if she'd had something good to say about this new life. But what could she possibly tell her?

Her father's position as head of an investment firm in Boston made weeknights as a family impossible. There existed the too-easy excuse of foreign markets and clients in locations where time was reversed, requiring her father to go without sleep in order to keep the world economy running smoothly.

In the beginning, her mother would go into the city to meet him several nights a week. She would take a late-afternoon bath and shave her legs, a small tumbler of vodka perched on the lip of the tub. She always left the door open just enough that Suzie could see her hand as it reached for the glass. The humid, lily-scented air would drift into the bedroom, and Suzie could feel her hair frizzing as she burrowed in her parents' bed, the sound of her brothers arguing filtering fuzzily through the closed bedroom door. Suzie would switch channels with the TV on mute while her mother volleyed questions about her day. There was nothing to tell so Suzie made things up: a new friend to have lunch with, a club she might join, tryouts for the tennis team, a possible run for student council. She enjoyed these little white lies where anything was possible. Her mother never asked any follow-up questions, too absorbed in applying makeup to the contours of her face and perfume to the hollows at her throat, as if she had never had children, as if Suzie were her girlfriend.

Those nights there was always money on the counter for take-out. Suzie spent it all on food until she figured out that her brothers were just as easy to please with a bucket of fried chicken and cylinders of spongy, fluorescent macaroni and cheese. Six months in, she had amassed a couple hundred dollars that she kept stuffed inside a tennis sock in her top drawer.

The spring of Suzie's sophomore year, just barely into this new life, her mother's trips into Boston began to trickle to every other week, until, by the summer, they ever so quietly ceased to exist at all. Her father showed up in Brookline to shower and change, to remove pressed shirts from cardboard boxes, and to refill the dry cleaning bag. By the time they had lived in Brookline for an entire cycle of seasons the routine was set: he paid someone to mow the lawn in the summer, rake the leaves in the fall, and shovel the snow in the winter. He congratulated himself and anyone who would listen for not buying a house with a pool and therefore not needing to pay someone to maintain that, at least.

Instead Suzie's mother joined the JCC, where Suzie's brothers took swimming lessons in an Olympic-sized pool before they were shipped off to New Hampshire for summer camp, and a temple, where she baked challah bread with the rabbi's wife on Fridays. In their previous life they would have been hard-pressed to find the menorah in their house, but here it became apparent, at least to the outside, that the Epsteins were observant.

Without Suzie's brothers to supervise, her mother spent summer weekends entirely behind her closed bedroom door. On

Monday mornings she emerged, showered, a little pale in the face. Her first stop those mornings was the grocery store, from which she would return with a brown bag containing a fresh bottle of vodka that she carefully placed in the freezer, a carton of milk, a box of Cheerios, and a bunch of bananas.

The pretense that there were groceries in the house seemed to convince Suzie they were doing just fine as they bumped up against a year in this new place. Even her father's rare appearances made it look like he was a willing participant in the charade. At the beginning of summer Suzie had been startled to find him at the kitchen counter in the middle of the night, a silver spoon with a slim quarter moon of milk nestled in its bowl as he lifted it to his mouth, a bowl of Cheerios and a soft brown banana in front of him on the counter. "Suzie Q," he said as he slurped the cereal, blotting the corner of his mouth with the back of his hand. He had a sunglasses tan, with lavender smudges beneath his eyes and hair that curled over the collar of his shirt, too long to be fashionable.

Suzie exhaled. It was hard sometimes to reconcile the father who had once punched a hole in the screen door with the man wolfing down Cheerios at the kitchen counter. She wanted to ask him why he wanted this second-chance family so badly when he was never here, but she supposed she already knew that he didn't like to lose.

"What do you want to do with your summer?" he asked.

Suzie moved across the room and filled a glass with water. "Well, I guess what I've been doing."

One half of her father's mouth went up in a reflexive attempt at a smile. "And what is that?"

"I go to the pool, I swim laps, I read." She hesitated and added a lie. "I play doubles with a girl from school."

"Oh yeah? Are you fierce on the court? I should come watch."

"Sure," Suzie lied again, shrugging. "I'm fierce."

"You should be playing singles, then; always have an exit strategy, Suzie Q."

"Really?" She took a shallow breath. "Maybe I'll make varsity this year, since I'm a junior."

He nodded as if it was a given. "Do you need a new racket?"

Suzie shook her head but her father's hand was already rummaging around his back pocket for his wallet. He opened it and fingered through the bills, then extricated one and dropped it on the counter. "Ask the guy at the shop for the best racket. If it costs more than that let me know. Don't buy second best, Suzie. You will regret it."

Suzie didn't realize she had been holding her breath until she reached for the bill. She picked it up and felt light-headed: one hundred dollars. Closing her hand around the money, she tucked her fist into her armpit. "Is Mom sleeping?"

Her father raised his chin slightly and wiggled his jaw from side to side before he answered. "That's what we're calling it?" There was a click followed by a low hum as the air conditioner cycled on. "Then, yes, she is sleeping."

Suzie finished her water in one long swallow and placed her glass in the sink. When she turned around her father had pushed his cereal bowl toward the edge of the counter. She reached for the bowl and put it in the sink alongside her glass and then turned the faucet on to get rid of the milk at the bottom of the bowl. When she looked back over her shoulder her father was gone.

During the week her mother worked side by side with the gardener, kneeling in the freshly tilled earth, planting and then rearranging row after row of perennials, filling the wheelbarrow with mulch and gravel, creating gardens within gardens until sweat saturated her T-shirt and shorts and the yard resembled a patchwork puzzle that always appeared to be a few pieces short. Suzie's mother was the only mother in the neighborhood who worked outside, as far as Suzie could tell, unless tanning and tennis were considered work. In their old neighborhood most of the mothers did some sort of gardening, but here it was always a bunch of guys in a pickup truck who decamped with so much machinery that it looked like a mini military operation was about to take place. In the first muddy, bright days of spring it took all of Suzie's limited high school Spanish to explain to the panicked gardener that her mother was not firing him but wanted to help.

When the milk turned sour in the fridge and the bananas blackened, Suzie would toss them out on her way to the JCC pool. There she worked her way through Freud's *Interpretation of Dreams* while camped out on a lounge chair. She did fifty laps two times a day and existed on lemon ice. Her body was brown, toned, and leaner than it had ever been in her life. She took notice of the hourly rotation of lifeguards, and when she tired of Freud, she appraised their flattened stomachs with the gradation of muscles, and the sharp jut of their hipbones from where their trunks hung in effortless suspension. At least once a week one of them would casually toss her an invite to a party, but she never took any of them up on it.

Though she didn't mean to, she thought of Sam. She wondered why she had always stopped short of going all the way with him. She knew his feelings had been genuine from the beginning, when hers had not. She remembered how his hands shook the first time he touched her breast through her bra, how his entire face had softened, how he had kept his eyes on Suzie as if what they were doing was special, as if Suzie was special. His eyes would widen as his hands grew bolder, although he stopped short of asking permission. There was a real tenderness to Sam that nearly made Suzie forget she didn't care about him. She could tell she confused him, and how scared he was to ask her what they were doing for fear it might stop. She knew he wanted more, whatever more was. He wanted to be a real boyfriend, not just the guy she hooked up with in her basement. The times he attempted to talk about the future she unzipped his fly or took off her bra. Anything to stop him from saying what he felt out loud. She had started out by telling herself she was using him. By the time she realized that things had changed, it was too late. But maybe the real reason was that it had always made her just a little bit angry that Sam was so pliable and that he cared about her feelings, when she had no idea what they were. In the end she hated how she had treated Sam. She hated the person she had become in Sam's eyes and there was no way to take any of it back.

In the late afternoon on her way home from the pool Suzie would stop at the grocery store and make two large salads from the takeout bar. She tried to mix up the ingredients depending upon what they had that day so that dinner held an element of surprise. She and her mother shared the two salads at the iron table on the back patio, the legs uneven on top of a swath of slate, irregular and iridescent, with stones that shimmered like scales in the waning light.

One evening, Suzie picked at her salad, waiting for the moment to tell her mother about the letter from school. Her mother's mood was light, which was surprising. Suzie's brothers were done with camp at the end of the week and school was starting a week after that. Suzie's father had originally said he would pick the boys up, but now he was going to Asia instead. So her mother was driving alone to New Hampshire. Suzie felt pressure to go with her, but she couldn't make herself offer.

"Mom," Suzie started. "I got this thing from school."

Sarah looked up from chasing a chickpea around the container. "A thing?"

"Did you know that I could double up on classes and graduate early?"

Sarah's tongue darted out the corner of her mouth and disappeared again. "How early?"

"A year."

"What?" Sarah's eyebrows shot up, accentuating the dirt trapped at her hairline. "And you would want to do this?" She shook her head. "How does it work?"

"I have a four-point-five GPA and I've taken AP everything since we got here. I'm bored out of my mind. I would just have to double up on my core classes, which would be nothing."

"And then what?"

"Then I go to college a year early." Suzie was relieved to say it out loud. "My guidance counselor thinks I could go anywhere, so why waste a year?"

"Wow," Sarah said slowly as she reached for her glass of iced tea. "You would be gone?" Her voice was low.

Suzie sighed. "I probably won't go that far, Mom. I would still be able to help you out."

Sarah frowned. "I'm sorry."

Suzie shook her head. "What are you apologizing for?"

Sarah sighed. "For making you feel like you have to help me out."

"Mom, I just want to be done with high school, really, I just want to be done." Suzie took a deep breath and tried to keep her voice sincere. "It's nothing about you or, you know, anything. Really."

Her mother looked at her like she was going to say something more, but didn't. Instead she reached across the table for Suzie's takeout container and piled it on top of her own. She pushed back her chair, the iron legs dragging on the stone, and stood.

Suzie stayed seated. She was anxious, but trying not to show it. "Will you sign the papers?"

In the dim light of the porch her mother's eyes looked watery, but Suzie couldn't be sure. She didn't want to make her mother cry. Really. She meant what she said. She just wanted to be done with high school. She wanted to be out of this house. She wanted to be free.

On the afternoon before her brothers came home Suzie added more than the takeout salads to the grocery cart. Sarah had still not said whether she would sign the papers, and Suzie was trying her best to figure out how to ask again. Getting groceries couldn't hurt. It would be one less thing for her mother to do before she left for New Hampshire.

She was standing before the boxes of macaroni and cheese thinking about all of this when someone tapped her on the shoulder. She jumped and turned around. One of the lifeguards from the pool was grinning and trying to reach around her. Their bodies were so close she smelled the suntan lotion wafting off his skin and the heat through his T-shirt. He had been the boldest of the lifeguards throughout the summer: offering lotion, commenting on her reading material, reminding her to hydrate, keeping count of her laps. She looked forward to his quips, although she tried hard not to show it.

She pushed the cart with her hip and moved aside. He laughed and picked two boxes off the shelf and held them out to her. "How many?"

"Oh." Suzie bit her lip, embarrassed all of a sudden for the two of them to be out of context. She liked that he saw her at the pool, not buying mac and cheese at the grocery store. "Uh, four?"

"You're pretty hungry, huh?"

"My brothers," Suzie explained as he dropped the boxes in her cart.

He grabbed two more off the shelf and shook them at her. "Well. These are all for me. I'm starving and broke, so mac and cheese it is."

Suzie smiled and started to roll away, but he put out a hand to stop her. "Hey, where you going?"

"I have to get home."

He nodded slowly and gave her a funny little frown. "You never came to any of the parties we invited you to. Tonight's your last chance. We all go back to college this weekend."

"What about the pool?"

He laughed. "Not my problem, but I think they got it covered. Or kids drown."

Suzie laughed. "Well, the JCC pool is pretty crowded, so they could stand to lose a few . . ." He laughed with her and Suzie felt a little thrill in her gut.

"Smart and funny." He grinned again and leaned on the cart. "How many books did you read this summer anyway?"

Suzie felt her cheeks get hot.

"Come on, you have to come out tonight." He paused and smiled. "You know where 2424 Merrywood Lane is?"

Suzie nodded. The address was in a development a few streets over from her own. She knew from driving her brothers around that the houses were large and similar to hers in newness, but closer together on smaller, less wooded lots.

After he got a maybe out of her, he moved aside so Suzie could continue shopping. She pushed past him, randomly taking things off the shelves, acting as if she knew all along what it was she was looking for.

It was true that Suzie felt a little less sorry for her mother the second time around. It was hard to muster sympathy for someone who knew exactly what it was she was willingly getting back into. If Sarah Epstein couldn't remember what it felt like to be called names, to have her screen door punched in, to have the police called, she should have asked Suzie. All Suzie knew was that if she ever trusted another human being enough to become his wife, she would never choose someone like her father, and certainly not twice.

As she pulled into the driveway she vowed to try hard not to get in an argument with her mother tonight. She thought about how they were more than this one moment, this one lousy dinner of takeout salads on the patio at dusk on a summer night in a place that was as random as any on the map. She hated how this place now had become more than geography, how it held the weight of starting over, and the stink of disappointment.

Sarah was at the table on the patio when Suzie walked in. She put the perishables away, left everything else on the kitchen counter, and carried their salads outside. Her mother had a map spread out on the table before her and was diligently writing down directions on the back of an envelope. She waved a hand away when Suzie tried to set the salad down. "I'm not hungry."

Suzie fought the urge to drop the salad on the patio. Instead she made room next to Sarah's elbow on the small table and set about opening her salad and digging in. She wasn't even that hungry herself. But she would eat even if she threw up. She wouldn't sulk like her mother.

After a few minutes of silence Suzie said, "Do you want me to do that for you?" She pointed to the map with her fork. A piece of spinach was caught in the tines.

"I'm good," Sarah answered quickly. "How was your day?" She didn't look up, although she had stopped writing.

"Fine. Good."

"Did you play today?"

"I hate tennis, Mom."

Finally, Sarah looked up.

"But I won every match."

"Why do you play if you hate it?"

"Why do people do anything they hate?"

"I'm not sure, Suzie."

"Neither am I." Suzie felt the prick of tears at the back of her throat and swallowed hard, refusing to allow herself any weakness.

"Listen." Sarah leaned forward across the small table, smoothing the paper beneath her palm. "I don't think it's a good idea for you to try to finish high school early."

"What?" Suzie said it quietly, although in her mind she slammed her fists down on the tabletop and sent their salads flying. "Why?"

"Because later on you are going to regret that you gave up this time. That you tried to rush your life. It's going to come at you sooner than you think. Why not give yourself time to get used to the idea of being an adult?"

"Why are you doing this to me? What do I ever ask you for?"

"Suzie—please, be reasonable. You are not ready to go out there yet."

"Out there? You mean the big, bad world? Are you serious, Mom? Are you serious with that crap about being an adult? How would you know?"

"What?"

"How would you know what it's like to be an adult?"

"Suzie!"

"From everything I've seen, every stupid decision you've made has been decidedly un-adult. Moving us here? Getting back together with Dad? Do you even think he's in Asia or alone? Do you really convince yourself that he is working every single night?"

"Suzie!"

Suzie looked at her mother. Sarah's face was white, her lips tight and tinged with blue. "Stop," she cried. "Please."

"Mom—"

"Where is this coming from?" Sarah put her palms up to her face. "You don't know what you're talking about."

"I was there," Suzie said, unable to stop herself even though she knew she should. "Is this the kind of husband you hope I'll find? Is this what you want for me? Do you want me to hang around here for another couple of years so I really know how to do everything just like you?"

Her mother's shoulders shook; her face was still hidden in her hands. She said something, but Suzie couldn't make out what it was.

"I don't want any of this, Mom. I didn't ask for any of this. If you don't give me permission I will find another way." Suzie took a deep breath. "Because the last thing I want to be is you."

✦ ✦ ✦

Later, Suzie found the house and the lifeguard easily enough. The house belonged to a girl she had noticed all summer at the pool, always the center of a large group. She was friendly, filling Suzie in on where she went to school (Tufts), where her parents were (a cruise to Alaska), and where the bar was (the kitchen island) before she disappeared out a set of sliding glass doors.

The lifeguard's name was Trent, although in Suzie's head it was better if she thought of him as simply "the lifeguard." He made her a vodka and lemonade and they walked outside to the far back corner of the yard, past the pool, past people twisted together on lounge chairs, past tightly huddled groups passing joints and laughing. He wanted to talk, to get to know her better. She told him she was about to start her senior year. He asked about colleges and a major and she found herself saying Harvard and premed even though she really didn't have a clue. She found out he was at BU, a sophomore. He was studying environmental science, a major he offered shyly. He said that Suzie was probably way smarter than he was, and she said no, even though she thought differently. When he stopped walking and gestured to the ground Suzie sunk down into the grass and looked back at the house. They were far enough away that they wouldn't be noticed and yet close enough that she could hear music and smell the weed. She finished her drink, aware that he was watching her. She nestled the empty cup into a fist of ivy, then turned to him and smiled.

"You are really pretty," he said as he reached out to tug on a corkscrew of hair by her chin.

"So are you," Suzie shot back. She leaned closer, the vodka doing an excellent job of warming her belly and making her less afraid.

"So why did you never come to any parties before tonight?"

" 'Cause I didn't want to."

"So why tonight?"

" 'Cause I wanted to."

He laughed and shook his head. "Suzie."

"Trent." She smiled. "What are you waiting for?"

He leaned into her, holding his drink between them. His lips were cold but soft. They kissed slowly, like they would have all summer. When Suzie pulled back he brought his drink to his mouth and finished it off. She watched his throat move as he swallowed, and she wanted to trace it with her finger down to the hollow. When he was done drinking he reached across her and put his cup into hers, dragging a hand against her bare legs as he did so. His fingers grazed the inside of her knee and she jumped.

He immediately began to apologize, but he kept his hand there, his fingers stroking up toward her thigh. She was surprised how every part of her body seemed to be at attention. She closed her eyes and leaned back on her elbows and he covered the upper part of her body with his. She shifted beneath him, encouraging him to get closer, and though his mouth was hard on hers he still seemed hesitant. She pressed the palm of her hand against his lower back, and a sound escaped from deep in her throat as their lower bodies met. It was then that he said "Let's go," and he helped her up off the grass and kept her hand in his as they walked back toward the house. Even though the lights were dimmed, Suzie blinked hard as they walked against a tide of people. She ducked her head against Trent's shoulder, her chin bumping up against his shirt, which smelled fresh like detergent, as he led her through the rooms and up the stairs, and she was all too aware that he had done this before and that he knew exactly where to go.

Afterward, Trent tried to walk her home, but Suzie put him off with the idea of an angry father pacing before the windows because she had missed her curfew. She cut through backyards, imagining herself a stealth midnight hurdler as she jumped shrubs and sprinkler heads until she reached her own. She got into her dark house through the broken latch on the sliding glass door. That tight, headachy feeling had returned and she wanted nothing more than to take a bath and crawl into her bed. But when she went into the bathroom, instead of running the water she got into the tub fully clothed and rested her cheek against the cool porcelain. She needed to talk to Bella. Without thinking about the time, she grabbed the phone and brought it back into the tub. She dialed Bella's number as if they had last spoken only yesterday and not a year ago.

Bella's mother answered on the second ring, as if she were waiting for a call. And then Suzie remembered that some of the medicine Mrs. Spade took made it difficult to ever truly sleep. Her insomnia had made sleepovers tricky as the girls had gotten older, especially whenever she and Bella had tried to sneak out in the middle of the night.

Suzie pressed the phone hard against the side of her face, as if Bella's mother were in the room. "Mrs. Spade," she whispered, "it's Suzie."

"Suzie? Suzie Epstein?"

Suzie nodded, grateful that Mrs. Spade had remembered her. The fuzziness of the dead air between them made her realize that she needed to speak into the receiver. "Yes, yes. I'm sorry; I know it's late. And it's been a long time."

"Nonsense," Mrs. Spade said. "Sometimes you just need to talk when you need to talk. Bella's not here, though, I'm afraid." She paused. "They are all out enjoying the last nights of summer."

"Oh." Suzie felt an irrational rush of sadness at being left out of whatever her friends were doing.

"I'm sorry, sweetie. Is everything okay?"

Suzie closed her eyes. She knew what Mrs. Spade meant when she asked if Suzie was okay. Everyone had known; it would have been impossible not to know about Suzie's family. She heard a clacking sound and remembered the individual cellophane-wrapped mints that Mrs. Spade kept in her pockets to ward against dry mouth, a side effect of a medication. How could she have forgotten so many details only to remember them all at once?

"Suzie?"

They were coming fast now, little snapshots of a life once lived: a dish of chocolate kisses on the nightstand next to Mrs. Spade's bed that she and Bella always used to take from when they were younger. It had become a game to see how small they could make the foil, so as not to be found out. But no matter how many they took, the dish remained full, and it wasn't until much later that they figured out that Mrs. Spade was in on their game. By then they had started worrying about how they looked in a bikini and had stopped eating candy altogether.

"Everything's fine. I was just really missing Bella."

"I'll tell her you called."

"Thanks."

"Suzie?"

"Yes?"

"It's good to hear your voice."

Suzie swallowed hard, choking back a sudden rush of tears. Mrs. Spade sounded so kind and so caring. As if what Suzie was going through actually mattered. "You too."

"It's going to be okay, you know. Whatever it is. It will all work out."

Suzie laughed. "That's what every adult says."

"Well." Mrs. Spade laughed back. "Do you want to hear that sometimes it doesn't work out?"

"I guess I already know that," Suzie said softly.

"I guess you do," Mrs. Spade answered. "I guess you do."

When Suzie woke she was curled on her side in the bathtub, the phone on the bath mat, her neck sore from the strange angle at which she had fallen asleep. She closed her eyes briefly, trying to remember the sound of Mrs. Spade's voice. Yes, that had really happened. She unfolded slowly, stretching each limb before she opened the door, and staggered, a little stiffly, down the hall to the kitchen.

It was a surprise to both of them when Sarah Epstein entered the room. At the sight of Suzie, Sarah stopped short and blinked rapidly. Suzie watched shock, anger, and sadness flit across her mother's features like the spinning images of a slot machine: Suzie knew right then that there would be no escape.

"You're coming?" Sarah said, her voice casual, softer than Suzie expected it to be, but not entirely forgiving. Suzie watched her mother's attention shift to the items she must have placed on the counter before going to bed: her purse, the sheet of directions, a map, keys, gum, and an empty to-go coffee mug. Sarah took inventory, touching each piece, before she crossed to the coffee machine and flipped the switch.

Suzie nodded and put her hands on her hair, attempting to pat it down into obedience. She was trapped now; there would be no backing out of the drive to New Hampshire. "I'll be right back," she mumbled.

In her room she avoided the mirror as she lifted her T-shirt over her head and caught a whiff of detergent, sweat, and grass.

She stumbled into the bathroom with her shorts around her knees, surprised again by the violent swath of blood, a mixture of brown and red, collected in the cotton crotch of her underpants. She recalled the look on the lifeguard's face when he realized she had been a virgin, and right then in his eyes he had been so much like Sam that she could barely look at him again. He seemed to be struggling to say something afterward, but Suzie had already begun the search for her clothes and wouldn't give him the chance.

She cleaned up, washed her face, brushed her teeth, and pulled her hair back into a ponytail; in fresh clothes she felt present-able, and invisible. When she returned to the kitchen she was surprised to find it empty, her mother gone. The counters had been swept clean; the light on the coffeemaker was still on. She poured herself a mug of black coffee and turned off the pot before she went into the garage. The door was open, and she could hear the car idling in the driveway. Suzie held up her free hand to shield her eyes from the sun as she walked toward the car. At the passenger's side she was surprised to be greeted by her mother, seat belt clicked in place, map spread out across her lap, travel mug of coffee in hand.

"Why don't you drive?" Sarah said.

"Are you sure?" Suzie asked, but she walked around to the driver's side door without waiting for an answer. The keys were in the ignition and the car in park. She was about to get in but then realized she would not be able to drive and hold a mug of coffee, and if she put it between them on the console it would most likely spill. She blamed lack of sleep for the fact that she had taken a regular mug, too fat to fit into the base of the cup holders. She took a deep swallow before dumping the rest on the driveway. As she settled in, she tucked the empty mug under the front seat and closed the door. She adjusted her seat belt and put her hands on the steering wheel. Her mother leaned over and pressed the garage door opener attached to the driver's visor and they watched the door close together.

When it was shut, Suzie turned and looked at her mother. "Are you ready?"

Sarah nodded.

"I'm going to need you to tell me where to go."

Her mother tapped the map with her index finger. "Got it."

Suzie backed down the driveway slowly and stopped at the curb. The automatic sprinklers had come on in their yard as well as in their neighbor's. Suzie noticed plastic bagged newspapers dotted along the driveways. The late-August sun seemed mellow at this time of day, but Suzie knew in an hour or so it would be brutal. For now, though, they could drive with the windows open. "Mom?"

Her mother turned to her, a single eyebrow raised in question above her large dark sunglasses. They looked at each other for a long moment before finally she nodded, urging Suzie to go on.

THREE

Scouting for Boys
Sam—1999

They arrived together at Penn Station. With the ticket to Rhode Island crumpled inside his jacket pocket, Sam shifted his backpack higher onto his shoulder and double-checked the departure board. When he looked back to the space where his father had been standing, he was gone, lost in a trench-coated army shuffling toward the exits. *Lemmings in London Fog,* Sam's mother had remarked once as they sat at the station watching the neighborhood men file off the commuter train.

They'd still had the station wagon then. Sam remembered sliding across the canyon of a backseat, the pleated and dimpled leather creating perfect troughs for marbles and plastic army men. Watching for his father, Sam had rested his chin on the high back near to his mother's scratchy wool-covered shoulder. It was past their usual dinner hour and Sam had been hungry and distracted, wanting his father to hurry up, resentful that he wasn't old enough to stay home alone like Michael. For some reason that car had always smelled like breakfast cereal, slightly sweet with the tang of warm milk. Sam had been too little to understand what his mother meant when she called the men lemmings, but old enough to know that the smile she gave him as she said it wasn't genuine.

Now, Sam bought a bag of chips and a soda for the trip at Duane Reade and finished them before he boarded. When the train arrived in Providence he took his time gathering up his stuff. He had fallen into a deep sleep soon after they pulled out of Penn Station and his cheek had a red sleep crease where he had used his backpack for a pillow. He had to switch trains in Boston to get to Providence and he had stumbled onto the next train and fallen asleep again. Sam wouldn't have known they had stopped if the conductor hadn't tapped him on the shoulder.

Originally this was supposed to be a weekend for the three of them, but last night his father had said he thought Sam should spend time with Michael alone, have Michael show him the real college life that he wouldn't if their father came along. When his father announced this change in plans, he and Sam had been eating ravioli, a dinner Sam had prepared by boiling water and dumping sauce from a jar into a pan. Sam had overcooked the ravioli a little bit and the water held a skim coat of cheese and starch, but they tasted fine masked by excessive amounts of Parmesan. The kitchen was a man's domain now. There was an ever-present stockpile of condiments centered on the table: salt, pepper, the green can of cheese, hot sauce, soy sauce, and a sticky mound of duck sauce packets from the Chinese takeout place next to the train station. Unless there was a big spill, sweeping the table for crumbs was often forgotten, and the surface of the table was always tacky to the touch. Still, in the eighteen months since Sam's mother had left them, Sam and his father managed to eat together at this table three nights a week. A triumph, his dad called it, each time they sat down for a meal.

The last time Michael had been home was winter break. Even

though his semester didn't start until mid-January, he left the day after Christmas to meet some friends whose parents had a ski house in New Hampshire, and he had returned to school from there. Before he left he spent most of his time sleeping or raiding the fridge late at night. Aside from the occasional late-night drive-by, Sam had seen Michael only twice over the break: the neighborhood Christmas Eve party at the Coles' house that they had been going to since Sam was in diapers, and Christmas morning, which was really late afternoon.

Christmas morning/afternoon had been as depressing as a Swedish movie, yet oddly comforting. Sam and Michael had opened the boxes of socks, underwear, and identical Norwegian wool sweaters from their grandparents, along with the cards containing their dad's checks to them, by the glow of the flickering lights of the television, having abandoned the pretense of a tree. If Michael had looked at Sam even once with any interest Sam would have begged to go to New Hampshire with him the following day. But he didn't, and instead Sam had spent the week between Christmas and New Year's in Peter Chang's basement along with Frankie Cole, Stephen Winters, and Johnny Ross. Each day was a minor variation on the day before.

Sam wasn't looking forward to spending three days with his brother. He couldn't remember if he had agreed to call Michael and tell him that he was coming alone or if his father was supposed to. Either way, Sam was pretty sure Michael wouldn't be waiting for him at the station. The truth of it was, without their mother, there was no one to remind them that they once shared something other than a fist bump as they passed in the night.

Michael lived with two other guys in an apartment on the top floor of a five-story building on Benefit Street. After Sam rang

the buzzer ten times and no one answered, he went to the sandwich shop on the first floor and spent twenty minutes reading
the chalkboard menus filled with sandwiches named for people
he didn't know and whose only similar characteristic was satire.
His stomach rumbled from the chips and the soda, so he ordered
a Godfather sandwich with the money his father had given him
to take Michael out to dinner and sat at a table, hunched over the
mound of bread, meat, and cheese, not coming up for air until he
was done.

When he tried the bell again at Michael's he was surprised to
be buzzed in. The paper on which his father had scribbled the
address said top floor, number nine. Sam glanced at it before he
started up the stairs and then shoved it back into his pocket. He
didn't want to arrive on his brother's doorstep with a piece of
paper pinned to his jacket like a kindergartner.

The sandwich was heavy in his gut and Sam burped his way
up. After the air cleared he discovered he was still hungry. He
could never seem to get enough of anything these days. On the
top floor he hung a right down a hall that had only three doors,
one on each side and one at the end. For a place that housed college students, the halls were surprisingly quiet. He'd expected
something out of the movies: open doors, music blaring, guys
walking around in their boxers.

The door to his brother's apartment swung open before Sam
had even raised his hand to knock, and then Michael stood before
him in bare feet, shorts, and a T-shirt. It was March and cold outside, but waves of heat snaked out the open door around Sam's
ankles.

"Sammy," Michael said casually, as if they were used to talking
to each other. He turned and Sam followed him over the threshold, closing the door behind him. Sam was careful not to follow

too close, not wanting to seem eager, the last puppy picked from the pound.

Michael stopped in the center of the large living room. One entire wall was taken up by stereo equipment, shelves of record albums, two turntables, speakers and receivers, and several pairs of headphones. On the opposite wall was an old red couch that dipped in the middle, covered with a tapestry.

"Your bed," Michael said when he saw Sam looking.

Sam shrugged out of his backpack and his coat and tossed them on the floor by the couch.

"You might want to take that off." Michael pointed to the sweater Sam was wearing, a stretched-out navy blue pullover that Bella Spade once told him made his eyes look really blue. "In case you didn't notice, it's like Africa in here." He shrugged. "That's what you get for living on the top floor in a student slum."

Sam did as Michael suggested and peeled the sweater off and added it to his pile. Under the sweater he was wearing the Smelly Eddie's T-shirt that was so old it was nearly transparent. Smelly Eddie's had been a bar that their parents had frequented during college. When their parents had been together they liked to tell the story about how Hunt won this T-shirt in a game of quarters the night he met Elizabeth. Sam had rescued the shirt from the bottom of a pile of laundry his mother had left to mold in the basement. When his dad saw him wearing it he averted his eyes but said nothing. Michael, however, narrowed his eyes and raised an eyebrow at Sam, as if to say, *seriously?*

Sam crossed his arms over his torso and waited for the tour to continue. Kitchen, bathroom, and three bedrooms. Michael's was farthest down the hall with its own separate entrance. The light in the room was dim, with one small window placed high to the left, like it was trying to escape. The only thing illuminated was the desk, which was just as well, considering the floor was ankle deep in everything else. The surface of Michael's desk was covered in textbooks and notepads split open with edges curled, stacked one atop the other in winding piles, pencils and pens cradled in the cracks. Tacked to the wall above his desk were multicolored index cards, at least fifty of them, maybe more, each covered in scrawl that already looked like a doctor's handwriting.

Michael flopped down on his mattress. The sheets were bunched up in a ball at the end of the bed. There were stains all over the exposed mattress like tiny archipelagoes. Sam waded through clothes and books to the desk chair and sat down, continuing to look around. Several large, abstract paintings hung on the wall opposite the bed, along with a pencil sketch of what looked like Michael's profile. Michael's bike leaned against the back door.

"I signed you up for a tour of campus tomorrow," Michael said.

"Oh," Sam said. "I guess I thought you were showing me around."

"I have a heavy load all day tomorrow. Fridays are my worst day, I told Dad that. But we'll hang out tomorrow night. Okay?"

Sam nodded. Hang out? Them?

Michael sat up and leaned back on his elbows. "Do you want to go to Brown?"

"I don't know." Sam shifted in the chair. "This was Dad's idea. He wanted me to get started."

"Get started? You should be making the decisions now on what colleges you want to apply to . . . get started?" Michael shook his head.

"Hey, don't blame me. Dad's been a little preoccupied, okay?" Sam and Michael had never talked directly about their mother leaving, about Mr. Epstein and the pictures of their mother, and definitely not about Suzy Epstein. Michael had been at Johns Hopkins that entire summer and then he went right to college. Sam had no idea how or when he found out about everything that happened, and he never thought to ask.

Michael sighed and looked across the room at the paintings. He looked like their mother, the same coloring, the same eyes and cheekbones. Slowly he turned his head to look at Sam. "Your grades? Are they good?"

His grades barely landed Sam in solid B territory. "I guess."

"So that's a no. What about your guidance counselor? What does he say?"

"*She* says that the CUNY and the SUNY schools are great."

"Ah," Michael said.

"There's nothing wrong with a state school," Sam said defensively. Truthfully, he had no vested interest in the CUNY or SUNY schools, but Michael's sounding like a self-important junior at an Ivy League college was starting to annoy him.

Michael shrugged and rubbed at his eyes. "You can still take the tour."

"You mean I don't have 'state school' written all over my face?"

Michael ignored him as he rolled off the bed and went to the doorway. "I have to study. I'm making coffee; if you want some it'll be here." He nodded his head in the direction of the kitchen before he disappeared.

Sam met Michael's roommates and had a cup of coffee even though he hated it, and then hung out on the couch staring at the wall of albums while Michael studied in his room. After a while he picked up a paperback from a pile next to the couch and leafed through the curled, damp pages. He was surprised that he became as absorbed as he did in the story of the Russian officer and his family. He was startled out of the book when Michael re-appeared wearing a coat.

"Hey—I'm going out and I might not be back tonight. Why don't you go sleep in my bed?" He nodded at the book in Sam's hands. "You a Tolstoy fan?"

Sam nodded even though he had no idea what Michael was asking. Where was Michael going all night? What happened to studying?

"Oh, and I called Dad and told him you got here safely. So don't worry about that."

Sam nodded again and felt stupid that he hadn't thought about calling. Would he ever think about the right things? He pictured their father in his chair by the television, chopsticks poised over a carton of black bean chicken. No triumph tonight, that was for sure.

Michael went back toward the bedrooms. Sam heard a door slam and realized that Michael must have left from his room. When Sam got down there Michael's bike was gone, but he had tossed a sheet over his mattress and straightened the pillows. Sam almost felt as if he cared.

Sam was awake when Michael came back. It was too hot in the room to sleep and he had stripped down to his boxers. He was weighing how much he wanted a glass of cold water against his feeling too lazy to get up and get it when the back door opened and a bike tire appeared, followed by his brother.

"You're missing something," Sam said as Michael leaned the tire against the wall without explanation and shrugged out of his jacket. Without acknowledging Sam he plopped down on the edge of the mattress and dropped his head into his hands. "You okay?" Sam asked.

"Fucking exhausted, my eyes are on fire."

"Too bad, I'd rather be exhausted from fucking." Sam chuckled at his lame attempt at a joke.

Michael lifted his head and twisted around to look at him. "Are you a moron?"

"It was a pun. A play on words. You know, wouldn't most people want to be exhausted from fucking? Not just fucking exhausted?"

"What are you talking about?" Michael ran his hands through his hair and slowly stood up. From the look on his face Sam could tell Michael was not even going to comment on what he'd said.

Maybe Sam was a moron. He'd had sex with Bella Spade after the winter dance when she told him his eyes looked blue when he wore that navy sweater. It had been the first time for him, but he wasn't so sure about Bella. If he was to believe Johnny Ross, Johnny had had sex with her in the deserted pool house at the club in ninth grade and again the summer after tenth grade. He thought that piece of information wouldn't bother him, but it did.

Before Bella, Sam had considered himself only a semi-virgin because of Suzie Epstein. They might not have had sex, but they had done everything but. As it was, that night with Bella they did it twice and he could have gone again and again if they'd had more condoms. Sam would have liked to experience exhaustion from fucking, but he wasn't about to tell Michael any of this.

"Jesus Christ, Sam." Michael was staring at Sam strangely. "I have class at nine. I'm going to take a shower. Your tour is at noon and meets on the steps of the library near the admissions building. If you want food you can take whatever you want from the middle shelf in the refrigerator, that's mine, and the cabinet next to the stove without a handle, also mine." As he talked he grabbed clothes and a towel and left the room.

Sam realized his boxers had formed a tent over his dick and

he batted it down out of embarrassment. Obviously that was the reason for Michael's annoyance. Well, nothing he could do about it now. He closed his eyes, remembering Bella Spade that night. They had gone to the high school winter dance in their usual group, attending mostly as a joke. They had made screwdrivers in Peter's basement before they left, and they were buzzed but not drunk, as they walked through the streets. The houses were already lit up for Christmas even though it was only the first week of December. Sam had been surprised when Bella caught up to him and slipped her hand into his jacket pocket, curling her cold fingers around his. There had been something so innocent about that gesture, reminding Sam of the games they used to play in the closet during sixth grade. Her breath had smelled like the licorice they had been eating moments before. He had kissed her on the cheek and they had held hands for the remaining minutes in silence, letting everyone think what they wanted when they emerged from the closet.

What happened after the dance was unexpected, but also somehow not at all. Sam was attracted to Bella for sure, and she was always so nice to him. He noticed her sometimes in the library writing in a marbled composition book that she carried with her everywhere. But she had also been Suzie's best friend. It was hard for him to see her and not think of Suzie. As far as he knew, none of them had heard from her. In the beginning the girls still talked about her like she was still around, but that eventually stopped. He hadn't bothered writing Suzie even though he really wanted to ask her why she had given him the photographs like she did. Sam realized he already knew the answer: Suzie hadn't cared for him at all. The private humiliation was enough. He didn't need written confirmation.

Still, that night after the dance, it had seemed stupid for Sam to stay away from Bella because of what had happened the summer he was fifteen years old. No one even knew about it; it was like it had never happened. Certainly Bella would never have to know.

Sam sat up and swung his legs over the side of the bed. If he gave any thought at all to Bella Spade's mouth and hands he was a goner. He needed to get up, get dressed, eat, and then go find the fucking library and admissions office. It was the least he could do for his father.

Almost everyone in the tour group was with one or, in most cases, both of their parents. From where Sam was standing, alone, the parents seemed to want to go to Brown way more than the kids. The tour guide, Carrie, a junior English major, did her best to answer every one of the parents' questions, and made it seem like she hadn't answered these same exact questions a million times before.

The last part of the tour was cookies and coffee and informal discussion with some other Brown students. Carrie caught Sam at the cookie tray, his hand hovering over the Milanos. "Only one per prospective student," she said from behind his left shoulder just as Sam snatched up a handful of cookies.

Sam dropped the cookies back onto the tray before he heard her laugh. "Oh man, that was way too easy." He felt his face go red and then she nudged his shoulder like they were old friends. "I'm sorry. I am so tired of doing tours today." She wriggled her jaw from side to side. "My mouth hurts." Sam gave her a side-long glance and picked the cookies back up. She laughed again. "Where are you from?"

"New York."

"Is your lifelong dream to come to Brown?"

Sam paused, trying to figure out how not to sound like he'd

never get in, not in a million years, and she said, "I'm teasing again." She picked a cookie off the tray and studied it before she nibbled an edge. "I'm just the tour guide working for my work-study dollars. Not admissions."

"My brother goes here, so . . ." He shrugged.

"Who is your brother?"

"Michael Turner."

"No kidding? Why didn't you say something?" She squinted at Sam through a fringe of bangs that fell into her eyes. "Then you must know Kate."

Sam frowned and shook his head.

"His girlfriend?" Carrie said. "She's one of my roommates. He must talk about Kate. They've been together for at least a year by now."

"Michael talks?" It slipped out before Sam thought about it. Michael had had a girlfriend for a year?

Carrie laughed. "You are funny." She nibbled some more of the cookie. "So I'll probably see you tonight. Then you can meet Kate. You're coming with Michael, right?"

"Uh, sure, yeah. Tonight." Michael had said the previous day that they were hanging out, so maybe he was planning on telling Sam later that they were going to a party, and about his girlfriend.

Carrie popped the rest of the cookie into her mouth. "Okay, well, my tour duties are officially over. I'm just going to hand out these info packets to the parental units and then I'm out of here." She put her backpack down on the floor and pulled out a sheaf of folders with the Brown University logo, offering one to Sam before she wandered away. He watched her calves in diamond-patterned tights squeeze and release as she bounced up and down on the balls of her feet in her scuffed black Doc Martens. Then he turned back to the cookies and swiped half a dozen off the tray and a can of Coke. It wasn't until he was back at Michael's apartment that he realized he had left the folder she had given him on the table.

Their father went about the business of divorcing their mother like he did everything else: silently and away from the house. He worked as an attorney for a large firm in Manhattan. He never talked about his work, and Sam's childhood memories of him consisted of a bulging briefcase and progressively bad eyesight.

Sam found out about the divorce one night after dinner. His father was at the sink; it was his turn to wash because Sam had cooked. His shirtsleeves were rolled to the elbow and suds clung to the hair on his forearms. Sam was hunched over the table, pretending to do his English homework and hoping he could sweet-talk Mindy Stevens into letting him see her vocabulary paragraphs, when his father started talking about things being official.

Sam looked up and tapped his pencil on the table. "Huh?"

"I just want you to know that you are mine. Officially."

"What does that mean?"

"It means I have custody of you. Your mother has visitation."

Sam tapped his pencil again. Since his mother left, there had been several awkward phone calls. So far he had refused to join her for the meal she kept offering to buy him.

"She has you for a week in the summer and one weekend a month, if you want."

"And if I don't?"

His father turned back to the dishes without answering. Sam noticed a smear of salsa on the back of his pants from their taco dinner and he felt sorry for him, but not sorry enough to tell him. "What about Michael?" He assumed his parents had divided their children and his mother had chosen Michael.

"What about him?"

"Does she have Michael too?"

His father sighed. "That's a little more complicated. Or a little less, depending upon who you are, I suppose. Michael is over eighteen, so he can choose what time, if any, to spend with your mother."

"Why didn't anyone ask me?"

His father sighed again. "I didn't think you wanted to go to court, Sam."

Sam slapped his notebook shut. "I need to go out for a little bit, okay? Just for a walk." What he really needed was to get the homework from Mindy, and he knew his father wouldn't stop him from going out on a school night. He had been very lenient since his mother left. If Sam let him think he was more upset about his mother than he really was, well, so what? He stood and gathered his books and turned to leave the room.

"Sam?"

"What?"

"I won't keep you from your mother. However much time you need, you take that? Okay, son?"

"Sure."

"We both still love you very much."

"Okay."

"I'm here if you want to talk. Or you can always call your brother."

Sam shook his head without speaking and let the back door slam harder than he intended. He immediately regretted the effect it would have on his father.

He stayed at Mindy's that night until he knew his father would be snoring in his chair in front of the television, a lukewarm cup of tea by his side, just so they wouldn't have the chance to talk.

When Sam got back to Michael's apartment, Michael was waiting for him with a beer. "Happy hour, bro," he said as he handed him a frosty can. "Fucking Friday."

Sam closed his hand around the beer and Michael tapped his beer against Sam's and took a long swill. Sam watched the muscles in Michael's neck constrict as the liquid flowed. This was the most enthusiastic greeting he had gotten from his brother in a long time. Possibly ever.

"Drink up," Michael commanded. "We have places to go and be seen."

Sam lifted the can to his lips and drank even through the stabbing pain in his left eye from the shock of the cold beer. He finished about half and then came up for air, squinting over at Michael. His brother laughed and opened the refrigerator, grabbing two more beers and opening one. "Come on, put this in your pocket." He tossed the unopened beer to Sam and walked out of the kitchen.

Sam ran to catch up. His empty stomach churned from the beer. He would have liked some food, but Michael didn't seem to be offering. He wondered if their father had told Michael to expect a dinner.

Michael jogged down each flight of stairs and waited briefly on the landings for Sam to catch up. By the time they hit the front door to his building Michael had finished his second beer and Sam had finished his first. "Hey," Sam said, already beginning to feel a little buzzed from the beer. "You hungry or—?"

"There will be food, Sammy, never fear."

Sam drained the second beer as they walked up College Hill. Michael walked slightly ahead of him, just far enough that Sam couldn't ask where they were going. He veered left abruptly in front of a small clapboard house surrounded by an iron fence.

Michael's bike, without the front tire, was chained to the fence.

Michael opened the front door into a dimly lit, cramped hallway that smelled sharply of curry and made Sam's left nostril begin to run. He followed Michael up a steep staircase to a landing where three open doors were shrouded with tapestries and an even stronger aroma of Indian spices prevailed. Against the walls were canvases of all shapes and sizes, some turned in, exposing the T-bar of stretcher, and others facing out. The paintings looked a lot like those Sam had noticed in Michael's room.

Michael lifted the corner of the closest tapestry and beckoned Sam inside. The room was decorated with a thousand twinkling white Christmas tree lights. People were everywhere, more people than Sam imagined could fit into the space, along with even more paintings. The mood was festive but mellow.

Sam sniffled and followed Michael deeper into the apartment, where the smell of food intensified. Sam was practically drooling when they reached a table laden with exotic-looking dishes. "Go ahead, grab a plate," Michael said, pointing to a stack.

Sam's stomach was growling and he set about following the crowd around the table, piling his plate with rice and naan and curried vegetables. He couldn't find a place to sit, so he leaned against the wall and started shoveling food into his mouth. Once he had cleaned the plate and pacified his stomach, Sam took a breath and looked around. His brother was across the room wedged into a corner talking intently to a dark-haired girl. Every once in a while he reached out and touched her: her shoulder, her cheek, or her hair. She smiled when he did that and bit her bottom lip, as if Michael's hand on her arm was worth the wait.

Sam was about to make his way over to them but something in the way they leaned toward each other stopped him. They didn't look like they wanted company. Sam returned to the food, devouring another full plate, and then went in search of a beer, then, beer in hand, went out and sat on the front stoop and studied Michael's bike chained to the fence. He wondered where Carrie was, if this was her place.

He'd been out there only a few minutes when he heard footsteps. "Hey, Sam, there you are." Michael came up behind him and tapped him on the shoulder. "Where did you go?"

He shrugged. "Nowhere. I couldn't find you so I came out here."

"Chill, dude. Are you mad? I thought you'd just hang, have a beer, eat some good food."

"I'm not mad. I just don't know anyone, you know?" Sam said, feeling like the high school kid that he was. He had just been a little bit afraid that someone was going to ask him what he was doing eating their food and drinking their beer.

"Everything's cool." Michael shrugged. "It's weird only if you make it weird." He stared at him until Sam nodded back. "You ready to go?"

Sam stood, tucked his empty bottle behind a planter on the stoop, and followed Michael down the path. "You taking your bike?"

"Huh?"

"Your bike?" Sam pointed to the fence.

"That's not mine," Michael lied.

"Seriously, dude? That's your bike. You came home with a tire last night and this bike, your bike, is missing a tire."

"Okay, detective, it's my bike." Michael's voice was flat. "Come on." He shoved his hands into his front pockets and leaned forward as he walked, as if he were trudging through snow. In that moment Sam saw what else Michael and his mother shared. Each of them had a life that was entirely separate from the one they lived day to day with Hunt and Sam. Sam knew only the side of

Michael that Michael wanted him to see, while their dad and Sam put everything out there.

"So who is she?" Michael stopped walking and looked over his shoulder at Sam. "That girl back there?" As soon as Sam said the words he flinched.

Michael shrugged. "Vera is my lab partner. We studied really late last night, and I left my bike at her house because there is something wrong with the gearshift and I didn't feel like dealing with it." He raised an eyebrow at Sam but offered nothing else.

"It looks like she's into you."

Michael shrugged and started walking again. "Possibly, but . . ." He shrugged again, as if Vera's liking him wasn't important. "She's just like that. Flirty. Vera likes everybody and nobody. I told her I would stop by tonight for some food, that's all." Michael smirked, as if explaining things to Sam about the opposite sex was funny. "So, you talk to anyone?"

"Huh?"

"Girls? Back there? You talk to anyone? What's your type?"

Frantically Sam searched his brain for his type, something to offer up to Michael. But the only type Sam could come up with was Suzie. And he didn't want to bring her name into this; he didn't want Michael to connect the dots between his old desire for Suzie Epstein and whatever their mother had been doing with Mr. Epstein.

"Don't sweat the answer, Sam. The best thing about college, or being anywhere away from where you grew up, is that you can be who you want to be and no one can tell you that you can't." A corner of his mouth turned up in a shadow of a grin.

Sam was silenced by this brotherly advice. But he did walk faster to catch up to him. Maybe he needed to give Michael more credit.

They went back down the hill to a section of town he had never been to before. Michael had said earlier that they had places, plural, to be seen, so he guessed this was another stop. This party was noisier, spilling out onto the sidewalk.

Michael circumvented the crowd and wove around to the back of the house. On the packed back porch Sam saw Carrie, perched on the railing with a joint poised before her lips. Their eyes met and she waved the joint. "Hey, it's the Turner brothers."

Michael shot Sam a look that he couldn't read. Carrie popped off the railing and came over to them. "Did you read your folder of material?" Her words were slightly slurred, but Sam didn't think she was messy drunk. She offered Sam and Michael the joint, then, when neither of them made a move to take it, handed it off to some guy walking past.

"I lost it," Sam said, swallowing hard, wishing for a beer.

"Bad boy," Carrie teased, but she was looking at Michael. "What's up with you not telling me your brother was coming to see the school?"

"I signed him up for your group, didn't I?"

Carrie rolled her eyes but she was smiling. "Busy, busy Michael. Such a busy boy." She said it like she was joking but her face looked anything but. "Kate's in the kitchen, I think. Trying to make nachos the last I saw."

Sam glanced over at Michael at the mention of Kate, but Michael's face didn't change. Was this Kate really his girlfriend? Why was Michael acting so weird and secretive?

They picked up beers out of a cooler on the porch and Sam followed Michael into the kitchen, where a girl with a high blond ponytail was shredding cheese into a bowl. She was wearing a sleeveless top despite the weather and her biceps flexed slightly each time she ran the cheese over the grater. Her jeans were low on her hips and revealed a smooth lower back and the hint of something lacy peeking out. She looked like one of those girls whose attractiveness came without trying. Sam shuffled his feet and coughed and she turned around, saw Michael, and gave him a wide, easy smile. "Hey, you. Study break?"

Michael leaned over and pressed his lips in the vicinity of her lips. His hand rested proprietarily on her hip. The girl craned her head around his shoulder and smiled at Sam. "Is this your baby brother?"

Sam felt his cheeks redden. "Hey, I'm Sam."

"Sam I am," she joked. "I'm Kate. Nice to finally meet you, mystery brother."

"Huh?"

Michael twisted around and gave Sam a look that seemed to say, please, don't embarrass me.

Sam shrugged. "I'm not that mysterious, but thanks, I guess." He smiled at Kate and she grinned back at Sam as if he had just said the most brilliant thing. At least she seemed nice.

Michael's shoulders relaxed as he looked at Kate. "What are you making?" He nodded toward the clump of cheese.

"Carrie was starving and I was bored, so I decided to make her something to eat." She picked up a bag of chips and dumped them onto a tray and then sprinkled the cheese over the top. "There," she said. "Let me just put this in the microwave."

"You forgot the salsa," Sam said, pointing to the bottle on the counter.

"Oh!" She turned quickly and plopped the tray back on the counter so hard the chips and cheese bounced.

"Let me," Sam offered, taking the jar of salsa from her hands and pouring it over the chips.

"I have an idea, Julia Child, why don't you nuke this and take it out to Carrie?" Michael was already leading Kate out of the kitchen as he said this over his shoulder.

Kate yelled, "Thanks, Sam I am," and then they were gone. Sam looked down at the smear of cheese and bloody, chunky salsa. His brother had certainly perfected the disappearing act.

Sam stood in front of the microwave watching the nachos twirl around as if he were a guard at Buckingham Palace. When the cheese melted he held the plate aloft and went in search of Carrie. She hadn't moved from the back porch and she squealed when she saw what he had in his hands. They sat on the steps and rested the plate on their knees and ate all of it, pretty much in silence. When they were finished Michael and Kate reappeared.

"Let's roll, Sam." Michael tapped him on the shoulder as he squeezed past.

Sam looked at Carrie, who shrugged, and back at Kate, who was smiling at Michael.

"Brunch tomorrow, the usual?" Kate called. Michael nodded. She turned to Sam. "Don't let him stay up all night studying."

"I'll try," Sam said as he stood and followed Michael.

"Goodbye, Turner brothers," Carrie called after them.

Sam caught up with Michael on the sidewalk. "That was fast." Michael shrugged.

"You really have to study?"

"Yes, Sam, I really have to study." He paused. "I'm going to the library. You can have my bed again, okay?" He added the last bit softly and Sam wondered if Michael was asking his permission.

"Kate seems nice."

"She is."

"How long have you known her?"

"A while."

"Is she your type?"

Michael stopped walking and turned around and glared at him. Sam shrugged and held his hands up in front of his face. "Hey, I'm just trying to figure this out. You asked me what my type was, I'm asking you."

Michael didn't answer, but he didn't move either.

"Do you think Mom was Dad's type? Do you think Dad was hers and then she changed her mind?"

The muscles in Michael's jaw twitched. "You'll figure that out for yourself."

"Did you?"

"Sure, yeah, I figured it out."

Sam shook his head. "That's not what I was asking. I meant, did you ever change your mind after you thought you'd figured it out?"

Michael turned and started walking again. At the entrance to his building he handed Sam the keys. "I'm going to get my bike." He paused. "I'll just take the couch when I get home. Don't worry about it."

"I thought you said you were studying." Sam called after Michael as he walked away. Sam watched him for two blocks, and just as he was about to turn the corner and start the climb back up College Hill, Sam realized Michael didn't have his books.

"Michael! Hey—" Sam took a step forward. "Michael!" His voice echoed in his ears, and the strain made something behind his eyes throb.

Michael slowed down at the crest of the hill and kicked at the crumbling curb. Randomly, Sam recalled a day with their mother. She had taken them to the quarry to look for flagstones for the front walkway. While she debated the merits of veining and thickness and color, Sam stood close to the edge to watch the prehistoric jaws of the earthmovers lift gigantic chunks, sediment spilling over the sides, confetti-like, to reveal a bedrock of uneven slate below the surface. Beneath his Converse the combination of dust and gravel was even as glass, and as he leaned out to get a better look he slipped. Before he could panic—before he even realized what was happening—Michael tugged on the neck of his T-shirt, yanking him back from the edge.

All the way home their mother drove slowly, as if the stones weighed her down. Sam waited for Michael to brag that he had saved his life, but he never did. They unloaded the stones from the car, the shapes reminding Sam of the puzzle pieces in his map of the United States. Their mother paid them in Popsicles, and they sat on top of the rocks and licked them quickly and quietly before they melted. The pile of stone remained at the end of the driveway for so long that it began to look like an impromptu wall, and no one complained when Sam eventually used the stones to support a piece of plywood for a bike ramp at the end of the drive.

"Michael," Sam yelled again. "I leave tomorrow. Dad gave me money for food, for us. So I can pay for brunch, if you want."

Michael held up three fingers palm out and touched his temple in the Boy Scout salute, and it was then that Sam finally accepted that what he wanted Michael to do and what he was going to do were two entirely different things.

FOUR

If Only I Told You One Thing It Would Be This
Bella—2000

Bella's mother had a thick leather diary in which she had kept track of social engagements, dinners, menus, meetings, and appointments for herself, her new husband, and eventually her children. It was swollen from the years, creased with age, its pages yellowed on the way to fragile. Every year she had carefully added more pages to the book, and it was so thick that she'd had to replace the leather tie that kept it all together. As Bella well knew, her mother had purchased the book her junior year of college on her first trip abroad, a semester in Barcelona, where her rudimentary Spanish grew adequate. She told Bella that when she held it in her hands she imagined the diary as something she would have her entire life, the leather growing soft with age.

Whenever Bella's mother spoke of Barcelona her entire demeanor changed. She admitted to Bella she had been terrified to go. She still left Vassar on the weekends to see her parents. Her father put gas in her car, kicked the tires for air, and changed the oil. Her mother took her shopping for new clothes, monogrammed her cashmere, noticed when she needed a haircut or a teeth cleaning, and made her appointments.

It had been her art history professor, an enigmatic man not much older than his students, bearded, corduroy wearing, who convinced her to go. His lectures were full of romantic tirades about Gaudí, the people of Barcelona, the beauty of the nights, and the heady indulgences of food and wine, unlike anything their pedestrian American palates had ever experienced. The class was mostly young women like Bella's mother, and that year nearly twenty of them signed up for the semester abroad. The plane ticket was purchased, and the passport ink dry, by the time Bella's mother realized what she was about to do.

When she returned after six months it was not an understatement to say that she was an entirely changed person. Instead of spending the summer before her senior year at home in Bedford with her parents, she took a share in an apartment on Bank Street in Greenwich Village with two girls she had traveled with. She got a job in the library at NYU, where she met Bella's father, then in his second year of law school.

By the time she returned to Vassar that September she knew she was going to marry him, which she did, five days after her graduation, in the backyard of her parents' home, in the center of the heirloom rosebushes her mother so carefully tended and in view of her childhood bedroom window. One hundred guests drank and ate and danced beneath the tents well into the night.

Bella knew the story of her parents' wedding so well she felt as if she had been there. She supposed her friends would think it was weird to be envious of the romantic life of her parents. But it was all Bella had. Bella's mother's pregnancy with Bella was what had inflamed her illness, and afterward her body never recovered. Bella's father and her two older brothers had known a different wife and mother. Bella had only her mother's stories, the diary, and the photographs.

There were boxes and boxes of photos of her parents, the extras that didn't fit into the many albums Bella's mother had carefully curated. There they were in Central Park on a plaid blanket, her father reading a thick law text and her mother reclining next to him smoking a cigarette, her ankles crossed, one hand resting on his knee. In another her father was asleep, the tent of the book open on his chest. And later, that same day, her mother lay curled on the blanket, her head resting in the crook of her arm and her eyes closed. There were pictures of her mother feeding a carrot to a horse in front of the Plaza, of her perched atop a low stone wall, looking away from the camera. Her mother was long and lean, and wore classic clothing that didn't age. She favored V-neck sweaters and slim skirts, cropped pants and flats, scarves tied around her head or her neck. In some of the pictures she was wearing what looked to be Bella's father's dress shirts, knotted at the waist, sleeves rolled to the elbow.

There were honeymoon pictures from a week in Maine, where her father's parents once had a house. Bella's parents standing at the water's edge with fishing poles, her mother squinting at the camera. On clay courts surrounded by ocean, dressed in tennis whites. In one, her father was bending over a pile of empty crab shells in the center of a table.

There were too many years of memories: her mother blowing a kiss to the camera, her mother with a fat barn cat on her lap and a faraway look in her eye, her parents at their wedding laughing and linking arms like the joke was on everyone else, her mother in an impossibly slim sleeveless shift dress and a small hat, her father in a dark suit, a small clutch of flowers between them. Then Bella's mother was hugely pregnant with Bella's oldest brother. She wore a black turtleneck and pants, and her face was soft and round, her hands resting lightly on her distended belly. She looked surprised that she had been caught by the lens, but happy.

In recent years her mother had stopped writing in the diary. She no longer kept track of her own doctors' appointments, let alone Bella's, and especially not her brothers' now that they had families of their own. The social engagements, the invitations, the dinner parties, the to-do lists, the shopping lists, and the birthday notations had disappeared. The diary was a record of before, while Bella had been living in the after for almost as long as she had been alive. There were only a handful of years in the beginning of Bella's life when her mother had tried to keep up the pretense of running the home and their lives, but eventually the entries stopped.

Bella kept it all tucked between her mattress and box spring. She wasn't sure if her mother would even care that she had it, but still she said nothing. Sometimes when she came home from school and the house was too still, Bella would make herself a snack and curl up on her bed and pull out the book. She studied the rhythm of her mother's days, memorized the cooking instructions for a roast beef dinner. Bella assumed her mother had cooked this dinner for her father, since there was a sloppily drawn open-ended heart next to the ingredients list, but she had never asked. Asking felt like an acknowledgment that one day her mother wouldn't be able to answer.

In a few weeks Bella would turn eighteen and graduate from high school, and in the fall she would be going to Vassar just like her mother. She knew that had made her happy, that Bella would be attending her own alma mater. It had actually been an easier decision than Bella had led her parents to believe. She liked that she would be a train ride away from home, far enough but not too far. She also liked the proximity to the city, and the English department was regularly visited by an impressive roster of writers, allowing Bella to visualize a sort of utopian college life in which she would spend her days reading great literature and having intellectual conversations.

But graduation and college really weren't on her mind. She had become one of those girls who worried what would become of her high school relationship.

Bella knew that Sam had been a virgin when they first slept together. She had finally grown tired of waiting for him to make the first move, so she surprised herself by reaching for his hand as they walked to the dance. The weight of his hand, the warmth, the way he stroked her palm with his thumb, made her sorry she had waited so long. At the dance they had stood side by side, bumping into each other as they swayed to the music, laughing and talking to their friends. But when he brushed up against her she felt her skin tingle all over.

In her mind that night, as Sam buried his face in her neck, sighing against her ear, the weight of him pressed against her, there had never been anyone else. All those awkward kisses, the fumbling beneath clothing, the push and pull of what she would or wouldn't do, no matter the desire, no matter how sweet the boy, had led her here. Sam was someone she had been waiting for her entire life, even if neither of them had known it before that moment.

✦ ✦ ✦

Bella made tomato soup and grilled cheese sandwiches for dinner. Her father was in the city for a late meeting with a client and her mother's evening nurse's aide would be late due to car trouble or a missed bus, her excuse something Bella couldn't quite make out when she answered the phone. Bella had a graduation party to go to that night, but she wasn't in a rush. While the end of high school was bittersweet, there was a sameness to these parties that was mind-numbing. She knew Sam and the other boys would drink too much and act stupid and she and Mindy and Ruthie would leave early, go to the diner, pile into their usual booth in the back, and order way too much food. The boys would stumble in later, smelling like booze, only to fall on the half-eaten plates of greasy leftovers as if they were attending their last meal.

Bella carried the tray of food into the room, set it down on the table at the end of the bed, and parted the curtains so she could open the windows. Her mother's room always smelled like cold cream and menthol, the menthol likely from the balm for the bedsores that the aides were constantly wrapping and re-wrapping, afraid of infection or worse. The television was on low, turned to the local evening news, a recitation of burglaries, attempted assaults, and accidents. Bella thought she might like to write a poem like that, a roll call of crime headlines taken from the news. She turned back to the bed and glanced at her mother.

"I have to go to the bathroom." Her mother winced, her eyes large and liquid, magnified behind her thick glasses.

Bella nodded. She knew, they both knew, that if her mother used the bedpan it would be easier. But she also knew that her mother must have waited until the last possible minute, hoping she wouldn't have to ask Bella to help her get out of bed. Bella didn't blame her for holding on to what dignity she had left. She brought the wheelchair close to the bed and pulled back her mother's blankets, then helped her swing her legs over the side of the bed. Her mother's legs were atrophied from the disease, red and scaly where the skin was dried. Her calves had shrunk to the size of Bella's forearm, her toes were permanently flexed upward, and her legs spasmed every so often in an uncontrollable bicycling movement. Bella tried to think of anything but what she was about to do as she brought her mother to the bathroom. They avoided eye contact as Bella helped her mother onto the toilet. She left the room, taking the wheelchair with her and pulling the door shut behind her.

"Are you okay?" she called through the door.

"Yes," came her mother's faint reply as Bella turned and walked a few steps away, attempting to give her more privacy. When she heard the toilet flush she waited a few minutes before she knocked and her mother gave her the go-ahead to open the door.

Bella wet a washcloth, squirted soap into the folds, and handed it to her mother, who washed her hands. Bella took the cloth and wrung it out under running water before handing it back again so her mother could rinse.

"Thanks, honey," her mother said into Bella's shoulder as she leaned against her and they did the dance again, into the chair, out of the bathroom, and back into bed. Bella tried to fix the blankets and pillows but her mother held up a shaky hand. "It's fine."

By the time Bella remembered their tray of dinner the soup was congealed and the toasted cheese was dry and hard.

"I'm not very hungry anyway, Bella. Don't worry."

Bella picked up the tray. "It will take just a few minutes, Mom; I'm going to heat up the soup again and make new sandwiches." She walked past the bed and out of the room before her mother could stop her. If her mother weighed one hundred pounds it was a miracle. They were always trying to get her to drink milkshakes or the little cans of high-protein drinks, but it was hard to tell if any of that was working or if it even mattered. She wasn't going to get better. Sometimes Bella thought it was crueler to keep her mother like this, this insistence on maintaining the semblance of a life.

When Bella brought the food back she was surprised to see her mother sitting up against the pillows, her hands folded in her lap, alert and waiting. The television was still on, the news replaced by *Jeopardy!* "Changed your mind? My cooking skills swayed you, didn't they, Mommy?"

Bella was rewarded with a smile as she set the food down on her mother's tray table. She handed her mother a cloth napkin and then helped her tuck it in at the neck of her robe. Then she slid the bowl closer to her mother and handed her a spoon. "Do you want me to cut your sandwich?"

"Yes, please." Her mother picked up her spoon and dipped it into the soup. "Looks good."

Bella smiled. "I'm in with those Campbell's Soup guys, you know." She crossed her middle finger over her index finger and held it up for her mother to see.

Her mother brought the spoon to her lips slowly, careful of the slight tremor in her hands. After she swallowed she said, "Cooking is overrated. That brain of yours is what matters."

Bella thought of the roast beef recipe in her mother's handwriting. "Did Grandma tell you that?"

"Oh no, my mother thought the 'wifely arts' to be very important. How to run a house, care for your husband and children, that sort of thing." She hesitated. "Not that there is anything entirely wrong in that, Bella. But you, my fabulous girl, you can do so much more, I'm sure of it."

"Did that make you mad? What your mother wanted?"

"Mad?" Her mother cocked her head to the side. "I don't know. Times were different. Expectations were different. This is going to sound awful to say, but I never gave much thought to any of it." She paused. "Until I had a daughter."

Bella felt shame for dismissing her mother as just her physical body. There was so much she should be talking to her about, and she didn't. "My mother the feminist," she half joked, wondering what her mother would have done with her life if she hadn't been chronically ill.

"An excellent title for your first book," her mother laughed. "Tell me, did you get a dress for graduation yet?"

Bella arranged the slivers of grilled cheese sandwich on the napkin next to the soup. "I have one. It has to be white. I can wear this sundress I bought last summer."

"But you should have something new! You only graduate from high school once. Linda or Ellen can take you shopping."

Bella shook her head. As much as she liked her sisters-in-law, an outing with them meant their babies came as well, turning the event into a large, messy affair with enormous strollers and crackers and bottles and diaper bags bursting with baby paraphernalia. She'd rather wear what she had than spend a day trailing them around with a bag of animal crackers to keep the kids quiet.

"I'm sorry, Bella. You know . . ."

Bella nodded and took a large bite of her sandwich to avoid answering. Her mother was eating mechanically, dipping the long pieces of sandwich into the soup and bringing them shakily to her mouth. There was a crime scene dribble of tomato soup on the cloth Bella had placed on her mother's chest.

When they were done eating Bella cleared the dishes and carried them back into the kitchen. She set them in the sink under running water and stared out the windows. The day had been warm but slightly overcast, the clouds swollen and low. But now the sky looked silver in the early-evening light. Bella got a lump in her throat and suddenly she needed her mother to see the sky.

Bella walked back into her mother's room. Her face must have betrayed her because her mother looked alarmed. "What is it?" she said in a shaky voice.

Bella moved to the bed and picked up her mother's hand. "I want to show you something. Outside." Bella couldn't remember a time her mother had been outside for anything other than a doctor's appointment. There had been an aide once who insisted on what she called the fresh air cure, but she hadn't been employed long enough for her methods to see results.

"Bella—"

"I can lift you into your chair. I just did it. Please?"

Her mother looked around the room as if someone else would speak on her behalf, talk sense into Bella, and allow her to stay in bed watching television.

Bella moved the wheelchair close to the bed. She straightened the oval of foam and the lambskin in the seat and she grabbed a blanket, even though the temperature had to still be in the seventies. She looked at her mother. "Trust me."

Bella navigated through the house slowly. Theirs was a one-story house, low and modern and open. Her mother peered at the rooms in a detached, polite manner, as if she were visiting a museum.

At the sliding door to the deck Bella struggled, slightly tipping the wheels over the track and onto the wooden floorboards. But it was only a moment, too short for her mother to protest, before they were out the door. Bella pushed her mother toward the railing and carefully put on the brake. When she looked at her mother her eyes were closed.

Bella touched her arm. "Mom, are you okay?"

Her mother opened her eyes slowly and blinked as if she had woken from a sound sleep. "Yes."

Bella pulled a chair up next to her mother and sat down. "This is nice, isn't it?"

"It is."

"Are you warm enough? Do you want the blanket?"

Her mother shook her head. "No, I'm fine, honey."

Bella exhaled. From inside the house she heard the phone ring. She ran through the possibilities: the night nurse, again, with another explanation, or Ruthie or Mindy wondering when they were going to Frankie's, or her father checking in. She waited for the beep of the answering machine and then she heard a click. Her bet was on the night nurse. Her father or Ruthie would have left a message.

Her mother seemed not to have heard the phone. "You know, when we first moved into this house that line of trees wasn't there." She nodded toward the back edge of their property, where a column of towering pines swayed almost imperceptibly. "We planted them ourselves and they couldn't have been more than five feet back then. Your father thought it would be easier to put in a fence. But I really wanted those trees. I had a vision." Her mother laughed. "And that was the extent of my green thumb."

Bella jutted her chin out in defense of her mother's ambition. "I like the trees. They used to be a great hiding place when I was little." As soon as the words were out of her mouth she wished she could take them back. The more incapacitated Bella's mother had become, the more a much younger Bella had retaliated by going places her mother could never reach her, testing to see if her mother was really wheelchair bound or if she could get up and walk if she wanted to. Bella recalled not only the shelter of the trees but also the top of the jungle gym and the maple tree, which had been lost to rot years back but where the tire swing had provided a boost up to the branches and beyond.

Bella's mother laugh turned to a cough, a cough that quickly turned into an uncontrolled fit. The dry mouth was a symptom of one of the many medications she took, and Bella had forgotten to bring along some of the lozenges her mother sucked on all the time. As her mother's face turned bright red and her entire body shook with the effort, Bella jumped up and ran inside, returning with a glass of water and a handful of lozenges.

She tilted the glass at her mother's mouth so she could get a drink, repeating the action several times until the high color in her mother's cheeks slowly receded and her cough was only a raspy tickle.

Bella unwrapped a lozenge and slipped it into her mother's palm. She watched her pop it into her mouth, then sat back down, unsure of what to do next. Bella knew how to perform the simplest of tasks for her mother, but it scared her to imagine anything worse than a coughing fit if they were alone.

They sat in silence for a while until her mother said in a weak voice, "It's Friday night. Don't you have plans?"

Bella shrugged. "Frankie Cole is having a graduation party. It doesn't matter when I get there."

"Is it safe to count his chickens before they hatch?"

It took Bella a moment to figure out what her mother meant, but then she laughed. "He is the smartest dumb person I've ever met. Third in the class, can you believe it?" Bella's mother raised her eyebrows and Bella laughed again. "If you ever saw any of them at a party you would have some serious doubts."

"Well, boys are a little slower catching up. Your brothers were such fools."

"That doesn't even seem like it happened in my lifetime, you know? They were both so much older than me."

"You were my surprise." Her mother's smile was so wide it covered half her face, making fishtail pleats of flesh at the corners of her eyes.

"Some surprise," Bella said softly.

"I wouldn't have changed a thing, Bella."

"Seriously, Mom?" Bella said. "How can you even say that? If you hadn't had me you might not have gotten sick."

"Bella, listen, tomorrow is not a guarantee for anyone."

Bella rolled her eyes. Her parents had been holiday-only Episcopalians and that was how they had raised her brothers and Bella. But the sicker her mother got, the more phrases acknowledging a spiritual world had entered her mother's lexicon.

"Doctors try their best with the science at hand," her mother continued, "but they can't tell you what it's going to be like to live with your decisions while you wait out their medical conclusions. I wanted you before I knew who you were. It's important for you to know that."

Bella looked down at her feet. She didn't want to have this particular discussion with her mother right now. Her once-white sneakers were now gray and smelly from being caught in too many rainstorms and wading at the shore, and were decorated with designs in Sharpie marker. The laces were shredded and the rubber was worn off in places. But she didn't want a new pair. She hated the look of new sneakers. "Do you want a bowl of ice cream?" she asked abruptly, standing without waiting for an answer. It was mean, this upper hand that she played, and she knew it and regretted it, but it still didn't prevent her from doing it.

She took the carton of vanilla from the freezer and scooped

until her hand hurt. She filled two bowls and carried them back outside, handing her mother a spoon along with the bowl. She placed a dish towel on her mother's lap and watched as her mother rested the bowl on her thighs.

Bella sat back down and buried her head in her bowl of ice cream. She didn't look up until she had three brain freezes and the bowl was almost empty. When the sliding glass door opened behind them she twisted in the seat, surprised that the light had faded so quickly. There was a milky film over her teeth and tongue and she wished for a glass of water.

"Ladies," her father said as he walked toward them, trying hard to contain the surprise in his voice. He was without his suit jacket and his tie was looped around his neck untied, but his face bore the exhaustion of a day that was never-ending.

Bella looked over at her mother. The ice cream was nearly untouched and was now a puddle of white cream that threatened to overflow onto her lap. Bella reached for the bowl and put it down on the deck.

Her father steadied himself by grabbing on to the handles of the wheelchair before he bent over to kiss her mother lightly on the top of her head. Bella looked away. It was just as awful to witness a completely asexual kiss as it was to see a passionate one.

"Where's Sasha?" Her father squinted into the corners of the deck as if the nurse's aide were hiding.

Bella shrugged. "Broken car, no bus, I don't know." Her mother was looking down at her lap. Bella knew she hated the presence of the nurse's aides in the house. She had reluctantly agreed to someone during the day and evening but refused to have a night nurse, making do from eleven until seven, when the day aide came in.

Her father sighed. "I'll call the agency, get someone new tomorrow. Should we go inside?" His hands reached for the wheel-chair's brake.

"Why don't you go make a drink and bring it out here?"

Bella and her father glanced at each other, surprised by Bella's mother's suggestion. Bella looked away quickly, collected the ice cream bowls, and stood up. Suddenly she felt an overwhelming urgency to run away. She walked back into the house without a word and deposited the bowls in the kitchen sink. When she looked back outside her father had taken her seat. His hand was on the armrest of the wheelchair, his legs splayed out in front of him. She could tell from the movement of her mother's head that she was talking. Occasionally her father nodded, even laughed. It should have made Bella feel better, but it just made her angry.

In the way, way back of Frankie Cole's backyard, which was really a second lot that had remained wooded and undeveloped, there was a tremendous bonfire in the fire pit and constellations of people dodging stray sparks. Bella searched for a familiar face and almost immediately ran into Stephen Winters and Peter Chang carrying cases of beer.

"Take one," Peter urged, his face red and puffy. "Or six."

Bella took a can even though she really didn't want it. Peter huffed with effort and walked by, Stephen in the rear. He carried three cases to Peter's two and it barely looked like it was an effort.

"There you are! Finally!" Mindy grabbed Bella's arm. "What happened?"

"Nothing," Bella said, handing Mindy her beer.

Mindy took it and popped the lid. She took a large swallow before she sighed. "We're never going to see each other again."

Bella laughed. "Min—we live within blocks of each other. All of us."

"Ugh, can't you just let me be dramatic for once?" Mindy smirked. "We are all going off to discover the world and then what? We've been together our entire lives!"

Bella shook her head and looked back toward the fire for Sam. "Vassar is in Poughkeepsie. Sarah Lawrence is a few train stops away in Bronxville. The world? Really?"

"The world is out there waiting for us. My guidance counselor, my parents, and *Seventeen* magazine have told me so." Mindy frowned. "Whoa, why are you so bitchy?"

"I'm sorry," Bella said quickly. It wasn't Mindy's fault that Bella wanted to get as far away from her house as possible tonight.

Mindy smiled again and squeezed Bella's arm. When she did, the beer she was holding tipped and spilled. She righted her hand quickly, only to spill more beer all over her shirt. "I'm drunk, I think." Mindy burped. "Have you seen Peter?"

Bella pointed in the direction he had gone.

Mindy swayed. "You okay if I go? Ruthie is over there by the fire with a hundred of our closest friends, and Celia is around somewhere outrunning Johnny Ross."

"Okay, I'll go find them. You don't need any help?"

"Bella, Bella, Bella." Mindy lunged toward her and cupped Bella's face in both of her hands. "You are a gem. A true friend. But no, I am fine. I am going to find Peter Chang and we are going to kiss. It is probably a mistake, but I'm feeling it and I think he is too."

"Are you sure that's a good idea, Mindy?" Mindy had made Bella and Ruthie swear that they would rescue her from herself where Peter Chang was concerned. But maybe, Bella thought, maybe Peter Chang wasn't such a bad idea for Mindy. Maybe she just didn't know it yet. Bella reached out and grabbed Mindy by the sleeve. "Hey, if you want Peter Chang, who am I to stop you?"

Mindy gave her a wide, sloppy smile and then shrugged off her arm and drifted toward the house. Bella turned and continued walking, although she had no real plan until she saw Sam. His back was to her, and though he was surrounded by people on all sides, it was obvious to her he was alone, staring into the fire.

She walked up behind him and slipped her arms around his waist and pressed her cheek to the dip between his shoulder blades. Bella closed her eyes for a second, grateful for Sam's quiet, steady presence. After a few minutes she let go and Sam twisted around to face her. "Hey there," he said. He pressed his lips to hers and she felt, as she had the first time, that they were meant to do this very thing forever. "Where've you been? I was just going to start looking for you."

"I just had some stuff to do at home," Bella whispered as she found his mouth again. Sam tasted like beer and smelled like woodsmoke. He tightened his arms around her and squeezed, lifting her slightly off the ground before putting her back down. Bella felt fused to him, the length of his thighs against hers, the hard angles of chest and arms. She felt soft, molding her body into his. They leaned their foreheads together and swayed back and forth.

"My dad is up at the lake," Sam said in a low voice.

"So?" Bella teased.

"Later on? Can you spend the night?"

"Will you make me pancakes for breakfast if I do?" Bella grinned, enjoying the moment. Of course she wanted to spend an entire night with Sam.

Sam laughed. "Bella, you're killing me."

Bella smiled and kissed his cheek; there was a little bit of stubble and her lips stung from the tiny cluster of hairs.

"DUDE! Turner! There you are!"

Bella and Sam swung around as Peter Chang and Frankie Cole came toward them. Frankie held aloft a bottle of vodka. "SHOTS! Now!"

Bella shook her head. She looked behind Peter for Mindy, but she wasn't there. Peter thrust a cup at Sam and Frankie began pouring. Bella disentangled from Sam. "I think I'm going to find Mindy and Ruthie."

Sam hooked a finger through her belt loop and tugged. "No."

"Yes," Bella said. "Enjoy your shots." She smiled and looked over at Frankie. "Where are your parents, anyway? This is getting kind of crazy." In the short amount of time she'd been at the party the woods seemed to have grown even more crowded.

"Everyone needs to leave by midnight. They're in the city for a play and dinner." Frankie poured vodka into the cup. He seemed sober, but even Bella knew that was impossible. "I figure that gives me until one to clean up."

"Are you kidding?" Bella looked over at Sam, who shook his head and shrugged. She leaned over and glanced at Peter Chang's wristwatch. "It's after eleven. Have you seen how many people are here?"

"It's a little nuts," Peter Chang admitted as he squinted toward the fire.

"Really?" Frankie looked up. "Can you do me a favor, Bella, and start telling people they need to get going?" He grinned at her and then passed the vodka bottle to Peter Chang. "Pretty please?"

Bella rolled her eyes. She twisted Sam's T-shirt into a knot and brushed her fingers against his stomach before she pulled away. When she looked back at him he was staring at her from over the cup he'd raised to his lips.

It was after two when Bella and Sam staggered into his darkened kitchen through the back door. They had managed to get rid of everyone before the Coles arrived home, but Frankie would have to craft a convincing story when the sun rose of why there was a confetti spill of beer cans and cups in the backyard, not to mention the enormous circle of blackened grass where the flames had overshot the fire pit.

Bella had her arm around Sam's waist and his arm was slung across her shoulders as they tripped over the threshold. He'd had way too many shots, so it was Bella who led the way through the shadows to Sam's bedroom. When they got there Sam pulled Bella down onto the bed and rolled over on top of her. "Finally," he said softly against her hair. "Finally."

Bella laughed and pushed Sam slightly off of her so she could breathe. Their legs were still entwined but their heads were side by side on Sam's pillow. If she turned her head she could press her lips against his without moving. Sam reached down and grabbed her hand and brought it up to his mouth, kissed her fingers, and then held it against his chest. "Bella," he whispered.

"Sam," Bella whispered back.

"You're here. In my bed."

"And you're very drunk."

Sam moaned. "Give me a minute."

Bella laughed quietly. "How many of me can you see right now?"

"I don't know. I'm scared to turn my head too quickly."

Bella closed her eyes. She could smell the boy-ness of Sam on his sheets: shampoo mixed with sweat and detergent and foul sneakers and another layer of whatever he'd had to drink that night. "Hey—do you feel like you're going to be sick?"

Sam didn't answer. His limbs were like lead weights on top of hers. Bella nudged him gently, afraid to make it worse. "Do you need a bucket?"

Very carefully, his words measured, Sam said, "I don't think so."

Bella attempted to disentangle so she could get up and get the wastebasket just in case. But Sam roused himself enough to stop her. "No, no. Don't."

"I'm coming right back."

"Promise?"

"Promise." Bella tried again to move but Sam wasn't cooperating.

"I ruined everything."

"It takes more than some vodka to ruin everything." Bella kissed Sam's neck below his ear.

"That's so nice."

Bella kissed his neck again.

"Really nice."

Bella rolled onto her side and curled up against Sam, bringing her knees toward her chest, careful not to place them anywhere near his stomach. "Mindy is worried that we're never going to see each other again. She said we're flinging out to the far corners of the world."

"Like pinballs?"

"Yeah, something like that."

"Pinballs roll back and bounce off each other again before they find a landing place. Over and over and over."

"Is that what you think we're going to do? Bounce off each other until we find that landing place?"

Sam bucked against the bed and the mattress moved beneath them. "You know I like to bounce off you." He laughed.

Bella laughed with him. "Hold on, cowboy, you're going to puke."

"Not going to puke," Sam said quietly. "Why do you like me?" He let go of Bella's fingers and brushed the back of his hand against her bra over her shirt. With his other hand he fumbled with the button of her jeans and when his fine motor skills failed him he slid his hands up under her shirt and cupped her breasts. "Off," was all she heard him say as he slid down beside her until his mouth was level with her bra. He bit at her nipples through the fabric. Bella put her hands on his shoulders to get his attention. He stopped what he was doing and stared at her from beneath heavy lids as she sat half up and lifted the shirt over her head and unhooked her bra. She tossed it over the side of the bed, and before she could even lie down Sam's mouth had found a nipple, while his fingers slowly drew out the other.

"You," Bella gasped.

"What?" Sam stopped what he was doing and looked up at her, a boyish little grin on his lips, his cheeks flushed a deep red. When all of a sudden he swallowed hard, Bella saw in his eyes a rising panic. She rolled off the bed and dove for the tin wastebasket under the desk, sliding it to the bed just as Sam's head came over the side. She turned away, but from the sound of it he managed to get it all in the can.

Bella scrambled around the room and grabbed at a pile of laundry still unfolded in the basket at the end of Sam's bed. There had to be a T-shirt in there. Her clothes were somewhere on the floor by the trash can. Finding one, she slipped it on over her head and ran to the bathroom for a towel.

When she returned to the room Sam was sitting up in the middle of the bed with his head in his hands. It smelled awful. Bella opened the windows and moved the wastebasket away from the bed with her foot. She handed Sam the towel and he dabbed at his face.

She tried to hold her breath as she moved closer to him. "Are you okay?"

He nodded, his face buried in the towel.

"You want some water?"

"I'll get it." He swung his legs over the bed and steadied himself before he stood. He was wobbly as he made his way to the door, so Bella moved to support him around the waist. He was pale and shaking as they made their way to the bathroom. When they got to the door Sam turned to her. "I'm good, better." He tried to touch her face with his hand but he missed. "I love you."

Bella nodded, too stunned to respond. Sam shut the bathroom door and she sank down on the floor outside the bathroom. Had it only been tonight that she'd waited in the exact same place for her mother? She leaned her head back against the wall and closed her eyes. "Sam?" she called.

"Yeah?"

"I'm going to go home."

He didn't respond right away. Bella stood and pressed her ear against the door. She tapped her fingers lightly. "Sam?"

"I heard you. I was trying to think of something to say to change your mind. But there's puke in my bedroom. So . . ."

Bella smiled. She heard the squeak of the faucets turning on and then off. Soon afterward Sam opened the bathroom door. His face was damp and he rubbed his hands against his jeans. She caught a whiff of toothpaste. He smelled better but he still looked terrible.

Bella laughed nervously. "I can't go back in there. I'm sorry."

"I know." Sam shook his head and winced. "Not a good idea." He put a hand on her elbow. "I'll walk you home."

Bella shook her head. "I'm okay. You're not."

"I'll walk you to the end of my driveway."

Bella frowned. "Watch me from the window."

Sam laughed and then held a hand to his head. "Oh, I wish this was funny."

"Okay, Mr. Pitiful." Bella tugged on his hand and smiled. "Walk with me."

When they got outside Sam took a deep breath. "That's good."

"Remember how the air smells before you go back inside."

At the end of the driveway Sam leaned against the mailbox. "So, let's do this again soon, okay?" he joked.

Bella smiled and leaned over and kissed Sam on the cheek. In his ear she whispered, "When you find my bra, will you give it back?"

Sam laughed. "Not on your life."

Bella began to walk backward down the middle of the deserted street. With each breath she could still smell the bonfire from Frankie Cole's party. She waved to Sam. He looked so small as she moved farther away. It was hard not to run back down the street to him. She could feel the world that Mindy was talking about pressing in on all sides, and then the crazy crooked line that ran from her mother to Sam. They had known each other all their lives. They were in each other's DNA. This place was all she had ever known. And she wondered how she was ever really and truly going to leave.

FIVE

When Dinosaurs Ruled the World
Sam—2003

Mrs. Spade died in the winter of their junior year of college and they all returned home for the funeral.

Mrs. Spade had been sick as long as Sam could remember, so her death shouldn't have been that shocking, yet it hit him harder than he expected. He guessed that her illness, always unspecified, had tricked him into thinking you could be sick forever, almost as a way of life. When he considered that now, Sam realized what an idiot he was.

Bella had called from Vassar to tell Sam. He'd picked up the phone and heard his name and then nothing, just a rush of air across the wires followed by what sounded like a faraway howling. Bella and Sam had continued, despite distance and any real commitment, to find their way back to each other. She surprised him first at school, showing up at his door, and they had fallen back onto his twin mattress as if they were starving. It felt exotic, somehow, to be in a place where no one knew them as a couple. To hold hands as they shared crummy food off Sam's meal ticket at the dining hall, to drink dollar pitchers at the Rat, to wake up next to each other and have sex without talking, as if they had the map of what they liked inked indelibly in their brains. By the time Sam's roommate returned from his girlfriend's place, the weekend ended, the buzz would wear off, and Sam would think they wouldn't do it again. Until one of them showed up on the doorstep of the other's room and it started up all over again. Sam thought this thing with Bella was casual, comfortable. They had never labeled what they were or talked about where it was going. He thought that was what they both wanted. Or maybe they were just too scared to bring it up. Sam liked things the way they were until something like this happened, and he had no idea how to act or what they meant to each other.

When she called, it had been the longest they had gone, since before Thanksgiving break. Sam hadn't been home for Thanksgiving that year; instead he and Michael had visited their mother in Vermont, where she had incongruously found her passion making goat cheese and living with a writer twenty years her junior. At Christmas, Michael went back to the goat cheese farm and Sam went with his father to Boca Raton to be with his grandfather, since his grandmother had died in September and his father couldn't convince his grandfather to come north. So Bella and Sam hadn't been in touch, and he was surprised to find himself missing her.

The night before the funeral, the Spade house had been crowded with people Sam mostly recognized: plenty of his friends' parents, pre- and post-divorce, a librarian who'd kicked him out of the stacks once for a whoopee cushion prank, Tina from the reception desk at the club, the lawn guy who hated Frankie and Sam for trying to start a rival business one summer, and their old mailman, Sy, who had carried a sack of dog treats in a bag around his belt. Running in and around all these people were the Spade grandchildren, six or seven blond kids who seemed identical in age. According to Sam's father, there had been a steady stream of neighbors bearing bottles of liquor along with casseroles in aluminum tins, who automatically received an invitation to stay by Mr. Spade, for whom the prospect of being alone to mourn his wife appeared unappealing. The alone part he could remedy, at least, considering the odd collection of mourners in their home pre-funeral.

When Mr. Spade had offered Sam a martini he'd replied, "Oh, God, no!" and then couldn't help feeling that his reaction had made Bella's father more uncomfortable, as he had excused himself quickly and disappeared into the crowd, one small blond child attached to his pant leg.

Sam scanned the main rooms with no luck, then turned a corner after narrowly avoiding his eleventh-grade English teacher, who was leaning against the wall by the pantry whispering into the ear of his twelfth-grade trigonometry teacher. He took off down the long hallway that led to the back of the house and the bedrooms. The Spade grandchildren had left nothing untouched: most of the doors had been flung open and toys and books were scattered across the floor. A television blared from one of the bedrooms; the high-pitched singsong voices led Sam to believe it was most likely a cartoon. He peeked in as he passed and was surprised to see Bella's oldest brother reclining against the pillows of his parents' bed, drinking a beer. Their eyes met and Bella's brother raised his beer in greeting and Sam did nothing, embarrassed to be caught looking.

When he finally found Bella she was sitting on the back deck outside her room, wrapped in an enormous fur that smelled like a combination of piss and mothballs. She was curled up inside the coat, her legs pressed to her chest, her arms around her knees.

Her mouth and chin were buried in the massive collar and all that showed was the tip of her red nose and her eyes. Her eyes were rimmed pink and Sam was pretty sure there was frost on her eyelashes. It was easily the coldest day of the winter so far.

"Hey," Sam said. "Mrs. Francussi is whispering in Mr. Holt's ear outside your pantry."

Bella tipped her chin up out of the coat to reveal a shockingly painted mouth outlined in a heavy scarlet lipstick. "They're probably fucking."

"Well, thanks, I could do without that visual." Mrs. Francussi wore flesh-colored stockings that made her legs look like sausage casings while Mr. Holt favored cardigans in shades of rust. The amount of nudity they should share was nil. They should shower clothed, as far as Sam was concerned.

Bella moved over and Sam sat down next to her, grateful for her fur-cloaked body against his side, adding another layer of warmth. Even if he had to breathe out of his mouth. "What are you doing out here?"

The entire fur ball that was Bella shrugged.

"I'd be hiding too. Where did all these people come from?"

"My feelings exactly. Where the fuck were all these people when my mother was dying? She fucking died in her bed, alone. My father was in the city. At work. She was here all day. Alone. Dead. Alone and dead."

Sam flashed on Bella's brother reclining in his parents' bed watching cartoons. Mrs. Spade had died in that bed? He didn't know what to say.

"She had a heart attack." Bella's voice sounded weak, like she was running out of anger. "After everything she had been through, she had a lousy heart attack."

"I am so sorry." Sam put his arm around the coat, but he

couldn't even feel Bella inside of it. He tried to pull her closer but he just got hair in his mouth. "Do you want to go for a walk? Get out of here?"

Bella shook her head and stood up. She held out her hand and Sam took her fingers, tiny and cold, and she led him through the sliding glass doors and into her room. She pushed aside piles of clothing and books and photo albums and flung herself on her bed, facedown. Sam followed because he didn't know what else to do. He tried to find any part of her that he could touch but he just ended up patting the top of her head. "What can I do for you, Bella? Tell me."

There was a long silence and then Bella rolled over to look at him. "Nothing, Sam. I'm going to be fine." The lipstick had smeared across her teeth. She looked the furthest from fine Sam had ever seen. "Oh, by the way, your mom sent some cheese."

Sam nodded. Of course she had.

"And a really nice note." Bella nibbled at her lip, leaving tiny exclamation points of red along her top teeth. "But she was good like that. She always wrote my mom notes. I think that cheered her up, you know? That she wasn't forgotten?"

Sam had no idea his mother kept in touch with anyone from the neighborhood. He nodded again because all of a sudden there was a lump in his throat. Bella's mother was dead, while his had left them to make goat cheese and fuck a guy who looked like his RA.

"I've been going through her things. I can't even remember the last time she was well enough to wear this coat, but I love it and I am never taking it off."

Sam held back the sigh that threatened to break loose. Parts of the coat looked like they had mange.

"So the service is tomorrow. At noon."

"I know. My dad told me."

"Good." Bella looked like she was waiting for Sam to kiss her, but he couldn't imagine touching that red mouth. He felt bad. He felt fucking awful. He felt like he wished he could run as far away from this as possible. What role was he supposed to play here? Doting boyfriend? Did her father and her brothers think he was that? Shit.

"What are you thinking?" Bella asked.

Sam shook his head.

"Come on, tell me."

"That I don't know what to do or how to act."

"Thank you." Bella nodded solemnly, her eyes huge in her face. "I get that."

Sam fell back on her pillows and closed his eyes. He was suddenly so fucking tired he could have slept forever. Bella stirred next to him but he couldn't gather the strength to move. It wasn't until he felt her hand on his zipper that he realized what she was doing. He couldn't even raise his arms to pull her on top, but when she peeled back his fly and reached into his boxers he immediately sprang against her palm. He felt the fur cuff, softer than it looked, as she dug deeper and freed his balls.

Bella climbed on top. The coat fell open as she lowered herself slowly down until they were connected. She stayed still for what seemed like forever. Sam's dick throbbed inside of her until she began to rock back and forth. Sam bit the inside of his mouth to keep from coming too fast. He thought about her brother watching cartoons in his dead mother's bed. He thought about the martini. He thought about what the fuck he was doing in Bella's house fucking her while the cocktail party of death raged on all around them. He hoped one of those little kids didn't yank open the door. Was the door even locked? *Fuck fuck fuck fuck. Bella,* Sam thought. *You feel so fucking amazing. Fuck. So fucking amazing.*

When Sam woke up the room was black and Bella was asleep on top of him, her head beneath his chin and the coat covering both of them. His dick was wedged where it had fallen out of her and as he rose to consciousness it did the same.

"Bella," Sam whispered into her hair. "Bella?"

He could feel her hot breath against his neck. She mumbled into his collarbone something he couldn't understand.

"Wake up, Bella."

Bella placed her palms against Sam's chest and raised herself up just enough to look at him with one eye. The lipstick was now all over her chin. "What time is it?"

"Dark." Sam half struggled to see the clock on her bedside table but Bella moved at the same time, accidentally rubbing up against him. Sam took a chance and hooked a leg over hers and rolled her over onto her back. Bella looked up at him with a lazy half smile and stretched an arm above her head. Sam reached down between her legs. She arched her back slightly and closed her eyes.

"Please."

He was inside her before she finished saying the word.

Sam left as Bella was running water for a bath. They had stayed in bed for a while, talking about nothing important, and she had seemed calmer. She had even laughed a little when she caught her reflection in the mirror above the sink as the small bathroom filled with steam. She insisted to Sam that he should go, that she was going to spend some time with her father and brothers. But even as he was leaving he couldn't shake the feeling that he should be staying no matter what Bella had said.

Sam made his way over to Peter Chang's basement. Peter was at MIT, having already developed and sold several video games that were providing him more than enough money without the degree, but Sam somehow always saw him in his mother's basement, where the best of their teenage years would live on suspended in time.

Being at Peter's was like one giant exhale. Almost everyone had come back for the funeral. Frankie Cole, Ruthie Newman, Stephen Winters, Johnny Ross, and Mindy Stevens were all there. The exceptions were Celia Newman, Ruthie's little sister, on exchange in France, and Suzie Epstein, of course, whom no one had heard from since she left. Sam took the Sucrets container that Bella had dropped into his coat pocket as he was leaving and placed it on the trunk in front of the couch. "A gift," he said.

Everyone looked at the tin but no one did anything to open it. Finally, Stephen Winters grabbed and opened it, revealing four neatly rolled joints. "Shit."

Ruthie and Mindy looked at each other. Ruthie said, "That's Mrs. Spade's, right?"

"What do you think?" Sam asked.

"Don't be an asshole, Sam." Ruthie narrowed her eyes. "This is hard for all of us, not just you. Bella is like our sister."

Sam wasn't sure what she meant. Was he giving the impression that Mrs. Spade's death was hard on him, or that tending to Bella was hard? Ever since Ruthie had declared women's studies as her major, everything had become an argument. Sam was too tired to go there tonight.

Frankie stared intently at the tin before reaching for it and slipping out a joint. "I heard she had cancer, that the pot helped with chemo."

"Nah," offered Peter Chang. "MS or some shitty disease like that, I think." He looked to Sam for confirmation.

Sam shrugged. "She had a heart attack, that's all I know."

"It doesn't matter now, does it? Are you going to light that thing or what?" Stephen tossed a pack of matches at Frankie. Frankie, a philosophy major at Rutgers, looked at the joint and seemed to consider the possibilities. Sam thought the consensus in the room was obvious: they had smoked Mrs. Spade's weed before, and it was some really good shit.

The room was silent as Frankie struck a match and raised the joint toward the ceiling. The paper sizzled as he took that first long drag. They passed the joint around the room, not speaking. When it was done Sam stood up, pleasantly buzzed, and walked up out of the basement and into the empty street.

He walked back over to Bella's house, stoned and feeling bad about leaving Bella all alone to take a bath. The windows were dark in front, but that didn't mean everyone was asleep. He held up his hand and waved. Then he felt like a fool and dropped his arm down by his side and shuffled off down the road.

At home he found his father sitting at the kitchen table dunking Chips Ahoy! into a mug that said #1 Dad. His eating habits, never great, had deteriorated while Sam was at school. Soy sauce packets threatened to take over the entire kitchen table.

Sam sat down across from him. His father pushed the package of cookies in his direction. Sam took one and they chewed in unison. Sam scraped the chair over to the counter to get a glass for milk. When he got back to the table he ate three more soggy cookies and made a flower pattern out of sauce packets on the table.

"How's she doing?" his father asked.

"Okay, I guess."

His dad nodded, a cookie halfway to his mouth. "It would have to be hard to be a daughter and lose your mother."

Sam squinted over at him. Did he think it was any easier to be a son and lose your mother? "I wouldn't know." He still couldn't get the picture of Bella with smeared red lipstick all over her face out of his head. What was wrong with him? He had real feelings for Bella. He just didn't know what to do with them.

His father closed his eyes briefly and then reopened them. "Do you want to go to the funeral together? Or are you going earlier?"

Sam looked at him, horrified at the thought of having to return to the Spade house before the funeral. He'd been planning to meet up with the boys and sit in the back of the church. This would be only the second funeral he had ever attended in his life, the first being his grandmother's memorial service, where Michael read an excerpt from *Walden* and afterward they went out for lunch. A week later UPS had delivered his grandmother's ashes in a brown box.

Through cookie crumbs Sam mumbled, "I'll go with you."

His father nodded. "Everything okay? Did you talk to your professors and tell them you would be gone?"

Sam winced. He had just received a notice in his campus mailbox from his counselor saying that he was yet again treading the waters of academic probation. He doubted he and his professors would have anything positive to say to one another at this point. "I'm good, Dad."

His father nodded. "You'd better get some sleep, Sammy. You look wiped out."

Sam pushed back his chair and carried his glass to the sink. Before he left the room he looked back at his father. He was mid-dunk and he caught Sam looking. He raised a cookie in salute and Sam waved back, then shuffled off to his room, dropped onto his bed fully clothed, and fell into his second hard sleep of the night.

The blazer Sam had worn for his high school graduation was still hanging in his closet, a navy-and-gold-striped tie looped around the hanger. He went into Michael's room and found an acceptable white shirt and pair of khakis and dressed for the funeral. The sleeves of the blazer were too short, but Michael's long-sleeve shirt made up for it. Sam was probably just a little over six feet by now, closing in on Michael's six-two. He was still waiting for the angles of his body to fill out. No matter how much food he consumed it didn't seem to stick. He knew from seeing his father's high school graduation photo in his grandfather's bookcase that he looked exactly like him at that age.

Sam nicked his chin shaving, took two Advil, and borrowed a belt from his father, and he was ready. He needed a haircut, but there was nothing he could do about that now. His father looked solemn in a navy suit and overcoat, the same outfit he wore to work every single day.

They left so early they stopped off for coffee and doughnuts and ate them in the car with the heat running. The temp on the dashboard read eleven degrees. Before his dad slipped on the defroster the windows fogged around them, and Sam appreciated being hidden from view for those few minutes, even if it was only in the parking lot of the doughnut shack.

They found a seat closer to the front than Sam would have liked, but his dad slid into a pew and he had no choice but to follow. He didn't want to look around, so he kept his head down. Before he did he caught a glimpse of the altar, with pots of that pointy red Christmas flower surrounding the coffin that held Mrs. Spade. The coffin was a deep, shiny wood. Sam wondered if the flowers were left over from Christmas or had been purchased especially for this occasion.

Behind Mrs. Spade was an organist playing an appropriately somber few chords over and over again as the pews slowly filled in. When the family finally arrived at the church, the pews were packed. Bella walked in beside her father. Her hair, usually a mass of waves, was pulled back into a severe clump at the base of her neck. Her skin was pale, her blue eyes appeared to take up most of her face, and her lips were unstained. She was wearing the fur coat.

Sam watched Bella take her place among her nieces and nephews in the front pew. One of them tugged on her shoulder and another climbed into her lap and the coat slipped, revealing a pale shoulder and a strap of black. Sam flashed back to her body beneath the coat the night before, the way it had opened to reveal Bella in nothing but a pair of panties. He felt a twitch in his crotch and, embarrassed, twisted away from his father, willing it to go away, focusing instead on a stained glass window of a saint crying tears of blood.

During the service Sam contemplated Bella's perfectly straight posture as she stared at a place beyond her mother's coffin. He had no idea what was said. When the service was over Mr. Spade got up and approached the coffin with his sons and touched the spot near the top, near Mrs. Spade's head. His sons followed their father, but Bella remained seated. When the organist played louder, Bella finally stood and gathered the children, who stayed clustered around her, and she ushered them forward, her head down. One of the smaller kids turned and waved, but Bella continued on, carefully avoiding eye contact with either the attendees or her mother's coffin.

At the reception Sam and his father parted. Sam was surprised by how pulled together the house was less than eight hours after the previous night's gathering. There was a fresh bar set up on the large kitchen island and platters of food covering the lengthy dining room table. Bella's brothers' wives seemed to be running the whole thing.

Sam ran into Frankie Cole and followed him out onto the back deck, where Bella was curled up in the coat on the lounge chair, flanked by Ruthie and Mindy. Everyone else was huddled around the fire pit trying to get something started. Sam looked around; they all appeared to be wearing a variation of their graduation clothes.

"The wood is wet, morons," Frankie offered as he poked at the firewood stacked on the deck, covered only by an icy shelf of snow. "Snow, ice, all of it makes water." He shook his head as Peter Chang lit another twisted piece of paper and held it up to the kindling. There was a sizzling sound followed by a tendril of smoke and then nothing.

"Just let it go," Mindy said, coughing and waving a hand in front of her face. "Please, know when to stop." Mindy and Peter had been an item briefly the summer before they went off to college, and ever since then she spoke to him like she was his ex-wife.

"Here, this will keep us warm." Stephen produced a bottle of vodka from inside the folds of his voluminous gray coat. He set the bottle down on the deck and wrestled a stack of plastic cups from his pocket. No doubt he had swiped everything from the bar on his way through. He poured generous shots and handed them all around.

Everyone, including Bella, raised a glass. No one spoke, and Sam fixated on Bella's bottom lip as it trembled. "To Mrs. Spade," he said in a rush as everyone tossed back the shots. The vodka burned going down. Sam knew that alcohol was the worst thing to drink when you were cold, that it triggered some sort of false positive effect in your bloodstream, but it wasn't as if they were going hiking. They were sitting on Bella's deck, their own houses all within a two-block radius. So they filled their cups again and again until the bottle was empty and they were all feeling the heat.

Mindy and Ruthie refused to relinquish their spots by Bella. Sam looked over at her and mouthed the words *Are you okay?*

She nodded and smiled back and then looked away as Ruthie whispered in her ear.

"Hey, you have any food in that coat?" Peter pointed at Frankie, who flattened his pockets with his palms and shook his head.

Sam was closest to the door, and everyone looked at him expectantly. He shrugged. "Fine, I'll go."

On his way down the hall he passed the bathroom and went in and shut the door to take a leak. The medicine cabinet was open, as if someone had been looking for something. Sam took a survey. There was the usual spare razor and blades, the half a dozen hotel soaps and tiny bottles of shampoo that seemed to collect in every spare bathroom, a bottle of Tums, and aspirin. He closed the door and blinked at his reflection, surprised to see himself there. It was entirely possible that he'd had too much to drink on a stomach of doughnuts and coffee.

Just like the night before, being in the back of the house and walking to the front was like entering another world. The decibel level was higher and people were everywhere. Sam caught sight of his father leaning against the wall near the front door, a sandwich raised to his mouth, nodding at something Henry Wild was saying. Mr. Spade, Mr. Wild, and Sam's father all worked for the same firm. Sam's father swallowed his giant mouthful and laughed at what Mr. Wild had to say before he took another tremendous bite of his sandwich.

Sam picked up a plate and began to make his way around the table, filling it with two of each kind of sandwich that was left. He balanced the plate in one hand and grabbed an unopened bag of potato chips with the other as the front door opened. He heard a chorus of greetings, and then his father shouted his brother's name above the noise. The door must have still been open, because there was a sweep of cold air along the floor, swirling around Sam's ankles. He headed toward the door, pushing through knots of people, curious to see if Michael had really shown up. His father had said he was too busy; the third year of medical school was too intense to even dream about asking for time off.

But now Sam could see that there was a commotion at the door, too many people attempting to funnel into one space. There was his brother in the center of it, his father reaching for him. Michael's cheeks and nose were pinched red from the air. He had a blue plaid scarf wrapped around his neck and a striped long-sleeve shirt tucked into his jeans, nothing else, nothing like a coat or a sweater that would protect him from the cold. He leaned back and said something to someone behind him, but Sam couldn't tell whom, because just as he did Mr. Wild stepped forward, blocking his view.

Sam started to back up, figuring he would have time to talk to Michael later. His friends were waiting on the food, and he didn't want to have to hear everyone fawn all over Michael's arrival.

But then Mr. Wild stepped aside and the person behind Michael moved forward. She had dark, wavy hair and was wearing a long navy wool coat. Her back was to Sam but in her posture there was something familiar. Sam stepped closer just as his father looked up, made eye contact, and motioned Sam over with an exaggerated movement. Sam pressed forward, the plate in front of his chest, the chips tucked carefully under his arm. As he did his father said something to the girl with Michael and she pivoted slowly in Sam's direction. Even from a distance he could see the S formation of freckles on her left cheek.

Suzie Epstein.

"Sam!" His father pointed at Michael and Suzie as if Sam couldn't see them from five feet away. "Surprise, huh?" His cheeks were red and his voice was strained. Sam was unsure if it was a few drinks that had done him in or the fact that his son had shown up with the daughter of the man who had broken up his marriage.

"Hey, hey, yeah. Big surprise." Sam looked at Michael and Suzie quickly, afraid to land his gaze in one specific place. Michael and Suzie?

"Thanks, I haven't eaten since last night." Michael reached for a sandwich on the top of the stack. Dimly, Sam offered the plate to Suzie, who just shook her head.

"Wow, Suzie. Wow."

"Wow, Sam." She grinned. "Wow."

"How long are you here?" Sam's father asked.

Michael held up a finger in response, swallowed, and said, "Got to leave tomorrow first thing."

"Where is Bella?" Suzie asked in a soft voice.

Sam gestured over his shoulder. "Come on. I was bringing food to everyone out back." He turned quickly and then felt too shy to check and see if Suzie was behind him. Of course she didn't need him to tell her where "out back" was located; she had spent more of her childhood in this house than in her own. Once they hit the long hall to the bedrooms she tapped him on the shoulder, and Sam nearly dropped the plate of sandwiches.

"Want me to take those chips from you?"

He'd forgotten he was holding chips between his side and arm. The bag felt kind of flat. "No, it's fine."

At Bella's bedroom door Suzie reached around and twisted the knob. They stepped into the room and Sam tried to avoid looking at Bella's bed. Heat was rising up from his back to his neck and he was sweating under the collar. But Suzie wasn't paying attention to him. She was sprinting around the piles, her hair and coat flying behind her, getting to the deck steps before Sam.

Sam heard Mindy scream, then Ruthie. He stepped outside just in time to see Suzie take Bella in her arms as the girls burst into tears.

"It's about fucking time, dude." Frankie grabbed the plate of sandwiches from Sam. He took two off the top and handed the platter to Peter.

Sam dropped the chip bag onto a chair. Stephen sidled up next to him and said under his breath, "Holy shit, she is hot. I mean, I always thought she was. But you know, this is even better than I imagined." He gave an approving nod.

Ruthie tapped Suzie on the shoulder and, when neither Suzie nor Bella responded, she tried to pull them apart. "All right, all right, you need to tell us how you got here and how you knew! Where have you been, Suzie Epstein?"

Bella pulled Suzie down with her onto the lounge chair, and

Suzie leaned back against Bella's fur-covered knees. Just like that they were fifteen all over again.

By the time Sam stumbled home it was midnight. He had learned that Suzie's parents had lasted only another year after their attempted reconciliation in Massachusetts, and that Suzie had graduated from high school a year early and been accepted to Harvard, where she now was a senior, premed, studying to become a psychiatrist. She had bumped into Michael in line for coffee two days before, and Michael had told her about Bella's mother.

Sam stood at the sink and tossed back two aspirin chased by a large glass of water. He squinted out the window, through the dull spray of a streetlight, and wondered what Bella and Suzie were doing. Suzie had not left Bella's side all evening. He imagined them inside now, curled together on Bella's bed, whispering into the shadows, wrapped in that damn fur. Suzie hadn't made eye contact with him again all night, and he wondered what that meant, if it meant anything. It probably meant nothing.

The television was on, an infomercial for weight loss on the screen. Michael was asleep on his back on the couch, one hand resting on his chest, the other grazing the floor. Sam stooped down, picked up the channel changer off the floor, and clicked off the sound.

At the sudden silence, Michael snorted awake. "Hey, hey. What time is it?" He fumbled at his watch.

"Midnight. Sorry."

"It's okay." He waved his hand in the air. "I'm used to sleeping for five minutes at a time." The usual snap of sarcasm in his voice wasn't there. "Medical school. One of the perks." He snorted again and smacked his stomach. "Damn, I'm hungry."

"I could make you something." Sam couldn't remember the last time he and Michael had spent any time together, and making him something to eat seemed like an easy enough way to do that. Besides, he was curious enough about Suzie and Michael that he was hoping for some more information.

Michael cracked open an eye and looked over at him. "Seriously?"

Sam nodded and moved past him into the kitchen. "Egg sandwich okay?"

"Ah, Sam-man, seriously, that would be fantastic."

Sam opened the fridge and pulled out a carton of eggs, a jar of salsa, a block of cheddar, and butter. From deep in the freezer he found a bag of bagels—grocery store version, but they would do. He heated the griddle pan and sliced the bagels, putting them facedown on the butter to slowly toast before he cracked half a dozen eggs into a bowl.

Sam heard the scrape of a kitchen chair and looked over his shoulder to see Michael slumped at the table. Michael poked at the pile of soy sauce. "Dad is going to get high blood pressure if he doesn't stop eating this shit." He gathered the packets up, leaned over for the trash can, and swept the packs in.

"There will be more next week," Sam said as he set the plate in front of him. Steam rose from the sides of the bagel, off the eggs. Cheese and salsa oozed onto the plate. His own mouth watered as Michael lifted the sandwich and took a large bite.

He was still chewing, head down, when Sam sat across from him with his own sandwich. He ate half and then pushed it toward the middle of the table. Michael was licking salsa from his fingers and he looked up at Sam as he lifted the remains from the plate. A piece of egg was on his chin, slick with grease. "This is amazing."

Sam laughed. "Did you even chew?"

Michael shook his head. "I'm telling you, medical school, especially the last two years, fucks with everything. Between rotations and classes and studying, you can't sleep more than an hour at a time and you eat like a pack of wolves is at your back." Sam handed him a paper towel and he wiped his mouth and chin. "And at the end you get a diploma."

"And a cushy life." Sam knew his perspective was probably ignorant. But considering his future looked less than bright, anything seemed cushy in comparison.

"Hey, yeah, but it takes years to get to that life. And frankly, health care and insurance being what they are, I don't know that the monetary rewards of being a doctor even exist anymore."

"I'm flunking more than half of my classes," Sam said. He didn't know where the confession came from, but he wasn't entirely sorry it was out there.

"What the fuck?" Michael looked concerned, but not shocked.

Sam shrugged. "I know some of it's my fault. But, I don't know, I just can't get it."

Michael shook his head. "There's a difference between can't and don't want to. Do you need a tutor? Do you need to change your major?"

"I don't know if that would help." Sam hesitated. "I just don't think I'm you, Michael. I'm not cut out for the books, never have been."

Michael made a face. "Nobody is asking you to be me. But, Sammy, it is so freaking hard to get a job without a college education. Have you told Dad?"

"No."

"You have to talk to Dad."

"And what is he going to say? Try harder?"

Michael ran a hand through his hair. Sam noticed that he too needed a haircut. "Is that impossible?" He squinted at something past Sam on the wall before he turned his attention back. "So you finish in five years instead of four. You take summer classes."

Sam sighed, pushed back his chair, and stacked their plates in the sink. "Feels like impossible is the answer."

"What are your options: make goat cheese?"

Sam grinned. Michael and he rarely brought up the topic of their mother. He looked over at his brother and was surprised to see him smirking. "Would that qualify as learning a family trade?"

Michael threw back his head and laughed. Sam watched his Adam's apple move up and down. When Michael stopped laughing he snuffled a few times and said, "I mean, when I think about Mom, I still picture her with Dad. Quiet, sad, moody. And then I remember where she is now."

"You remember her like that?"

Michael nodded.

Sam swallowed hard. He remembered their mother singing silly made-up songs, lining up his plastic army men on sheets of newspaper and spray painting them crazy colors, letting him drive the old station wagon while sitting on her lap, allowing ice cream to dribble down his arms on a hot day and then hosing him off. Sam knew she could be quiet and sad, but that wasn't all he remembered.

"Shit, Sammy, look at your face. We had it pretty good. Even after, we did, you know?"

Sam nodded. What would Michael know about after? He had been away at college. But he was right. They had survived more or less intact.

"Was it awkward with Dad tonight?" Sam asked, then clarified, "because of Suzie?"

Michael stopped mid-yawn, his hands above his head, his shirt untucked to show a hairy slice of his lower belly. "What do you mean?"

Sam stared hard at Michael. Was he kidding?

Michael shook his head from side to side. "Sam?"

"That summer Mom left was the summer the Epsteins moved. I think Mom and Mrs. Epstein were close, or, you know, Mom felt bad for her when Mr. Epstein left." Sam knew he was stammering idiotically, but Michael had already seemed to lose interest. If Michael didn't know about their mother and Mr. Epstein, now didn't seem like the time to tell him.

Michael stood again, shrugged, and yawned. "You going to crash?" Sam asked, eager to get off the subject.

"Yeah. I have to be back in Boston for nine A.M. rounds. So I'm leaving in"—he checked his watch—"three hours."

Sam didn't want to ask if he was taking Suzie with him. He nodded and said weakly, "Any time you need an egg sandwich . . ."

"You rock, Sammy-boy. Thanks for that." Michael patted his stomach, then started down toward his room. He paused at the door and looked back. "And talk to Dad. Don't worry, I won't spill your secret." He reached up and tapped the molding and then he was gone.

The spray of something hard against the window above Sam's bed woke him. He thought it was raining until he remembered how cold it had been, how cold it was even right now in the house because his dad turned the thermostat down to fifty-eight while they slept. He had just tucked his comforter back around his shoulders and legs when the sound came again.

Sam sat up and lifted the shade. The window was smeared with ice and water and seeing anything was impossible. He kneeled to squint out of the upper part of the glass that remained streak free and saw someone in a long, dark coat hurrying back down the driveway toward the Epsteins' old house.

Sam yanked on a pair of jeans and a sweater. Downstairs he shoved his feet into his dad's shoveling boots, which he kept on a plastic tray by the back door. When he got outside Suzie was standing with her back to Sam at the edge of her old driveway. She wore a knit cap topped with a giant puffball. Her head was tilted back as she took in her house.

He touched her on the shoulder and she turned around. "Sam."

"Suzie." He noticed she was wearing the plaid scarf Michael had been wearing earlier.

She smiled. "I know I'm going to sound like every person who goes back to look at her childhood home, but I'm going to say it. Looks smaller."

Sam nodded. It looked exactly the same to him.

"So," she said, and shrugged. "Your brother wants to leave at three. I wasn't sleeping. I thought I'd come early."

Sam glanced back at the house, but it was dark. No light from the bathroom or Michael's room.

Quietly Suzie said, "We have some time."

Sam didn't know what to say. Would asking how much time sound like he was expecting something?

"You grew up handsome, Sam." Suzie gave him a tentative smile that broke into a grin. "Not that I ever doubted that."

There were puffs of frost in the air between them. Sam felt the heat rise to his cheeks despite the cold and Suzie giggled.

"I'm glad to see you haven't changed, Sammy."

"That's what you think," Sam said weakly.

"That's what I see. You and Bella? I'm glad about that, glad that it's you she has to lean on. I'm glad she is with someone who has a good and generous heart."

"Bella's a cool girl," Sam said, and stared at the ground. He didn't want to talk about Bella with Suzie. "So, a psychiatrist, huh?"

She looked embarrassed and brought a hand up to her mouth. "Am I that transparent? Do I sound like one of those jerks who takes a class and diagnoses everyone they meet?" She put her hand on his arm. "I'm not, really. If anything it has taught me to say what I mean."

Sam nodded, concentrating on the feel of her hand through his sweater. He wished he could tell her that after all this time, after all these years, she still had the same effect on him.

Suzie looked back at her house again, her hand still on his arm. "I spent most of my life right here in this spot, and I feel like I can't remember anything about that time at all. It's like my life has only started now, and nothing before has any significance." She dropped her hand and Sam stepped back. Suzie didn't look at him, and right then he knew she hadn't meant a single word she'd just said.

Sam took Bella back to Vassar because the last thing he wanted to do was return to school, although he admitted that to no one. When he went to her house to pick her up Mr. Spade patted him on the shoulder and called him a "good man" for seeing Bella safely back.

On a snowy day, they boarded a nearly empty train. Sam nudged Bella toward a window covered in crystals and stowed his backpack and Bella's small leather satchel above. The satchel contained some of Bella's mother's things, and as far as Sam could tell from the bulk and the heft of it, there was no clothing at all inside.

Bella put her hand against the window and pressed hard, leaving an imprint. "It's like being inside a snow globe," she said before putting her head on his shoulder and closing her eyes. She was still wearing the fur, and either he was getting used to the smell or the coat was actually airing out.

Back at Vassar Bella returned to classes right away. She was a serious student, serious about her English degree and her dead poets and her writing. She mentioned several times, first in a tone of awe and then of envy, that she was amazed Suzie had skipped a grade, that she was a soon-to-graduate senior on the cusp of her real life. That if Bella had known that was an option she would have taken it. Sam realized then they all had someone they measured themselves against, and even the brightest weren't immune.

Sam stayed because he was hiding and then he stayed because he couldn't leave. He made Bella breakfast before she left for class each morning. One morning, as he was pouring them each a mug of coffee, he glanced over at Bella, sitting at the table, framed in the curtainless window that looked out over the parking lot. Her hair, like his, was still wet from the shower. Sam's muscles felt warm, pulled, like ribbons of saltwater taffy. Bella was bent over a book, wearing a white long-sleeve T-shirt, loose at the neck, without a bra. She held a piece of cinnamon toast halfway to her mouth. As Sam slid her coffee across the table at her she looked up at him and smiled wide.

Sam sat down opposite her and returned her smile. He genuinely cared for Bella; if he focused on that, on living with her and making her breakfast, he could ignore the fact that the rest of his life seemed to be imploding.

The phone rang and Bella leaned over, squinting at the caller ID screen. She frowned. "It's your dad, again."

Sam shook his head and brought his coffee to his lips.

Bella frowned again and pressed ignore. "Sam, you never called him back?"

Sam put down the cup.

"Sam, you can't ignore him forever."

"It's only been two weeks."

Bella sighed. "Forever, two weeks, what's the difference?"

Sam sighed. "You're right. He doesn't deserve this." He ducked his chin to his chest. "I think I need to go."

For a moment Bella looked scared, but she quickly straightened her shoulders, her small breasts brushing against the cloth of her shirt. There was a damp circle above her right breast where a tangle of wet hair had fallen. "Then you need to go."

Sam reached across the table and grabbed her fingers in his hand. "Hey. You have class. And I have to go see my dad."

Bella took a deep breath and exhaled. "Pretending was nice, wasn't it?"

"Were you pretending?"

She bit her bottom lip. "Only if you were."

Sam laughed. "Oh, is that how it is?"

Bella giggled. "Oh, that's how it is."

They stared at each other. The air smelled of cinnamon, coffee, heat from the radiators, and Bella's shampoo. Sam inhaled. Trying to remember it all.

Sam had intended to go home, and then he didn't. It took a train and two bus transfers to get there, eleven hours in all. The snow was deep and the walk unpleasant in sneakers. There was an absence of streetlights, although the moon was low on the snow.

When he got to the house every window was an inked rectangle, and he hesitated, but figured, as he put his fist against the old wood, that he had come too far to go anywhere else that night.

When the door finally swung open Sam saw him first and immediately thought he was wrong to have come. Then from the back of the long, narrow hall she came rushing toward the door. Her hair was loose and long; it fell around her shoulders like a blanket. She flung her arms out to her sides as if she were going to hug him and then changed her mind.

Sam opened his mouth to explain why he was in Vermont on a late snowy night in the dead of winter. But the only word that came out of his mouth as he fell against her shoulder was "Mom."

SIX

We Only Move Backward
Bella—2003

Years ago on a December night in their junior year of high school they had been in Peter Chang's basement before the winter dance, and Sam had turned to Bella, his eyes as navy as his sweater, and said, "So?"

It began as simply as that, friends who had known each other since they were in diapers. Sam made her happy. Just the sight of him as his cheeks flushed a deep shade of red was all it took. She wanted to kiss him and she knew that he probably wanted to kiss her too. Later, when they had all stumbled from Peter's basement, wandering through the streets of their neighborhood to the high school, Sam had bumped up against her shoulder and she had found his hand down by his side and grabbed hold of his fingers. He wound them through hers and hadn't let go, and right then in that moment she had been so sure of everything she had ever wanted.

Since her mother's funeral, Bella had been stuck on that memory, and she didn't know why. Maybe it was only the ache of nostalgia. That night, coming in late after the dance, straddling the threshold of her mother's room to tell her she was home, she apologized for missing her curfew. Her lips had been swollen from kissing. She wanted to lie in bed alone and go over every minute she had spent in Sam's arms. But then she had noticed the way her mother was looking at her and instead she had crawled into bed with her and whispered about Sam. The mustard light in the room was diffused by the angle of the bathroom door, and she caught a glimpse of her mother's face in the shadows. She was smiling but there was also something sad in her expression. Bella had pled exhaustion then and gone to bed, not wanting to give her mother a chance to say what she had been thinking. She was sure her mother had never felt anything close to the way Bella had felt that night. She hadn't seen the way Sam had stroked her cheek with his fingers, and looked into her eyes before the first time he kissed her.

But here she was, weeks after her mother's death, without him. And now when she thought about everything she had once believed, she just felt raw and foolish.

She knew her father was worried that she would end up alone, curled up like a snail on the bathroom floor, a weeping, wilting mess. Her brothers had wives and children, full lives that extended into every single minute of their days, and he wanted that for his only daughter. So he called her every morning, usually from the train. And Bella began to look forward to the sound of his voice. There was something comforting about the two of them sharing the quiet part of their morning together.

She also had Suzie. Bella and Suzie had fallen back into their friendship as if the gap in years meant nothing. That night after her mother's funeral, after her sisters-in-law had wrapped the leftovers, cleared the counters of cloudy wineglasses, after the kids had fallen asleep in midmovement, with food-smeared faces, shoes missing, half dressed in their funeral clothes, after her father had taken a drink into his study and asked to be alone, after the last drunken mourners had left and her oldest brother had locked the front door, Suzie and Bella had lain in her bed. Bella couldn't remember the last thing she had said to her mother. She had never returned the call she promised she would, begging off on the pretense of studying when instead she'd gone out. These things were playing on a loop in her brain. So Bella had asked Suzie to talk. She didn't care about what, she just wanted to hear the sound of her voice, she just wanted anything but the quiet, and Suzie had obliged.

Suzie was interviewing at medical schools in the city and had convinced Bella to take the train in from Poughkeepsie and meet her for the weekend. Bella, saddled with one last year at Vassar, was envious that Suzie had something concrete to move on to. After everything that had happened, Bella couldn't help but think that her English degree was somehow trivial.

They were staying on the Upper East Side in an apartment owned by the parents of someone Suzie knew from Boston. When Bella rang the bell Suzie greeted her at the door in a suit and heels, holding a bottle of wine, looking the part of an adult. She drew Bella inside quickly with a bright smile and squeezed her forearm. "I'm so glad you're here."

Bella set her bag on a bench in the hall and followed Suzie into a long, narrow kitchen off to the left. Suzie rummaged around in the drawers until she found the corkscrew. She held it up, triumphant, and grimaced as she wound the metal into the cork. Next to Suzie Bella felt even more like a college student in her tan corduroys, stretched-out sweater, and bulky scarf, and her mother's fur coat.

While Suzie secured glasses and poured their wine, Bella shrugged out of the coat. "Bathroom?" she asked.

Suzie looked up. "Down the hall to the right."

In the bathroom, Bella closed the door and sat down on the toilet. Across from her was a stack of *New Yorker*s that looked unread. She picked up the top magazine and flipped to the table of contents. The slick pages were virginal, and Bella wondered if *The New Yorker* was the only magazine that seemed always to be subscribed to but never read. She replaced the magazine, flushed, washed her hands, and frowned into the mirror. Her hair, which had been wavy her entire life, had mysteriously gone straight since her mother's death. She smoothed it down, wishing she had a hair tie, and pinched her cheeks, and then felt ridiculous that she was acting as if she had to look attractive for Suzie.

When she opened the door Suzie yelled, "In the living room."

Bella walked down the hall to an open room with large panes of glass, a grand piano resting on a faded oriental carpet, floor-to-ceiling bookshelves, and an enormous L-shaped couch covered in brown velvet. In front of the couch was an old trunk that held precariously uneven towers of books. Behind the trunk sat Suzie, a wineglass balanced on her knee and another in her hand, which she held out to Bella.

Bella took the glass and positioned herself on the couch so that she could face Suzie, who had taken off her suit jacket and kicked off her heels. Suzie raised her glass and Bella did the same. The wine was tangy and she let it pool on her tongue before she swallowed. Growing up, she and Suzie had shared many days and nights on the couch watching television and consuming bags of junk food until they wanted to puke. If no adult was around to shoo them outside, and frequently none was, they could sit silently for hours, the only noise the rustling of the bags. Bella wished they could sit like that again. If only for a moment.

"So," Suzie said, "you found it okay?"

Bella nodded, taking another sip of wine. She looked over at Suzie, her expression expectant. Then Bella remembered the reason Suzie was in the city. "Did everything go okay with the interviews?"

Suzie nodded, as if she had been expecting Bella's question. "Good. Nerve-racking, but good."

Bella knew that Mount Sinai was Suzie's first choice, but she had also interviewed at Columbia and Hunter. Bella also knew, because Suzie had told her, that Michael was hoping to secure his residency at Mount Sinai. Other than that Suzie had been quiet regarding their relationship. Bella wondered if it was out of deference to her struggles with Sam.

Bella took another sip of wine. "You will have multiple offers, Suzie, I'm sure."

Suzie shrugged. "I'm not fishing for reassurance here, Bells, but you just never know."

Bella nodded. "You'd think I would get that by now." She twisted her mouth into what she hoped looked like a smile.

"You look thin," Suzie said, changing the subject.

"I'm not," Bella said, even though when she put on her pants that morning she was surprised to feel them slip down to her hipbones. She looked at Suzie and admitted, "Maybe a few pounds lighter."

Suzie leaned forward and twisted the stem of the wineglass between her palms. "How do you feel?"

Bella gave a sharp little laugh. She ran a hand across the smooth velvet couch cushions. "Like I've been locked out of my house without any hope of getting the keys."

Suzie sighed. "You haven't heard from Sam?"

"No," Bella said. "And I don't think that's going to happen." She shook her head. "We're not like that."

"Then why the hell did he go back to school with you?" Suzie sounded a little angry as she reached for the wine bottle.

Bella had always thought that maybe something had happened between Sam and Suzie in high school, before Suzie moved. But so far they had skirted around the whole thing. She supposed anything that happened before was really a nonissue at this point. Bella held out her glass for another pour before Suzie refilled her own. "I don't think Michael has heard from him either. Their dad is worried." Suzie paused. "Especially since he seems to have ditched school."

Bella knew how Sam felt about school. Her mother's death and Bella's neediness had temporarily given him the excuse to prolong the inevitable. "He'll show up eventually." She really believed he was fine, even if she didn't think he would turn back up in her life.

Suzie looked like she was about to say something but instead clamped her mouth shut, her lips squished into an uneven line.

"What?" Bella asked.

"He's so unlike Michael."

"I guess. I don't really know Michael, but Sam said they were pretty different. He always described Michael as goal oriented," Bella said.

"That's true." Suzie smiled. "Michael knows what he wants. He has a plan. I like that about him, you know?" She paused. "Does this seem totally bizarre to you, that I would end up with Sam's brother?"

"Only in a who-ever-would-have-guessed kind of way." Bella was curious where Suzie was going.

"We were fifteen a long time ago." Suzie laughed awkwardly. "And it really was nothing."

It took Bella a minute to realize that Suzie was acknowledging that there had been something between her and Sam. "Does it bother Michael that you were once with Sam?" she said carefully.

"No," Suzie said softly. "I wasn't with Sam. I mean there was hardly a relationship. We made out in my basement for a few weeks." She shrugged. "I mean if I hadn't moved, you know, maybe things would have ended differently."

"Sure," Bella said, wondering why Suzie had never told her.

"But that was high school," Suzie said, "history. No one stays with their high school crush."

"Right," Bella said. Suzie chose Michael. Sam chose to run away from Bella. Whatever it had been was over. There really was nothing left to tell.

Bella woke up curled on the couch. The lights were off in the room, but there was a marine-like glow from the curtainless windows that overlooked Central Park. Bella blinked to clear her vision and stretched her legs out as she settled deeper into the cushions. Her stomach growled. She wondered where Suzie had gone but lacked the urgency to get off the couch, and closed her eyes again, dozing for a few more minutes until she heard a snorting sound, and then a door opening.

Suzie shuffled down the hall toward the living room; she had changed into jeans with a hole in the knee and a plain black sweater. She had a strange look on her face. As she got closer, Bella could see that her eyes were swollen, like she had been crying. She saw Bella looking at her and wiped the back of her hand under her nose.

"Hungry?" Suzie asked. She stood with her head bowed and

her hands shoved deep into the front pockets of her jeans. It was a childish posture and made her look like a vulnerable, sulky teenager.

Bella nodded at her oldest friend and sat up. Whatever was wrong, Suzie wasn't going to talk about it right now.

An hour later they sat knee to knee at a small table in a hole-in-the-wall place in Chinatown, dim sum for an army crammed between them on the chipped Formica tabletop. They had fallen on the food wordlessly as the plates came out one, two, three at a time, and now they were still eating, but the pace had slowed. Bella's stomach was full to bursting and she was grateful for her too-big pants, but she couldn't keep her chopsticks out of the food.

As they filled up on pork dumplings and Chinese beer, Bella noticed that Suzie looked a little better, but she still wasn't totally present. Bella thought about all the moments of their life they had shared together: bad haircuts, ugly clothes, crushes, first periods, braces, and big pimples. Bella had hidden Suzie in her closet when things got too bad at her house between her parents, and Suzie had come to the hospital every time Bella's mother had been admitted, playing War with Bella on the floor of the waiting room. They had spent endless hours discussing what it was going to be like to be kissed, and what it would feel like to have sex. Nothing was off-limits, or so Bella had thought, but Suzie had kept Sam a secret, so maybe they hadn't told each other everything.

Bella poked the air between them with a chopstick. "Are you going to tell me what's up?"

"It's the same old thing. My mother." Suzie rolled her eyes. "She can't handle my brothers and they take advantage of her." She paused. "They have been asked to leave yet another private school.

Really, the school isn't asking, it's insisting they leave. And my mother is running out of options. Just another reason for me to get the hell out of Boston." She poked at the translucent little pile of ginger. "Do you know she went as far as to have them bar mitzvahed? I think she thought that whole 'you're a man now' shtick would jolt them into acting responsibly. When in reality it just provided them with boatloads of bar mitzvah money to spend on dope and booze."

"What does she expect you to do about it?"

Suzie chewed her bottom lip. "She doesn't think like that. She just wants someone to do something and I happen to be that person." Suzie smiled, but she didn't look happy. "Cash buys a lot, but not even my father's kind of cash can help them there."

"I'm sorry you still have to deal with all this," Bella said. "So where is he now?"

"The patriarch?" Suzie gave a short little laugh. "Well, that would be anyone's guess. I don't know, we really don't speak." She picked up her beer and took a swallow. "There was a rumble of illegal trading, a misallocation of funds or something like that, but it never stuck." She sighed. "He always lands on his feet."

"Does he pay for school?"

"For me? No, no, no." She shook her head. "I have some scholarships and loans."

"Really?" Bella was shocked. Harvard, and now med school, couldn't be cheap.

"I don't want him to touch my life any more than he already has. It's just been one humiliation after another. I can't stand it. My mother and my brothers will always give him the benefit of the doubt. But I can't."

Bella leaned forward, her head nearly touching Suzie's. It was a relief to not be focused on her own problems. "Does your mother still want to be with him?"

Suzie made a face. "God, no. She finally let that part go. But she still accepts his money. I wish she would get her own life, get away from that damn dependence on him. But then most of her days she spends in a vodka bath, so . . ." She sighed. "She's way past the point of changing."

Bella put down her chopsticks and leaned back in the chair. She was stuffed to the point of being immobile and she wondered how she was ever going to get up and away from the table. She admired Suzie's handling of her complicated life, but she had sunk so deep into her own misery over her mother's death and Sam's disappearing act that she offered none of those sentiments to her oldest friend.

Bella paid the bill, courtesy of her father. They wandered slowly through the narrow streets of Chinatown arm in arm, sluggish from dinner. They were in no hurry, had no particular plan until Suzie spotted a sign for psychic readings above a store that sold beauty supplies. She practically skipped the few steps to the door and held it open for Bella.

Bella peered inside before she moved forward. It smelled like dust and heat and rancid wok oil. In front of them was a narrow storefront lined with shelves. The atmosphere was like that of a low-rent Duane Reade.

Suzie took Bella's hand in hers and led the way to a makeshift counter along the back of the store. A young woman with a Hello Kitty T-shirt was bent over a textbook. The inky hair on top of her head was cluttered with brightly colored plastic barrettes. She didn't look up from her book.

Suzie tapped her fingers on the counter. "We're here for a reading."

The girl looked up and slowly looked Suzie and Bella up and down. "For two?" she finally asked.

Suzie nodded quickly.

"Fifty."

Bella tugged on Suzie's arm. It was too much. But Suzie was already digging through her bag for her wallet. She placed the bills on the counter. The girl stood up, jammed the bills in the pocket of her jeans, and sat back down.

"Where do we go?" Suzie asked. "Here?" She looked around the room.

The girl blinked and ran a hand over her eyes as if she were hoping Bella and Suzie would disappear. Bella was starting to feel a prickle of sweat on the back of her neck. She noticed a series of stains across the top of Hello Kitty's head right below her pink bow on the front of the girl's T-shirt. From the pages littered with charts, the textbook on the counter appeared to be chemistry. When the girl removed her hand from her face she peered up at Bella and pointed. "You."

Suzie swiveled around. Bella swallowed hard and nodded. "Yes?"

"You have too many questions." The girl shook her head. "Not good."

"Really?" Bella was irritated. Any idiot would know she had questions. But too many? How could she have too many questions?

"Too much back there, too much." The girl looked beyond Bella, over her shoulder. Bella felt a trickle of sweat between her breasts. The girl winced, looked back down at her textbook, and shook her head.

Bella wanted to demand an explanation of what "too much back there" meant, but she felt like she couldn't catch her breath. She didn't want this girl in the dirty T-shirt to be the one who told her Sam didn't want her. She turned to Suzie and said, "I can't," and then she bolted from the store.

Even though she heard Suzie behind her calling her name, she didn't stop running. Suzie finally caught up to her in a funny little alley shaped like an elbow because Bella, coming around the blind corner, had tripped on an overturned plastic milk carton. She was bent over, her hands on her thighs, panting loudly, when Suzie put a hand on her back.

"Bells! Are you okay?" Suzie rubbed Bella's back. "What happened?"

Bella's ankle throbbed, her lungs hurt, and she felt like she might throw up. She tried to stand up straight. "I'm fine," she managed. She didn't know whether she wanted to cry or scream. What the hell was wrong with her?

"I'm sorry." Suzie looked like she was about to cry. "I'm sorry I freaked you out. I thought it would be fun, I guess. I don't know. I'm so sorry." She rubbed Bella's back. "Do you want to sit someplace?"

Bella shook her head. "I'm tired."

"Sure, " Suzie said, her voice relieved, as if it was obvious that was what was wrong with Bella. Her mother was dead. Sam had disappeared. Her life was shit. She was tired.

"I'm just really tired," Bella said again, willing herself to believe it. She hobbled back toward the main street. Her ankle was sore, but not horrible. She could walk on it. She put out her hand to Suzie.

When they were younger she and Suzie had followed their horoscopes with religious fervor. During sleepovers they always pulled out the Ouija board. Of course all of their questions had been about boys. Why had they never asked what they were going to be when they grew up? Why had they been so consumed with who they were going to kiss? Who they were going to marry? Had things changed at all since they were thirteen?

She had no idea what that girl was going to tell her. But if it was anything close to an answer she couldn't bear it. The unknown was the weight that was keeping her here. Without it, she would surely float away.

The apartment had two bedrooms but Suzie and Bella shared the king-sized bed in the master suite because it was what they had always done. After dinner it took everything Bella had just to change and wash her face before she dropped onto the bed. Suzie made her prop her foot on a pile of pillows and handed her a bag of corn she'd found in the freezer. She wouldn't quit fussing with the pillows, the corn, the lighting. She brought Bella a glass of water she didn't ask for, and then opened the window for air circulation. Eventually she stopped moving and stood by the curtains, rubbing her feet back and forth against the carpet, as if she were running in place.

"Suzie, please relax," Bella said, testing her toes as she wiggled them beneath the bag of corn. "I'm fine."

Suzie twisted a wad of curtain fabric in her fingers. "I feel awful. I thought the psychic would be fun, a diversion. I didn't want to make you feel worse."

Bella shrugged. She wanted to stop talking about the psychic, but she didn't want to draw any more attention to her freak-out. And Suzie had paid a lot of money and hadn't even gotten anything out of it. "What would you have asked?"

"Oh." Suzie hesitated and looked up at the ceiling. "Probably something stupid like: Am I going to get into med school, or is this thing with Michael real . . ."

"I don't think you need the psychic for those answers."

"No?" Suzie said. "You think, really?"

"Ugh," Bella said. She rolled over onto her side away from Suzie. The corn slid somewhere into the tangle of blankets around her legs. "I think it's pretty obvious that you are going to get into med school and that Michael is totally into you."

"Bells," Suzie said, and then she was quiet for so long that Bella finally rolled over to look at her. Suzie's face was pale, and she looked terrified. "I love him," she whispered.

Bella struggled to sit up. She kicked the bag of corn. She missed the girls they once were, dreaming about happily ever after, never imagining that they would get scared or hurt or need to be saved. "Life is surreal, Suzie. But you picked the right Turner brother."

"I did?" She cracked a slow smile as she walked toward the door. "I did." She said emphatically. "I really did."

Bella watched Suzie go. It wasn't long before she heard the low murmur of her voice from the other room. Michael must have been sitting on his phone, waiting to hear from her.

Bella stared at the ceiling. She wasn't so much a realist as a coward, afraid of everything. She thought of all the things she might have said to her mother, or to Sam. All the wrongs she could right, all the possibilities that had passed her by, all the chances she'd had to make something, anything, more meaningful. There were too many blank spaces to count, and too many regrets.

SEVEN

I Thought You Said You Loved Me
Sam—2003

S am's mother gifted him a handful of days when no one knew he was in Vermont. Although she didn't say why and he didn't ask, he felt generosity there between them.

What he should have done was get in touch with his father, with Bella. What he did was find a bar tucked away in a dingy, beat-up bowling alley in the basement of a building, just blocks off the town green, and drink.

Middlebury, with its mix of privileged college students and farmers, was easier to hide in than Sam imagined, especially in winter. Quickly, he established a pattern of sleeping till mid-afternoon, walking into town, and drinking all night. The trek back along the winding roads to the home his mother shared with her goats and Tom was just enough to sober Sam up so he didn't get hit by a car or freeze to death in a snowbank.

Every one of those nights, Sam sat at the bar listening to the crash of pins, the swoop and click of the electronic setup. With each drink he was more aware of his body forming an apostrophe. A woman who worked the dinner shift always pushed a basket of fries his way even when he didn't order them, and stopped serving Sam when he'd hit his limit. She also asked him questions he didn't want to answer. On his fifth consecutive night on the same stool she said, "You know, I can tell you really don't have your heart in this."

Her comment made Sam blush. He felt like he'd been caught with a fake ID, even though he was a fully legal twenty-one. Even worse, he felt like a moron.

A cheer came from the tables behind him and Sam turned to see a group of women in matching T-shirts scanning the electronic scoreboards with rapt attention. "So, what are you hiding from?"

Sam looked down into his piss-colored beer. He didn't even have the balls, or the resources, to order hard liquor. "Well, I flunked out of school, which I haven't shared with my father yet, and I left my girlfriend's apartment under the pretense of going to tell my father and then instead came here to visit my mother." He paused. "I haven't talked to either of them since I got here." He left off the part about the recent death of Bella's mother.

She looked disappointed, as if she had expected him to cop to something else. "First, you need to get in touch with that girl. Even if you don't want to see her again, that's not right." She stopped wiping the bar with a sour gray rag long enough for Sam to know she was serious. "And who cares that you flunked out? You don't think that half the kids at this college aren't doing the same thing?"

Sam held up a finger to make a point. "Big difference between them and me."

She gave Sam a funny look. "Big difference between you and me." She shrugged and walked down the bar and refilled another beer. "And you're still here."

✦ ✦ ✦

Sam sent Bella a letter that said: *I'm sorry. I'm at my mother's house. I'm really sorry. Sam.*

A week later Tom handed him a small square envelope in return. Inside on a torn sheet of notebook paper it said:

> Whatever happens with us, your body
> will haunt mine—tender, delicate
> your lovemaking, like the half-curled frond
> of the fiddlehead fern in forests
> just washed by sun.

Sam folded the paper into a slim rectangle and stuck it in the back of his wallet. He wished he understood what she was really trying to tell him. Was that forgiveness for his stupidity? Was it anger? He thought of Bella sitting in the winter sunlight eating cinnamon toast in her apartment. He wasn't sure anyone would ever be as generous about his failings as a human being again. The words felt like something he should keep.

He helped his mother care for her goats. He trailed her to the pen. He learned their names. As soon as the goats heard the gate latch lift they stumbled over one another to knock against his mother's legs. His mother made clucking noises of greeting deep in her throat.

Sam collected the warm pale blue eggs the hens laid, and he listened as his mother told him how to make goat cheese. He remembered none of the details but he was grateful that she kept up the conversation even though he said nothing in return.

His mother was alone a lot, but Sam didn't necessarily think she was looking for company. Tom was teaching a beginning fiction class at the college this semester as well as freshman composition, and was editing his new book. So he stayed late at his office at school, leaving Sam to cook simple dinners for his mother: omelets and toast, or frittatas with goat cheese and herbs. They ate them in front of the woodstove, in a small room tucked off the kitchen, where his mother had a crowded desk covered with books and papers and photographs of Michael and Sam when they were younger. Most were unframed, their edges curled, and a few had the remains of tape left yellowed in the corners, as if she had grabbed them quickly on her way out. In a way they reminded Sam of Mr. Epstein's photographs in the shoebox.

Sam stopped going to the bowling alley. Instead he accompanied his mother to the ice-covered pond that sat behind the barn, cupped in a pocket between two slopes slick with crusty snow. She and Tom always skated after dinner, and she hated to miss it. Sam wore Tom's skates, which were a size too big. His ankles wobbled as he made his way out on the ice, where his mother, a lumpy yellow scarf wrapped twice around her neck, skated figure eights around him and laughed. She seemed to always swoop in to save him just as he began to fall.

Sam remembered the skating rink in their town, where everyone took lessons together until the boys split off for hockey and the girls for figure skating. His mother always stayed for the adult free skate afterward, bribing Michael and Sam with hot chocolates and candy bars from the vending machine. The boys had sat thigh pressed to thigh in the bleachers, sweat trapped under their collars as icy tips formed in their hair, candy wrappers crumpled at their feet and wisps of foam mustaches dusting their lips, as she skated lap after furious lap, stopping only when the horn blew, signaling the end of free skate.

Every evening after skating Sam made drinks: herbal tea for

his mother and coffee for him. His mother looked through seed catalogs and made notes on a yellow legal pad for a future garden. Sam listlessly flipped through a stack of magazines that bore Tom's name on the labels: *Poets & Writers, Farmer's Almanac, The Atlantic, Bon Appétit.* Their feet, clad in heavy socks, shared an old footstool covered in woven strips of fabric, and the only sound came from the radio tuned to NPR. At first, Sam slipped into his mother's life, hoping she wouldn't notice he was an interloper. Yet he could tell from the way he caught Tom staring at him at breakfast sometimes that he had plenty of questions for Sam, but out of respect for Elizabeth, he didn't ask.

After two weeks where the sameness of his days and nights had begun to wear, Sam was restless. He couldn't continue to hide there. But he didn't know what to do. Frankly, he was surprised by his mother's lack of prying into his future. "Mom?"

"Hmmm?" She didn't even glance up from the catalog in her lap.

"Don't you want to know? Aren't you even curious?"

She stopped writing, her pencil poised above the pad. "About?"

Sam exhaled in a fit of frustration. Vermont was too quiet. His mother's world was too quiet. He hated the way people enunciated on NPR. He could not take another night like the previous six. "Can we stop this?" He gestured around the room, claustrophobic from her full new life.

"What, Sam? You came here. I opened my home. I figured you would tell me if you wanted." She shrugged, seemingly perfectly willing to allow him his secrets.

Sam stood up and paced the small room. "I should have known."

"What should you have known?"

"Uh, okay. You left, remember?"

"Of course, I remember. I'm not following you, Sam. If you want me to understand something, you need to tell me." She put down the pencil and the catalog. "It's about school?"

"Well, Christ. You already know?" If she knew what he was running away from, why hadn't she said anything? Why was she refusing to be his parent?

She shook her head. "I know you're supposed to be in school and obviously you aren't."

Sam nodded. "I'm not going back." He looked over at her to gauge a reaction.

His mother didn't so much as blink. "It sounds like you've already made a decision. Why are you so angry?"

"You really did give up everything, didn't you? You walked out the door and you just gave up mothering? Is that really all you have to say to me? That I made the decision?" Sam was pacing the room now, his voice rising. It was hot, way too hot. The wood-stove was stifling.

"You are twenty-one years old. If you don't want to finish school, you don't want to finish school. What am I supposed to do?"

"BE MY MOTHER!" Sam's voice bounced off the walls, so he lowered it to add, "Fuck."

"Hey—everything okay?" Tom leaned against the doorframe. He had a bulging canvas bag full of papers and books slung over his shoulder. He was still wearing his coat and boots and he was frowning, his brow creased. He must have heard Sam from outside. "Lizzie?"

"We're fine," Sam's mother said.

Tom looked at Sam for confirmation and he nodded back, offering a weak "Sorry."

Tom gave Sam another, longer look but then turned and left the room. Sam could hear him climb the stairs and walk around the bedroom up above them. The toilet flushed and the springs of the bed creaked.

"I should go," Sam said. "I wasn't thinking when I came here."

"Sit down, please. Can we start again?" his mother asked gently.

"I don't know what more there is to say," Sam said, but he did as she asked. He looked over at his mother. She was resting her head against the high back of her chair. Her lids were heavy. She was up at four every morning and she had to have been tired, sitting here at night keeping him company. Her hair, in a thick braid, was flipped over one shoulder. Sam blinked, trying to remember what she looked like years ago. But he couldn't find the image in his memory bank.

"You were always the easier baby, the easier kid. Michael felt everything so deeply. Even as an infant. You were a relief and a joy." She hesitated, so Sam waited to see where this was going. He certainly had nothing to add. "So maybe I took advantage of your easiness. In you, I saw your father. In Michael, me. I thought you would be okay. That Hunt would be better for you anyway. Michael was done. He was gone. He knew what he wanted."

"That sounds like a bullshit excuse that made it easier for you to leave."

"Maybe, but it wasn't." She hesitated and licked her lips. "Are you trying to say that you can't finish college because I left? Or that I somehow made college difficult?"

Sam shook his head, a little ashamed that he'd tried to blame her. "No."

"Okay, then," she said quietly. "Okay."

Sam shrugged. "What about you?"

"What about me?"

"You get to start over here? You get to make a new life with someone closer to your sons' ages than your own? Are you going to have babies again? What is this all about?"

Sam's mother leaned forward and gripped the arms of the chair, a small smile on her lips. "I am very protective of this life," she said. "But there is no such thing as starting over. Everything that makes me who I am, who you are, began at birth. You cannot lose that, and you cannot escape that. You take it with you." She paused and pointed a finger at Sam. "Our problems aren't the same, Sam. Why does it bother you how old Tom is? We are committed. Age doesn't mean so much now."

Sam felt heat rise to his cheeks and the prick of tears in the corners of his eyes.

"It might matter to him one day," he said huffily, regretting the words when he saw her flinch.

"Perhaps," she said with enough weight behind the word that he knew she thought about that.

"I don't care. I don't care about any of this." Sam stood up, his fists clenched. He bit the inside of his mouth hard to stop the tears. "Sleep with whoever you want. That's what happened with Mr. Epstein, right?"

His mother slumped back against the chair. "I may have done some stupid things. Questionable things. But I didn't sleep with him." She paused. "He wasn't the reason why I left. But he helped it along. I hadn't been happy."

Sam put his hand up. "Don't tell me: Dad was ruining your life."

"Sam, no. Not at all. I was ruining his." She paused. "But then I suppose I didn't lead you to believe anything different. It was easier to make you think Hunt was the bad guy without saying anything at all."

"I never believed it was Dad's fault."

His mother looked a little surprised by Sam's confession, which just confused him even more. So she wanted them to think it was Hunt's fault but then when he said he never did, she was hurt? Sam couldn't stand to hear another moment of this. "I'm going to bed." He turned and headed out of the room. The hallway was freezing and he stopped and leaned against the cool plaster walls. He heard his mother come up behind him. "I just wanted my mother, that's all," Sam mumbled against the wall. "I just wanted to see you."

"Sammy—"

Sam pushed himself away from the wall and pulled himself up the stairs by the banister. "It's all good. Seriously. 'Night, Mom." He took the stairs two at a time and slipped inside the unwelcoming, narrow guest room and fell onto the bed. He waited until he heard his mother's footsteps on the stairs, the clank of the water pipes, the flush of the toilet, and then he waited some more. When he opened the door he could hear Tom's low voice, a sigh, and then later the soft snort of his mother, a heavier rattle from Tom. Quickly, he grabbed his backpack up off the floor and then yanked open the one dresser drawer that held a few of his possessions, cramming them all into the bag before pulling hard on the drawstring.

He was briefly paralyzed on the top step, his backpack straps tightened across his shoulders. He listened for the rhythm of Tom's snores and ran down the steps so that the creak of the wood was hidden in the sounds. He was too far down the road toward the center of town before he remembered to take one last look back, and by then it was too late.

In his wallet Sam had an emergency credit card from his father and thirty-seven dollars in cash. The bus ticket to Boston ate up thirty-six dollars, and the coffee he'd had with his mother kept him awake. The bus was full, an odd mix of travelers, and most of them slept save for an older man across from Sam who rattled a sandwich bag on his lap, folding and unfolding the waxy creases, occasionally taking from the bag a saltine cracker that he ate thoughtfully, slowly, as if he was savoring each bite.

Sam refused to use the credit card, so he trudged through the slushy streets until he found Michael's apartment in the attic of a crumbling brownstone. Lucky for him, he'd happened across his brother's address scrawled on an envelope on his mother's desk. The neighborhood had narrow streets, parking laws that only a veteran cop could figure out, and a variety of ethnic restaurants that papered the nearby buildings with menus. Years before, Sam and his father had helped Michael move in, driving a U-Haul full of cast-off furniture from home. On a steamy August weekend they had set up his couch, his bed, a table and chairs, and a desk. They had gone to the grocery store and filled the refrigerator and at the end of the day they had sat on his small fire escape and grilled hamburgers as if Boston had transformed the three of them into an all-American family unit.

The double doors of the building were wedged open with a brick. Sam climbed the stairs to the top, the heat hitting him in layers. By the time he had arrived at Michael's door he had removed his coat, hat, and gloves.

He had barely knocked when the front door swung open. Suzie Epstein stood in front of him in an oversized cardigan sweater, a Harvard T-shirt, and skinny black pants. "My God, Sam! Everyone has been crazy worried about you!" She threw her arms around his shoulders. Sam had his coat clutched against his chest, so he leaned forward from the waist, finding his face in her hair, nearly nuzzling her neck.

Suzie let go of him as fast as she had attached herself to him and pulled him inside the apartment. Sam took a quick look around. Books and papers fanned over the couch and onto the coffee table. A mug of unidentifiable liquid and a plate of comma-shaped crusts were also on the coffee table, next to a stack of Post-it notes. The television was on, but muted.

Suzie followed his glance. "I'm a mess when I study. I like to spread out." She shrugged almost sheepishly. "Michael isn't here. He's at the hospital." She chewed her bottom lip. "He'll want to know right away that you're here, though. Maybe I should leave a message."

Sam shook his head. "No, forget about it. I'm not going anywhere." He could see down the short hall to the bedroom. There was a large pile of clothes on the floor and the bed was a twisted pile of sheets and blankets. Suzie was watching him when he turned back to her and asked, "Can I use the bathroom?"

She nodded and pointed down the hall. Sam closed the door and sat down on the edge of the tub to think. The bathroom didn't have a window and the air was moist. A rubber duck sat on the ledge next to a bottle of bubble bath.

Sam turned on the bathtub faucet and splashed water on his face. The back of his skull was beginning to tighten and hum from lack of sleep. He closed his eyes, just for a moment.

When Suzie knocked at the door Sam jerked awake. "Sam? You okay?"

Sam looked down. The tub was clogged, so the water wasn't draining. He twisted off the water, then slipped the duck off his perch and watched him bob around.

"Sam?" This time Suzie tried the knob. Sam hadn't locked it and she came right in. "Sam?" she said again. She didn't seem surprised to see him on the edge of the tub.

"Hey," he said weakly. "I'm pretty tired." Suzie's face looked fuller, and her hair was way past her shoulders. Sam slipped his hands beneath his thighs.

"Of course. You can crash in the bedroom. I have class in twenty minutes, so I'm leaving. It will be quiet."

"Do you live here?" Sam asked.

Suzie took a step back. "No."

"You stay here?"

"Sometimes."

"You just didn't happen to run into Michael a few weeks ago, did you?"

She gave him a little half smile. "Well, we did run into each other that way. But it wasn't a few weeks ago."

"How long ago was it?"

She bit her lip. "Eight months ago."

"Wow. So you guys just clicked, huh?" Sam attempted indifference even though he was burning with curiosity.

Suzie's cheeks flushed. "Sam, we should have talked about this. Or I should have told you I was coming home with Michael. I know it's a little weird. But, Sam—we were babies."

"Yeah."

"What you and I did when we were fifteen has nothing to do with my relationship with Michael."

"Yeah."

"I mean . . ." Suzie swallowed hard. "I had feelings for you, sure. I hated to leave you."

"But you gave me a hell of a going-away gift. One that my brother seems to know nothing about."

"What does it matter now?" Suzie whispered.

She took a step closer.

Sam grabbed her hand. She didn't pull back. "Does Michael know what we did in your basement?"

She shook her head. Her eyes were huge, liquid. He brought her hand to his mouth and kissed it and she did not squirm away. He kissed it again, harder. And then Sam took his tongue and pressed it against her palm. He heard her sharp intake of breath and thought he could probably kiss her mouth, maybe even slip his hand up beneath her Harvard T-shirt to cup her breast.

But when he looked up at Suzie there were tears streaming down her cheeks. Sam dropped her hand and stood up. Without a word he walked out of the bathroom and across the hall to the bedroom and shut the door in her face.

Sam woke up in his brother's bed with the realization that Suzie slept there with Michael. He stretched his arm beneath the pillow and his fingers found an abandoned hair tie. He pulled it out and examined the strands of thick, dark hair before he tossed it onto the floor. He had been an idiot to think Suzie Epstein had been pining away for him because they'd enjoyed some fun times in her basement.

Sam rolled over and reached for the phone and called his dad. The phone rang and rang. Sam pictured the kitchen, the garbage overflowing with takeout containers, the empty lounge chair in front of the TV where his dad fell asleep most nights still dressed in his work clothes. He let the phone ring until the machine picked up, and then he thought to look at his watch. His father was most likely at work. He dialed the office number and waited for the voice mail. "Dad," Sam said as his voice echoed into the receiver. "I'm at Michael's."

After he hung up he dialed Bella's number. She picked up on the second ring.

Sam dropped the phone when he heard her voice. He fumbled with the receiver and slammed it down before she said anything else.

In the kitchen Sam found a canister of beans and a grinder, stale Italian bread, and a container of curried chicken that looked too old to reheat. He made coffee using a paper towel for a filter, toasted the bread, and stood over the sink peering out the triangle-shaped window tucked up under an eave. The view was all angles and rooftops. Sam heard the front door open and close, a bag drop, and then the heavy shuffle of someone who was dead tired. He didn't have to turn around to know it was Michael.

"Dude," Michael said slowly, "what the fuck is up?"

Sam turned around to see him pouring a cup of coffee. Michael raised his mug in greeting and then his face disappeared as he drank.

"I guess you were right," Sam said. "I should have just talked to Dad."

"Everyone deserves the right to disappear, I guess." Michael sighed and ran a hand through his hair, but he looked unconvinced. "At least once." He leaned back against the counter, crossed his ankles, and looked at Sam. "But you could have called."

Sam had not expected this response at all. He'd thought Michael would come in guns blazing, calling Sam a loser. This probably meant that Michael had told their father about Sam flunking out of school. "You told him?"

"I had to." Michael shrugged. "I wasn't going to, but he had no idea where you were or what you were doing." He paused. "I had to give him a reason. You could have been dead. You could have done something stupid, he didn't know. I mean, what the fuck, Sam?"

"Did Mom call?"

"I called her."

"But she didn't say anything?"

"No." Michael shook his head. "She didn't give you up."

Sam shrugged. Apparently Bella had kept that secret as well.

"I think you may have fucked things up with the father of your girlfriend, though; no one likes to see his daughter upset." Michael gave Sam a strange look. "Bella said the last thing she knew you were heading to see Dad."

"She's not—" Sam stopped. Why was he denying that he had treated Bella like a girlfriend? What was the point? He had made a mistake thinking Suzie still thought of him. He had treated Bella like she was his second choice, when that wasn't the case at all. But now he had screwed that up too. "We're not together."

"Not now you're not." Michael snorted. He tipped the mug to his face, finished his coffee, and set the mug in the sink. "Should we go get a bite? Come on. I'm starved." Michael turned and Sam followed him because he seemed to leave no other choice.

At the diner they were served massive plates of food that both of them barreled through as if it was their first meal in days. When Michael was done, his plate wiped of any edible residue, he pushed it into the center of the table and leaned back against the red Naugahyde booth. "Fuck, medical school is going to kill me." He shrugged. "Residency is going to be a cakewalk if I survive the next year of med school.

"What's up?"

"I finish my oncology rotation in a week. It's been brutal. As of right now . . ." He glanced at his watch. "I haven't slept in twenty-seven hours."

Sam wasn't sure exactly what he meant by *rotation*. But he didn't ask.

"How do you do that?"

"Coffee and willpower. Next up is gyno." Michael rubbed his face as if he were scrubbing it with a washcloth. "Waaaaaa," he said, and shook himself awake. He lifted his mug at a passing waitress, who stopped to give both him and Sam a refill.

"So what does this rotation involve again?" Sam genuinely cared, but he didn't want to sound stupid either.

"I see patients on rounds, all under the supervision of a doc, and then I have to take an exam after each rotation and I have to do really, really well. Because I want to get my first-choice residency."

"Which is?"

"Mount Sinai or New York–Presbyterian. I want to specialize in pediatric cardiology, and those hospitals are among the best."

Sam nodded, feeling lost.

"And Suzie is applying to NYU, Columbia Med, Harvard, natch, Johns Hopkins."

"So." Sam cleared his throat. "Suzie . . ."

Michael grinned and his entire face changed. "Yeah, Suzie. Surprise, right? How did I fall in love with the girl next door?"

His question didn't seem to beg for an answer. Sam took a swallow of his coffee as Michael took a twenty out of his wallet, tucked it under the bill, and waved away the change as the waitress slid it off the table.

As Sam watched the simple transaction he realized that both the dollar he had in his wallet and Michael's twenty were courtesy of their father. A third-year medical student had no time to pick up a part-time job; the earnings from every crappy summer job Sam ever had never lasted past November. The bank accounts he and Michael had existed because their father supplemented them. If ever he had any illusion that he could survive in the world without his father, Sam was dumber than he already felt.

Sam made an agreement with his father that he would return to school to officially withdraw from classes and pack up his things. On a Thursday morning Sam dropped his father off at the train and took the car. During the drive he had imagined a heart-to-heart with the registrar, and he tried to think up a good excuse for being a total fuckup, but when he got there all he had to do was sign a paper that said he was voluntarily withdrawing and that he understood his ID card would be deactivated. No one asked him why or to rethink his decision. The RA let him into his old room and stood out in the hall talking to his girlfriend on the phone while Sam shoved clothes into a duffel bag and left a note that his roommate could have the microwave.

When Sam got in the car he looked at the clock on the dash and was surprised to see that officially changing his entire life had taken less than an hour. He turned the key in the ignition and sat and sifted through the papers. Three quarters of the way through his junior year his GPA had been a 1.6. Sam crumpled the papers from the registrar's office and dumped them in the trash.

By default, Sam became the odd-job man/boy of the neighborhood. Only Mrs. Schwartz with the schnauzer named Colonel asked Sam why he wasn't in school. Sam told her he'd had a little freak-out, but she didn't seem to buy it. She told him to read the newspaper to keep up with the world, and handed over Colonel's leash.

Frankie Cole's mother paid him to walk her Yorkshire terriers, Spencer and Kate, twice a day. One day when Sam was out with Spencer and Kate he watched as a Realtor spiked a For Sale sign into Peter Chang's front lawn: Peter Chang's mother had decided she'd had enough of winter and was moving to Florida. After that, Spencer and Kate each lifted a leg to the sign on their morning walks and the reliable Kate managed a dump. Sam had to say he felt the same way they did. It was hard to believe Peter Chang's basement would no longer be his.

His friends trickled home from college at the end of their junior year. Peter Chang was first. When Peter came home Sam was in the basement enjoying the many perks that Peter's Japanese video game deal had purchased, among them a flat-screen and multiple game consoles. Mrs. Chang had made him a lunch of Tater Tots and hot dogs like she did when they all were younger, and then sat across from him at the table and made lists of things he could do. As an odd-job man for hire so far he'd emptied the attic and made several trips to Goodwill and one to the dump. Mrs. Chang was not the least bit sentimental. Sam had gone to the basement to get rid of the old TV in the massive stereo cabinet and had gotten distracted.

"Man," Peter said as he descended into the twilight of the basement, "you need to get a life."

"Got several," Sam said as he took out five of his enemies with one fell swoop of the game stick.

Peter sat down beside him and watched. Sam could hear him counting the number of fatalities under his breath. He knew his brain was tracking the level of intensity, the effort, the skill sets.

Peter swayed back and forth with each hit as if he were in the game. Sam, distracted by Peter, was mortally wounded.

"You know what you did?" Peter reached for the game stick and held it in his palm, frowning. "Want me to tell you for the next time?"

"How would that be any challenge?"

Peter shrugged. "It's just a game."

Sam stood and stretched. "Want to help me haul this thing out? Needs two people."

"Seriously?" Peter eyed the cabinet. "I think I'm going to get emotional."

Sam glanced down at Peter and was about to laugh when he saw his friend's crumpled face.

"It's been here forever," Peter said. "That turntable still works! Shit, remember all those albums we used to play?"

Sam nodded. Mrs. Chang had an odd collection of Broadway show tunes, some comics, notably Lenny Bruce and Phyllis Diller, an album that featured Mr. Ed the talking horse, and a few old ladies warbling love songs. Sometimes, out of boredom or frustration, they'd put on an album and laugh until they cried. Sam looked around the basement, and for just a second, he saw them all there as they used to be.

"You're going to be around this summer, right? So you, me, Frankie, and Johnny, we should go somewhere, rent a house on the water, you know? I have the cash. I have more than enough cash." Peter licked his lips. "What do you say? You in?"

Sam watched Peter's mouth move, and he heard what he was saying, but all the while he was thinking: *I have to get out of here.* Someone else would walk Spencer, Katie, and Colonel. Peter could help his mother clean the house and move to Florida. Sam's father would order takeout and eat packaged cookies with or without him. Bella would continue to hurt. Michael would still be in love with Suzie. Sam thought of his mouth pressed against her hand, her tears, and how easily he could have found his way back to her body. He could feel the heat rising, the friction of skin against skin, the effortless tug on a nylon string revealing a milky curve, a tight amber nipple, and the unique smell of that airless basement room, the musty blankets, the brightly colored afghans they kicked to the floor. Sam had been there first. No matter that Michael was there now. Sam had been first.

The very first time Michael slept over, Suzie woke to an empty bed. Right about the time she had belatedly come to the conclusion that Michael had turned out to be a giant shit, he had shuffled into her bedroom wearing only a pair of plaid boxers and carrying two mugs of coffee. He handed her the mug that said Cambridge Bank & Trust and he kept the Horseman for Senate mug. Suzie had inherited the dishware when she rented the apartment.

Michael perched on the edge of the mattress, his thigh touching hers as they sipped their coffees. The way he looked at her then was still new, but it would soon become so familiar. Everything about Michael was close to perfection. The coffee, however, had been weak. He had since learned to make a much better cup.

It was Suzie who brought up to Michael the summer his mother left, the second time they met for coffee in the square. That meeting Suzie had to acknowledge was an actual date, not just a chance encounter.

"You can ask me anything," Suzie had said, and then waited

while Michael looked puzzled and a bit unsure of what she was offering. "About that summer?" she prodded.

She watched the recognition settle into his face, recognition of a memory that, before Suzie had brought it up all these years later, had been unformed, dormant. Tentatively she admitted to the discovery of the shoebox of photos. Michael nodded, pushed his coffee toward the center of the small table, and listened without speaking. When she got to the part about giving Sam the envelope of photos of their mother, Michael glanced up at her and exhaled.

He played with an empty straw wrapper, wrapping it around his index finger, before he spoke. "When I left for Johns Hopkins she was there; when I came back she was gone. And honestly, it wasn't all that different. My father was quiet, pretty beat up, but he told me they were getting a divorce, he was straightforward, and that was that." Michael cleared his throat. "Are you saying that your father and my mother?" He swallowed hard. "I knew there were photos. I heard what happened. I wasn't sure what or why, but I didn't know that my mother—"

"I don't know anything for sure," Suzie whispered quickly, barely able to get the sentence out fast enough.

Michael nodded slowly. "My father never pointed a finger. But?" He shook his head. "Do the details even matter at his point?"

"I don't know," Suzie said again. "I was a stupid kid who thought I knew everything."

"You were not a stupid kid," Michael said softly. "You were just a kid."

Suzie was humbled by Michael's generosity. "It was my fault. Everything. If I had just left the photos alone, if I had been less of a snoop, but I never knew what was going on. And I was determined to find out. Either my parents were fighting or my mother was locked in her room crying. I had to know, but I was just making huge leaps, you know? Connecting the dots where maybe there was no connection?"

Michael reached over and grabbed Suzie's hand on top of the table. He squeezed her fingers gently. At his touch, Suzie hesitated, but then found the courage to forge ahead. "I gave Sam the photos of your mother, but my father also had photos of almost all the other neighborhood mothers. I tossed those photos out the sunroof as we drove away. My father was furious. Here he was driving off into the sunset to start over again." She thought of the mottled red flush on her father's neck, the angry rope of cords that rose to the surface. Even her brothers, immune to the most heinous parental arguments, had been flattened by their father's fury over what Suzie had done.

"Sam picked them up, you know."

"What?" After she was done, after the box was empty, Suzie had tossed that as well, and had fallen back into the car, scrunching down into a ball in the backseat as if prepared to deflect a blow. She hadn't had the courage to turn around. Her chest was heaving, adrenaline coursing, too late to take it back. She thought about her mother still left behind in the neighborhood and hoped she wouldn't come out of the house.

"Sam." Michael nodded. "He picked them all up."

Suzie shook her head slowly as she considered this. She had no idea why she had never given much thought as to what had happened to the pictures. "How do you know?"

Michael shrugged, as if trying to minimize something painful.

"What happened to them?"

"He destroyed them up at our place on Paradox Lake. We were up there with our dad, right before I graduated from college. I came across Sam building a bonfire. He burned them."

"Really?" Suzie felt the heat of embarrassment flush her chest and her face.

Michael nodded slowly, but he didn't seem like he was going to divulge the circumstances, and Suzie didn't want to push it. "I didn't know," she whispered. "I didn't know what I was doing. I just wanted to hurt everyone." She looked at Michael. If he wanted to get up and walk away from her she would get it. She would hate it, but she would get it.

Michael leaned across the table so their faces were inches apart. She could smell the slight tang of coffee on his breath. "Of course you did, Suze. You were protecting yourself."

The shock of tears felt hot on Suzie's cheeks. "I hate him so much," she said. "You have no idea." She was fumbling for a napkin when Michael pressed one into her palm. She blotted her face and wanted to run away. "I'm sorry."

"You don't have to be," Michael said softly. "Suzie, look at me. Come on." Suzie did as he asked and Michael smiled. For the first time she saw a hint of Sam in there. "We are more than our parents' mistakes. You were fearless, and proud and a little bit reckless. You did what you had to do in the moment. I admire that." He paused. "I've never had to think about anybody but myself. Well, maybe I should have. But I've only thought of myself. When my mom left I guess I saw that as my chance to remove myself as well. Sam seemed to need our father more, and I suppose I thought my father preferred it that way."

Suzie had only fond memories of Mr. Turner. He was the dad barbecuing at the neighborhood block party in a red checkered apron, he got in snowball fights with Sam and his friends, and he took everyone to see the new *Star Wars* at the Cineplex in the next town over when no other parent wanted to drive during a storm, piling them all in the station wagon. It was because of

Mr. Turner's inherent niceness that Suzie had hated to find Mrs. Turner among those pictures in her father's collection.

Until now, Michael was the only Turner she didn't really know. When they'd run into each other on Church Street in Cambridge, he had approached her, and it had taken a moment to register that he was from her other life, and that he was Sam Turner's brother. Growing up, their age difference had made any cross-over social interactions nearly impossible, so she had only had a few memories of Michael: when he got his license and he drove Sam and Peter to the mall, picking Bella and Suzie up along the way, and when he had posed on his front lawn with a prom date and allowed his mother to take picture after picture, their odd frozen smiles like the bride and groom statues on the wedding cakes in the bakery window.

Suzie had stared at Michael then across the tiny table, before they had even kissed, before they had lain in her bed, a little shy but very much in awe of what they'd done, and she saw a glimpse of what he was offering her. Suzie imagined that one day he might see the foolishness in his decision. But she had been eager to force those thoughts to the back of her mind.

But then they had gone back home together for Bella's mother's funeral and walked into the Spades' house, and the months she and Michael had in Cambridge fell away like false walls. Whatever future they had whispered about, tucked beneath the blankets in Michael's drafty apartment, seemed insubstantial in the face of his family and her friends, and she had panicked. Suzie had made Michael go around the block three times before she had mustered enough courage to walk in the door. Michael had done so without complaining, driving with one hand, the other wedged between her thighs, his thumb rubbing against her tights. Suzie had leaned her head back against the seat and closed her eyes. She had never thought anything would ever bring her back. But she had come for Bella. Only Bella. No matter that Sam would be there. That Suzie would arrive with Michael. It was all for Bella and nothing more.

Michael had left a note tucked under Suzie's coffee mug on the counter in their tiny New York kitchen. The stove was just wide enough to roast a chicken, with a dorm-sized refrigerator and a slanted butcher-block counter, and the bed doubled as their couch, but it was their first real place together. Michael had left the apartment around five to make rounds, and Suzie hadn't even heard him get up. She had been studying until three, when she had finally admitted defeat and crawled into bed.

Suzie poured her coffee and squinted at Michael's scrawled *good luck, I love you.* She smiled. The exams and rotations, the lack of sleep, the pressure to get a decent residency, everything was coming at her at once. This year of medical school was taking her down. Instead of feeling ready to tackle the next step she felt defeated on a daily basis by her own overthinking. There were days she was sure her cognitive abilities had rearranged into an approximation of madness—even more so when her professors assured her this was all entirely normal. Surely, they saw the contradiction of it all?

Michael, a third-year resident at Mount Sinai, was getting ready to start a fellowship in pediatric cardiology, so he was even busier than she was, and yet he still managed to express himself in the tiniest of gestures. There was the time he had picked up a bundle of bodega flowers and left them in a glass on the bathroom sink, there was the much-improved morning coffee, and he always insisted on carrying the grocery bags and always switched places with her when they walked so she was on the inside of the sidewalk and he was closer to the street.

And in bed he loved her fiercely. From the start she had been overwhelmed by the attention he lavished, and the pleasure he derived as he made her tremble beneath his hands and his mouth. On the nights when their schedules synched and they slept together in the same bed, he had this habit of tucking her head beneath his chin, as if loving Suzie was all he ever wanted. As if all along the secret to everything had been this simple.

Later that night when the phone rang, Suzie thought it was Bella returning her call. Since Bella had moved to Iowa for grad school, their weekly calls never seemed sufficient. One or the other of them forgot to say something, and it had gotten so bad on Suzie's end that she kept a list of things to tell Bella. She had hoped now that Bella's two years were up, she would be coming back north, but she had fallen in love with a poet named Ted, and they were for the indefinite future blissfully ensconced in a cabin in the woods, writing their hearts out.

Michael was at the hospital, and Suzie, asleep, thought the ringing phone was in her dreams. Slowly she woke, rolled over, and fumbled along the nightstand. "Bells?" she mumbled, her eyes still shut.

"Suzie?" It was her baby brother Joshua, and suddenly Suzie was wide-awake.

"What? What time is it? What's wrong?"

"Uh, it's Mom."

Suzie sat up. Her chest felt tight. "Go on."

"She got in an accident tonight. She's in the hospital."

Suzie was already out of bed looking for something to put on. She grabbed the pants and shirt she had tossed on the chair before bed and began stepping out of her pajama bottoms. "How bad?"

"I don't really know. But the police are here and they won't let me talk to her or see her yet. It's kind of confusing."

"The police?" Suzie spoke carefully to make sure she heard him correctly. "The police?"

"Yeah, like I said, it's confusing."

"Is she hurt? Did she hurt someone else?" Suzie knew her mother should probably not be driving, ever, given the amount of vodka that was coursing through her bloodstream on a daily basis. There had been two prior incidents; if this was a third it wouldn't be good.

"They aren't telling me anything." Joshua sounded exasperated. "I told you."

"Where's Eli?" Eli was the older of her two brothers by a year, and often the least reliable.

"At a concert."

"Fuck." Eli had gone to Cornell to play lacrosse. He had transferred all his intensity to a hard little ball and a netted stick. He did everything to excess, but that seemed to be acceptable on the lacrosse field.

"What? I tried, I can't get him."

"No, I know. It's just, nothing. You can't get a nurse to tell you anything about Mom?"

"I mean, she's alive and well enough to talk to the police, so I guess she's not that bad?"

Suzie counted to ten and closed her eyes. Josh had been misdiagnosed for years, or just ignored. But finally he had been diagnosed with dyslexia, and he had just finished his sophomore year at a small private college in Vermont that specialized in students with learning issues. He had calmed down a lot. But he smoked too much pot. "What hospital? You know it's going to take me at least three hours to get there, right?"

"I know, Suzie, I'm not stupid." He paused. "Beth Israel. And you're going to be mad at me."

"Why?"

"I panicked and I called Dad."

"Oh, fuck, fuck, fuck."

"But he didn't pick up."

Suzie exhaled. Her brothers had a relationship with their father that Suzie would never understand. It was like he was their much older brother who paid for everything, who got them good tickets for sporting events and concerts, who never passed judgment on their lives. Josh, the earnest baby of their tattered little family, claimed their father had reformed, that he worked all the time and still loved their mother, that it was their mother who would have nothing to do with him. Suzie doubted the integrity of the story. Since she had left Boston four years ago, she had tried hard to be emotionally as well as physically distanced.

Quickly she put the phone down and reached for her bra and shirt, dressing as if the house were on fire. She calculated what it would cost her to miss her classes the following day, when the next Amtrak left for Boston, whether she could get a hold of Michael. Tomorrow night was their only time together for the next ten days and he had hinted at something special.

She grabbed the phone. "Josh, go find out what you can. Be a bulldog, make something up, I don't care. But don't give up and don't let them put you off no matter what. Tell them I'm on my way. And then call me back. I'm headed to Penn Station. Can you do that?" She reached for the bag that she kept for overnight shifts at the hospital and double-checked that she still had a stick of deodorant and an extra toothbrush and toothpaste in the zippered compartment. She yanked open a dresser drawer for a change of underwear and shirt. She had no idea how long

she would be there. Damnit. She did not want to see her father.
"Josh?"

"I'm here, I'm here."

"Can you do what I asked?"

"Yes, but I already told you I—"

"Damnit." Suzie cut him off. "Try harder, Josh. Try fucking
harder. Call me back. Okay? Call me back the second you know
anything."

He mumbled something and hung up. Suzie grabbed her bag
and headed out the door.

The ER entrance at Beth Israel was insane even at five o'clock in
the morning, and so Suzie cut Josh some slack. Her brother had
called about half an hour after she got on the train with the news
that her mother was being charged with an OUI, third offense.
Her blood alcohol was twice the legal limit. She had pulled into
the wrong driveway and run over a child's bike and banged into
a garage door, so there was property damage, but thankfully no
human damage other than to herself.

Suzie hadn't been able to talk to Michael at all, which she expected. She'd left him two voice mails, one in which she said
where she was going and another that said what had happened.
She had been working off very little sleep and her second large
black coffee by the time of the second message, and she hoped
she had at least been coherent.

When the elevator doors opened she saw her brother directly
across from her, leaning against the wall, his hands shoved into
his front pockets, ankles crossed, his chin touching his chest.
If anyone could sleep standing up in a busy hospital corridor it
would be Josh. Suzie approached him slowly, afraid if she startled
him he'd fall over. "Hey," she said softly. "I made it."

Josh looked up and blinked. He reached out and touched Suzie on the shoulder. "You're here."

"Where is she?"

Josh yawned, pushed off from the wall, and jutted his chin to the left.

"Does she know I'm coming?"

"She's out of it. They gave her something to sleep."

"Okay."

"They think she has some internal injuries, I think. I don't know, they're not really clear."

Suzie reached over and squeezed his forearm. She felt bad about yelling at him before. "We'll figure it out. Okay?"

Josh nodded and yawned again.

"You're alone?"

"He's not here."

"You talked to him?"

He shook his head. "Nah." He touched Suzie's elbow and they started down the hall. "He hasn't called me back."

Their mother was unconscious and handcuffed to the gurney. Suzie knew from her own med school rotations that police juris-diction applied whether in the hospital or not. She had seen her share of handcuffs on a wide range of patients. But this was her mother.

She moved closer to the bed. She hadn't been home in over a year and a half. Even though she tried to call home at least once a week, the last few months had been insane. The best she could remember was talking to her mother on her birthday, and that would have been two months ago.

Looking at her mother now, Suzie could see how much physi-cal deterioration had occurred. Her mother had always been small-boned, but now she seemed to barely exist beneath the sheet. There were several deep lacerations on her face, one above her left eyebrow and another on her chin, and her skin had the telltale yellow pall of liver damage. Her hair, which had always been thick and dark, was wiry and nearly all gray. If Josh hadn't been there, Suzie would have thought she had the wrong room.

She looked at her watch. The night shifts were beginning to wind down; she knew most nurses would be at the desk making their last notes on charts in preparation for the morning shifts and doctors' rounds. There was probably nothing to be found out until then, so she turned to Josh and said, "Let me buy you breakfast."

Over yet another cup of coffee, Suzie said, "What's been going on?"

Josh shrugged as he finished chewing a large bite of bagel. "I only got home from school two days ago. I think I surprised Mom. The calendar on the kitchen counter hasn't been turned since March."

Suzie blew on her coffee.

"The house looks pretty bad."

Suzie nodded. If her twenty-year-old brother had noticed the state of the house, things must be far worse than she imagined.

"Eli got home before me and paid some of the bills. I think the cable got shut off and he wanted to watch a game, so he took Mom's checkbook and paid off the gas company, the cable, the electric. If Dad didn't pay for school we probably would have been asked to leave already."

Suzie ignored his last remark. She felt the familiar reaction flaring up. She had been angry her entire life. In the years since she had left home she had tried so hard to reverse that, and yet here she was again. She picked up her coffee and took a large swallow. "Do you have any idea where Mom was going? Or coming from when she got in the accident?" The last two OUIs had been misdemeanor offenses. Her mother had gone to counseling, safe driving classes, and some sort of community service that Suzie couldn't immediately recall. But Suzie wasn't so sure the third wouldn't carry a more severe penalty, maybe even jail time. She would have to call the lawyer.

Joshua wiped his mouth with the back of his hand and then fumbled for a napkin. "There was a carton with vodka in the car, so likely she had gone to the liquor store. I didn't even know she had left the house, honestly. If she needed the booze I would have gone for her. I would have driven her."

Suzie shook her head and sighed. She couldn't believe that they had gotten to the place where providing their mother with the alcohol was preferable to getting her to stop drinking. "She's going to drink herself to death."

Joshua swallowed hard. "Don't be mad at me, please. I called Dad because I panicked. I know you don't want him to be involved, but he is, Suzie."

She shook her head. "That's your choice, not mine. He's unreliable. He's manipulative. He's a liar."

Joshua flinched. "It's not like I don't know what he's done. But Mom . . ."

"What? What about Mom?" Suzie lowered her voice. "He's not going to save her, Joshie, he's not." She hesitated again when she saw the defeat in his posture. "You have an entirely different relationship. He always treated me just like Mom. He likes his women subservient and obedient, and I am neither. Let's just fix whatever we can, Josh. We have to leave him out of it."

By midmorning Suzie had a throbbing headache and three missed calls from Michael. She left him a quick voice mail to let him know she was still trying to sort things out. She had been talking for what seemed like days to the doctors; their lawyer, William Bennett; the police; and briefly her mother, who was roused to acknowledge consent of her situation. Suzie had been standing at the end of her mother's bed, and when their eyes made contact her mother smiled vacantly, revealing yellowing teeth. Even though her mother said Suzie's name, Suzie wasn't sure her mother knew who she was.

The medical consensus seemed to be cirrhosis of the liver, advanced enough that Sarah was experiencing disorientation and confusion. The doctors wouldn't know how far gone she was until she really dried out and started a course of treatment. William Bennett seemed to think he could get her into a rehab facility to deter a medical jail facility. He had already approached the neighbors whose garage door and bike Sarah Epstein had destroyed. They had agreed to a check for damages and seemed not to want to press charges.

According to William, who pulled a sheet of rehab facilities out of his briefcase, they could get Sarah into a place as soon as twenty-four hours from now. Suzie's father still provided her mother with an excellent insurance policy; some of these programs were covered in full. William was going to pull strings for availability and then get back to Suzie. Suzie had no idea how he dealt with the arraignment or any of the other legal details, but she was too exhausted to even think about it.

By noon her mother's twist-tie handcuffs had been removed and she was coherent enough to respond when they told her what was about to happen. She had nothing to say when she found out she would be transferred to a facility the following morning for an indefinite stay. Suzie thought it was just as well. She'd had enough of her mother's histrionics to last a lifetime.

She and Josh drove home in silence. Suzie fidgeted in the passenger seat, unable to sit still, and approached the house with an increasing sense of dread. She hadn't spoken to Eli at all, but Josh had finally been in touch with him and he was at home waiting for them. All Suzie wanted was to take a bath and a nap. But she doubted she was going to get either one of those things anytime soon.

The first thing that she saw as they turned down the block was the overwhelming jungle that had once been her mother's carefully tended gardens. To look at it you would never know it had once been meticulously and obsessively cared for. But if there was one good thing to say about the bramble and chaos of the gardens, it was that at least it took your eyes away from the mess of the house. The shingles on the house had weathered and curled like cornflakes, and the shutters, gap-toothed in sections, needed to be either replaced or painted.

Eli met them at the front door. Suzie noticed that Josh didn't even try to open the garage door, which meant that it was either broken or overrun with stuff. Eli towered over Suzie, and when he moved to give her an awkward hug, she felt the hardness of his arms and chest and was shocked that he was so grown up. "Sorry about last night," he mumbled.

Suzie stepped back and shot him a look, but Eli's remorse seemed genuine. She shrugged. "We didn't all need to stand at her bedside. There will be plenty of time for that." She pushed past her brothers and into the hallway. It was obvious Eli had made an attempt at cleaning. The surfaces had been cleared, and the windows were open to the fresh air. It did nothing to hide the shabbiness, but at least it wasn't horrifying.

She could tell Eli was watching her take it all in. He said, "I've got about thirty garbage bags piled high in the garage. I guess I have to see if I can get someone to pick them up." He paused. "Your room was actually in pretty good shape. It was stuffy but untouched. I don't think Mom ever goes in there." He waited for her to say something. When she didn't he added, "I got rid of all of the booze."

"There was booze in the house? Why did she go out, then?"

Eli looked at her like she had asked a stupid question, and Suzie probably had. He had likely found the bottles their mother had hidden and then forgotten about.

Suzie's throat was scratchy and hot. She didn't want to seem ungrateful for what her brother had attempted to do, but she couldn't stand up anymore. She moved past them down the long hallway to her room, kicked off her shoes, and fell facedown onto her bed. A faint breeze from the open windows lifted the curtains, exposing the splintered wooden frame. Sounds of a suburban spring afternoon drifted in: a neighbor's sprinkler, a basketball hitting asphalt, a child crying. Suzie wasn't sure if it was the influence of being back in her teenage room, but all she wanted to do for a little while was disappear.

✦ ✦ ✦

The three of them went back to the hospital during evening visiting hours. Suzie wasn't planning on going but then, with a pang of empathy, thought it might be nice for her mother to see her children together.

Sarah Epstein was sitting up propped by pillows, her long, bony fingers picking at the woven cotton blanket around her bloated midsection. Eli and Josh had been ahead of Suzie, so she didn't realize until they parted that their father was sitting in a chair next to the bed. When she saw him she took a step back.

"Suzie Q," her father said.

Suzie ignored his greeting and looked at her mother. Her eyes seemed brighter, more alert, probably due in part to the meds. "How are you feeling, Mom?"

"Better," Sarah said quietly. "I wish I knew you were coming. I need some clothes. For tomorrow." Her voice was thin and raspy.

Suzie wanted to scream at her mother to stop playing the victim. But instead she nodded and said, "We can do that, don't worry."

"I was just talking to your mother about tomorrow," their father said.

Eli and Josh looked quickly over at Suzie and then down at the floor. "We have it covered," Suzie managed in a voice that was barely controlled.

Their father gave a curt little nod. "I told Sarah that if anything extra needs to be done, just let me know. Although I really think your mother can beat this on her own. She's strong."

"Fuck off," Suzie said. "She has a disease. Can she cure that on her own?"

Sarah made a noise that sounded like a baby bird. Suzie shot her mother a look, incredulous that she could still fall for her estranged husband's bullshit.

Suzie knew she should stop, but she couldn't. "Or would you like to take another shot at it? 'Cause I think if you do, the next place we'll be gathered is her funeral."

Their father looked at Suzie's brothers as if to garner support, then hung his head in a show of shame. Suzie didn't believe it for a moment.

"Rehab is your only choice, Mom. The last stop. You do understand that?" Sarah Epstein looked down at the blankets and nodded. "Rehab keeps you out of jail. You could have killed someone, and somehow you didn't. Not this time, anyway. So we're clear, right?" She looked over at her father before turning back to her mother. "I'll get you some clothes and bring them back tomorrow." To her brothers she said, "I'll wait downstairs."

When she got down to the lobby she made a dash for the double sliding doors at the entrance. She just needed to breathe. She walked along the perimeter of the grounds until she came to a row of benches, all unoccupied, and chose the one at the far end. She wanted to think that her father didn't affect her after all this time, but he did. He always would. Had it really been seven years since she had seen him? Since her freshman year at Harvard, when she told him she didn't need his help?

Suzie sighed. She half thought that she should just walk away from this entire mess right now. Let her brothers and father take on the rehab of Sarah Epstein. Let them do whatever the fuck they wanted. But no matter how badly she wanted to, she couldn't totally abandon her mother.

She rummaged in her bag for her phone. Michael had left two voice mails. The first said he loved her. The second said he was on his way to Boston. Suzie dropped her face into her hands and cried in relief.

The next morning Suzie arrived at the hospital before anyone else. William Bennett would be the only one accompanying Sarah Epstein to Silver Hill, so Michael had gone to the cafeteria on the pretense of needing coffee, to give Suzie some time alone with her mother.

The plastic bag the hospital had given Sarah with her belongings contained a dirty canvas tote bag covered in wildflowers that proclaimed: A Weed Is But an Unloved Flower. Seeing it made Suzie cringe, especially after seeing the state of Sarah's gardens. Before Suzie gave the bag to her mother she had gone through it to make sure she didn't have a hidden bottle or mouthwash, anything that could contain alcohol. But there had been only her wallet, some used tissues, and an old issue of *People* magazine.

Suzie had not been prepared for what she found in her mother's bedroom. When she'd opened the door the stench hit her immediately, like a bar the morning after, except this accumulation had been building for years. The instinct to gag was overwhelming and Suzie had to put her hand over her mouth and nose. There were piles of filthy clothes, books, magazines, newspapers, plates, and takeout containers. Bottle after empty bottle of vodka was strewn across the room. The mirrored closet doors that Suzie remembered her mother pirouetting in front of before a date with her father were broken; one was cracked, as if her mother had thrown something at her reflection, the other completely gone. The sheets on the bed were slick and stiff from spilled food and drink. Suzie pushed the bathroom door open with her foot and peered inside. The tub that was large enough for two looked like a tarry black crater.

Suzie backed out of the room and shut the door quickly. Then she asked Josh to take her to the mall. At the drugstore she picked up basic toiletries, a new hairbrush, mini bottles of shampoo and conditioner, and at the last minute a pale pink lipstick, as if her mother were going on some fantastic trip. In a clothing store she had chosen several pairs of pull-on pants because of her mother's bloated belly, and simple sweater sets to match. She bought everything in size extra-small. Before they returned to the house she had Josh take her back to the hospital so that Sarah would have the clothes for the morning to avoid any delays.

Now, in the hospital, Sarah was nervously pawing at the pressed fabric. She was dressed in a pale blue and brown combination, and even the extra-smalls hung from her wasted frame. Suzie felt defeated. She'd done the best she could, but it wasn't enough. It would never be enough.

Suzie sat on the corner of the bed. "Mom? About Dad? You don't need him. Let yourself get better. Let the doctors help you."

Her mother winced. "I don't want to be alone."

Michael returned, carrying a small clutch of carnations from the gift shop. He handed them to Suzie's mother, kissed her cheek, and said something quietly into her ear. Sarah looked dizzy, and Suzie thought she saw her mother blush like a little girl. Michael glanced over at Suzie, caught the look on her face, and excused himself again, ostensibly to go and check on the paperwork that Suzie knew was already completed.

"Mom?" Suzie tried again. "You're not alone."

Her mother waved a feeble hand. "What do I have?"

Suzie looked at her mother. There was nothing she could say. She wasn't moving back home.

Moments later Michael, Eli, and Josh arrived along with William Bennett. The discharge papers were signed, the court papers filed. William patted his briefcase as Suzie handed him an envelope with a check and all the documentation for her mother: medical records, phone numbers, insurance cards, bank account routing numbers. She looked over her shoulder for her father, afraid at any moment he could show up and derail the plans.

Suzie relaxed only when her mother was loaded into the transport van that would deposit her safely in New Canaan, Connecticut, on the doorstep of Silver Hill and William Bennett took his seat next to the driver. She could see the top of her mother's head through the glass, as well as her own reflection. Suzie stood on the curb and watched the van pull away before she took a deep breath and slowly turned back to where Michael and her brothers stood in a knot by the entrance to the hospital.

On the train back to New York, Suzie rested her head on Michael's shoulder. He let her talk without interruption. She went over the last twenty-four hours, the scene with her father, the condition of the house, the looks on the faces of her brothers when they realized she really had to leave.

Late last night over pizza and beer, she, her brothers, and Michael had come up with a plan for the house. Or really, it had been Michael who organized their thoughts, yellow legal pad at his elbow, who made the lists of things to be done: Dumpsters to be ordered, contractors to be called, a Realtor to be found. There was plenty of money in the bank; Suzie didn't really want to think about the fact that it most likely was from her father. When Sarah got out of rehab, if she was able to live alone, she needed a fresh start, not the house that stank of failure.

Her brothers had committed to making the improvement and selling of the house their summer job, and while Suzie didn't really hold out much hope that they would stick with it, she had no other choice. She and Michael would come back and forth when they could to help, and that would have to be enough.

Now, on the train, Michael held Suzie's hand in his lap. When she was done getting it all out, after they had been quiet for a while, he said, "I want you to marry me, Suzie."

Suzie said nothing at first. The pulse at the base of her throat fluttered and she pressed a fingertip against it.

"I was going to ask you the other night," Michael went on, "when we both had off. But then, well—" He shrugged, and Suzie's head slid off his shoulder. Quickly she repositioned it, in time to hear him say, "Somehow this is better." He pressed his lips to the top of her head.

Suzie rubbed her cheek against the soft cotton of his shirt. She thought about how the night before, Michael had held her in the same bed she had slept in as a teenager, how he had told her that he would help, that he wouldn't leave no matter what happened.

When her parents had agreed to try again, Sarah Epstein had explained to Suzie about *bashert,* the Yiddish term for people brought together by fate. At the time Suzie had thought her mother had just been looking for a reason to welcome her father back. She'd had no idea about what it meant to believe you had found your soul mate. And if that's what her mother really believed she'd had with Suzie's father, then Suzie wanted no part of it.

But now she knew differently. Michael had changed what she thought she knew about love, had shaped the idea of love into something kind and generous and caring. The idea that he could love her forever felt impossible and unpredictable. And still, it was real. No matter what happened next, she could never undo what he had given her. Suzie sat up and leaned back a little so she could see Michael.

His expression was sheepish. "I'm embarrassed I don't have a ring. I hoped we could do that together?"

She touched his arm and smiled. "Yes," Suzie said quietly, watching Michael's face change as he heard her answer. "Yes," she said again, laughing as his smile grew. "Yes, yes, yes."

NINE

Renovation
Sam—2007

S am, come here, take a look." Marguerite waved to Sam from the makeshift table in the backyard, a tube of blueprints spread out across the plank of plywood. She and his father were in the beginning stages of a massive remodel that was to include a master suite, a mini gym, and a vaulted-ceiling family room open to a gourmet kitchen. After they put the house back together there were plans for a pool, a pool house, and a hot tub. Sam's father, according to Marguerite, was finally going to live like he deserved. It sounded obnoxious, as if Hunt had no idea how to live until he met Marguerite, but Sam knew that wasn't her intention. She just wanted to make his father happy. Sam had no idea where she planned to put the takeout menus and soy sauce packets in the new kitchen, but he was pretty sure his father would claim a drawer.

The back wall of the house was open to the late-spring breeze, the tarps flapping like flags as Sam walked past the picnic table his mother had found years ago abandoned on a curb. She had made Sam help her lift the table into the back of the station wagon. All the way home she talked about summer dinners outside, hinting of campfires and s'mores to keep his interest. Now Sam could recall only one dinner on that table. The bugs had been so bad his father and Michael had retreated into the house with their plates, while he'd sat in the flickering candlelight slapping his arms and legs, waiting for his mother to finish a bottle of wine.

Marguerite wanted to include Sam in the kitchen planning process because he worked in a restaurant. He had noticed an awkwardness when she addressed him directly. She seemed very aware that Sam and his father had been alone a lot of years before Marguerite, so she tried even harder. Which was why he guessed that every attempt to engage him seemed based upon his interests, as if he were a well-behaved child at a cocktail party, instead of twenty-four years old. She and Sam had been reduced to having conversations about Marguerite's favorite restaurants, as if he were a Zagat guide and not a line cook in a shitty tapas bar. The kitchen remodel gave them something else altogether.

"Sam!" Marguerite pointed at the drawings again. "Sam, what do you think about soapstone for a sink?"

Sam reached the table and smiled as genuinely as he could. "I don't know a damn thing about soapstone. Professional kitchens are all stainless steel."

Marguerite frowned at this piece of information. Sam knew she really didn't need his opinion on anything. They both knew that Marguerite had assisted in the building of multiple kitchens because of her family's construction business. She had met Hunt when he represented her family in a wrongful death suit against the manufacturer of the scaffolding that had given way and caused the death of Marguerite's father and two workers.

Sam's stomach gurgled. His father and Marguerite had lured

him out with the promise of lunch, and he was starved. Over Marguerite's shoulder was an earthmover, its pterodactyl-like neck and basket poised to attack. To the left was a Dumpster filled with shards of the back wall of the house. Marguerite, in her crisp white shirt and slim gray skirt, looked impossibly clean amid the destruction. She tapped her index finger against the blueprints. Sam admired the nail, short and buffed to a pale pink.

Sam turned around. He could see his father standing at the open refrigerator as if he might find something inside. The kitchen cabinets and pantry had been cleaned out, most everything passed on to Goodwill. All the doors yawned open as if a gang of hungry people had ravaged the place.

Marguerite smiled widely. She wore no makeup on her tanned face that Sam could tell, and her shoulder-length brown hair was streaked with strands of gray. He genuinely liked her and was really trying to get her to see that. He hoped she would relax soon. "You'll be the first to cook in the new kitchen, okay, Sam? We'll have a party and invite some of the neighbors, your brother and Suzie." A crease appeared between her eyebrows. "I'll have to see when would be the easiest time for them. Doctors' schedules leave no time for lives."

From what Sam knew, Marguerite was a widow with no children. She had once been married to a surgeon, but he died when he was only thirty-two, in a car accident on the Hutchinson River Parkway with a tractor-trailer that he never saw coming. Sam hadn't heard much more than that, and he certainly wasn't about to ask.

"Hunt?" Marguerite lifted a hand to shade her eyes. "Hunt? Hunt!" The panic in her voice the last time she called his father's name made Sam turn around. His father was leaning against a support beam, a hand to his chest. He lifted his head only slightly in acknowledgment. Marguerite ran past Sam and yelled, "Call 911!"

Sam stumbled after her, only to see his father straighten up and wave her off. By the time he got to them Hunt was totally upright, his cheeks ruddy as if rubbed raw from the wind. Marguerite had her hand cupped around his elbow and he had reached out to touch her cheek. Sam, embarrassed by the tender gesture, almost took a step back. "Dad?" he asked.

Hunt turned from Marguerite to Sam. "I'm fine. I only had coffee this morning. I'm fine, really."

"It doesn't matter what you say, Hunt," Marguerite said. "We need to get you to the doctor."

"Marg," Hunt said gently, "I'm really fine. What I am is starving. Besides, you know Frank Ross is on the golf course right now, it's Saturday, and I don't need to go to the ER and explain my medical history to a stranger only to have them tell me to go home."

Marguerite did not look convinced. Her fingers went for Hunt's wrist and Sam could tell she was feeling his pulse rate. Sam relaxed at the mention of Johnny Ross's father. He had been the family doctor for years, and Sam had never given it much thought. But now the offhand way in which his father had mentioned him seemed enough to keep them all safe.

"Can we go eat now? Please?" Hunt laughed. "If you let me eat I will allow you to take my pulse all through the meal."

"That's not funny," Marguerite said. "At all." She grabbed her purse off the kitchen counter and rummaged around inside, ultimately producing a small bottle of aspirin. She shook two pills into her palm and handed them to Sam's father. He accepted them and waited for her to give him the bottle of water that she also pulled from her bag.

Sam watched him swallow and then turned back to Marguerite. The tip of her nose was red and her eyes were watery. She returned his gaze and released his father's wrist, but not before she found his fingers and threaded them through her own. "Hunt, maybe we should call Michael," she said softly. "He can check you out."

Sam's father held out his tongue as proof he had swallowed the aspirin, and then laughed as if he was hoping to lighten the mood. "Come on, we can talk this over in the car on the way to Stern's. My mouth is watering for pastrami on rye. How about Sammy drives and we sit in the back?" He winked at Marguerite while he fished his keys out of his pocket and tossed them to Sam.

Sam caught the keys midair and turned away from them to walk around the house and to the driveway. He wasn't quite sure who had won back there, if he was driving to the ER or to Stern's. It had scared the hell out of him to see the blood drain from his father's face. Suddenly, instinctively, Sam spun around. "Dad?" Hunt looked up and smiled. His color was back, his eyes looked clear. Sam needed to believe he was okay. He returned his father's smile and joked, "Can you hurry it up? I'm starving."

Peter Chang purchased his family home, unable to see himself living anywhere else, and when he graduated from MIT he moved back permanently. By then, Mrs. Chang was happily settled in the Villages, a city-like complex in Florida for retirees that had enough daily activities to fill several bucket lists. Peter and Mrs. Chang joked that the Villages' motto should be: Keep Them Moving Until They Can't.

The formal living room, where Mrs. Chang had kept two white couches and marble end tables with glass figurines, and where they had never been allowed as kids, now functioned as Peter's office. The large room had been taken over by a leather sofa, three long conference tables, five laptops hooked up to tremendous viewing screens, and notebooks and notebooks of scribbled code. Peter still used the basement as his primary place to unwind, and it was there they sat on the same old broken couch that afternoon before Sam returned to the city. He was tired, feeling the effects of gorging at lunch, and enjoying the silence that only old friends will give each other without question. They passed a joint while Peter showed Sam his latest game, the second in a trilogy. He offered to give Sam a demo copy to take home, and when Sam told him he didn't have a computer or a TV, Peter looked at Sam as if he had suggested technology didn't exist, which Sam supposed for him it didn't. Even his cell phone was a throwaway, and half the time Sam forgot to charge it.

When Sam went upstairs to retrieve some beers he wasn't surprised to see that the kitchen, without Mrs. Chang, was home to a tower of pizza boxes stacked neatly by the back door and a trash can filled with empty takeout coffee cups. The refrigerator held three six-packs of Sam Adams and that was it. He grabbed two beers and went back downstairs. "How do you survive?" he asked Peter.

Peter shrugged and took the beer Sam offered him. "I don't need much. Coffee, pizza, and beer. What else?"

Sam took a swig from the bottle. "Nice kitchen gone to waste."

"Then you cook in it." Peter slid a notepad off the trunk in front of the couch. "Anytime, seriously." He scribbled something while frowning and tapping his foot. "And don't start sounding like Mindy. She shows up from time to time to spend the night and in the morning complains I don't have coffee or even a coffeemaker."

"What? Like how often?" Sam knew Mindy and Ruthie had

joined Bella on a backpacking trip through Europe after college graduation. Then Ruthie went off to Chicago for a graduate degree in women's studies and Bella to Iowa for an MFA. Sam thought Mindy had stayed in Europe.

Sam made it a point to never ask about Bella, not even to Peter. It was easier that way. But his father always managed to somehow drop her name and whereabouts into their conversations, information most likely culled from Mr. Spade over the watercooler. Thinking about how he had behaved toward Bella felt like poking a hot stick into his soul to see if it was dead yet, so Sam tried very hard not to think about her. But she showed up sometimes in his dreams. Dreams that felt so real he'd spend days afterward trying not to dial her number.

"Once a month?" Peter said.

"Man." Sam shook his head. Not at the revelation that Peter was content to continue screwing the girl who had treated him like shit since forever, but that he had no one else and a pretty low sex drive. Despite Sam's allergy for attachment, he was horny all the time. "Where is she?"

"Grad school, Sarah Lawrence."

"Huh."

"What?"

"You could buy a coffeemaker."

"Why would I do that?"

It occurred to Sam that maybe Peter was enacting his own revenge for how Mindy had treated him all those years by refusing to buy the coffeemaker. "I have an idea. Come into the city and hang out with me some night. I can introduce you around to the group I work with now." Briefly, he thought of Clara the pastry chef and the tattoo on her lower back that had been revealed to be an owl sitting in the branches of a tree. For a few nights they had burned fast and furious and then it had died to a simmer when her shift had changed, and he hadn't minded at all. "Maybe you need to get out of here."

"Why would I do that, Sam?" Peter looked around. "I have everything I need. I like routines. You know me, I've never been a seeker."

Sam closed his eyes and leaned back against the couch to enjoy his buzz. He realized he had no argument for what Peter had said.

Two days later, after a morning in court, Sam's father had a heart attack in the lobby of his office building. The security guard whom he had greeted moments before watched Hunt crumple to the floor as if he were, as the guard put it, "taking a knee."

Sam was the last to arrive at the Mount Sinai ER. He saw Michael and Marguerite in the hallway, but no sign of Suzie, for which he was first relieved, then ashamed. Shouldn't he be thinking of his father, not Suzie Epstein?

Marguerite was standing with her back flattened against the wall. Her eyes were closed and her chin tipped to the ceiling. Sam had no idea if she was religious, but it seemed like she was praying, so he approached mutely. Michael's head was bent over a clipboard. He was wearing his white doctor's coat, a stethoscope draped around his neck. When Sam joined them the first thing he noticed was the gray tint to his brother's skin. He was either terrified or exhausted.

"Where is he?" Sam asked too loudly, feeling a cold sweat break across his back and in his pits.

"Upstairs for tests." The muscles in Michael's jaw pulsed furiously. "The surgeon is on his way down here now. He's the guy we want."

Sam nodded. "As in the best?" Marguerite had yet to open her eyes or to acknowledge his arrival.

"Yes, I told you. He's the guy we want."

Sam nodded again. He wished Marguerite would look at him. "Do you know about Saturday?"

Michael narrowed his eyes at Sam. "Yes, I was told. Today. What the fuck were you thinking?"

Sam thought he heard Marguerite whimper, but he couldn't look at her. He tilted his head in her direction and then shook it from side to side. "We were listening to Dad. He seemed fine. He ate his usual lunch."

Michael frowned. The pulse throbbed again in his jaw. "Well, he shouldn't have. Technically, Dad has atherosclerosis. Three arteries are almost completely blocked. He presents as a classic case; naturally, his blood pressure is off the charts, that's worrisome but not a surprise. Bypass surgery is the most likely course of treatment."

"Did you talk to him?"

"I did, but it was quick. He was lucid, though. So that's good."

Sam stared hard at Michael. "What did he say?"

"That he loved us."

"Fuck." Sam bit the inside of his mouth and stared down at his feet. He was still wearing chef pants, an apron, and his food-splattered clogs. He had no recollection of leaving the restaurant or getting in the cab. He had thought when he got to the hospital his father would be dead. But Sam wouldn't admit that now. He still didn't know if he was going to pull through, and he was afraid to say out loud what they were all probably thinking. It was childish, he knew, but if he didn't ask the question it meant everything was going to be okay.

In the surgical waiting room Sam avoided the faces of the other people waiting for news and went to get coffee. Michael disappeared for half an hour, saying he needed to check in on his patients, but then he was back waiting with them. He had a stack of folders on his lap, a pen in one hand poised and ready. Sam noticed for the first time that his brother moved his lips ever so slightly as he read.

Sam extended a cup of coffee to Michael and he reached up and took it, wincing through a sip before he set it on the empty chair to his left and returned to his charts.

Sam had too much energy to sit. He stood before his brother and Marguerite and rocked back and forth on his heels. He stared at the clock on the wall behind them. A bad idea, he thought, for a waiting room. By his estimates, their father had been in surgery for two hours. Michael had said it could take three to six hours.

"Maybe you've had too much of that," Michael said.

"What's that?"

"The caffeine."

"Impossible." Sam drained the last of the cup. "Have you ever noticed that we both wear white to work?"

Michael squinted at Sam as if he might not be human. Marguerite, for the very first time since Sam got there, smiled. Sam shrugged. "Just an observation."

Marguerite stood and smoothed the creases from her tan trousers. "Would either of you like to accompany me to the cafeteria? I think I should stretch my legs and check out the Jell-O options."

"Sure," Sam offered, eager to have something to do. He followed her from the room and kept his head down until they reached the elevator bank.

"You need to remember to breathe, Sam," she said as they

stood shoulder to shoulder in the elevator. "Go on," she urged. "I mean it, take a deep breath. You'll feel better."

Sam inhaled and held it too long and then felt light-headed on the exhale. Marguerite was wrong. It didn't make him feel any better.

In the cafeteria they fell into line and slid their damp, steamy trays along the counter. At the table Sam looked at the food between them: two Greek salads, a bowl of tomato soup, macaroni and cheese, a fruit cup, and a yogurt. He wondered how it had gotten there and which one of them had been drawn to the fruit cup.

Marguerite opened the clamshell lid on a Greek salad and eyed it suspiciously, poking an olive with a plastic fork.

"Are you mad at me?" Sam whispered.

"No!" She dropped the fork and leaned forward. "No, Sam, no. Absolutely not."

"I'm mad at me." He felt a flush of heat that started at his chest and rose to his face. The back of his throat felt scratchy. He thought of all the crappy dinners he made his father that he was so grateful for; every order of takeout; the sweet cereals, cookies, and candy that Sam was happy to purchase once his mother left.

Marguerite pushed aside her salad and put her hand out on the table, palm up. Sam put his hand in hers and she folded her fingers over his.

When they got back to the waiting room Suzie was seated next to Michael. Their heads were together and they seemed to be whispering in each other's ears. Sam looked at the clock behind them on the wall and was shocked to see that he and Marguerite had been gone for only forty minutes.

Suzie jumped up as they walked in and held her arms out to

Marguerite. Sam quickly stepped aside, surprised by her display of affection.

Marguerite hugged her back. "How's your mother?" she asked.

Suzie frowned. "It's hard to tell. She's there because she has no other choice." She paused. "If it's not one thing . . ." She trailed off and shrugged.

"You never leave the hospital," Marguerite added, and made a sympathetic sound. "And your brothers?"

Michael looked over at Suzie, and then up at Marguerite. "Trying to be helpful."

Suzie laughed softly. "Nothing much gets done if I'm not there. And I can't be, but yeah, Michael is right, I guess they are trying. The house is empty, so that's a start."

Sam wanted to ask what they were all talking about, but he was caught off guard as Suzie turned to him. Sam gave her the classic one-armed hug of avoidance, patting her awkwardly on the shoulder. "Hunt is strong," Suzie said brightly to Sam, as if he were a child and yet to understand that sometimes life turned out like shit. She picked a backpack off the floor by her feet and slung it over her shoulder. "I have to get back. But I wanted to see how Hunt was doing." She addressed Marguerite more than Sam, which he was grateful for.

"I'll walk you out." Michael gathered his folders and put his hand on the small of Suzie's back.

Suzie ducked her chin to her chest and her hair fell forward, big, loopy tendrils that she swatted away from her eyes and tucked behind her ear. Sam's gut tweaked and he had to look away.

By midnight their father was out of recovery and in a bed in the cardiac ICU. Michael was the only one allowed in with him, so Sam was surprised when Michael returned to the waiting room and beckoned to him from the doorway. Marguerite had fallen asleep curled in a chair, her head resting in the crook of her arm, and Sam felt bad leaving, but Michael shook his head when Sam leaned down to wake her.

Michael greeted the nurse at the desk as they passed. He led the way into a room where he directed Sam to dress in gauzy scrubs, covering even his head and his feet. It was noisier than he expected in the ICU, with the constant click, whoosh, and beeping of machines. There was a faint smell of chemicals and burning plastic. The lighting was low, and as Sam's eyes adjusted to the forms in the beds he couldn't help but think of a horror movie. The hoses, tubes, and bandages rendered the bodies nearly anonymous and Sam panicked that he wouldn't be able to recognize their father.

Michael suddenly stopped at a bed, then turned and motioned for Sam to come closer. Hunt was hardly recognizable, adding to Sam's panic. He had tubes coming from his nose and a hose in his mouth that was taped on either side. Other tubes jutted from his chest, his arms, and his hand. A sheet covered his father from the waist down. Sam could see purple and green cauliflower-like blooms on his father's chest and arms. Even though it was warm in the ICU he had the urge to cover Hunt with a blanket.

Michael flipped through the chart and then looked up at the monitor that was beeping above his head. He exhaled with such force it was as if he had been holding his breath his entire life. "Looks good. Everything looks really good, Sammy." His voice caught when he called Sam by name.

"Except Dad," Sam whispered back.

"Yeah, I know. It's a lot to take in. But he's pretty heavily se-dated now, and any pain is under control. If he's on track by tomorrow they'll take him off the vent and really wake him up. He might be out of bed by tomorrow night."

"It's a miracle."

"It's science." Michael slipped the chart back into the slot at the end of the bed. "I was thinking we should call Mom."

It took Sam a moment to register what his brother had said. When he did, he shook his head so hard his paper hat nearly flew off and he had to reach quickly to grab it. "Why?"

"He was her husband. She might want to know."

Sam shrugged. "I think if she wanted to know anything about Dad she wouldn't have left."

"Come on," Michael said, his voice scratchy.

"I don't think you should, but I can't stop you." Sam kept his eyes trained on his father's sleeping form. He felt Michael shrug beside him and then he turned and began to walk away from Sam and back toward the door. Sam stayed by the bed a moment longer. He knew Michael was going to call their mother whether Sam agreed or not.

Carefully, he inched his hand across the sheet until he was touching his father's leg. Sam was careful to apply only the slightest pressure. He just wanted him to know he was there. He couldn't think of anything to say except *don't go*.

Marguerite's house was in Tarrytown, New York. The place had originally belonged to her grandparents and when Marguerite's husband had died, her brother offered to split the house into two separate apartments. She lived on the first floor and her brother on the second.

Their father moved in with Marguerite to recuperate. Michael, as well as Hunt's doctors, stressed the need for more sleep, more exercise, and a better diet. Sam offered some dishes that Marguerite could freeze and was surprised when instead she asked him to teach her how to cook healthier food.

Tarrytown was a thirty-one-minute express train ride from Grand Central Terminal. Sam got on the train with two minutes to spare, found a seat, and jammed his iPod buds in his ears to discourage his seatmate from making conversation. Over the past couple of days he'd had three missed calls from Michael, which was unusual but not necessarily alarming. Sam had been in daily contact with his dad or Marguerite, so he knew it was nothing about them. Sam should have used the train time to call Michael back, but he put it off. He didn't have the energy to have a serious conversation with his brother.

That morning Sam had woken after only a few hours of sleep next to someone he barely knew. He'd had another dream in which he and Suzie were sitting in her basement with the box of photos: he was about to lift the lid when Bella came into the room and surprised them. He'd startled awake, panic in his gut that had only been compounded when he realized he was in a strange bed. But luckily the girl was a heavy sleeper, and Sam had easily extricated himself without waking her.

Sam had been feeling increasingly claustrophobic, even at work. The kitchen he'd grown fond of was closing in on him ever since his father's heart attack and he wasn't sure why. Sam wondered if people who had a real life plan ever felt this way, or if it was just a symptom of his own life.

Marguerite picked Sam up at the station in a red Honda hatchback. She honked and waved out the driver's side window. Her hair was back in a ponytail and she had on large sunglasses. She wanted to go to the grocery store first, she explained, which was why she hadn't brought his father.

She was an efficient shopper, armed with the list Sam had

scribbled on the train, and they were back at her house in under an hour. As he reached for the bags from the trunk Sam's gut twitched. He was nervous. He hadn't seen his father since the day he was discharged from Mount Sinai, although they'd had a daily phone conversation while his father was enjoying a juice drink after his doctor-approved walk. It had been a month and he had yet to return to work. Sam knew he was restless.

"Sammy!" Hunt appeared on the porch. He was wearing his weekend summer outfit of madras pants and an untucked white oxford-cloth shirt. The pants looked funny at the waist and hips and Sam noticed Hunt was wearing a belt that he'd tightened a couple of extra notches.

His father held open his arms, and Sam lifted the grocery bags like he was lifting weights. His father took one from him and they hugged. Sam was shocked to feel so much less of him in such a short time.

Sam followed Hunt to the kitchen and they deposited the bags on the table. On the window ledge over the sink there was a row of orange prescription bottles. His father caught Sam looking at them. "Yes, I am officially an old man."

"Dad—" The word caught in Sam's throat and he couldn't go on.

"Aw, Sammy, I know." Hunt put his arm around Sam's shoulder and pulled him against his chest. They were almost the same height and the engagement of limbs was awkward. "I'm fine," he whispered. "Good as new."

Sam pulled back and wiped his face with the back of his hand. He was as surprised as his father that he'd had this reaction. He focused on unpacking the groceries while his father took a seat at the table, watching.

Marguerite entered the room just as they were done. "Sorry about that," she said, smiling and holding a plate aloft in one hand. "The neighbors, checking up on you." She showed him plastic-wrapped brownies and Hunt's face brightened. Marguerite shook her head and flipped the lid on the trash, sliding everything into the can but the plate. "You can say they were delicious," she called over her shoulder from the sink as she ran water over the smear of chocolate.

"That might have been worse than the heart attack," Hunt said.

Marguerite snorted and handed him a glass of water and two of the pill bottles. "It's noon," she said quietly.

Sam leaned back against the sink and watched the two of them. After Hunt swallowed his pills, Marguerite stood behind him and rested her chin on the top of his head. He reached around and patted her ass and she jumped, her cheeks flushing a deep red. "Hunt!" she said, but she was laughing, they both were, and Sam realized in that moment something his father must have known the entire time he was married to his mother: he had loved her more than she had ever loved him. Seeing him now with Marguerite, the difference was obvious.

"Well, I think I will leave you two to cook this food, if that's what we are calling it," his father said. Marguerite stepped away to allow Hunt to push back the chair. "Sam, watch her with a knife." He laughed at his own joke as Marguerite swatted his retreating form with a dish towel.

Marguerite turned out to be an excellent sous chef. By the time Sam's father had risen from his nap they had a quinoa salad with roasted vegetables, black bean burgers on whole grain rolls, a green salad, and new potatoes with lemon laid out on the table in the backyard underneath the grape arbor. When they were all seated at the table Sam admired the age of the gnarled vine, in

some places as thick as his forearm. Marguerite said, "My grandfather and uncles used to make their own wine and sit at this very
table drinking it out of jelly jars, eating shaved slices of Romano
from a tremendous wheel they kept covered on the center of the
table. They would be out here for hours at a time, and at night,
sometimes when it's quiet, I can still hear their voices, a hybrid
of English and Italian, even though all of them are long dead."

Hunt smiled, as if he'd heard the story before and enjoyed it
in the retelling. He lifted a fork of the salad, a thread of eggplant
poised on the tines. "This is really good, Sam. Really."

Sam smiled. "Dad, in all the years I've been cooking for you
I can't remember a time when you ever told me something was
awful."

His father raised an eyebrow and cocked his head to the side.
"Are you sure?"

"Positive."

Hunt took another black bean burger. "Huh," he said as he
held it up and examined it before taking an enthusiastic bite.

Marguerite laughed and lifted her glass of club soda in Sam's
direction. Sam toasted her back just as he heard tires crunch
over the gravel in the driveway. It was only just dusk but the arc
of headlights was obvious even in the backyard.

"Who's that?" Marguerite wondered aloud while Hunt, head
down, continued to fork red potatoes into his mouth. "Tommy
is still in Syracuse." She looked as if she was about to get up and
check when a car door slammed and then another.

Sam's father put down his fork and touched Marguerite's arm
so she would sit back down. "I'll go." Moments later he reappeared with Michael and Suzie.

Marguerite jumped up. "What a surprise! Sit! We have so much
food. Healthy food!" She pulled out a chair next to hers and mo-

tioned to the one next to Sam, then rushed into the house. Sam was relieved when Suzie chose the seat next to Marguerite.

Michael elbowed Sam in the ribs. "You don't answer your phone?"

Marguerite hurried out of the house, plates and silverware cradled to her chest. She set them on the table but neither Suzie nor Michael made a move to take any food. They looked at each other and smiled, almost shyly, and Michael reached across the table and grabbed Suzie's hand.

Marguerite looked from one to the other and then over at Hunt, who was smiling. "What gives, you two?"

Sam took a deep breath, louder than he intended, and Suzie glanced at him. He shook his head. He just wanted to know what was going on other than an impromptu family dinner.

"There's been a lot going on these past couple of months," Michael said. He paused and cleared his throat, acknowledging his massive understatement. "Suzie's mom, and of course, Dad." He gave a nod toward Hunt and smiled, with a shadow of relief. "It's given me more than enough reason to think about the things that are important in life, something I admit I usually don't do a lot, or even at all." He hesitated and finally allowed a genuine toothy smile. "Oh shit, I'm horrible at this." He looked like he was about to burst. "I asked Suzie to marry me."

"OH!" Marguerite twisted in her seat and threw her arms around Suzie. "Oh, I am so happy for both of you! Congratulations."

"Surprise!" Hunt called out, looking anything but surprised.

Michael got up and went around the table to Marguerite and then Hunt, allowing each of them to hug him before he stood behind Suzie and rested a hand on her shoulder. She reached up and stroked the inside of his arm. Sam had yet to say anything.

He knew what he was expected to say, but he was unsure of how to say it sincerely.

Michael looked over at him. "You should have answered your phone."

"I'll never ignore it again." Sam hesitated. "Congratulations, really." He pushed his chair back and went into the kitchen. He knew there were champagne flutes in the pantry; he had noticed them earlier when he was getting a platter for the burgers. He dropped raspberries into the bottom of five flutes along with lemonade and sparkling water, then put them all on a tray and carried them back outside. Holding up one of the flutes, Sam said, "To true love."

Over her champagne glass Sam caught Suzie staring at him. When they made eye contact she looked away and moved closer to his brother. Marguerite was asking about the details of the wedding; his father leaned in, listening to their answers. Sam heard nothing but the sound of his own blood pounding in his ears.

TEN

Ladies in Waiting
Bella—2008

Y ou look so beautiful."

Bella caught Suzie's eye in the mirror and made a face. She was sitting on a rose-colored velvet tufted stool with her knees to her chest, watching Suzie get her final gown fitting. The seamstress worked down around the hem, a wide bracelet of pins circling her wrist. Bella was definitely not feeling very beautiful in cutoff denim shorts, one of Ted's V-neck T-shirts, and sandals that showcased unpolished toenails. Her hair, which had never gone back to waves, was pulled back into a messy bun. She had been traveling for what felt like days to get there from Montana.

Suzie made a face back and laughed. "Seriously, whatever it is: Ted, mountain air, clean living, good sex. You look amazing."

Bella shook her head and caught the eye of the seamstress, who smiled. "Enough about me," Bella said. "You are the princess today, tomorrow, the next day . . ."

"Ugh," Suzie said. "You know I never went in for any of that crap."

"Spoken like a true anti-bride." Bella laughed.

"Seriously, though, I'm so glad you're here." The seamstress stood and stepped back and Suzie turned around to look at Bella. "It's okay?" She picked at the material that gently hugged the curve of her hips. The dress was simple and elegant, and the color, neither cream nor white, made Suzie's skin shimmer, turning it a flattering shade of rose.

Bella nodded. Her eyes filled with tears. Suzie was getting married. It was no longer an abstract idea dissected during their weekly calls.

Suzie shook her head when she saw the waterworks. "Bella, don't."

Bella swiped at the corners of her eyes with the hem of Ted's T-shirt. She shook her head. "I'm not a real grown-up person yet and here you are getting married. How did that happen?"

"Do you really believe that?"

"You're going to be a doctor. You will have a husband who is also a doctor. You have a real home." Bella smiled, thinking of the apartment Suzie had so proudly showed off, so new the couch and mattress were still wrapped in the delivery plastic and bore stickers from Macy's. "These are all really good things."

"It sounds scary when you list them like that."

"Good scary, though, right? Like you never ever believed that this would happen?"

"Yeah," Suzie whispered. "But what about you?"

Bella smiled. "I'm happy," she insisted. "But I don't quite feel there, where you are, you know?"

Bella hadn't thought Ted would come with her to Suzie's wedding. His writing was going well, so well that he had been living alone in the cabin while Bella had gone back to Iowa City for work. She was the only one with a job, a temporary teaching gig, a last-minute replacement for a famous writer who had just had a baby. There was disappointment on all sides, students and Ted alike, when she showed up for her first day. The students were disappointed because she was no one who could further their careers. Ted was disappointed because he had lost his daily reader/editor.

Bella took the job because she wasn't doing any of her own writing anyway, and she was tired of her father's supporting her and Ted. Her work on turning her thesis into a publishable book had stalled, even more so after she found out that three people in her graduating class already had agents and book deals. Even Ted had an agent. Bella lost all enthusiasm for editing her own work and instead pored over Ted's pages as if they were her own.

Ted's cabin, which he had built with his own hands, was so remote that the only way Bella could communicate with him was to send a letter to the post office in the town where he kept a PO box. Once a week Ted trekked into town for supplies. If it was an emergency, Bella could call the general store/post office and they would leave a message tacked up on the bulletin board in the store. But Bella hadn't considered Suzie's wedding an emergency, so she had written Ted a letter with the dates and what she hoped sounded like a no-pressure invitation. He had called her collect from the pay phone in the store and told her to come back. He said he missed her and he couldn't sleep at night. He promised they would leave in time for the wedding. Through the receiver she heard the sound of paper crinkling. She imagined her words crumpled in the palm of his hand. She was so surprised that she did as he asked without thinking.

After the dress fitting Bella dropped Suzie off at the country club in Rye where the wedding and reception were being held. Suzie and Michael had rented all of the quaint clapboard guest cottages that circled the golf course for their out-of-town relatives, and that was also where Suzie was staying with her mother and brothers. Suzie wanted to check on Sarah, six weeks out of Silver Hill, and take a nap before Bella met back up with her for drinks with Mindy, Ruthie, and Celia.

When Bella arrived home she found Ted on the deck outside of her room. He was sitting in a green webbed lounge chair, the cat wedged between his splayed legs. On the floor around the chair were Bella's laptop, the charger, two empty beer bottles, and a plate with a gelatinous smear of tomato innards and a lone saltshaker.

As Bella wrenched open the sliding glass door, Ted, whose back was to her, twisted around and offered up a lazy half smile. Bella noticed the yellow legal pad shoved beneath his thigh and wondered if he was trying to get some work done. She hesitated, not really wanting to interrupt him, but he held out his hand and said, "Baby, where have you been?"

The cat jumped down off the chair and disappeared into the backyard as Bella approached and leaned over Ted. She kissed him on the lips. He tugged on her belt loop and she fell on top of him.

He laughed as he nuzzled her neck. "Just what I was dreaming about."

Ted's three days' growth of stubble tickled as he moved his mouth down past Bella's throat and into the deep V of her T-shirt. Bella could feel the sun beating down on her head and shoulders and she relaxed under Ted's hands. The old chair creaked beneath them and Bella heard something pop just as the footrest collapsed, tipping the chair forward. Bella laughed and Ted groaned. His fingers tugged on a nipple and Bella shivered.

They managed to get off the chair and into Bella's bedroom, the glass door protesting loudly on the uneven tracks. For all the words Ted put on paper, he was quiet in his pursuit. Before they even made it to the bed he had stripped off Bella's shirt and shorts so that she stood before him in a lacy bra and underpants, her only nod to femininity lately. Their breathing was shallow and labored in the closed, stuffy room as Ted pushed Bella down onto the bed. She heard his shorts drop to the floor and her eyes flew open in time to see him kneel down at the edge of the bed between her legs. He ran his hands up and down inside her thighs and Bella closed her eyes, enjoying the familiarity in knowing what came next, where the only unknown was how long it would take.

Ted had fallen asleep when Bella got out of bed in search of a fan. She picked the inside-out T-shirt of Ted's off the floor, pulled it over her head, and left the room. Ted swore he could survive without modern conveniences, but Bella knew her limits. Even though she had made it sound to Suzie that being in a remote cabin in Montana was pure bliss, it wasn't. Right now, she was hot and thirsty and in no mood for roughing it. At least here she had a choice.

When she got to the kitchen her father was standing at the island mixing a martini. He was as surprised to see her as she was him, and so she had no time to back out of the room. She tugged at the hem of the T-shirt and he looked down at his drink. "I'm meeting Hunt and Michael for golf," he said quickly, his eyes trained on a point past the kitchen. "I asked Ted, but he said he doesn't play." He paused. "He said he has work to do."

Bella nodded. She heard the slight way her father emphasized the word *work*. She knew he wouldn't say what he thought: that writing with no guarantee of money seemed more like a hobby than a job. She imagined Ted sharing his feelings about the environmental hazards of golf courses with her father. When she told him that Suzie and Michael's wedding was at the country club he had shaken his head in profound disappointment in their lack of ecological awareness.

"So I'm leaving now," Bella's father added. The ice cubes tinkled against the sides of the glass as he drained the drink and turned away from her to place the glass in the sink.

"Okay," Bella said quickly. She spun around and ran back down the hall and into the bathroom, where she pressed her face up against the cool tile wall and waited until she heard the door to the garage open and close. Why was she hiding as if Ted were her sixteen-year-old boyfriend? She was old enough to have sex. Certainly her father knew she was having sex. But she didn't want to have a conversation with him while standing in his kitchen wearing nothing but her boyfriend's T-shirt just after having sex. Especially since she had an idea of what her father thought of Ted, and it wasn't great.

Mindy, Ruthie, Celia, and Suzie were already at the bar in their summer dresses when Bella arrived. They smelled of cocoa butter and roses, the scent of girls who do not live in a cabin in the mountains. Bella inhaled as she hugged them and remembered when she used to smell like that too.

Ruthie ordered gin and tonics for all of them as they settled at a black iron table on the wide front porch. The breeze lifted Bella's ponytail off the nape of her neck and she flicked her hair back over her shoulder. Her mind wandered as her friends talked. Bella was still unnerved from the run-in with her father. She wondered what her mother would have thought of Ted, if somehow she would have made things easier. She thought about how Ted had asked her to look over his work before she went out, and how she had forgotten to go outside to retrieve the pad off the deck. She hadn't meant to, but she wondered what Ted would make of that. If he would think she didn't care. It had been so long since they had even talked about her work. But that was her fault. She had shut him down the last few times he tried to bring it up.

She took a sip of her gin and tonic and looked across the table. Mindy had handed Suzie a small shopping bag and Suzie was sifting through the layers of tissue paper. Finally she revealed a pewter-colored silk slip, the delicate edges rolled and hand stitched, shoulder straps as thin as threads. "It's beautiful," Suzie said, unable to hide the surprise in her voice.

Mindy smiled. "It's definitely you, darling."

Everyone at the table murmured in agreement. The waiter arrived and they ordered another round. They talked about their lives since they had last seen one another, what they had imagined for themselves all those years ago, and they marveled that Suzie was the first among them to be married. By the third round of drinks, when the solar lights hidden in the landscaping had begun to glow in the dusky gray evening light, Bella caught sight of her father, Sam's father, Peter Chang, and Michael heading down the cart path toward the clubhouse. Peter Chang was an odd addition to the threesome. Bella wished that Ted had accepted her father's invitation despite his moral opposition on behalf of the environment.

Michael greeted everyone but was looking only at Suzie and she at him. Suzie looked up at Michael, her eyes shiny, her lips swollen from the heat, her cheeks flushed from the gin. "Are you leaving soon to get Sam?" Bella felt a twinge in her belly.

Michael nodded. He tucked a tendril of Suzie's hair that had escaped her bun back behind her ear. Everyone seemed to avoid looking at Bella, or maybe that was just three gin and tonics and Bella's own paranoia.

Hunt offered, "I'll go, if you want."

Michael frowned. "I'm fine, Dad, enjoy yourself."

Bella's father slapped Hunt on the shoulder. "You know what that means. We can have martinis with our steaks, Hunt." He laughed, and Bella laughed with him. What would they have done if Bella said she wanted to go with Michael? What if she met Sam head-on at the airport full of gin and tonics?

"Loser buys," Hunt said, laughing back.

Peter, who had been hanging back from the table, tapped Mindy on top of the head, and she pushed back her chair and they disappeared inside the club, hand in hand. Ruthie looked over at Bella with a raised eyebrow and Bella laughed. They all might have aged, but they hadn't grown up.

There came a time later in the night when they lost their shoes somewhere on the golf course. They had been on their way to Suzie's cottage and then somehow collapsed onto the green, unable to go any farther.

Bella burped softly. "Does anyone else have a splitting headache?" Her head already hurt and she was still a little drunk.

Ruthie and Celia moaned. They were on their backs on the green, arms thrown over their faces. Bella looked at Suzie. "You are a doctor. Why does my head hurt?"

Suzie shrugged and laughed.

"Thanks," Bella said. "I have to pee."

"Me too," added Ruthie.

"Same," Celia echoed.

"I had sex with Peter in the bathroom at the club," Mindy said.

Suzie and Bella laughed. Ruthie groaned again. Celia was quiet.

"What?" Mindy shrugged. "Friends with benefits, it's the best sex." She must have thought they looked unconvinced, because she felt the need to add, "We knocked over the basket of pot-pourri. I didn't pick it up."

"I had sex with Ted this afternoon, and my father surprised me," Bella said.

"What?" Suzie and Mindy said in unison.

Bella shook her head. "Well, I mean it was after. I went into the kitchen wearing Ted's T-shirt and he was standing there."

"Awkward," Ruthie said.

"Did he say anything?" Mindy asked.

"About me having sex? No." Bella made a face. "God, no. I wasn't going to tell you guys that and now I did, so obviously I am an unreliable keeper of secrets."

"It was your own secret, so you didn't promise anyone but yourself," Celia pointed out.

"True," Bella agreed. "But if you can't keep your own secrets, isn't that worse?"

"No," Mindy said with a hint of authority in her voice. "It just means you changed your mind, dummy."

"Oh," Bella sighed. "I changed my mind; that sounds better, I guess." She didn't really think so, but she wanted to get off the subject. "What about you, bride-to-be?"

"What, is this Truth or Dare?" Suzie asked slowly. The rest of the girls busted out laughing, but Bella could see she blushed deeply.

"Oh my God, remember playing that in Peter's basement?"

Ruthie said. She pointed over at Mindy. "You and Frankie Cole. I so remember you and Frankie."

Mindy rolled her eyes. "Okay, you and Johnny Ross?"

"Lots of saliva." Ruthie looked solemn. "I wonder if that ever improved."

"It has," Celia piped up. They all turned and looked at her. "What? He's cute. Have you seen him recently? He plays guitar."

"Why can't we leave each other?" Mindy asked. "Is this normal?" She poked Suzie on the thigh. "You're the head doc."

"Bella has Ted, he's not one of us," Ruthie said.

"But she had Sam first," Mindy said.

"Oh, did she ever." Ruthie laughed. "For all of his awkwardness that boy is walking sex."

"You think Sam is awkward?" Celia asked. "I think he's cute."

"Well, compared to Michael, the handsome, handsome Michael, he is," Ruthie said.

Mindy laughed as if she'd just processed what Ruthie had said. "Walking sex?"

Bella squirmed. Her dress was sticking to her body. She avoided looking over at Suzie. She had thought about Sam when she was lying next to Ted. She remembered in detail the night after her mother had died. She would never forget that.

Thankfully Suzie jumped in. "No one is normal, okay? Everyone is always worried about being normal, but we are all abnormal." She pointed at each of them. "Every single one of you. And me."

"I think you might want to work on that bedside manner," Ruthie said.

Suzie held up her finger. "Duly noted."

Bella sat up and waved her hands in front of her face. "I'm hot. Can we go swimming?"

"The pool is closed," Celia said.

"All the better," Mindy said. She stood and offered Bella her hand.

They straggled as a group off the path and cut over the tennis courts to the pool. The moon was low, the air was thick, and it was only a couple of hours before dawn. If the weather continued like that for the next twenty-four hours the wedding day was going to be brutal.

Bella got to the gate first and stood on her tiptoes to pump the release on the latch. As it swung open they skittered across the concrete deck to the edge. Suzie lifted her dress over her head and dove in first, hitting the water so seamlessly that it took a moment for Bella to realize she had gone in. When she popped up, her head was as dark and sleek as a seal.

One by one they shed their summer dresses and jumped into the pool. The water was warm, like the middle part of a perfect bath. Bella swam the length of the pool underwater, back and forth, and then floated on her back in the deep end. The only sound she heard was her own breath in her ears. She wished Ted were there with her. She wondered what he would think when he woke and she wasn't beside him. She was probably sober enough now to go home. But she couldn't bear the thought of leaving.

ELEVEN

I Knew You When
Sam—2008

S am should have left Paris three days earlier, but he missed his original flight out of the South of France because of a string of storms and a lack of urgency, so all the connecting flights fell like dominoes. He finally arrived at JFK on the evening of the rehearsal dinner. He called the moment he landed, but his change of plans had left Marguerite and his father no other choice but to go on ahead without him. By the time Sam caught the shuttle and then a cab to the house, he had been without any decent sleep for thirty-six hours.

Sam stepped inside the front door and realized that while the outside remained the same, everything inside was different. If he hadn't been so tired he was sure he would have been sufficiently warned by the metaphor. He spent way too much time wandering through the downstairs, admiring the surfaces and the light, the marble countertops in the kitchen, and the carefully placed art. He took a beer from the refrigerator and went upstairs, peering in the open door of the impressive master suite. The bed was unmade, sheets and blankets forming a bridal train to the floor, and a nightgown draped over a chair. On a sleek, low modern dresser stood framed high school graduation pictures of Sam and Michael that had once been on Hunt's old dresser.

Sam finished the beer in the master bathroom and studied his reflection in the wall of mirrors above the double sinks. He hadn't spent any time concerned with his appearance in the past months, so what he saw was a surprise. He was thinner but stronger, his arms and legs ropy and hard, his abdomen visibly muscled from swimming in the warm Mediterranean waters, which he did whenever he wasn't cooking. His skin was dark, nearly olive, and his hair a lighter shade of brown, nearing blond at the tips, and shaggy to the point of badly needing a haircut. His beard looked like a small animal and would have to go. He wondered how late that would make him, how much time he had before he really pissed everyone off. When Michael had asked Sam to be his best man, right after he was offered the job that would take him a continent away for nearly a year, Sam had imagined the wedding would never happen. He'd thought there was a possibility he would never have to stand by his brother and watch him marry Suzie Epstein. But now they were here, and Sam had already shirked most of what he imagined were traditional best-man activities. The least he could do was show up for the rehearsal.

He took a shower in the master bathroom and tracked water across the hardwood floors to the old part of the house, where his room remained intact. On his bed were a dark suit and a white shirt, below on the floor a pair of shoes. Sam guessed Hunt must have left everything out for him. He slipped on his clothes and glanced in the mirror, rubbing his smooth face. It had taken several passes with the scissors and another few with a razor until he got a close shave. His skin was pale where his beard and mustache had been, and he didn't know what looked worse, the beard or the two-toned effect. He finger-combed his hair back off his face, but it was so long it brushed past the collar until the ends turned up.

His father had left the keys to Marguerite's Honda. On the way to the club Sam passed the strip mall where his mother used to take him and Michael to get haircuts before school started. There had been a glass jar full of baseball cards and candy on the counter. Sure enough, the jar was still there. Sam handed over all the money he had in his wallet with a request to make him look presentable. On the way out, he grabbed a lollipop from the jar and slipped it into his pocket. Everyone in the shop had mistaken his level of panic and thought he was the groom. They called after him with an avalanche of best wishes for a wonderful wedding— wishes Sam accepted without bothering to correct them, which probably damned him to a lifetime of bad luck.

At the end of the long gravel drive Sam gave the Honda over to a jumpy kid in a white jacket and a crooked black tie, and then stood looking up at the grand clubhouse with its pearly white shingles and black shuttered windows. Everything, the rehearsal dinner and the wedding and a brunch on Sunday, was happening here for convenience's sake. Vines and flowers spilled from elaborate stone planters, and the air smelled sweet. People were gathered on the wide front porch, arranged in groups as artfully as the wicker; the sounds of their voices and the sudden swell of a string quartet made Sam want to run after the Honda and ask the kid if he had any weed. Instead, he jammed his fingers in his pocket and came up with the lollipop from the hair place. He ripped off the plastic and put it in his mouth: root beer.

Sam sucked on the lollipop as he walked through the lobby to the screened-in back porch that ran the length of the clubhouse and overlooked the rolling hills of the aptly named Rolling Hills Golf Club. The porch was filled with white flowers, twinkling white lights, and candles that seemed to be the source of the sweet scent he had caught a whiff of before. The string quartet was at the far end of the porch in front of a massive stone fireplace. The cello player had an *I'm not really here* look that Sam envied. He hung back, looking for a familiar face before he took the plunge.

The first person he made eye contact with was his mother. Sam recognized the trapped look in her eyes only because it mirrored his own. She came toward him smiling, slim and tall, her hair now entirely silver. She was wearing a pale blue dress with a skirt that moved as she walked. Her face was clear of any makeup except for a gloss on her lips. She had never looked better.

"You look pretty," Sam said as he moved into her open arms.

She pulled back, laughing softly, and held him at arm's length. "So do you, Sam. So do you."

Tom appeared at her side holding drinks in his hands. He tipped his chin at Sam in greeting and handed a glass to Elizabeth. "How was the South of France?"

"Beautiful," Sam nodded. "Good. Great, actually."

"Great opportunity."

"Absolutely." Sam figured he didn't need to tell him that for the first six months he'd peeled carrots and potatoes and dressed salad greens and only got to really cook when the chef had had too much to drink, which as the year went on increased in frequency.

"What are you going to do now?"

Conversation with Tom was like playing volleyball. Sam knew he didn't think much of him, of the way Sam fell in and out of his mother's life. He wanted to say to him that she didn't exactly call

Sam every week either, that she left when he was fifteen years old, but he had a feeling that didn't matter to Tom.

Sam's mother saved him from answering Tom's question when she said, "The gardenias are overwhelming."

"Is that what smells so sweet?" Sam could feel a headache forming behind his right eye. Jet lag was almost definitely to follow.

"SAM?"

Sam spun around at the sound of his father's voice and was immediately crushed against his chest. The force of Hunt's hug nearly lodged the lollipop stick deep into Sam's throat and Sam gagged. Hunt thumped him twice between the shoulder blades while Sam disengaged the stick. "Prodigal Sam, you made it."

"I did," Sam smiled. He accepted the cocktail napkin that had suddenly appeared before him from his mother and wadded it together with the stick into his pocket. "I did, finally. I'm sorry about the confusion, my flights." His father looked thinner than when Sam left; Sam wondered if his heart felt bruised a year later.

"You're here now. Have you seen your brother?"

"No, I just got here and I ran into . . . Mom." Sam pointed to his mother, who was looking at them over the rim of her glass. When was the last time they had been together? Sam's high school graduation?

Hunt smiled in her direction. "Elizabeth, doesn't our boy look great?"

Sam's mother returned her ex-husband's smile. "He does. It's good to see him."

Sam wasn't sure if they had agreed before the wedding to act as if they were the most cordial divorced couple in the world, but it felt like it. He peered past his father for Marguerite, but he couldn't find her. There were a lot of people on the porch but no one he immediately recognized.

Hunt put a hand on Sam's shoulder. "Let's get you over to Michael. He'll be glad to know you finally showed up." He hesitated, and then said as if he were asking permission, "Elizabeth?"

"Go, go on. Make your brother calm down." Elizabeth ignored Sam's father and smiled at Sam as if this night, all of them together and his brother marrying Suzie Epstein, was entirely normal. "I'll catch up to you later."

Sam's father barreled through the crowd, pumping hands and introducing Sam like a politician at a fund-raiser. "Who are all these people?" Sam asked as soon as there was a pocket of air. He gulped frantically, like a goldfish breaking the smooth surface. Everyone was drinking and his hands were empty. The bones in his skull felt tight. He needed a damn drink.

His father looked over his shoulder but, like a shark, kept moving forward. "Friends, business associates, neighbors. You name it, they are here."

"I'm never doing this," Sam said to his father's back.

"What?"

"I said: it's great that they are doing this, having so many people and all."

His father finally stopped and turned to smirk at Sam. "Absolutely."

"What?" Sam feigned innocence.

"I've missed you." Hunt laughed. "It's really good to see you, Sammy, really good." He paused and then pointed. "Come on, there he is."

Sam followed his father's finger. Michael and Suzie stood surrounded by a group. Suzie's arm was slipped through Michael's, and she was leaning forward at the waist as she listened to some-one standing to the left of Michael. She wasn't doing a thing to get attention, yet she had Sam's. Fully. He took a deep breath.

"Here he is!" Hunt presented Sam to the group in a booming, cheerful voice, as if he had just been released from the asylum or born again.

As the group parted to let him in, Sam said, "Hey," and raised his hands in surrender. "I'm sorry I'm so late."

Michael reached out a hand as if they were going to shake and then pulled Sam in for a half hug. Sam smiled at Suzie and then turned back to his brother. Jokingly he asked, "Is there anything important I need to know for tomorrow?"

Michael shook his head as if this was typical of Sam, making a big joke out of everything. He pulled Suzie tighter to his side. She buried her face in his jacket and then peered up at him through a mass of wavy black hair as if no one else were present. From the back of the group came the unmistakable ring of fork tines hitting crystal, quickly multiplying. Michael and Suzie obliged the crowd with a kiss.

Slowly, Sam backed away from the happy couple and made his way toward the bar. He seriously didn't know how he was going to get through the next few hours, let alone the entire following day.

Sam wedged himself into a corner of the bar and ordered a beer. His headache was in full-force vise-grip mode. To his left was a platter of stuffed endive leaves; he rapidly ate three, even though the endive was bitter and the cheese was overprocessed and salted.

"So, it's fucking true. You're back."

"Peter?" Sam twisted around and made room at the bar.

Peter put a hand up to the bartender and signaled that he would have what Sam was drinking. "How long have you been gone, asshole? A year?"

"I just got here." Sam squinted at the clock over the register. "U.S. soil, that is, not even two hours ago. Two hours. I missed the rehearsal. And the dinner."

"I know, I was here."

"Why?"

Peter took a swallow of his beer. "Mindy's in the wedding. I'm her plus one."

"Mindy? In the wedding."

"What did you expect from Suzie? Mindy, Ruthie, and Bella." Peter craned his head around to scan the room. "Frankie Cole is here somewhere." He paused. "She invited the rest of them too— Stephen, Johnny, Celia. We'll probably see them tomorrow."

Sam dropped his forehead to the bar. He felt weak in the knees at the mention of Bella. Oh, why the fuck was he so stupid? Of course Bella was there.

"You okay?"

He lifted his aching head. "Jet lag."

Peter nodded solemnly. "I might have a little something that will help."

"I would be eternally grateful."

"I wouldn't expect any less from you, shithead."

They drained their beers and Peter motioned for Sam to follow him. They were cutting back through the porch again on their way out to the golf course when he finally saw Marguerite, in a conversation with Mr. Spade. As much as he wanted to say hello to her, he did not want to talk to Bella's father, but it was too late. She had seen him and waved him over.

"Sam, I am so glad to finally see you here!"

Sam hugged her, then looked over at Bella's father and extended his hand. Mr. Spade took it, but he didn't look entirely pleased to be doing so. "Sam," he said. "How's the cooking?" The way he emphasized the word *cooking* made Sam feel like he was the short-order fry guy at Burger King.

"Good, great."

"Good to hear it."

Marguerite smiled widely, looking back and forth between the two. "I was just bragging about your year in the South of France."

Sam nodded. "It is a beautiful place."

"Did you have a lot of time for sightseeing?"

"No, I worked pretty much all day and into the night. Because it was a charter boat nothing was ever really the same day to day. Lots of interesting people, though." Sam smiled stiffly. Marguerite brushed something off one of his lapels. "Well, we were heading out to catch up with some of the guys."

Mr. Spade narrowed his eyes at Sam and then Peter. Sam was sure he was wondering if Sam was including Bella under the umbrella term *guys*. Peter tapped him on the shoulder because he lacked the social skills to pretend he still wanted to be standing there, and for once Sam was grateful.

By the staircase that led off the porch Sam saw Suzie walking down a long hall back toward the party. He was surprised that she was alone. She raised a hand for him to wait. While she continued toward Sam he couldn't help but stare. Her dress was a pale gold, sleeveless and fitted to her curves. She was smaller than she had ever been and around her tiny waist was a fragile-looking belt made of chain links. Her eyes were big and bright, and there were two spots of color high in her cheeks. As she got closer Sam looked for the constellation of freckles that formed an S on her cheek, and wondered if Michael had ever noticed that about her, if he had ever traced it with his finger as Sam had.

"I'm so glad I caught you alone, Sam." She was slightly out of breath, as if she had been running. Her breath was tangy, her voice soft and slow.

"I was just on my way out with Peter." When Sam gestured behind him he noticed Peter was gone. He felt desperate to stop the pain in his head.

Suzie frowned. "It's the night before my wedding, so you have to do whatever I want." She giggled, and then Sam knew she was drunk.

"Suzie—"

She shook her head. "This is important, Sam. Please." She adjusted her belt and rubbed her palms against her dress. "It's about Bella." She looked around and so did Sam. They were alone, tucked in a triangle-shaped alcove before the staircase. "Tomorrow, please, tomorrow you have to act like you and Bella, well, that there isn't history."

Sam stiffened. "What kind of person do you think I am? I'm not going to be the one to ruin your wedding. I think there are potentially plenty of other people here who could. Your father, my mother, my father, your mother." He didn't add that he was upset that she was more worried he might hurt Bella than that he might be hurt she was marrying his brother.

Suzie bit her lip. "My father wasn't invited."

"What?"

"He and I don't have much of a relationship. We hadn't ever, really, since . . ."

"Oh." Sam had heard rumors, knew more stuff had gone down with her parents after they had moved.

She nodded and swallowed hard. "Anyway, I just wanted to

make sure that you and Bella could stand together for us tomorrow. Bella is totally fine with it. But I wasn't sure how you would, you know, feel." She searched his face with her enormous eyes until he had to look down at his feet.

"Don't worry, okay? Just don't worry."

Suzie reached out her hand as if she might touch Sam's arm and then retracted it fast. He could feel her fear, and he was sad that he was the cause. He motioned for her to step ahead of him into the room alone. He didn't want to give anyone a chance to think that the bride and he had any secrets.

Sam followed his nose and found Peter at the sixteenth hole with two guys in khakis, striped ties, and navy blue blazers. They looked slightly familiar, but he didn't care enough to ask for their names and no one offered an introduction. The four of them shared a joint for a bit, and then the two strangers wandered off.

Peter and Sam sat down on the green and finished off the joint. They were far enough away from the porch that no one could see them, but close enough to hear voices and the string quartet. Sam fell back onto the grass and shut his eyes. His headache was still there, but it felt further away. "Tell me what happened the last year of your life," he said.

Peter coughed. "Pretty much the same thing that happened the year before."

"So the thing with Mindy is still going on?"

"There is no thing."

"Um, you're at my brother's wedding with her."

"How was France?"

"I cannot tell one more person how fucking beautiful it was."

"Did I ask you that?" Sam heard the strike of a match and then the sweet smell of a fresh joint. Peter floated it over his chest. "Was it worth it?"

Sam took a long hit, exhaled, and handed the joint back to Peter. "Was what worth it?"

"Running away?"

"What the fuck are you talking about?"

"Hey, here you assholes are . . . having all the fun without me." Sam propped himself up on his elbows. Frankie Cole was heading across the green. "Turner," he said when he reached them. "Long time." They slapped hands in a misguided mid/high five.

Frankie reached over Sam and took the joint from Peter. "There are no single girls here except for the ones who already know me." He took a hit off the joint.

Sam laughed. "Same old story, Cole, same old story."

Frankie half snorted, half coughed as he tried to keep the smoke in. "Fuck, I've missed you guys."

"Ruthie has a lover, by the way," Peter said.

"Did you meet him?" Frankie asked.

"No, but I met *her*." Peter handed Sam the joint. "And I'm not making up the lover thing. She said, 'Peter, meet my lover, Lucy.' "

"Fucking women's studies," Frankie added. "Worst boner-killer major ever. They put all these hot girls together, teach them to hate men, and so they turn to each other."

"Did you mention that in your interview when they hired you at Rutgers?" Sam asked. Peter had told him that the philosophy department had offered Frankie a job after grad school and was allowing him to work toward a doctorate while he taught. Sam had no idea what being a philosophy professor entailed. Whatever it was, Frankie was supposedly brilliant at it.

They killed off the second joint. Sam listened while Peter and Frankie discussed the futility of mating with one person for life.

Finally Sam said, "What was going on inside when you left?" He was trying to figure out how much more time he was expected to stay. If he couldn't leave soon he was going to just spend the night on the golf course. The sprinklers could wake him in the morning.

"Toasts," Frankie said. "Long, boring toasts given by crying people." He paused. "What they don't understand is that love is an abstract idea. It is improbable as a long-term—"

"SHIT." Sam sat up, cutting off Frankie's tirade against love. He was pretty sure that at some point Michael had said the best man would have to give a toast. "I have to get in there." Sam tried to stand and fell back down on one knee, hard. He clawed at the green and got enough momentum to push himself upright. As he walked toward the clubhouse he realized he was stoned. Possibly more stoned than he had ever been in his life. Which was entirely the reason everyone turned to look at him as he fumbled with the latch on the screen door.

His mother saved him. She took Sam by the elbow and closed the door softly. He felt her brush off his shoulders and back and press something cold into his hand. "Drink," she commanded.

Sam did as he was told, grateful for the cold water. It was the best water he'd ever tasted in his life. He felt her hand on the back of his head, fishing something out of his hair, most likely grass. "Do I have to say something?" he whispered.

She shook her head and pointed to the front of the room, where Michael and Suzie stood arm in arm. Sam suddenly realized how quiet it was. The string quartet had finally stopped playing. Michael and Suzie shimmered, their affection for each other enviable, and yet they did it quietly, almost privately. They were standing in front of a hundred of their closest friends and family, but they might as well have been alone.

Sam shivered, and his mother reached up and massaged his shoulder. He wasn't sure how much she had been paying attention to him that summer she left, but he would be willing to guess she had known way more than he had given her credit for.

After the toasts were over, Sam sat at the bar with Peter and Frankie, inhaling a burger and fries. He had noticed Bella in the crowd of people closest to Suzie and Michael. She was standing next to a guy who kept bending down to say something in her ear. She smiled and laughed and one time reached up and fixed the collar of his shirt. The guy brushed her hand off as if she was annoying, but Bella didn't seem to notice.

Sam thought about going over and offering a casual hello to get it out of the way. But then he reconsidered. He had the feeling that maybe he had been thinking about Bella way more than she ever thought about him. Sam still carried that scrap of a poem in his wallet; the paper was so thin from being folded that the fibers had broken down to nearly transparent in places. He wasn't sure if what he was feeling was nostalgia or sleep deprivation. Tomorrow would be soon enough.

Michael was standing alone in the middle of the backyard when Sam finally got home. He had gone to Peter's with Frankie because Mindy was spending the night with Suzie and Ruthie in a bungalow at the club. When Sam finally headed toward home he was nearly catatonic with exhaustion. It struck him, as he walked the darkened streets of his childhood, that he had been taking this path forever. That his body would know how to find the way even if his mind wasn't cooperating.

Sam had been at the sink for some time when he noticed Michael. He had been looking at the framed photos of Hunt and

Marguerite on the marble countertop. In one his father was in the canoe at Paradox Lake waving at the camera, and in another he and Marguerite sat at a large round table surrounded by champagne flutes and flowers. There was also a photo of Michael and Suzie sitting together in the same lawn chair, and one of Sam frowning at the barbecue, his face nearly obscured by the smoke.

The back wall of the house, once solid, was now made of glass, and tiny lights outlined a stone walkway to the new patio. Michael was off the path in the grass. He was still wearing his suit, his tie slung over his shoulder like a scarf. He was barefoot. Sam watched his brother. When he didn't move in the time it took Sam to down four glasses of water, he went out back to join him.

"Hey."

"Hey," Michael answered without turning around.

"I'm sorry."

"For what?"

"Being late, being born, take your pick," Sam joked.

Michael laughed.

Sam craned his neck and made a show of looking around the yard. "Everything looks great here. I'd barely call it home."

Michael nodded.

"You okay?"

Michael opened his mouth but didn't say anything right away. Sam felt himself getting nervous. Finally Michael looked over. "I'm just taking a moment, you know?"

"Sure, of course. Big day tomorrow."

"Do you ever think you will do this?"

"What? Stand in the middle of the backyard contemplating the state of the universe?"

Michael grinned; he looked tired. "Get married, asshole. Suzie thought you might come home with someone, that that was the reason you missed your flights."

Sam thought of the nearly celibate year he'd spent in France. It had mostly been by choice, an attempt to change his ways of empty sex and strange beds. But in the end he was just frustrated, hardly changed, and lonely. "No, not this time."

Michael gave Sam a funny look and ran a hand through his hair. "I should sleep, right? I should sleep because tomorrow is going to go by so fast. I want to be present, you know? I want to remember everything."

"You will."

Michael stared at him. "It's okay, right?" he whispered. "Me and Suzie?"

Sam was confused by his question. "She's crazy about you. Everyone can see it."

"No." Michael shook his head, clearly agitated that Sam wasn't following. "I thought . . ." He hesitated.

"What?"

"When I used to think about the future, about my life, I always thought I would be alone. I just couldn't imagine being with someone in this way."

"And now?"

"Sometimes I still think it's not real." He shook his head. "And then I see her, you know? I see her, and I can't see my life any other way."

How could Sam tell his brother that at one time he knew exactly how Michael was feeling about his soon-to-be wife? "That's the way it should be," he choked out. The words felt hard, unyielding, a lump in his chest somewhere in the vicinity of where his heart used to be. "I should go to bed. I can't even count the hours I've been awake."

"Sure."

"You okay?"

"Absolutely. Hey, you talk to Mom?"

"Yeah, and Tom. He hates me."

Michael smirked. "Nah. Not once you get to know him."

"And you do?"

"Well, at least I try." He smirked again. "Go, get some sleep, write a toast, will you?" He yawned and gave Sam a sloppy grin.

"You coming in?"

"Soon."

Sam started to walk back to the house. At the patio he turned to look one more time at Michael. In that moment Michael reminded him so much of their mother and her mercurial moods. He almost said something, but then he thought better of it.

The next afternoon Bella came toward Sam in a halting step due to the uneven ground and the petals strewn in clumps on the walkway. Under a flower-draped arbor Sam stood to Michael's left in a suit and tie. The air was heavy like a late-summer afternoon at the beach. All morning Michael had been panicking about the impending storms. Hunt had the flat-screen televisions in the bedroom, living room, and kitchen tuned to the Weather Channel, where they could see the Peter Max–like radar screens shift and expand. There was a nearly 100 percent chance of rain. Michael had paced from room to room, his phone tucked near his chin, weaving alternate scenarios into the receiver until Suzie finally persuaded him to let go. She insisted on the wedding as it had been planned: the ceremony outside on the lawn, cocktails and dinner inside on the large wraparound porches.

The wind gusted, lifting the satin ribbons that tied the flowers to the folding chairs. The ribbon tails quivered gracefully as

Ruthie, Mindy, and Bella walked down the aisle. As the music changed the crowd turned in their chairs to see the bride. Sam glanced at Michael. He was smiling with abandon; any doubts he'd had the previous night were gone. Sam saw their father in the front row with Marguerite pressed against him, her hand held firmly in his lap. Before he even turned around to look at Suzie, his father's eyes were shiny with tears. Two seats away from Marguerite were Elizabeth and Tom. He had his hand on her shoulder, and she looked like she was trying hard to keep it together.

Sam took a deep breath and focused his attention on Suzie. Her dress had the translucency of eggshells, a shimmer of satin that fell deeply from her collarbone and then draped across her breasts and clung to her waist. Her hair was down, a tumbling mass of gentle waves that bounced as she moved. She walked arm in arm with the two guys Sam had smoked pot with the night before: her brothers, all grown up.

Sam felt that lump in his chest again. He avoided looking at Bella, even though she was barely a few feet away on the opposite side of the arbor. If it was possible to miss something you never had, Sam was feeling just that. As Michael stepped forward and took Suzie's arm, Sam looked up into a swirling mass of smoke-gray clouds and waited for it to be over.

After the ceremony they took endless combinations of pictures, representing all the fractured branches of the newly combined family trees. Sam hadn't seen Mrs. Epstein since the summer the Epsteins left town and he was shocked by how different she looked. For most of the pictures she offered nothing more than a vacant smile. Then, just as the last picture was shot, she reached over and wrapped her fingers around Sam's wrist. "I knew you when."

If she hadn't touched him he wouldn't have known she was talking to him. Her voice was low, her eye contact not great. Sam was paralyzed. And then the older of her sons reached over, lifted her fingers off Sam's wrist, and led his mother back to her table, his arm firmly positioned around her waist.

The storms started during cocktails. Sheets of water obscured the golf course and beaded up on the screens surrounding the porch. By the time Bella and Sam ended up in a pocket by the bar, alone, dinner was about to be served. Sam was stressing about the upcoming toast when there she was next to him, waiting patiently for the bartender's attention.

It was now or never. "Let me," Sam said, stepping up and catching his eye. He looked back at Bella and asked, "What do you want?"

She hesitated a moment, then said, "Vodka tonic," holding up two fingers and nodding when the bartender held up a twist of lime.

She moved back then, so he passed the first drink to her over his shoulder. "Thanks," she said under her breath, retrieving the other drink herself and then starting to walk away.

"Bella?" Sam stammered. "Hey."

Bella glanced over her shoulder, the drinks held aloft by her chest. She nodded indifferently and stepped into the crowd.

It felt as if the rain was never going to stop and yet when it did, after dinner and the toasts, the sky turned pink, like the inside of a seashell. Sam was pleasantly drunk, enough that he had stopped obsessing over Bella and her companion, whose name, he learned through Mindy, was Ted. Ted was a fellow in the writing department at Iowa. A poet. Sam felt the weight of that slip of paper in his wallet, and he was embarrassed. Ted was probably stellar with words. Ted would have come up with something other than a lame greeting after years of silence. Ted, he could tell, would never have disappeared on someone like Bella when she needed him most. Although, from where Sam was standing, Ted did seem like a bit of a jerk. He kept checking his watch as if he had to be somewhere, and he spoke to no one but Bella. Sam saw Bella try to pull Ted onto the dance floor a couple of times and Ted yanked his arm away from her and lurched toward the door. Apparently poets didn't dance.

Johnny Ross was chasing Ruthie's sister, Celia, around the wet lawn with the curious case of arrested development they suffered from whenever they were back together. The edges of Celia's dress were damp and dark and she was laughing, snorting, slowing down and waiting to be caught. Peter and Mindy, leaning against the porch banister, kissed in a way that said their relationship was anything but casual. As Sam walked over to Frankie to hand him his beer, the sodden ground felt spongy beneath his feet. He looked up at the sky; there were ominous gray streaks through the pink.

Ruthie clattered down the wooden porch stairs hand in hand with her lover, Lucy. "We have a problem."

Sam looked beyond Ruthie to Lucy, who appeared absolutely miserable. She was Barbie-doll pretty, with waist-length blond hair and a great body, but Sam had yet to hear her speak more than a drink order or offer a greeting when introduced. "What?"

"Suzie's father is here."

Frankie whistled against the top of his beer. "Shiiiiit."

"Did you tell Michael?" Sam asked.

"No, Turner, I did not want to tell your brother, the *groom,* that his persona non grata father-in-law is about to crash the wedding. I thought you might want to do something about that before Suzie loses her shit and he ruins her day."

Sam couldn't say he was thrilled at the thought of confronting Mr. Epstein. "Are you sure?"

Ruthie nodded. "I saw him in the parking lot, sitting in his car."

"Maybe he lost his nerve," Sam suggested.

"Do you really want to take that chance?" Behind Ruthie a flash of lightning illuminated the trees. Sam braced, waiting for the boom to follow. When it finally did he felt a spasm arc up his vertebrae. Ruthie squinted up at the clouds. "You need to do something now, Turner. He's in a blue sedan."

Another zipper of lightning that looked like it was about to gut the contents of the sky was followed by a bellow of thunder. Celia had allowed herself to be caught and she and Johnny ran past them to the stairs hand in hand, Celia holding up the edge of her dress. Mindy and Peter followed. Ruthie turned away from Sam and allowed Lucy to lead her to the shelter of the porch. She looked back over her shoulder and pursed her lips and raised her eyebrows in what Sam recognized as her *take care of it* look.

"Dude," Frankie said. He gestured with his head toward the parking lot. As the thunder and lightning ramped up, the sky had turned nearly black. Sam and Frankie made their way around the grounds to the parking light. As Sam looked out over the aisles and aisles of cars, the security floodlights dotted among the plantings flickered.

"How the hell are we supposed to find him?" Sam asked.

"Blue sedan?" Frankie yelled as a crack of thunder exploded. "Fuck, that was close."

With that crack of thunder came the rain, as unrelenting as before. Sam hunched over as water pelted the top of his head.

He ran up and down the rows, between cars, looking from side to side. He could barely see the make of the cars, let alone anyone sitting in one of them.

When Sam hit a parking marker, hard, he bounced back and was knocked on his ass. His clothes, his shoes, every inch of him was soaked. He realized as he lay there that there was no way he was going back into the reception, and so he gave in to the rain and stretched out on the pavement.

After a few minutes the strikes of lightning had subsided, although the rain was still coming down hard. Sam could actually see where he was, the clubhouse directly in front of him, about six rows of cars away. He grabbed hold of a door handle and pulled himself up, and as he did so he could just barely make out the outline of someone standing in front of the stairs. Sam pulled himself together and ran over. "Hey!" he shouted.

When the figure spun around his face was half hidden in the hood of a dark blue slicker, but Sam knew it was Mr. Epstein. He saw Suzie's nose in profile. "Hey—can you hear me? You have to go. Now."

Mr. Epstein was in bad need of a shave, and even in the storm Sam could smell the stink of alcohol rising off his body. He was trying to figure out what he should do when Frankie came up from the left, panting. "You found him?"

Mr. Epstein looked from Sam to Frankie. He opened his mouth but nothing came out.

"Hey! What's your deal?" Frankie pushed Mr. Epstein hard on the shoulder. Mr. Epstein crumpled against the post at the bottom of the stairs, his body collapsing as if he had no bones.

"Fuck," Sam yelled to Frankie. "What the fuck did you do that for?"

"He's shit-faced!" Frankie shouted over his shoulder as he

lifted Mr. Epstein's chin off his chest and peered into his face. Mr. Epstein raised his arms in front of him in an ineffective attempt to fend off Frankie.

It became obvious to Sam in that moment that Mr. Epstein was no threat to Suzie or Michael or his parents. Not that day, anyway. "We have to get him out of here."

"Ted! Please!"

Sam looked up. Had he heard Bella? He squinted through the rain toward the porch.

"TED! Answer me! Please! TED!"

Frankie was still crouched over Mr. Epstein. The rain seemed to distort everything. Sam didn't want anyone to see them with Mr. Epstein. When he heard the thud of footsteps he froze.

"TED!"

Sam looked up. Bella was coming for him, her head down, her hands up in front of her face. She was wearing a too-big long, dark suit coat over her bridesmaid's dress.

Sam took several large steps toward Bella and away from Mr. Epstein sprawled on the ground, but it was too late. Bella saw Mr. Epstein and ducked around Sam. From the look on her face he realized that she thought it had been Ted down on the ground. "What are you doing? What's going on?"

"He's wasted," Frankie yelled.

"Ruthie told us he was here. She told us to stop him so he wouldn't ruin the evening for Suzie. We didn't hurt him. We tried to stop him from going inside. He just sort of fell." Sam realized he was rambling and shut up.

Bella put her palm to her forehead and rubbed. As the rain lightened up Sam could tell that she was definitely wearing Ted's suit jacket. "What are you going to do?" she asked.

Sam felt helpless. "Don't tell Suzie."

"Why? Why would I do that to her, Sam?" Bella chewed her bottom lip. She half turned away from them as if she were going inside, but then she stopped and turned back around. "What can I do to help?"

"Go back inside and keep anyone, Suzie and Michael especially, inside too."

Bella nodded and pulled Ted's coat tighter around her chest. "I can do that. Do you know what you're going to do?"

Sam, who hadn't had a plan until that second, said confidently, "Absolutely."

"Okay," Bella said. "Okay." She turned and jogged back to the clubhouse.

Sam wondered what had happened to Ted: Why had Bella been shouting for him?

"Dude, come on!" Frankie nudged Mr. Epstein's hip with his foot, as if that would make him move along, then started going through his pockets. "What are you doing?" Sam asked.

Triumphantly, Frankie held up a ring of keys. "We click this, find his car, drag him there. Quickly, before someone else comes out and sees us here. We're lucky that was only Bella."

Sam shook his head. They hoisted Mr. Epstein up between them and Sam supported most of his weight as Frankie pressed the unlock button on the key chain. He had to do it several times before they finally saw the headlights flash on a car about ten rows back, parked in the middle of the lane.

Frankie took his place on the other side and they half walked, half dragged Suzie's dad to his car. When they got there it was obvious that someone drunk had parked the car. Sam opened the front passenger's side door.

"No, no, the back," Frankie said, gritting his teeth and leaning over to reach the handle. He swung it open and Sam pushed Mr.

Epstein headfirst into the backseat. The seat was littered with newspapers, clothing, fast-food containers, and beer bottles. Some of the trash fell to the floor as Mr. Epstein's body filled the space.

Together Sam and Frankie jammed Mr. Epstein in the rest of the way. He grunted when his head hit the opposite side door, as if he were the one exerting himself. He was wearing only one shoe, which meant the other shoe was lost somewhere between the steps and the car. Sam wasn't going back to find it.

Once Mr. Epstein was all the way in the car Sam slammed the door shut and then slumped against it. Frankie raked a hand through his wet hair, his face almost purple from exertion.

"Give me the keys." Sam put his hand out and Frankie dropped them into his palm. Sam walked around the car and got in behind the wheel. His wet clothes were beginning to feel stiff and cold.

Frankie opened the passenger door and leaned in. "What are you doing?"

"Driving him to the train station. I'm going to park the car there in the lot and let him sleep it off."

Frankie got in and shut the door. He tapped the dashboard three times and flipped on the radio. Sam pulled out of the country club lot and turned right.

"What a fucking day," Frankie said. He pulled down the visor and peered into the mirror, checking on Mr. Epstein. "What a fucking unbelievable day."

Sam drove slowly, carefully. The road was littered with debris from the storm. Traffic lights were flashing and ropes of black electrical lines were down. But the roads were passable. He hunched over the steering wheel to peer out the window, and over to his left, in a swath of clear sky, he caught the hint of a rainbow.

There was no way Sam or Frankie could go back inside the reception. But Marguerite's Honda, which Sam had driven to the wedding, was still in the lot at the country club and Sam had no choice but to return and get it. He wondered if Ruthie had covered for his absence, or maybe even Bella. Had he redeemed himself just a little?

They walked back slowly under a sky that was streaked with the remains of a sunset. Sam's suit was drying stiffly in odd places and made it difficult to walk fast. He and Frankie were quiet.

At the edge of the parking lot they stopped. "You want a lift home?" Sam asked.

Frankie pointed. "Looks like she has it all figured out."

Sam looked up. Bella was rushing across the lot. In her arms was a bulging plastic bag. She was no longer wearing Ted's jacket. The bottom of her dress looked dark, and her hair was now down around her face, but other than that she didn't look at all like she had been out in a rainstorm. She was beautiful.

"Here," she said breathlessly when she reached them, thrusting the bag against Sam's chest. "It's the best I could do. My dad keeps some extra golf clothes here. You can just say you were caught in the rain if anyone asks. "

Frankie laughed and grabbed at the bag, pulling out a pair of lime green plaid pants.

"Is everything, uh, did things work out okay?" Bella asked.

"If we tell you we'll have to kill you too," Frankie joked. He held up the pants, tugged on the waistband, and raised an eyebrow as if he were considering buying them.

Bella took a step back. "What?"

Sam laughed and shoved Frankie. "Bella, we left him in his car at the train station to sleep it off. By the time he wakes up and remembers where he is, Suzie and Michael will be long gone."

Bella smiled. "You did good, Sam."

"How about me?" Frankie asked. He had discarded the plaid pants for blue seersucker shorts.

"Both of you," Bella said, but she was still looking at Sam.

"So everything is okay inside?" Sam asked. "I mean, no one knows or . . ." He wanted to ask why Bella had been out in the rain screaming Ted's name earlier, but he couldn't think of how to phrase it tactfully.

"Don't worry. Everyone is drunk and dancing."

"Sounds like my kind of party," Frankie said as he discarded his shirt, jacket, and tie for a pale pink polo shirt.

Bella shook her head but she was smiling. "I'll let you guys change."

"Hey—what's your dad going to say when he sees us in his clothes?"

Bella was already walking toward the club. She waved a hand in the air. "Don't worry about it. I already told him you guys got caught outside. He thinks you're both dimwits anyway, so . . ." Bella was laughing and Sam started laughing too. *Dimwit* was a step up from *loser who abandoned his daughter when she needed him the most.*

"Save me a dance," Frankie yelled to Bella's retreating form. Sam wished he had gotten the words out first, but then he had no right to ask. Instead he picked up the clothes Frankie had left in the bag and turned his back modestly away from the club as he undid the fly of his ruined suit pants.

TWELVE

The Only Sure Thing About Luck Is That It Will Change
Suzie—2009

When Michael got caught up with a patient and had to cancel lunch with his father at the last minute, Suzie didn't mind. She enjoyed spending one-on-one time with her father-in-law, even if it was as simple as grabbing hot dogs from a cart and walking through Central Park.

After the hot dogs had been eaten, Suzie and Hunt took a bench by the entrance to the zoo. Suzie must have been staring too hard at the ice cream vendors, because Hunt got up and returned with two ice cream sandwiches. Suzie unwrapped the paper eagerly. Pregnancy was making her ravenous. She and Michael had agreed to keep it quiet until she hit the twelve-week mark, and she had four more to go before she could tell Hunt they were going to give him a grandchild.

"So, not the healthiest lunch, huh?" Suzie smiled at Hunt. "Michael is going to kill me for allowing you to eat a hot dog and ice cream. It's not like I don't know any better." She tugged on the lapel of her white lab coat.

Hunt shook his head. "I have to indulge every now and again; otherwise I couldn't face another bowl of quinoa and kale."

Suzie made a face. All she had wanted to eat since she found out she was pregnant were carbs, tangy meat, and sugar. She was already thinking about the pot roast she'd started before the sun had even come up that morning, when she was bleary-eyed from lack of caffeine. She had hoped for the best as she tucked the meat into the snug bowl of the cooker along with a pile of plump baby potatoes and carrots, thanking God that she didn't have any morning sickness. Surely a slab of veined bloody meat would have brought it on.

Maybe she would pick up brownies and ice cream for dessert. She had no idea if Michael would be home for dinner, and what she truthfully cared about most was eating that delectable soft, greasy meat and crawling into bed by eight. Food and sleep seemed to be the only things she craved. She was going to have to slow down if she didn't want to gain eighty pounds by delivery.

Hunt took the napkin Suzie offered him and wiped his mouth. A few pieces of shredded napkin dust got caught in his midday stubble. Suzie put her index finger to the corner of her mouth and Hunt mirrored her, ridding himself of the flecks of white. He relaxed back against the slatted bench in his suit and tie and raised his face to the late-September sun. Suzie smiled. Hunt had taken care of his sons when his wife decided she no longer could. He never seemed to judge anything either of them did. Suzie hoped she would be that kind of parent, the kind of parent she imagined Michael would be. She thought of Sam, still drifting. And how still Hunt seemed to be willing to let Sam figure it out. Would Suzie be that generous? She couldn't be so sure.

Lying to her parents had always felt too natural, the truth rarely a consideration.

As if he were reading her mind Hunt said, "I called Sam to meet us too, but he didn't answer." He paused. "Have you seen him?"

"Michael did, last week," Suzie said cautiously, not wanting to say anything else. She was pretty sure Michael had lent Sam money. She and Michael had a joint account, and she had noticed a withdrawal of five hundred dollars on the day he and Sam had met for drinks. She hadn't asked Michael about it, but had hoped he would bring it up to her instead. She had never told him not to give Sam money, so she wondered why he hadn't.

Hunt nodded, his shoulders relaxed. "That's good. I'm glad they make time for each other. Sam's working hard. They both do. I always wished I had someone growing up, you know? The perils of being an only child, I suppose."

Suzie did know. She had always felt like an only child. Josh was finally going to graduate from college after an extra semester, and Eli had graduated eighteen months before. He was living in Boston sort of near their mother's condo, bartending and selling solar panels and trying out for semipro athletic teams. But he was good to their mother, checking on her, bringing her food, and forcing her to leave the condo at least once a week for lunch or dinner. He was better to her than Suzie had ever been. After Sarah left Silver Hill, she seemed to blame Suzie more than her brothers for this drier version of her new life. So Suzie called once a week and stuck to a script they had been working on for years. When Suzie found out she was pregnant she did have a moment of panic: How would she become a mother if she had never felt mothered? But then she quickly pushed that out of her mind. She had to, that was all.

Hunt stretched his legs out and crossed them at the ankles. He didn't seem in a hurry to get back to the office, but Suzie checked her watch and he noticed. "Have to go?" he asked.

"I do. I have paperwork to finish before the shift change." Suzie didn't move. The last thing she wanted to do was paperwork. She could feel the midafternoon slump coming on hard and fast.

"Can I get you a coffee for our walk back?"

Suzie debated the offer. She wasn't technically drinking coffee, but there were professionals on both sides of the caffeine debate for pregnant women. She probably wasn't going to be able to get off this bench if she didn't have a little push. Besides, wasn't that hot dog she inhaled worse than coffee? She nodded at her father-in-law, grateful. One cup couldn't hurt.

They retraced their route out of the park at a slower pace, coffee in hand. As they approached the park exit, Hunt hesitated. He looked left, then right, but didn't make a move. A crowd of people crossing the street parted around them as they stood on the curb. Suzie touched him on the elbow. "You okay?"

"Yes, absolutely," Hunt said. But he didn't make eye contact with her.

"Is something wrong?" Suddenly Suzie felt a catch in her throat. What if it was his heart again? What if it was something with Marguerite? Hunt looked down at the coffee in his hand as if he had never seen it before. Slowly he raised the cup to his face, but didn't touch it to his lips before he lowered it again. "Hunt?" Suzie said again. "Are you going back to the office?"

"The office?" Hunt repeated.

"Yes," Suzie said slowly, wondering if she should assess him for a stroke or call Michael.

"Well, I suppose I have to." Hunt turned and smiled at her. Now he seemed fully present. He shrugged. "If only to set an example."

Suzie smiled back. Perhaps it was her hormones that were making her such an alarmist. Certainly her early-pregnancy brain had made her foggy. Hunt offered her his arm, a courtly gesture, as they stepped off the curb, and Suzie rested her hand on his forearm. It struck her then that Hunt was the closest thing she had ever had to a father, a father in the truest sense of the word, and she didn't know what she would do if she lost him.

Suzie had landed in the field of adolescent psychiatry because she was drawn to teenagers' tender souls. At first it was disconcerting to glimpse her vulnerable teenage self peeking out from behind the scrim of bravado; but then it became like seeing an old friend, one you were once close to, had moved on from, but still remembered fondly.

It was a pregnancy scare that actually made Suzie want to have a child. She and Michael were only a month into marriage and her shoulders still bore the shadow outline of her bathing suit straps from their Italian honeymoon. It wouldn't have been a surprise to be pregnant; Suzie wasn't on the pill because she hated what it did to her body, and they had been lazy about birth control. They had so much sex during that golden ten days that sometimes she wasn't sure where one orgasm ended and the next started. So when her period, regular to a day since she was fourteen, was ten days late and she had to bite down on her lip when Michael even gently grazed her breasts with the back of his hand, she was convinced she was pregnant.

Suzie had been so freaked out that she had called her mother, which turned out to be a disastrous idea. Instead of offering any sort of comfort or congratulations, Sarah Epstein had said ominously that now Suzie would have to start behaving like a mother. Suzie had no idea how to do that, no idea what her mother even meant. Instead Suzie bought a multipack of pregnancy tests, peed on three plastic sticks, and found them all negative. As if on cue, her period arrived the following day.

Suzie had been in an inexplicable funk for days after, and when Michael asked her why, she had blurted out that she wanted a baby. Her admission had taken them both by surprise.

They had moved to the bed, because the weight of the conversation felt manageable if they were touching. Neither of them had said they were in a hurry to have a family. Suzie knew Michael thought children were something that would happen eventually, later, in those hazy future years when they might own a car and live in the suburbs. They spooned beneath the blankets and talked about the impossible, demanding schedules of a resident and a doctor. They knew people in their programs who'd had babies during this time and it wasn't easy. But then Michael had asked Suzie another question: "When would it ever be perfect, really? Wouldn't we always find an excuse?"

Suzie had felt a fluttering of nerves. "So you're saying you want a baby?"

"I'm saying that sometimes you can't overplan." Michael paused. "I feel like I've been planning everything forever." He laughed. "I'm kind of tired of planning." He nuzzled her neck and that liquid feeling flooded her limbs. "Suzie, you are the best thing that has happened to me and you took me completely by surprise."

Suzie smiled. "I can say the same thing about you."

Michael pulled back from the exploration of her ear to look her in the face. "Then why shouldn't our baby be just as much of a surprise?"

"Our baby, really?" Suzie had said as she slipped a hand inside his boxers. "You're telling me the truth, right? I can take it."

Michael laughed, and then tried for a deep, sober voice even though Suzie was distracting him with her hands. "Scout's honor." He sighed as soon as she touched him. "But I'm easy," he said as he helped remove his boxers and lifted her T-shirt over her head. "Obviously."

Suzie shivered, giddy with anticipation as she climbed on top of him and showered his face and throat with kisses. Michael pulled her hard against his chest and flipped her onto her back as he slowly began to move inside of her. As her hips moved in sync with his, she rationalized that it almost never happened the first time. And then she forgot that they were even trying to make a baby.

After her mother's initial reaction Suzie never brought up the pregnancy again, and neither did her mother during their weekly calls. It was a testament to their powers of avoidance. Their relationship seemed to work only when her mother was happy with her own life, which she never would be sober. To make things even harder, Suzie knew her mother would never forgive her for excluding her father from her wedding.

Suzie's mother had been nearing the end of her rehab when Suzie had taken her out on a day pass to go shopping for a mother-of-the-bride dress. There was a quaint village shopping area in town, complete with cobblestone walkways, concrete planters filled with flowers, and striped awnings, and Suzie had planned an early lunch. She had called ahead to the restaurant to ask that they not offer her mother any cocktails. It turned out to not be that unusual of a request; the restaurant catered to a large clientele of patients on day passes and had a dry menu.

Suzie's mother had put on some weight while in the facility. Part of the program was three healthy meals a day, as well as cooking classes, which were intended to, as the center put it in all the literature, *enhance the quality of healthful living through hobbies*. Suzie thought her mother could afford to put on another fifteen pounds, maybe more, but at least some fullness was back in her face. At the dress shop she stood in her slip on the elevated platform. The flesh on her chest was mottled and freckled and her breasts had disappeared. She had looked a little overwhelmed, her veiny hands fluttering at her neck, the wedding rings on her fingers spinning round and round.

Suzie rifled through the rack of suits and picked three of her favorites. Two suits in shades of blue and one a pale violet. She held up all three for her mother's approval. Sarah pointed to the violet suit and Suzie handed it to her. As she took the jacket from the hanger she said, "Your father has always liked me in this color."

"Mom, you remember that he's not coming?"

Suzie's mother shrugged into the jacket. She fussed with the collar, frowning. "They have their own seamstress here, right? I think this needs a little something." She pulled back a handful of the suit at the waist.

"Dad's not invited, Mom. You know that, right?"

Her mother met her eyes in the mirror. "I assumed you and Michael would change your minds. I thought that was just you being you and making that typical first hothead response you always do before you calm down."

Suzie swallowed hard. She really didn't want to get in an argument with her mother today. "It was not an easy decision. But I can't."

"You mean you won't. You will deny him the right to give his only daughter away?"

"You really think he earned that right?"

"Did he not clothe you and feed you and house you?"

"Seriously?" Suzie asked, feeling fifteen all over again.

Susie's mother stepped into the skirt and fumbled with the button. Her torso through her hips was like a reverse hourglass, the bloated alcoholic belly and stick-thin legs. "Suzie, you always wanted something more than you had."

"How can you say that? I did everything you wanted. I helped raise Josh and Eli."

Suzie's mother sighed. "I think you exaggerate your role, Suzie."

"Okay, okay," Suzie said, wanting to appease and not argue. "But did I also hallucinate the emotional abuse my father inflicted on you? On us?"

"He never raised a hand to you."

"So, because it never came to that? No harm done?" Suzie couldn't bring herself to say any more.

"You'll find out what it's like to be married soon enough."

"I can tell you one thing. If Michael ever did to me what your husband did to you, I would be gone in a second. No, I take that back. If I even imagined he could ever be that kind of person I wouldn't be with him in the first place."

At that moment the salesgirl knocked, opened the door, and stuck her head inside. "How's everything going in here?"

Suzie stepped back and allowed her to open the door all the way. She kept her eyes on the carpet. She remembered how she would watch Sarah get ready for dates with her father. How she was nearly giddy with anticipation, how unaware she was of anyone but him.

"Can I see the seamstress?" Sarah asked. "I want this one, but it needs some reworking."

"Sure." The salesgirl seemed to be hesitating, waiting for Suzie's approval also, but Suzie didn't look up.

When Suzie heard the door click shut she said to her mother, "I want you at my wedding. But if you cannot be there happily, then you don't have to come."

For once Sarah looked at her and didn't immediately look away. Her eyes looked clear, as if she had understood what Suzie meant. "Mom?" Suzie prodded.

Sarah still said nothing. The silence was broken by a knock at the door: the seamstress. Suzie was prepared to send her away, to put the suit back on the hanger, to take her mother back to rehab without lunch, without ever saying another word again. They would walk past the flowers, across the cobblestones, into Suzie's rented car, and that would be that. No more forced attempts at mother/daughter pre-wedding bonding.

"Can you hold on a minute?" Suzie's mother asked, a tremble in her voice. She turned to Suzie. "Promise me you will give it some thought."

"I have," Suzie said. "I'm not changing my mind." She paused. "So you have to come knowing that. You have to be there for me, for Michael. Will you?"

Her mother was still fussing with the fabric. She didn't appear to be paying attention. But then she nodded to herself, took a deep breath, and said, "All right, then." She looked once again at herself in the mirror, the too-big suit falling from her frame. "All right."

It was the most Suzie's mother was willing to give her, and Suzie was willing to accept that this was it; this was all it was ever going to be. Sometimes she forgot, as in that moment of panic, elation, and confusion when she had thought she was pregnant.

That neither of them had followed up seemed the solution, rather than the problem.

Suzie and Michael were at a dinner celebrating Bella's job offer from Hunter. It was a job Bella had heard about from a former colleague in Iowa and had thought of as a long shot. But now here they were. It was too much good fortune for Suzie to comprehend and she tried not to jinx it, not even asking Bella about it until they knew it was a sure thing.

Suzie was late getting to the restaurant, and Michael had been even later. But they were finally all together. Suzie raised her glass of sparkling lemon water and clinked with Bella. Ted, who had seemed distracted since Suzie arrived, was looking the other way and chose not to join them in a toast. Suzie felt Michael put pressure on her elbow with his; he tried hard to like Ted for Bella's sake, but things like this always derailed him. She made eye contact with Bella, who smiled, but it was too wide, too bright, and a minute later Bella got up to go to the bathroom. Suzie followed her.

When Suzie opened the bathroom door Bella was standing at the sink staring into the mirror. She didn't turn to look at Suzie. Instead she said to her reflection, "Now, isn't this classic. Girl-friend hides in the bathroom because boyfriend pisses her off." She wiggled the faucets, splashed some water on her wrists, and then turned them off. "You don't see him storming off."

"You didn't storm off," Suzie said as she leaned back against the door. "What's going on?"

"Ted doesn't think he's a New Yorker. He's not sure he can commit to a year here." Bella's speech was clipped.

"But didn't he know when you came here that this was the

third interview . . . and that the third interview is usually when they want to make an offer?"

"Of course." Bella sighed. "Everything was fine. I think—" She stopped and shook her head. "I don't know."

"Did he think you wouldn't get the job? Is that why he's mad?"

Bella shrugged. "Ted loves me. He's a really great guy. I know you don't get to see that part of him. I can be difficult too, I guess, springing this on him. I don't want you to think . . ." She pinched the bridge of her nose and shook her head. "He's so smart, so brilliant, really. His poems, they are these delicate strings of words that just gut me. But his people skills . . ."

Suzie hated to see Bella so miserable. She looked as if she hadn't slept well in days; there were smudges of violet beneath her eyes. She hugged her. "Bella, we like Ted."

"Really?" Bella rubbed her face against Suzie's shoulder. "I sound like a fucking toddler." She lifted her head and pulled away, then glanced at her reflection and tried to fluff her hair. "Look at me, shit. I'm just fucking hormonal."

"You can be angry at Ted, Bella. I'm not going to hate him."

"I wanted this job, Suzie. I know it sounds lame, but I really like teaching."

"Why shouldn't you?" Suzie answered, and thought: *and Ted thinks real writers don't teach, they write.* But she couldn't go there. Instead she said, "Ted will get used to New York. All the best poets and writers have been through here. What's more poetic than this city?" She smiled. Her stomach growled so loudly Bella heard it and laughed.

"You know, I had these silly daydreams of you and me together again, meeting for coffee, lunch, a movie. I mean, okay, we both have to work, but still. I couldn't believe I was going to get a chance to be with you again. To talk to you every day just like we used to. To bitch about stupid things without making a phone call. So maybe I wasn't really thinking about how Ted would feel."

Suzie stared at Bella, trying hard to compose her feelings into a mask of neutrality. Bella had lived in a cabin without running water just to be with Ted. Surely Ted could stand some indoor plumbing for a year. "Being a couple means compromises. Tell him how much you want it, maybe agree to let him go to Montana for a month here or there if that's what he needs to recharge. It could be the best of both worlds." Suzie paused. "Show him some Woody Allen movies, early Woody, before he went European."

Bella laughed and shook her head. "I overreacted."

"He was being kind of a dick."

"He was, wasn't he?"

Suzie nodded, and Bella smiled. "What do you think he and Michael are doing out there?"

"Michael deals with children every day. I'm sure they're fine." Suzie said it quickly and a little more sharply than she intended. But Bella just laughed again.

"Can I tell you a secret?" Suzie asked.

"What? I should ply him with sex? Promise a blow job a week?"

"I'm pregnant," Suzie whispered. It was three weeks shy of the agreed-upon date she had promised Michael. She sent a silent prayer of forgiveness to whoever was in charge of these things in the universe.

Bella's mouth fell open. "Suzie!"

Suzie grinned and touched her flat stomach. Bella put her hand over Suzie's. "Pregnant? Oh my God. No way. No freaking way."

Suzie felt tears come to her eyes and before she could stop

they were spilling down her cheeks and running down her neck. "Now who's hormonal?"

"Oh my God, a baby!" Bella repeated. "We're happy? Right? You're happy? Michael's happy?"

"Everyone's happy," Suzie assured her, wiping at her face with the back of her hand. "Deliriously happy."

Bella leaned over, grabbed some paper towels, and handed them to Suzie. "I thought you were glowing. I thought something was up. I don't know what. Maybe I just always think you two look so much more in love than anyone in the room."

Suzie considered that Ted usually looked miserable or out of place, and felt bad for Bella. "You can't say anything yet. I promised Michael that we would wait until the first trimester was over."

"My lips are sealed. But how much longer do you have to wait?"

"Three weeks."

Bella threw an arm around Suzie's shoulders and squeezed. "I'm going to be an aunt! That settles it, you know. Nothing's going to stop me from moving to New York now."

Suzie tossed the paper towels in the trash. "That was my plan all along."

When they returned to the table Michael and Ted were talking as if nothing had happened. Ted appeared engaged, at least from a distance. He looked up at Bella with a contrite expression and pulled out her chair. Bella leaned down and kissed him on top of the head. Michael shrugged at Suzie and handed her a plate of quesadillas that had arrived while they were in the bathroom.

The room was hot and busy, full of people laughing and talking, striving to be heard over the music. Michael rested his hand on Suzie's knee under the table. He and Ted had ordered a variety of small plates that slowly began appearing in front of them.

Suzie leaned against Michael's shoulder, her cheek finding a familiar place against the curve of muscle. She was hungry and drowsy at the same time, and she could have closed her eyes for a catnap right then. But if she had she would have missed Ted smiling at Bella as if she were the only person in the room. She wanted her best friend to be loved. Really loved. She wanted everyone she loved to be loved. Suzie smoothed the napkin in her lap and placed her palm against her abdomen. As much as she couldn't wait to share, she loved the idea of a secret. *Hello, hello, hello, little one,* she said silently. *I cannot wait to meet you.*

THIRTEEN

You Are Always Leaving Too Soon
Sam—2010

Michael and Suzie had invited Sam to their apartment on the Upper West Side for dinner. The apartment was in one of those buildings with a name and a doorman. Michael and Suzie didn't have Central Park views, but everyone knew the park was right there, which was good enough as far as Sam was concerned. But then again, good enough had always been his problem.

Sam had been working for a caterer because he wanted to be back in a kitchen but didn't know if he wanted to commit to a restaurant. The prep kitchens were in a warehouse building near the West Side Highway, and the food was what you would expect at a wedding for a hundred or so of your not-so-close friends. There were always a multitude of chicken dishes on the menu, as well as salmon puffs and shrimp rolls, and roasted red potatoes. These dishes traveled well on the Long Island Expressway en route to their location. It wasn't exciting work, but it was regular, and because Sam came with the most kitchen experience, he often was left alone to do as he pleased in the kitchen.

His name was not with the doorman at Michael's building, and the doorman was new so he didn't just wave Sam up. He had to call Michael. Sam could tell from the way he said *brother* with a question mark at the end, and how he repeated his name into the receiver, that Michael had forgotten they had invited him over. Even after he got the go-ahead Sam thought about turning around and leaving. But he really didn't want to go back to his crappy apartment and spend the evening avoiding his roommates.

Michael answered the door on the phone and wearing his coat. He held up a finger but ushered Sam in as he walked away, leaving him to close the door. The room was large but dark, the blinds shut, the air suffocating. Michael disappeared into the back of the apartment as Sam stood in the center of the living room. In front of the long windows were a table and chairs with the remains of what looked like breakfast: several cereal bowls and a milky mug of tea, as well as a substantial pile of old *New York Times Magazine*s. In the galley kitchen Sam could see a raw chicken sitting in its plastic wrapping on the counter alongside a bag of potatoes. Dinner was most definitely not being prepared.

Sam was thinking about ducking out and cutting his losses when Michael reappeared. The phone was still in his hand, but he didn't seem to be on a call. He seemed surprised to see him standing there. "Oh, Sammy."

Sam grinned, but felt out of place. He wasn't sure if Suzie and Michael had had an argument or what, but he didn't want to be there to find out. He listened, but there wasn't a sound. No music, no one sobbing into a pillow. It felt weird. "Did I get the night wrong? Were we having dinner? I can go if it's not a good time."

Michael frowned. "Listen, it's, it's Suzie." Michael scratched the back of his head. "She, well, she had a miscarriage this afternoon." He squinted at Sam as he delivered the news, as if he didn't quite believe it himself.

Just a month before, Sam had met his father, Marguerite, Michael, and Suzie at a dim sum place in Chinatown to celebrate the pregnancy. They had raised their cups of green tea to the unborn Epstein-Turner. "Wow, oh shit. I'm sorry, Michael. Is she okay?"

"She's okay," Michael said with a scrap of hesitation. "She's resting. I just gave her something. I wasn't here when it happened." He shrugged. "If it's going to happen, this is the best way. Now, I mean. Rather than later."

"Sure." Sam nodded, although Michael looked entirely unconvinced by his own words. "Can I go get you guys anything? Food? What can I do? Leave? You name it."

"We never should have said anything so early. We should have known better by now." Michael walked over and collapsed onto the couch. He was still wearing his coat and it puffed up around him, the collar standing up around his ears. He held the hand with his cell phone over his heart. "I need a drink."

"By now?" Sam asked as he glanced over at the bar cart by the table. "What do you want?"

"Something hard. I called Bella, she's coming over. I just need to get out of here. Do you want to go down the street? One drink?"

Sam shook his head, hoping he hadn't heard correctly. "Bella?"

Michael shrugged. "It's what Suzie wanted." He sighed. "We've been through this before, I just don't know how much more . . ." He trailed off, shaking his head.

Sam didn't know what to say to Michael's revelation. He felt awful, but ill equipped to comfort or ease his brother's pain. All he knew for sure was that he wanted to get out of Michael's apartment before Bella arrived. "Are you okay with leaving Suzie alone?"

"She probably won't wake up anytime soon." Michael rubbed his face. "And anyway, she has Bella. She asked for her, that's what she wants." Michael pushed himself up off the sofa with a soft groan and headed toward the door, so Sam followed him.

Michael was drinking scotch on the rocks. He'd already finished two in fast succession and was now nursing his third. He and Sam were sitting in a booth by a pool table in a bar that was filled with people who looked like Michael.

As Michael drank he peeled off layers until he was down to a blue button-down shirt with the sleeves rolled to the elbow. On the table in front of him was his badge from the hospital, his wallet, phone, and keys. Sam had just started a second beer and had ordered them two roast beef sandwiches when Michael's phone vibrated. He tilted it toward him, peered at the screen, and put the phone back down. "Bella is there, says Suzie is fine."

"Good."

"This is the third time, you know? She knows what to expect."

Sam was shocked. "I didn't know, Michael, I'm, I'm really sorry." Suzie was a third-year resident in psychiatry at Mount Sinai, where Michael was on staff as a pediatric cardiologist, and Sam had thought this pregnancy was a surprise, considering everything they had going on.

"Yeah, well." Michael studied the glass of scotch but didn't take a drink. "She really wants a baby." He passed a hand over his glass, rubbing his pinkie along the rim. "She'll be all right."

The sandwiches arrived. Sam was too hungry to pretend he didn't want to eat. He inhaled the first half while Michael picked at his. "You should eat," Sam said, gesturing toward his brother's sandwich with a spear of garlicky pickle.

Michael stabbed the bread with a toothpick and picked up his scotch. "We talked about kids. But in a far-off-in-the-future way." He laughed. "And then in the moment I said: what happens, happens. But I didn't picture us here. Like this. Three failed attempts."

"But you want kids? Still, I mean?"

"It's getting harder the more shit happens." He shook his head. "Three miscarriages?" He frowned. "Is it all some master plan? I see kids every day, sick kids and their desperate parents. Do I want to be one of those?"

"Who says you would be desperate?"

"You can't fucking guarantee anything, Sam. Despite technology and intervention, we can't take away the chance that something will go wrong at any given time, or that I can't fix it when it does go wrong." He stuck the toothpick in his mouth. Sam watched the muscles work in his jaw. "The miscarriages? They are the natural rejection of the body. They are not an indictment of our marriage or our incompatibility or my lack of enthusiasm to procreate." He spit the words out along with the toothpick.

Sam had a feeling that Michael and Suzie had had this conversation before.

"Look." Michael's voice softened. "You don't get this because you have no obligations, no real life you are committed to. No other person who can take your morning breath and dirty boxers kicked beneath the bed and still want to fuck your brains out and forgive you when you forget to pay the mortgage or pick up the dry cleaning or buy milk." He paused and drew a circle with his index finger on the tabletop. "The thing about you is that you let go of everything. You step out of something if you don't like it. You disappear. How could you even begin to get it?"

Sam flinched. How had this become about him and his faults? "You're right, I don't get this at all." Sam picked up his beer and took a long swallow. What a romantic picture Michael painted of his marriage and Sam's wanderlust. "But maybe you are so critical of my life because you can look at it from the safety of yours."

Michael leaned forward and jabbed an index finger on the tabletop. "She thinks she failed me, *me*. How twisted is that? She is upset because she can't make me a father." He picked up his scotch and swirled it around once before he drained the glass.

Sam didn't want to know any of this. He wanted Michael to stop talking about Suzie. "Why don't you tell her?" he suggested. "You should be telling her this, not me."

"Fuck!" Michael slammed his palms on the tabletop, making everything bounce. "You haven't been listening to me at all." He swept his keys and wallet off the table into his lap. Spit clung to his lip. "I'm fine, Sam. It's not your deal."

"Listen—"

"Nah, we're done, right? We're done here." Michael opened his wallet, swaying slightly as he considered what to leave. He dropped a handful of money on the table. "That's good enough."

Sam picked the bills out of his sandwich. Two hundred and sixty dollars. "That's too much." He tried to hand most of it back but Michael waved him off.

"We invited *you* to dinner. Keep it. Keep the money. Give the money away. What the fuck do I care right now?" As he spoke he gathered all his clothes from the bench. His eyes were bloodshot little slits, the corners of his mouth clogged with spittle. There was a catch of a sob strangled in his throat that twisted Sam's gut. "I have to go home," Michael said quietly. "I just have to go home."

Sam walked beside Michael the two wide blocks back to his building. They didn't talk. From beneath the canopy Sam stood on the sidewalk and watched through the double glass doors as Michael brushed past the doorman, refusing assistance, and waited for the elevator. Once Michael was gone Sam felt stupid for still standing there, as if Michael were going to reappear. The doorman caught him waiting and walked to the door and peered out, frowning. Sam had the feeling that he barely believed he was Michael's brother.

Sam smoothed down the dark gray down jacket Marguerite had given him for Christmas, and adjusted the collar of the denim shirt that was caught in the folds, self-conscious of his appearance. Sam had had to dig the coat out of a pile of crap on the floor in his room, so it could look and smell like death for all he knew. The fucking weather was more like February even though it was late April, and he was sick of the cold, sick of waiting for the seasons to really change.

Feeling stupid for lingering on the sidewalk, he held up his hand and waved to the doorman. The doorman did not wave back. Sam turned and walked south toward the subway.

He was about to round the corner, heading toward Broadway, when he heard his name. He turned and looked behind him. Bella was leaning against a streetlamp, shaking something out of her boot. She was wearing a dark coat and pink scarf, and her hair, under the fizzy light, looked like a halo. When she saw that he had stopped, she raised her boot in greeting. "Hey," she called. "Sam? Can you wait up?"

She put her boot back on and shuffled over while he calculated the months (eighteen) between now and her witnessing his sloppy removal of Mr. Epstein at Michael and Suzie's wedding, and then before that (two, nearly three years) when they didn't speak. When they finally were inches apart she got shy and looked down at her feet, then up at Sam from under a fringe of bangs. He couldn't ever remember Bella having bangs before.

"You were with Michael, right?"

"Yeah. How's Suzie?"

She ran her tongue across her top lip. "She's okay. I mean, I think this time she really thought . . . so . . ." She shrugged and reached up and adjusted the pink scarf. "She really just needs Michael now."

"Sure." Sam paused. "Is your hair different?"

"From what?" She gave Sam a funny look but didn't answer his question. "You heading home?"

"Yeah, yeah. I live downtown."

She nodded. "Ted and I are in Morningside Heights. I'm teaching at Hunter, so it's kind of a pain-in-the-ass commute, but not too bad."

"Are you, I mean, is it a full-time job?"

"Well, it's an independent contract thing. I have the position through the end of the year but I don't know what happens beyond that. It sort of makes it hard to plan. Especially for Ted."

"Oh, what's he doing?"

"Well, he's working on a book."

"Great."

"Yes, yes it is. He is a brilliant writer." Bella said the words quickly. The tip of her nose was bright pink. "So I'm working and my writing is kind of on hold anyway. It's a good time for him to finish his book."

"Sure. Absolutely."

"And Ted really misses the West. Eventually we'll probably head back there. He lived for three years in a cabin without running water or electricity."

"Wow, impressive." Bella's enthusiasm for Ted's resume was exhausting. "But until then, nice that you're so close to Suzie."

"Yeah, and my dad, of course. He's glad I'm back for a while." She paused. "How's your dad?"

"Happy. He's happy."

"He looked great at the wedding."

"Yeah, well, you know, or maybe you don't, he had a heart attack a couple of years ago. But he's good now."

"I had heard that." Bella nodded. "So now he's a changed man?"

Sam laughed. "Well, yeah, sure." He wondered when Michael would tell their father about Suzie and the baby. Sam thought of the look on his face at the restaurant. His father hadn't said it out loud, but Sam knew he was thinking that he was glad to be alive to see his grandchild. "Hey, so was Michael okay when you saw him?"

"Just now? Well, he was a little unsteady." She gave Sam a half smile, as if she approved of his getting his brother drunk after his wife lost a baby. "Suzie and I were sitting on the couch and she was still a little groggy from the painkiller. But when he came in they sort of fell into each other's arms so I took it as my cue to leave."

Sam sighed and looked up at the night sky. Why did people always think you could never see any stars in the city? He could see plenty. "Well, I guess I'm going to head home then." He really wanted to touch her. He couldn't think about anything else but touching her. He missed her so much. But he had lost his chance. Before he did anything stupid he said, "Bye, Bella."

Bella looked surprised, but she echoed, "Bye, Sam."

They laughed at the awkwardness of the exchange, and Sam could see in her face that she was as relieved as he was that it was over.

Michael was always right. As summer hit the city, and with it the wedding season that demanded the need for endless trays of bite-sized food, Sam quit the catering gig, cleared out of the sublet with the few items he owned stuffed in a duffel bag, and went home. He managed to walk away with about fourteen hundred dollars in his bank account. Once again, New York had knocked him on his ass.

Marguerite and Hunt were in Italy for a month, and Sam had promised to check on the house while they were gone. He didn't think they expected that he would quit his job to bring in the mail and water the lawn, but the opportunity to have a place to be for a month with a pool and fresh air, and without the pressure of roommates or poaching endless filets of salmon, was too good to turn down.

Dozing in a lounge chair, lulled into a semiconscious state by the click of the pool filter and the soft strum of the compressor that kept the house a cool seventy-two degrees, Sam had plenty of time to consider his life. He had the vague idea that if he had his own kitchen he could do as he pleased. But Sam knew there were as many failures as restaurants, guys like him who were passable cooks but who couldn't run a business. Sam couldn't fool himself into thinking that the odd success story would be him. Which brought him to the realization that maybe he just wasn't enough of a dreamer, that somehow he had become careful to the point of being paralyzed, and that was sobering.

When Hunt and Marguerite returned from their trip they didn't have much of a reaction upon discovering Sam had moved back into his old room. The fact that this was simply part of their expectations where he was concerned was annoying yet true. So how was Sam to be offended? As it was he was spending most of his waking hours by the pool or at Peter Chang's house, and he kept to that routine when they returned.

Hunt looked tanned and rested from the trip. He and Marguerite brought back several outstanding cases of wine, and in the summer evenings they sat out on the patio side by side in matching lounge chairs, going through photos and enjoying a glass. Sam usually ducked out before they could offer him one. He knew they wanted to talk; he could see the concern in Hunt's face. It was just that his topics-to-avoid list was growing.

For the first time in a long time Sam had run out of ideas. But then Peter rented a house in Chatham out on the Cape for the month of August and invited anyone who was around to join him. Frankie, Peter, and Sam drove out together and met the real estate agent for the keys. She walked them through the house, pointing out the two-sided gas fireplace, sunken bathtubs, sauna, remote control skylights, gourmet kitchen, and the long table that sat twenty. Peter followed dutifully while Frankie took the steps two at a time to the second floor to get the first pick of the six bedrooms. Sam went outside to check out the view. The house sat on the curve of a bluff overlooking the ocean. It had a wraparound deck on each of the two floors. With the sliding glass doors open, the breeze pulled the white curtains horizontally until it appeared as if they were floating.

After the real estate agent left, Sam went to the store to pick up provisions. Even after spending six hours trapped in the car to get to the Cape, he appreciated the quiet, meandering drive into town: the salt-tangy breeze of the stop-and-go traffic on the narrow two-lane road, the classic New England architecture of weathered shingles and painted shutters.

The grocery store was flooded with people who, like them, had just started their rentals. Food and children perched precariously in overloaded carts that reminded Sam of the Grinch's sleigh after he had looted Whoville. The only bags of charcoal left behind had been gutted. He weeded through what remained and left the grocery store with thick, bloody steaks marbled with fat, gold potatoes, greens, lemons, parsley, butter, several six-packs of locally brewed beer, coffee, milk, and cereal. At a roadside farm stand he stopped for a dozen ears of corn and a bushel of warm tomatoes to round out the meal.

When Sam got back to the house there was another car in the driveway besides Peter's. Bella, Ted, and Suzie were on the deck with Peter and Frankie, an already empty bottle of wine in front of them and a second bottle uncorked between them. Sam wanted to ask where Michael was, if he was coming later or at all, but he didn't.

Sam and Ted had never officially met at Suzie and Michael's wedding, so Bella performed an introduction. It seemed odd, and slightly suspect to Sam, anyway, that he was the only one of Bella's "friends" who hadn't met Ted. From the way Ted kept his arm wrapped around Bella's waist, Sam thought Ted must feel the same way. As soon as Sam could, he escaped to the kitchen.

For dinner Sam grilled the corn and steaks, pulverized the parsley, lemon, garlic, and oil into a pesto that he drizzled over thin slices of meat and roasted potato, and served everything on the deck. As the sun dipped into the water the breeze slowed, but the air was cool. Unwilling to abandon the gorgeous views, Peter dragged blankets from the house and they sat huddled over their plates until there wasn't anything left.

Sam's impression of Ted from the wedding was that he was unlikable. Sam wanted him to remain unlikable to his friends. So far, Ted stared hard at his plate, concentrating on his food, and only looked up when Bella spoke. Then he appeared overly attentive, a ghost of a smile hovering over his lips before he added a comment or reached over to whisk an errant strip of hair off her cheek. Sam, at Ted's glimpses of humanity, consoled himself with the notion that charm was a trait held by sociopaths. Especially when Ted directed a sudden stream of conversation toward Sam. They talked about the feasibility of eating locally, sustainable organic farms, and Sam's mother's award-winning goat cheese. Ted seemed enamored with the idea that Sam's mother had taken such a risk.

"When I was a kid I didn't really think of it as a risk, I thought of it as abandonment." Sam felt the impact of his sentence as everyone got quiet. "Anyway, I guess that's old news now."

"Hey, sorry, dude," Ted offered. "I didn't realize it was a tough subject still."

Sam shrugged. "A lot of shit went down that summer, that's all." In his peripheral view he saw Suzie squirm in her seat and take a large gulp of wine. Was she worried that Sam was going to bring up her father? He looked down at his plate. She was his sister-in-law now, and he had to protect that familial bond. He could feel Bella's eyes on him, but he couldn't look at her and see disappointment yet again.

When the bottles of wine they had brought with them were almost gone, Ted stood. As he stretched and yawned he invited all of them to take a day trip the next morning to Martha's Vineyard. A college friend of his had recently moved there to work the family farm. To make amends for being such a giant prick, but all for Bella's benefit and not Ted's, Sam heard himself agreeing, and immediately regretted it. Peter and Frankie begged off, claiming they had to wait for the rest of the group to arrive the next day, and Suzie said she just wanted to sleep on the beach. By then it was too awkward for Sam to try to get out of taking an excursion with Bella and Ted.

Sam stacked plates and carried them into the kitchen as everyone cleared the deck. He pretended not to hear Ted and Bella shuffle upstairs to a bedroom. Frankie and Peter had come inside and were bent over a chessboard in front of the fireplace. Sam went out to the deck to retrieve the last of the glasses and was surprised to see Suzie still there. She had nearly disappeared into two large blankets; her hands and a glass of red wine were all that was visible.

Suzie nodded toward the bottle on the floor by her chair. "Have one more drink with me?" Her words were soft and slurry.

Sam sat down next to her, picked up the bottle, and took a long swallow.

Suzie giggled. "Good man."

Sam shook his head at the taste. He had been drinking beer and the wine tasted sour. "So, how are you?"

Suzie closed her eyes and leaned her head back against the blankets. "I'm sorry about that night." She opened her eyes and squinted over at Sam. "I wasn't thinking very clearly or I would have called you."

"Hey, come on." He shrugged off her apology.

They sat looking out at the water without speaking for a long time. Suzie finished her wine and tucked the empty glass inside the nest of blankets. Sam wanted to go to bed. But he didn't want to leave her alone. "Where's Michael?"

"On call."

"Too bad he couldn't come."

"Yeah. So, how do you like Ted?"

"He seems great."

She laughed quietly. "Liar."

"What?"

Suzie put her fingers to her lips like she was about to tell a secret. She shook her head.

Sam felt a rush of fatigue that made the back of his head hum. He could close his eyes and be dead right here, or find a bed now. "I think I'm going to turn in. Did you drop your stuff in a room?"

"I'm all set, Sammy. Don't worry about me." Suzie extricated a hand from the pile of blankets and waved her fingers. "I'm going to sit here a while longer, stare at the churning sea, and ponder the enormity of the cruel universe." She gave him half a smile before she turned away to face the water. She was either dismissing him or saving him.

Sam hesitated. "You know, for the record, I think Ted's a dick."

Suzie smiled. "There's my boy."

"I'm not your boy," Sam said, irritated. "Don't say that."

"I'm sorry. I didn't mean anything by it. I was just waiting for the real Sam to appear."

"I don't know what the fuck you're getting at, Suzie." Sam had never been this annoyed with her. But it occurred to him in that moment that maybe he didn't like Suzie all of the time.

Ted's friends had fifty-five acres in Edgartown on Martha's Vineyard where they planted a variety of crops, including corn, beans, squash, tomatoes, potatoes, carrots, beets, lettuce, spinach, and potatoes, along with a culinary herb garden and berries, peaches, and plums. On the farm was a tremendous post-and-beam barn, inside which was a kitchen where they produced seasonal dishes and baked goods for sale as well as eggs and freshly slaughtered beef and lamb from the farm in Chilmark that another son ran on family-owned land. The owners, Brian and Lori, had raised four kids on the farm, and all of them had their hands in the family business in some capacity. Zeke, the son that Ted knew, had gone to school for aquaculture, which in Sam's limited understanding of Ted's rambling explanation had something to do with irrigation systems.

Out behind the barn an extension of the kitchen opened to the outdoors, where there was a roasting pit, grills, and, beneath an arbor crosshatched with vines, a long table made of planks of reclaimed wood resting on sawhorses, surrounded by stumps that could accommodate at least thirty people. The view over neatly plowed fields and shimmering expanses of green was stunning.

Lori insisted they stay for lunch. Sam devoured a zucchini and tomato pie, arugula and kale with lemon dill dressing, a delicate quiche threaded with scallions, and a peach tart. Everything they ate was from farm to table, and while Sam savored the flavors, he also ate ravenously, as if he couldn't get enough. After lunch, while Ted went off on a tractor with Zeke, and Bella sat at the table with Lori, Sam invited himself into the kitchen. Brian told him they had recently doubled the size because they were considering adding special-event dinners to their currently all-takeout menu; that part of the business was thriving, and the demand was only growing.

Sam fell in love in that kitchen. The surfaces were gleaming lengths of professional stainless, as were the walk-ins and ovens, but the walls were still the rough barn board. Overhead, notched beams crisscrossed the ceiling. Industrial-sized fans spun in lazy circles from those beams. What sealed the deal for Sam were the windows above the sinks, an expanse of glass that looked out onto a generous swath of the fields and beyond. The windows at the catering kitchen had looked out on a brick-walled alley.

The chefs, two women in their early twenties, showed Sam

around. One was going into her final year at Boston College and had spent the last four summers working there, and the other was new to the farm this year. She had tagged along with a boyfriend who planted and tended crops, but Sam recognized her starry-eyed look as his own as she talked about the farm. They allowed him to skim through the recipe notebooks, all the evidence of trial-and-error dishes recorded in each chef's hand. Because of the seasonal work, a lot of the chefs had used the farm kitchen as a launching pad to other kitchens, yet a few returned, their handwriting showing up in six-month cycles in the lined notebook pages.

Sam went back outside. Bella was sitting at the table alone. When she saw him she grinned. "You love this, don't you?"

Sam sat on a stump across from her and rested his elbows on the table, inexplicably remembering that last morning in her college apartment. They had taken a long, hot shower together and then he'd made breakfast. Sam remembered condensation on the naked windows, a spray of cinnamon toast, coffee, Bella sitting across from him at the table, the curled wisps of wet hair leaving damp circles on her shoulders, her smile. He realized as he looked at her now that in the time they had been apart he had mastered so many more ways to fail her. "It's a lot more than I expected," Sam admitted, not giving Ted any extra credit.

"You know you could work here, right? I mean, Lori and Brian said they hire people all the time. There are never enough hands. Wouldn't that be amazing?"

Sam laughed at how simple she made everything sound. "Well, look who's planning my next step."

"Oh, God, Sam." She blushed and ducked her chin to her chest. "I was just saying I could see you here, you know, cooking, surrounded by all of this." She swept her arm out to her side.

Sam nodded and looked beyond Bella to the fields. He heard the rumble of a tractor in the distance, most likely Ted and Zeke on their way back. "How's Ted liking the city?" he asked, wanting to steer the conversation away from him.

Bella stuck out her chin. "Fine," she declared, as if Sam were crazy to ask.

Sam left it at that as Ted and Zeke reappeared. There was a certain swagger to Ted's step that made Sam want to punch him. Since they had been at the farm Ted had quoted Thoreau at least four times. Sam couldn't imagine Bella digging his act, but apparently she did.

Ruthie, Mindy, and Celia were at the house with Suzie when they got back from Martha's Vineyard. The girls were on the beach below the deck, stretched out on their backs on brightly colored blankets, chins tilted to the sun. Frankie and Peter sat in low webbed chairs under a large umbrella with a cooler of beer between them. Bella hung over the railing calling out to the girls, while Ted hovered at her side, cupping her elbow in his hand, urging her away from her friends and upstairs for a nap before dinner. He had nuzzled her neck the entire ferry ride back, and Sam was beginning to take it personally.

Sam had brought bags of produce and meat from the farm, enough for several meals. He took the bags and went into the kitchen to unpack everything, cracking open a cold beer and cranking up the music. When the food was spread out on the counter he felt an anticipation and excitement he rarely felt for anything else in life. He decided to use the lamb chops for dinner, seared with a nice salted crust but still a little pale pink in the center, along with a vegetable strudel made of squash, onions, basil, tomatoes, eggplant, and goat cheese, a roasted potato salad with a lemon, garlic, red pepper, and olive oil dressing, and a sausage and minestrone soup. Dessert would be warm berries and fresh cream. He whistled as he put the ingredients he wasn't going to use away and began to set up the chopping stations.

As Sam slid the pan of potatoes into the oven to roast, he heard a familiar voice behind him. "Can I help?"

Sam turned from the stove to see Bella on the far side of the kitchen. The bridge of her nose was sunburned. He must have looked startled, because she laughed. "Have you turned into one of those chefs who can't have anyone else in the kitchen?"

Sam laughed, thrilled to see her standing in front of him without Ted. "God, no." He pointed to the onions. "Can you chop?"

She smiled. "Give me a knife." She pointed to the magnetic strip where a line of German knives (easily the cost of one month's rent in Manhattan, Sam could not help but notice) was waiting. She selected a medium-sized knife and Sam slid a cutting board toward her. "Large or small pieces?"

"Small, please."

She grinned and rubbed her face, the blade of the knife close to her cheek.

"Jesus, Bell, put the knife down first."

She gave him a half smile. "Relax."

"Blade down on the cutting board, and I will consider it."

"You lied. You are so one of those chefs who doesn't want anyone else in the kitchen."

Sam looked up from salting the cubes of eggplant. She was grinning at him. Where had this Bella come from?

"Seriously?" he asked, teasing her back. "Me?"

Bella rolled her shoulders forward and put her head down in earnest. She sliced the onion in half and then proceeded to make hash marks lengthwise before she turned the onion and made them again in the opposite direction.

They chopped in assembly-line order. Sam slid vegetables in Bella's direction and she made neat piles along the granite counter. When she was done she put down her knife, grabbed two beers, and handed one to Sam while he prepped sauté pans and a stockpot just as everyone began filing in from the beach. More beers were opened, the girls, including Bella, went off to shower, and Frankie and Peter picked up their long-running chess game.

Sam set the table out back, fired up the grill for the lamb chops, and turned everything else to simmer while he sat on the deck to finish his beer. He heard the shower running through the open bathroom window and tried hard not to think about Bella's naked body under the spray.

✦ ✦ ✦

From the far end of the table Frankie raised his beer. "To Sam: without you there is only cold cereal in my life."

Peter banged on the table until dishes and glasses rattled and a bottle of beer tipped over into an empty dish. Mindy smacked him on the shoulder playfully and then leaned in to kiss his cheek. Just as her lips grazed his skin he turned to kiss her hard on the mouth.

Frankie whistled for attention. "But seriously, you guys, how is it that I'm still looking at your same damn faces after all these years? Why don't we have any other friends?" He paused and looked over at Ted. "No offense to you, Teddy."

Ted had been hanging on Bella all through dinner. Right now he had an arm slung around her shoulders and their chairs pushed as close together as possible. "Is Ted our friend or Bella's date?" Sam spat out involuntarily, and then tried to avoid looking directly at Bella.

Ted didn't take Sam's middle school bait. Instead he nodded his chin at Frankie and said, "None taken."

Sam shifted in his seat and caught Suzie's eye. The expression on her face was blurry in the candlelight. He thought she smiled at him. Sam crossed his arms over his chest and leaned back in the chair.

"I love you guys," Frankie crooned. "I love you."

Celia pushed back her chair and stood up. "Who wants to go for a walk on the beach?"

Ruthie lifted her hand, which was still attached to Suzie's. They giggled as one stood and the other fell back down before they righted themselves.

Frankie pushed back his chair. "I think you ladies need an escort." He offered his arms and Celia and Suzie grabbed ahold of the sloppy sleeves of his sweater. "We don't want you to get in some unfortunate Natalie Wood type accident."

"We are not going out in a boat. And who says we need an escort?" Ruthie shook her head vigorously. Sam knew she was softer than she looked. Bella had confided in the kitchen earlier that Lucy had recently broken Ruthie's heart by sleeping with a man. Ruthie had sobbed to Bella that she had done everything Lucy had wanted, she had changed everything so Lucy would love her more, but she couldn't grow a dick. Sam realized that he had never changed for anyone; his answer was always to leave. What kind of person did that make him?

"Never mind the details," Frankie called after the girls as he stumbled over his own feet to keep up as they moved ahead of him toward the stairs. "You don't need a boat to drown."

Sam left the two couples at the table and went into the house for another beer. Once he was inside he started to fill the dishwasher. He purposely made a lot of noise; he didn't want to know where Bella and Ted were, or if they had gone upstairs. After a while, Mindy came in carrying a stack of bowls. She set them down near the drainboard and reached for a berry from the strainer as she left again. Peter trailed after her, and soon Sam was alone in the kitchen as they disappeared upstairs. Sam kept at the task of cleaning up, getting lost in the repetitive motions until there was nothing left to do. Not yet feeling tired, he stretched out on the couch with the intention of watching a movie.

He was surprised, then, when he felt a pressure on his shoulder like someone's hand pressing him down into the cushions. Sam opened his eyes to the kind of dark, still quiet that happens only just before dawn. When had he fallen asleep? It took him a moment to figure out that Michael was sitting on the coffee table, leaning over him, whispering his name.

"What the fuck?" Sam said.

"Sammy, I'm sorry. Where's Suzie?"

"Asleep, I'm guessing."

"I don't know which room."

"Neither do I. Fuck, Michael, what are you doing here now?" Sam's eyes adjusted to the lack of light. He expected Michael to appear haggard after an on-call shift and driving all the way out to the Cape, but he didn't. In his dark polo shirt he looked like he did when they were kids. For a second, in Sam's sleep fog, he imagined Michael telling him he knew where their mother had hidden the Christmas presents.

"Can you help me?" Michael whispered.

"Can't it wait until the morning? Pick a couch." Sam pointed to the opposite side of the room, where an empty couch was Michael's for the taking.

"I need to see her." Michael shook his head. "I need to see her now, Sam."

Sam sighed, and sat up and motioned for Michael to follow him upstairs. The hallway was an elongated L; the master bedroom, where Peter and Mindy were sleeping, faced the ocean. Sam pointed down the hall to the rest of the rooms. The first room on the left was where he had dumped his duffel bag the night they arrived. The door was ajar, his bed empty. He could hear Frankie snoring in the room next to his. Suzie was going to be in one of the other two rooms on the other side of the hall. The only problem was he didn't know which one, and he didn't want to open a door and find Bella and Ted.

He could feel Michael's breath on his shoulder as he hesitated in front of the room across from his. Impatient with Sam's indecision, Michael quickly reached around Sam and pushed open the door. Inside were two double beds, a mound of luggage between them. Ruthie and Celia were curled like parentheses in the bed on the far side of the room. Closer to the door were Suzie and Bella.

Michael darted into the room and collapsed onto his knees next to the bed. He gathered Suzie in his arms, and Sam watched Suzie startle awake and then start sobbing into Michael's shoulder. Sam heard the words *I'm sorry,* and *I love you,* but he thought they said them at the same time. Either way, it was hard to tell who was sorrier.

Sam didn't want to be standing in the doorway, but he couldn't move. His mind kept chewing over the fact that Bella was sleeping in here and not with Ted. He turned his gaze from Michael and Suzie to Bella, and found that Bella was looking right at him, her eyes wide and unblinking.

FOURTEEN

Depth of Field
Bella—2010

Bella always felt like a little girl when she went to her father's office, especially if she had to wait for him, like she did today, in the reception area. When he was done with his meeting he came rushing toward her, shoving his arms into his coat sleeves and offering apologies even though Bella didn't need one. He bent down to kiss her and Bella tossed the magazine she had been holding on her lap back onto the side table. She offered him her cheek and said, "Dad, you need better magazines."

In the restaurant her father waited until Bella was seated before he sat down. She smiled at her father across the table, grateful for his manners. She wasn't hungry; her stomach had been twisted since she woke up. She hated asking for money. Hated that this many years out of college, even with a teaching job at a decent college, she wasn't making enough money to pay rent. That Ted was supposed to be carrying half but wasn't obviously was an issue, one that she most definitely didn't feel like bringing up. She opened the plastic-coated diner menu, sticky around the edges, and glanced over the top at her father. He was making a show of looking even though she knew he would order the Reuben. He always ordered the Reuben.

They managed to get through most of their food by exchanging family information. They talked about Thanksgiving, four weeks away, and what Bella's brothers and their families were doing, the many grandchildren and the two more on the way.

Just last week Bella and Ted had been in the park on an unseasonably warm October day, the kind of day that felt like the last of its kind until April. Ted caught Bella watching a toddler trying hard to lick his ice cream without making it fall off the cone. The boy's father had offered a hand but the child had stubbornly refused, and moments later, on their way out of the park, Bella heard the high-pitched wail of disappointment that could mean only one thing. Ted had heard it too and he'd given Bella a sidelong glance. "Reason number nine hundred seventy-three that I will never be a father."

Bella's inclination had been to dismiss Ted, to tell him that you never felt that way about your own child. But something about the way he said it made her hear what he was saying. That he wasn't waiting to be joked out of it by Bella. That he probably wouldn't change his mind. That he really didn't see himself being a father and Bella, if she was going to be with him, was going to have to accept it.

The crazy thing about all of it was that Bella wasn't so sure, like Suzie apparently was, that she was meant to be a mother. But still, she wanted to have the choice. Lately, being with Ted made her feel as if she had no choice about anything.

"So." Her father leaned forward over his plate, the last bite of meat and bread in his fingers. "How's Ted?"

Bella poked the lump of cottage cheese on her plate. She always ordered the salad special, and she always forgot it came with cottage cheese. She looked away from her food and smiled at her father. "Great."

"How's the writing?"

"He might be almost done. His agent thinks so, anyway."

Her father shook his head slowly from side to side. "Publishing is a mystery business, I guess. Not a lot of logic involved. Lots of delicate personalities." Her father smiled, but it was tight and not at all sincere. Bella was pretty sure the "delicate personality" he was referring to was Ted.

"I know the payoff isn't supposed to be about fame, or money even, but Ted's book is so beautiful." Bella believed in Ted, believed in what she was saying to her father, but she was also getting tired of defending him. If Ted were there he would tell her to knock it off, that he didn't need her sticking up for him, that he didn't give a shit what people thought about him and that Bella cared too much.

Her father frowned. "I hope so, Bella. I really do, for Ted's sake and for yours." He took a deep, gulping breath. "What about you? Your writing?"

Bella was always surprised that anyone remembered she was a writer. Her father always did, and Suzie. The only writing Bella did lately was correcting her students' papers and editing Ted's work. She had not felt the pull of her own work in years, and she had never enjoyed it in the way she enjoyed teaching. But she didn't have the nerve to admit to that out loud. It still sounded like too much of a failure. "It's always there, but I don't get a lot of time."

"It's hard," he acknowledged. "You will make it happen."

Bella nodded, afraid still to disappoint her father. The last time she had felt like writing she had been in love with Sam. She refused to believe that one had anything to do with the other.

Bella put down her fork. She was done mashing the cottage cheese. "Dad?" She twisted in her seat and looked across the room at a table where an elderly woman sat, her hair unnaturally red, her eyebrows dyed to match, a dish of cottage cheese in front of her untouched, a spoon held in a shaky hand over a cup of tea. Bella had to force herself to look away. "I'm sorry. I need some money."

Her father nodded.

"I'm sorry," Bella said again, wishing that Ted knew what this felt like. In all the years they had been together Bella had never met Ted's parents and had spoken to them only briefly on the phone, once, when they had called Ted for his birthday. Bella always had the feeling that Ted was mildly disappointed in the paths his parents' lives had taken: his father worked for the post office while his mother ran a dog-grooming business and kennel. Ted was an only child who as far as Bella could tell had never been denied a thing in his entire life, although he made a show of never taking anything from them as an adult. If Bella wasn't positive his parents existed, she would have thought he was an orphan.

Her father swallowed and wiped his mouth. "New York is expensive, Bella. Please don't apologize. I'm happy you are close to home." He tapped the top of the table with his hand. "Don't apologize," he said again.

"You make it too easy for me."

Her father smiled. "You want it to be harder?"

Bella shook her head. She felt miserable about the state of her finances.

"Bella, listen to me. You are my daughter. I love you. I would do anything for you, that's my job." He paused. "You don't believe me now, but everything will even out. You'll see."

Bella nodded. The unqualified love was almost too much to bear. She looked back across the room at the old lady, who was now daintily eating her cottage cheese. She smiled slightly after each spoonful. Maybe she had it all right, Bella thought. Maybe she was concentrating too much on what was wrong all the time instead of what was right.

She watched her father get up from the table and pay the check, and make small talk with the waitress, who had stepped behind the register. They were speaking loudly enough that Bella had no problem hearing everything they said, even above the noise of the restaurant. The woman had a glittery pumpkin pinned in place of a nametag and Bella's father commented on it. The waitress explained that her son had made it for her when he was five and now he was in college. Bella smiled as her father pointed to her back at the table.

The weeks leading up to Thanksgiving passed in a blur for Bella. She had a full course load and too many papers to grade. Every night she trudged to the subway feeling more and more like a hunchback, weighed down by her canvas totes and the voluminous winter coat and scarves. Snow had already stalled the city once in early November, leaving even the most hard-core winter romantic dreading the long months ahead. There was nothing wonderful about numb fingers and toes or frizzy hair from all the forced dry heat.

After that lunch with her father, and a loan that had paid November's and December's rents, Bella made a promise to herself that by the New Year she would be self-sufficient. That meant she and Ted had to have a real discussion about money, specifically about his intention to contribute. She had put it off night after night, but now that November was hurtling to a close she was going to have to bring it up.

She smelled the stew as she trudged up the four flights of stairs to their top-floor walk-up. Inside, Bella released her baggage onto the bench by the door and sighed as she massaged her arms and kicked off her boots. The music was loud, an experimental jazz station that Ted favored. She closed her eyes and took several deep breaths before she walked down the hallway and into the main room.

Ted was at the desk by the windows that overlooked the air shaft, surrounded by teetering piles of moldy old paperbacks. When he saw her he looked up, put down his pen, and smiled as if she was the best thing he had seen all day. Bella noticed, as she took the few steps across the room, that he had set the coffee table with place mats, real napkins, candles, and wineglasses.

Ted circled her waist with his arm and brought her down onto his lap. Bella put her head on his shoulder and closed her eyes. They were heading to her father's house the day before Thanksgiving and she hadn't realized how much she was looking forward to the long weekend away until that very moment. She loved the noisy, chaotic domesticity that was unique to her brothers' families.

Ted kissed the side of Bella's neck. "You smell like snow."

"Hmm," Bella said, wondering if dinner could wait as Ted found his way under her sweater. He kneaded her spine, then reached around front, brushing the outside of her bra with his thumb. Bella tried to shift in his lap, but Ted held her hip firmly with his other hand. Then abruptly he removed his hand and his mouth.

"What?" Bella mumbled, her eyes blinking open.

Ted laughed. "The stew! Wine or beer?"

"Beer," Bella answered reluctantly. "But can it wait?"

He shoved her gently off of his lap. "Go sit on the couch."

"You don't want help?"

"Nope."

Bella plopped down on the couch and reached behind her for the pile of mail from the sofa table. She turned on the light by the sofa, the better to read the mail by. Ted turned it off as he handed her a beer. "Ruins the mood," he explained.

Bella pushed the mail between the couch cushions. She was willing to shift the mood to whatever Ted wanted if it ended up getting her laid. They could talk about the rent afterward, when he was in a relaxed state of mind. She took several deep swallows of the cold beer; it was nearly half done and she was feeling a little buzzed by the time Ted returned with two steaming bowls of stew. The chunks of carrot and potato were coated in a glistening brown glaze that smelled faintly of red wine and bay leaf. Bella first had Ted's stew at the cabin in Montana, made with venison from the deer Ted had killed, not beef from the Fairway Market. She speared a potato and chewed, searching already for a hunk of bread to mop up the soupy bits of meat and gravy. Reading her mind, Ted tore off the end of a crusty baguette and handed it to her as he sat down, the remainder of the loaf balanced on his lap in a dish towel. They ate in silence, breaking it only to murmur appreciation and, in Bella's case, to ask for seconds.

When she was satisfied, when her stomach was pressing against the waistband of her skirt, Bella relinquished her empty bowl to the coffee table and leaned back against the pillows, watching Ted. He chewed slowly, methodically, like a prisoner savoring his last meal. She teased him about this habit, but it was probably why he was naturally thin. He tasted his food, and didn't inhale like Bella did. Bella was always hungry for more before her body had even registered that she had eaten.

Ted finished his stew and pushed everything to the center of the coffee table so he could put up his feet. Bella took this as a chance to extend her legs and put her feet in his lap. Ted massaged Bella's arches through her thick-cabled socks.

"Oh, that's nice," Bella said. Ted looked at her, distracted but happy, as if he had a secret. "What's up? Good day of writing?"

"You could say that."

"What?" Bella nudged his thigh with her big toe.

Ted took a deep breath. "I got an invitation to Essex."

Bella struggled to sit up. "What? Wow! Seriously? When?"

"A few months ago."

"Wait a sec—what are you talking about?" Bella shook her head. Ted was looking across the room instead of at her. "I don't understand."

"Essex offered me a residency. Two months. A cabin in the woods. My meals delivered in a dinged-up metal lunch pail, walks on the grounds where Capote and Mailer and their fellow writers once frolicked, and stimulating conversation in the evening with other like-minded individuals."

Bella was afraid to hear what came next. Essex was the residency most of the writers she knew aspired to. The application process was rigorous. She knew many talented people who had been turned down multiple times. She had no idea Ted had even applied. "When are you going?"

Ted finally turned to face her. "I turned them down."

"Why?"

"Because I agreed to stay here with you."

"So you're saying I kept you from Essex? I would never—" All of a sudden the stew that had sat so satisfyingly in her belly churned ominously.

"I'm saying that I have my own cabin. I certainly don't need Essex."

"But it's so—"

"Prestigious?"

Bella nodded and Ted made a face at her, as if she knew better than to use that argument on him. He held up his thumb and forefinger. "I'm this close to finishing."

"What's stopping you? You have all day every single day. You can have the nights too, if that's what it takes. I'm working. You have no pressures." Bella almost said *you have no pressure to make money,* but she didn't. He needed to pay rent, and this seemed like a great time to remind him. "You haven't given me money for rent in months, and I let it slide because I thought you were really pushing through to the end."

Ted ignored her comment about the rent money. "Essex's offer made me really reconsider all of this, Bell. I have to go back to Montana. I can't, I just can't work here."

"But what about my job?"

Ted sighed and shook his head. "If we are going to be together I just can't see it being here."

"I like my job."

Ted nodded slowly. "I know you do."

"Is that bad? That I like my job? That I like to teach?"

"No. I just could never choose that."

Bella felt as if she had been slapped. She removed her feet from Ted's lap and swung them off the couch and onto the floor. She put her head in her hands and rested her elbows on her knees. "I thought everything was going so well," she said, her voice barely above a whisper. "I like it here."

"Bella—"

"I'm good at my job."

"So am I."

Bella looked up, confused. "What?"

"I'm better than good, Bella. I haven't given myself a real chance. I met you. I fell in love. You were so passionate in Iowa. I allowed myself to be distracted."

"I'm a distraction?" Bella's heart pounded in her ears. It felt as if a chunk of potato was caught in her throat. She coughed, but nothing moved. "You don't want me anymore, just like that? After all this time?"

"Bella—"

"What? What happened? You don't touch me anymore. We never have sex. I thought maybe we were just in one of those ruts, you know? That if I tried a little harder we could turn it around."

Ted shook his head. "I don't know what to say to that."

"Fuck you!" Bella was incredulous. Was he agreeing with her? That he didn't want to have sex? That it was somehow her fault? "I thought we were going to be together forever."

"Did you really? You knew I didn't want kids. I can't be domestic all the time." He gestured around them at the apartment. "I can't be tied to this life, Bella."

"What life? You mean the one we created together?" Bella put her face in her hands. The enormity of what Ted was saying had begun to hit her in bitter waves. "Oh my God."

"I'm going back to Montana."

"Am I invited?" Bella asked.

Ted said nothing.

Bella inhaled. "Okay."

"Maybe we just need a few months." The sincerity behind Ted's words was so false Bella couldn't even look at him.

"Is that why you were so happy when I came home? Because you had decided to leave?"

"You have no idea how good it feels to have made a decision."

Bella stood up and walked the few feet to the alcove that

housed their bed. The sheets and pillows were tangled, the elastic stretched out at the corners of the bottom sheet. It looked as if the people sleeping there had wrestled the entire night. "When are you leaving?"

"Tomorrow."

Bella turned to look at Ted. He looked like a man who had broken the news about a fatal illness and was waiting for the patient to melt down once the information sunk in. And yet she could already see herself arriving alone for Thanksgiving, could picture the relief on her father's face. "I think you should take everything. Ship what you can't carry. I can't afford to stay in this apartment. I—we—haven't been able to afford to stay here for a while. My father has been helping us, in case you thought the bills paid themselves."

"You knew when we moved to New York that my income was limited."

"You said you would contribute," Bella said weakly, as if that would matter now.

Ted shrugged. "I knew you wanted this, so I said what you wanted to hear. I'm sorry. Your father has always helped you out. I assumed you didn't have a problem with that."

Bella looked around the small apartment. Most of the things belonged to her. Even her books she kept separate from Ted's. It would be easy for him to pack his duffel. They had been together for nearly three years and had nothing tangible to show for it. Not a joint checking account, a TV purchased on credit, or a couch they had deliberated over in a showroom. How had she never seen this before? This part, the less sticky part, would be easy.

FIFTEEN

You Deserve Everything
Sam—2010

Marguerite was nervous. She seemed unable to sit long enough to eat dinner, let alone have a conversation. If she was still, which was infrequent, her eyes traveled to Sam's father. When Sam tried to clean up after dinner, she pushed him toward the door, where his father was standing, already clad in a monstrous down coat and DayGlo yellow mittens, ready for a post-dinner stroll.

Sam shrugged into his jacket, declined his father's offer of a scarf and a hat, and followed him into the street. At the end of the driveway he stopped and looked up. Living on the Vineyard for the past four months had altered his view of the natural world. Even here, peering up at his childhood sky, the stars looked like confetti. Sam zipped his jacket to underneath his chin and exhaled, satisfied by the puff of smoke. An odd memory popped into his head of cold mornings standing at the bus stop near Frankie Cole's house. They had huffed and puffed and pretended to blow smoke rings. Their breath commingled and held the leftover flavors of their sweetened breakfast cereals. Hunt was three houses ahead because he had not waited for Sam, and now Sam hurried to catch up. It was the day after Thanksgiving, and most of the neighbors had already been busy exchanging one holiday for the next; strings of Christmas lights decorated several of the porches. Sam and Hunt wound through the familiar streets in silence.

Sam had missed Thanksgiving because he had cooked dinner at the farm for thirty people, as a farewell gift to the farmers who had so generously taken him in and given him free rein on their land and in their kitchen. He had left knowing he had a job on the tip of Long Island that they had arranged, working for another small organic farm that was trying to replicate the model out on the Vineyard.

Apparently, Michael and Suzie had come and gone on Thanksgiving within a couple of hours. Marguerite had said so in a torrent of words while shaking salt into the pasta water. Over a casserole of turkey Tetrazzini she'd added that they were headed to Mexico for a well-deserved vacation. There was no mention of a baby, and Sam wasn't going to bring it up.

All the windows were dark in Peter Chang's house. Peter and Mindy had gone to Florida to spend the Thanksgiving weekend with Mrs. Chang. Sam wondered if they were going to come back engaged, or even married. It was a mystery how Peter had managed to turn an ambivalent attraction into a long-term relationship that worked, while Sam could never seem to get past the occasional hookup.

What Sam had always liked best about walking around the streets at night was the glimpse it provided into other people's lives. Through half-opened curtains and the slats of blinds he caught the flickering lights of a television, people gathered around tables, kids running back and forth, grateful for the holiday weekend. Sam remembered exactly how that felt, knowing you had entire days ahead where you didn't have to do a thing.

Beside Sam his father stopped, transfixed by a window through which multiple generations of a family appeared to be gathered around a table piled high with pizza boxes. This house had recently sold; Mrs. Schwartz and Colonel the schnauzer had retired to Coral Gables, Florida. So the family was new, which explained the lack of window coverings (no time to put up curtains) and flattened cardboard boxes roped and tied at the end of the driveway (a miscalculation due to the change in recycling schedule because of the holiday).

Sam's father was not even trying to hide that he was staring, standing in plain sight in front of their large picture windows. "Life goes on whether or not you want it to," he said, then abruptly began to walk away.

"Dad?" Sam called, and hurried to catch up to him. Hunt's gait had increased, as if he didn't want to be next to Sam. "Dad?"

When his father turned around he looked delighted to see Sam, as if he had forgotten altogether that they had been out for a walk. He smiled broadly and rocked back and forth on his heels. "When we first moved into this neighborhood it was this time of year. You were a baby. It was snowing, and cold. Colder than this. I remember eating turkey leftovers on top of a tablecloth-covered box. Your brother was in one of those booster chairs and you were crawling around on the floor. Your mother wanted to take a walk after dinner. We did that a lot when you and your brother were small. We told ourselves it was to help you sleep, but really, I liked it more than you guys did. I was proud to show off my family. Proud to have married and bought a house and had two sons."

He had stopped moving and Sam finally caught up to him.

"We used to wrap you in so many layers and prop you and your brother in this sled that had high sides. We would take turns pulling you through the snowy streets." He paused and closed his eyes as if he could still see them as they were then. When he opened them he said, "I was your age. Can you even imagine that?"

Sam shook his head. His father reached over and cuffed him gently on the chin with a mitten-covered hand before they started walking again. When they turned the corner Sam could see Bella's house from all the way down the block. Every single window seemed filled with light, and there were multiple cars in the driveway parked at haphazard angles. Her brothers and their families must have come home for the holiday weekend. As they got closer Hunt slowed down. "Come on, let's stop in for a drink."

"What?"

"I told him I would."

"Now?"

"Why not?"

"Well, what about Marguerite? Wouldn't you rather have her with you?"

"But I'm here now." His father frowned, as if it didn't make sense to walk three blocks home to get Marguerite.

Sam looked at his father. If Sam gave him a plausible excuse not to go into the Spades' he probably would have walked on home without question. As it was, he had finally pulled the mittens from his hands and was standing on the front walk, waiting for Sam with a puzzled expression. Sam nodded for him to go ahead. Hunt pressed the buzzer, and as they waited for the door to open he turned to Sam and said in a low voice, "By the way, I'm retiring January first."

As soon as those words were out of his mouth one of Bella's look-alike brothers opened the door and enthusiastically ushered them inside. The house smelled like cookies and burnt toast. One child was crying while another was screaming, and two others were banging out "Jingle Bells" on the piano. There were people and platters of food everywhere and in the center of the chaos was a half-decorated Christmas tree. On a stool next to the tree, attempting to untangle a string of lights, was Bella. At her feet several blond children bent over a large box of ornaments, squealing as they lifted each one up.

Sam was still processing what his father had said to him when Bella turned and smiled in his direction. "Ho, ho, ho," she said, jiggling the string of lights.

"Only Santa says that," said one of the ornament fondlers. Sam noticed two thick rivulets of snot poised on his upper lip. The tip of the kid's tongue darted out and Sam looked away.

Bella grinned. "I've been served." She glanced down at Little Mr. Snot Nose. "Go get a tissue now. And don't use your brother's sleeve. Remember, he's watching." She pointed to the hallway. The kid dropped the ornament and trudged off. Sam was surprised that he had listened.

"Who's watching?" Sam asked.

"Santa Claus." Bella put her finger to her lips. "You can use Santa from the day after Thanksgiving until the night before Christmas. It's the only way to get through the month with kids." She stepped off the stool and left the knot of lights tucked deep into a branch. Her face was pink and her hair a large, fluffy halo. "When did you get home?"

"Today. You?"

"The day before Thanksgiving. Ted is at a writer's retreat in Vermont."

Sam nodded and shoved his hands into the back pockets of his jeans, trying not to show how thrilled he was about Ted's absence. "That's great."

"What?"

"Ted's residency." He hesitated and then joked, "He kind of makes me look good, showing up for a Thanksgiving drink."

Bella raised an eyebrow. "You want a drink?"

"Oh, sure, sure. Thanks." Sam started to follow Bella to the kitchen but then caught sight of his father standing in a circle of men that included Mr. Spade. Hunt was still wearing his puffy down jacket. He was holding a glass of something amber. Sam paused to watch him, still feeling unsettled.

Bella returned swiftly and handed him a beer. Sam lifted the bottle to his lips and drank, grateful for the cold liquid, but he was unable to take his eyes off his father.

"What's up, Sam?" Bella nudged him with an elbow in the ribs.

"Right before we got here my dad told me he's retiring on the first of the year."

"Seriously?"

"Is that odd?" Sam couldn't imagine his father not going into the office. Even when he'd had his heart attack, he hadn't been allowed to go into the office for six weeks and that had been five weeks too long.

Bella shrugged and took another swallow of her beer. When Sam looked over at her, her lips were shiny. She said, "Maybe he just wants to enjoy life with Marguerite. He's worked a long time."

"What about your father?"

"What, retire?" She scrunched up her face. "I can't see it."

Sam nodded. "My point exactly."

"What does your brother think?"

"I wouldn't know. I haven't talked to him since he appeared

in the middle of the night for Suzie. You probably see them more than I do."

Bella looked unsure of how to respond. "They really needed this Mexico trip."

"What does that mean? Marguerite said the exact same thing at dinner."

"Nothing," Bella said quickly. "They both work hard. They need time to relax."

"Oh, sure, of course." Sam drained his beer and changed the subject. Something still bothered him about the way Suzie had acted toward him on the Cape. He wasn't sure why. "How's Hunter?"

"Good, how was the farm?"

"Good, fine, life-changing." He ran a hand through his hair and looked over at his father again. Hunt hadn't moved, hadn't taken a sip of his drink, hadn't taken off his coat. "Maybe I should see if Dad wants to get going. Marguerite thinks we're out for a walk . . . she'll be worried."

"Go." Bella's tone had softened to a near whisper. "Go on."

Sam took a step toward his father and then turned back to Bella. "Can I call you tomorrow?"

Bella stared at him above the rim of her beer bottle, but she didn't refuse.

When they got in the door Sam could tell that Marguerite had just sat down on the couch. The paper she was holding in her lap was as put together as it had been when it was delivered that morning. Immediately, his father announced that he was tired. But he went to sit down next to Marguerite still wearing his jacket, and it was Marguerite who unzipped it and gently coaxed his arms from the sleeves.

Sam went into the kitchen for no other reason than to leave the room. After a while he heard them talking and laughing, so he walked back through and said good night. His father was stretched out on the couch with his head in Marguerite's lap. They were watching Jay Leno. They both acknowledged him with a smile, his father telling him to sleep tight, Marguerite adding that she had left an extra blanket in the closet. Nothing seemed wrong, but it didn't feel right either.

Sam arrived at the diner before Bella, and out of habit took the table in the back, the same table they had occupied during high school.

The house had been quiet when Sam woke. His father and Marguerite were gone, the only evidence they had been awake before him two empty mugs on the counter and the tang of ground beans in the air. There wasn't a note, but then, there was no reason for Sam to think they would leave one.

He ordered coffee just as Bella stepped inside the door, and was able to catch the waitress before she walked away and change the order to two cups. Bella looked to the back of the restaurant, as Sam knew she would, and raised a hand in greeting as she made her way around the tables and chairs. Sam looked away after they made eye contact, not wanting to make her feel like he was putting her on the spot. He studied the paper cutouts of turkeys and Christmas trees taped to the wall above the booth.

Before Bella sat down she slipped out of her coat and unwound her scarf and shoved them into the booth ahead of her. Then she slid in across from Sam. Their coffee arrived in thick white mugs, steam rising off the top. As the waitress set them down she said, "You guys know what you want?"

"I wish," Sam said, and to his surprise Bella laughed.

The waitress shrugged. "No rush. When you're ready let me know."

Bella reached for her coffee. "Existential crisis so early in the morning?"

Sam inhaled the steam from his coffee. "It's the age-old question: eggs or waffles?"

"Easy: eggs over easy, with a side of hash browns, bacon, and sourdough toast."

"Sounds delicious."

"That's all the convincing you need?"

Sam raised his hand to get the waitress to come back. "Apparently."

"Wow, you really have changed."

Sam looked at Bella to see if she was joking. She didn't seem to be. After the waitress had left with their orders Sam said, "I'd like to think I've learned something after all these years."

Bella nodded and looked down at her hands on the table. She flexed her fingers as if they were stiff. "Was your dad okay when you got home last night?"

"Seemed to be. I don't know, maybe it's my problem."

"It's hard to know what their normal is. I mean, you're not there. It's the same for all of us. We come home for a visit and things are slightly off, but we don't know why."

"He's getting old."

Bella nodded. "We all are."

"I don't know about that. If I'm in a new place and it's first thing in the morning I feel like I'm eighteen, nineteen, twenty."

"Ugh. I don't want to ever go back to those years." Bella lifted her mug to her lips. Sam couldn't read her expression.

"Because of me?" he asked. "Because of what an idiot I was?"

"What?" Bella said softly.

"I'm sorry." Sam hadn't planned to say it, but as soon as it came out of his mouth he knew there was no going back. "I'm so sorry."

Bella set her mug down carefully on the table as if she was afraid to spill.

"I'm sorry I left you like that, I'm sorry I never came back."

The waitress walked over with their plates and slid them in front of them. She pulled bottles of ketchup and hot sauce from her apron pocket and set those down in the empty space between the plates. Bella was staring at the wall when she asked if they wanted anything else and Sam shook his head for the both of them. As Bella turned back to him he saw that her eyes were shiny.

"Fuck you for saying that right now," she whispered. She looked down at her plate of eggs but did not pick up her fork.

"Bella."

"No, no, Goddamnit, Sam. You don't get to do this to me after all these years."

Sam leaned toward her so their foreheads were almost touching. "I had no idea what I was doing, Bella. I was flunking out of school. I thought the best thing to do would be to walk away. If I had stayed with you we would never be here now."

"There isn't a now, Sam. There isn't a *we*. There isn't even an *us* to remember. I've been with Ted for two years. Two years!" Bella spit out the last part and Sam felt her breath on his cheek. "He wants to be with me, he tells me every chance he gets. Can you imagine that?" Bella collapsed back against the booth.

Sam reached in his pocket for his wallet. He fumbled through junk until he found the piece of paper he was looking for. "Take it."

Bella took a deep breath, exhaled, and looked back at the paper turkeys.

"Bell, take it, please."

She held out her hand, and Sam dropped the paper into her palm. The creases where the paper had been folded and refolded, nestled inside his wallet, were nearly ripped all the way through.

"Adrienne Rich." Bella made a face. "I was so naive."

"What?"

"This." Bella's hands shook as she stared at the paper. "Adrienne Rich, she wrote this—it's part of a series of twenty-one love poems."

Sam sat back. All these years, he had thought Bella had written those words about them.

Bella folded the paper back up and held it in her hand. "Why now?"

Sam couldn't read her face. He swallowed hard. "I don't know. That's not why I asked you to breakfast. I just, there was this opportunity and so I took it."

"I can't." She shook her head as if she could get rid of him.

"At the wedding when I tried to talk to you, and we didn't—at all." Sam stumbled all over his words. "And then that whole thing with Mr. Epstein, you, well, I mean, I felt, I hoped you looked at me a little differently." Sam swallowed hard. "I never expected you to ever speak to me again. But then there was the night that you caught up to me in the street outside Michael's apartment? And then the Cape?" He tried to pick the right words. "There was so much I wanted to say, but I didn't think you would want to hear."

Bella cleared her throat. "I know you loved her. Suzie."

To hear Bella say it out loud sounded so foolish to Sam's ears. "My God, Bella, we were fifteen." He gulped. "I loved her only if love was all about getting to the next base."

"I knew all about it." She shrugged ever so slightly, carefully holding her body as if she were bruised. "But I liked you even though I knew I would be your second choice."

"How's everything here? Something wrong with your eggs?" The waitress led with her pot of coffee, frowning at their untouched breakfasts. Sam pushed his mug in her direction for a refill because he was unable to speak. Bella looked down at her plate. When neither of them answered, the waitress turned around and left.

Sam shook his head. "Bella, a lot of shit happened that summer. A lot of unresolved shit. I may have overromanticized those few weeks with Suzie; I may have carried that forward because it was easier to long for something I never had than to be in the moment. I don't know. Suzie was all tangled up with my parents' split. These are not excuses but I can't explain it any better than that. Nothing about that time has ever felt finished." He took a breath. "Was I shocked as shit that she showed up with Michael? Yes. That they had a relationship? Yes. It threw me for a fucking loop, I cannot deny that. But I've grown up. I miss you." He took a gulp of hot coffee and winced as it scorched its way down his throat and into his esophagus. His voice was scratchy when he asked, "Are you in love with Ted?"

"I told you. We've been together for two and a half years. Almost three, really."

"And that means you love him?" Sam paused. "You can do better than Ted."

"You don't know anything." Bella was still holding the piece of paper with the poem in her hand. She crumpled it up and tossed it across the table before she grabbed her coat and scarf and slid out of the booth.

"Then tell me," Sam asked. "Tell me."

Bella shoved her arms in the sleeves of her coat but left the buttons undone and the scarf unwound as she bent over and grabbed her bag from beneath the table. Then she strode out of the diner. It took seconds, maybe a minute tops, for her to get away from Sam. The door jangled as she exited, the bells swinging back and forth for a long time after she left.

Sam let her go. He had already said whatever he thought would have kept her, and it hadn't been enough. He picked up the crumpled piece of paper, which was nestled in a bed of home fries, and smoothed it out on the table as best he could. The dots of grease combined with the rips made it unreadable.

Sam extricated a twenty for the waitress and tucked the bill beneath his plate before he carefully folded the paper back up along the creases and put it back inside his wallet.

Apparently Marguerite and Hunt had gone to get a Christmas tree. When Sam returned home he found his father on his hands and knees under the tree, cursing at the screws in the stand. "Do you need help?" Sam asked.

Hunt crawled out from under the canopy of branches and sat back on his feet. His face was red and there was a sprinkling of pine needles across the shoulders of his Polartec jacket. He gestured to Sam with a pair of pliers. "I think I finally got the son of a bitch tight enough so it won't fall over. Give me a lift?"

Sam held out a hand to his father and hoisted him off the ground. Then they righted the tree in the stand, turning it all the way around while Marguerite found its best side. Sam tried to remember the last time they'd had a Christmas tree, or the last time he had helped to decorate one, but he couldn't recall. Marguerite had brought many things back into the lives of the Turners, holiday traditions among them.

Marguerite had the ornaments spread out on the couch and

the coffee table and was bent over the boxes searching for hooks. Sam was restless. The last thing he felt like doing was decorating a tree. He wondered where Bella had gone, if she had gone home, if right now she had a zillion little kids clamoring for her attention. He still wasn't sure how he had gone wrong so fast.

He needed to forget the fiasco of breakfast, so he went over to the bar and poured a finger out of a dusty bottle of tequila and then went into the kitchen and added ice cubes and a generous slice of lime. The tequila went down easier than Sam expected on a stomach of coffee and nerves. He could feel it turning him sideways. He went back to the bar cart for another and just decided to take the entire bottle of tequila instead.

Sam could feel his father and Marguerite watching him as he walked down the long hall to his room. The three of them knew that nothing good could come out of a bottle of tequila and his childhood bedroom. "Sam?" Marguerite called after him as he shut the door. "Sam?"

"Leave him alone," he heard Hunt say. "He'll come out when he's ready."

It was dark when there was a knock on his bedroom door. Before Sam could answer, the door opened, letting a sliver of light in across the bed. "Sam?"

Sam struggled out of the fog of sleep and tequila. When he did he saw his father leaning against the doorframe dressed in a tuxedo. "Hmm?" Sam mumbled, unsure of what he was seeing.

"Sammy? Hey? We're leaving."

"Where? What?"

"We're going to the city."

"To get married?"

"What?"

"You're wearing a tux."

"We're going to Marguerite's hospital fund-raiser. It's formal." Hunt stepped closer to the bed. He may or may not have nudged the empty bottle of tequila with his foot. Sam thought he heard glass tumbling against the floor. He closed his eyes.

His father touched Sam's knee. His limbs felt heavy, and it was impossible to imagine ever moving them again. "What's going on?"

"Nothing."

"A bottle of tequila isn't nothing when you start drinking before noon."

"I'm fine."

"You're a man." Hunt's voice sounded tired. "Do what you want. I just wish—"

"I was more like Michael?"

"Cut that crap. It's way too easy for you to place blame there." Hunt paused. "I want to help you, if you'd let me."

Sam rolled over onto his side and looked at his father. There was a slight pounding in his temple and a roiling in his empty gut. "I should be able to get my shit together without you by now. Hey, are you really retiring?"

"Yes." Hunt frowned slightly as he nodded, and brushed something off his lapel.

"What are you going to do?"

Hunt laughed. "Get my shit together. Want to help?" He turned toward the sound of Marguerite's heels tapping against the hardwood floor. "I have to go. I just wanted to make sure you were alive before we left."

"Tell Marguerite I'm sorry."

His father paused with his hand on the doorknob and said, "I think you can handle that yourself." And then he walked out of the room and closed the door softly behind him.

Sam made a dinner of scrambled eggs and toast and sat in the family room next to the bare Christmas tree, watching *It's a Wonderful Life*. After a while he felt so bad about the tree he decided to thread the lights on the branches. When he had done that he peered into the ornament box.

These ornaments were new, purchased by Marguerite in recent years. Sam had no idea what had happened to the wheat paste stars, paper chains, and clay dough handprints he and Michael had brought home every holiday season while they were in elementary school. Before she left, their mother would make a show of unwrapping those ornaments from the layers of storage tissue paper as if they were the most prized possessions she owned. Sam doubted she would have taken those with her on the way out the door. The most likely scenario he could come up with was that they had been thrown away during the renovation.

Sam considered hanging some of the ornaments until he found the white and red ceramic ball that said Grandbaby's First Christmas. That must have been purchased before Suzie's miscarriages. He rewrapped it and plunged it deeper into the box, covering it with a reindeer made out of twigs and a felted Mr. and Mrs. Claus. Sam tucked the box flaps back together and brought his dish into the kitchen just as the doorbell rang.

Bella stood on the front porch, her hands shoved deeply into her coat pockets. The bottom half of her chin was covered by the same enormous pink scarf she'd worn earlier. It was freezing, and in the streetlights beyond her head he could see a flurry of snowflakes. Sam remembered the storms after Mrs. Spade's funeral, the icicles on the windows of the train he and Bella had taken back to Poughkeepsie. He opened the door wide, surprised to see her there. "Do you want to come in? No one's here."

"No," Bella said, her words muffled against the scarf. She wiggled her chin from side to side to free it from the cloth. "I just wanted to tell you I was sorry for running out on you like that this morning." She shrugged. "I just have a lot going on right now."

Sam crossed his arms over his chest. "You don't have to—"

"I do, I do. Can we leave it at that, Sam?" She shuffled down the walk and out to the street. He held his breath and counted to ten but she didn't look back.

Without thinking Sam ran down the steps. When he caught up to her he was already feeling the ridiculousness of the gesture. Plus his feet, clad only in socks, were rapidly becoming wet and cold. "I can't leave it at that, Bella."

Bella spun around. "This isn't real, Sam. You aren't real. You aren't even fully formed yet."

"What does that even mean?"

"Nothing in your life is set in stone. You go whenever you want. You disappear."

"Is your life set in stone already, Bella? If it is, I don't think you would be standing here talking about mine."

Bella opened her mouth and then closed it. There were snowflakes caught in her eyelashes. Eventually she said, "Go back home."

"If you want to be with Ted, tell me, and I'll leave you alone. But I want you to come with me." The snow picked up with the wind, blowing the flakes sideways. The shoulders of Bella's coat were completely covered in white. "Come inside. Please." Sam began to walk backward toward the house, all the while watching Bella's unreadable face. He couldn't feel his feet and he stumbled, nearly falling to the ground before he caught himself and climbed up the stairs to the porch. He was scared to turn around to see if she was following. If he got to the door and she wasn't behind him he would have to forget her.

Sam put his hand on the door handle. When he finally got up enough nerve to look behind him, a mass of white filled the space where Bella had just been standing. She was gone.

SIXTEEN

Visibility
Suzie—2011

As Suzie stepped from the car her coat button popped, revealing the slight pouch of a pregnancy six months along. She touched a hand lightly to her belly, still in awe that this time, this time, she had stayed pregnant. She had felt sluggish all morning and now she watched Marguerite, who had been driving, gather items from the backseat instead of helping her. Suzie squinted over at the front windows of the restaurant. She could see Sam moving back and forth. He was so involved in what he was doing that she doubted he even knew they'd arrived.

Suzie stepped ahead of Marguerite and held open the door just as Sam came forward. He smiled at them in a distracted way. Against the long brick wall was a lineup of paint cans and drop cloths. To save money wherever he could, Sam was painting the interior himself, and Marguerite's brother had helped with the kitchen remodel. The actual dining space was small but charming, and as soon as the paneled walls were covered in the soft shade of white Sam had them all approve from a sheaf of paint cards he'd carried around for weeks, the interior would reflect the sage and lavender that huddled against the squat brick-and-shingled building.

The building that housed Sam's soon-to-be restaurant was a long, vacant tavern at the end of a small string of businesses in what Marguerite had called the quaint downtown corridor of Rye. Quaint or not really didn't matter to Sam, Suzie knew. Before he signed the lease Michael and Suzie had met him here at the restaurant. Sam claimed to know instantly when he walked inside that this was where he was meant to be, but he still wanted another opinion.

Across the street, out the front windows, the commuter train station that had been a fixture of their childhood stood guard. It was strange to hear how differently the brothers remembered those years of their lives. Sam had said that he and his mother had picked up his father most nights from that station. In the winter Sam would wear pajamas and slippers under a coat, and wrap himself in a sleeping bag that his mother kept in the far back of the wagon. Some nights while they waited, Elizabeth would quiz Sam on spelling words or multiplication tables, but mostly they sat in silence. Sam would stare down the tracks, but he knew the train was coming before he could see it; that first vibration of steel against rail, rippling beneath the concrete and coming up through the floorboards of the car, signaled the approach. That was the sign for his mother to toss her cigarette out the open window and check herself in the rearview mirror.

Michael claimed that he had been along all of those nights, and that he was the one who helped Sam with his math homework. Michael also said it was his idea to wear pajamas to the station so they would have extra time before bed for the glass custard cups of ice cream with chocolate sauce that their mother doled out for special desserts. Once home, before bed they would join their father in the kitchen while he ate his reheated dinner, saved in the same faded red pie plate night after night.

Suzie had listened to Michael and Sam as they had relayed their stories and seen a hint of defeat in Sam, a concession that Michael had the right memory. Michael seemed not to notice Sam's confusion. He was all about the facts, and confident in his own recollection. The difference in the way the brothers saw their world had never been so black and white as it had been in that moment, at least for Suzie.

Now Suzie smiled at Sam in greeting as he tried to take the things out of Marguerite's arms, even though she wouldn't let him. Suzie pointed to the kitchen and Sam nodded, so she headed back to look at the stove he had talked about the last time he had seen them, a few weeks ago in the city. The stove had cost more than two months of the restaurant's rent, but Sam said it had been worth the price.

When Suzie returned to the dining room Marguerite had set the box down and shrugged out of her coat near the painting supplies. She was bent over with her hands on her knees, squinting at the colors smeared across the lids. With a nod of approval she straightened up, smoothing the fabric down over her hips. "Look what I found," she said to Sam. She pointed down by her feet.

Inside the box was a stack of large dinner plates, somewhat irregular in shape, with an organic, handmade feel. Sam lifted one up and turned it over in his hands. The glaze was white with underlying facets of gray and blue, so the effect was like the warmth from a well-worn set of pearls. He smiled at Marguerite's find.

Marguerite grinned at his reaction and clapped her hands together. "I'm so happy! I thought they were the ones, but I didn't want to jinx it. I can have the lot of them, but I just took a few to show you. They're from a French place near Columbus Circle that went out of business. I went to the liquidation sale in Garden City yesterday, and I talked my way in before they opened it to the public. I put a hold on six cases of thick handmade green glasses with a cobalt lip, and the farm tables too." She took a tape measure from her pocket and began to walk the space from front to back. She snapped the tape and looked over at Sam. "Perfect! How many times does that happen?"

Suzie looked over at Sam. He gave Marguerite a wide, toothy smile that made him look goofy and impossibly young. Suzie felt a twinge in her gut at the glimpse of the boy she once knew. She shook her head and glanced out the window. The restaurant had been just as much Marguerite's project as it had been Sam's; she had invested an endless amount of energy to make everything happen. Sam had told Michael that he had run out of ways to express his thanks for all her generosity.

Before the restaurant, Sam had spent months at an organic farm out on Long Island planning for the growing season, but when the financing for the farm had disappeared, Sam had no choice but to retreat to Hunt and Marguerite's home once again. As Suzie understood it, the restaurant was born out of several late-night conversations between the three of them at that time.

Marguerite dug around in her bag for her phone. "I'm going to step outside and call them. I don't want to take any chances. This stuff is good, and cheap because they need to sell quickly." She disappeared out the door.

Sam moved over to a stack of notebooks piled on the bar that ran along the back of the room, and Suzie followed him. "We got the liquor license this week," Sam said as he flipped open the top notebook. He tapped his palms flat on the bar, a long stretch of gleaming chestnut, while looking for a pen, located a nub of a pencil, and scribbled something. "A friend of Dad's helped a lot," he added, and Suzie nodded, although he wasn't looking at her. "So I got Brooklyn Brewery and maybe one other local brewer doing some great organic IPAs."

"What's all that?" Suzie pointed to the notebooks.

Sam looked down at the stack under his hands. "Apparently I've been working on the menu for a restaurant my entire life."

"In there? You mean you've been making up recipes and—"

Sam snorted. "I never took notes in class when I was supposed to. But these books have been with me forever. Notes on what I cooked, what I wanted to cook, attempts failed and successful, sources for meat and veggies. You name it." He shrugged, closed the notebook, and shoved the pencil nub in his pocket. "You guys are coming next week, right? I'm going to cook the menu and invite friends and family for a taste test. It's helpful to know what works, what doesn't work. An opening before the opening, you know?"

"Absolutely," Suzie said. "I'm looking forward to it. I'm always starving."

"You want something now?"

Suzie pushed aside her pending doctor's appointment and weigh-in and what she had already eaten so far that day, and nodded. "I won't turn it away."

Sam beckoned for her to follow him into the kitchen. He opened the refrigerator and took out a bowl of hummus, opened the wire vegetable bin and grabbed a few carrots and peppers, sliced them quickly, and slid the cutting board toward Suzie. She scooped a red pepper into the hummus and popped it into her mouth. The hummus was thick and lemony with the right amount of bite from sriracha.

"Good?" Sam asked as he wiped his knife off on a towel.

Suzie nodded, her mouth glued shut with hummus. When she could speak she asked, "Are you still going to crash upstairs? Did you get any furniture? What do you need?" When Sam had shown Suzie and Michael the place, he was most excited about the small apartment above the tavern. It was dark, with an odd placement of casement windows at half height and a pitched ceiling that made it difficult to stand upright except in the middle of the room, but Sam had been thrilled that it was all his, not a room at his father's house and not a place with roommates.

"I got an old mattress, it's all good."

Suzie finished the hummus and sat back. Her face was flushed, her cheeks and neck a bright red, as she fanned her face with her free hand.

"You okay?"

She ducked her head, trying to downplay the fact that her body was reacting the way it was supposed to. "Oh, yeah, hormones are working overtime. So, your stove is beautiful and terrifying."

"Perfect, right?" Sam stroked the surface with the dish towel, buffing the stainless. "She's a studio apartment in Manhattan in a so-so neighborhood with no view."

Suzie laughed. "Well, you could probably sleep in that oven if you tucked your legs to your chest."

"I think I have," Sam said, laughing. "You never saw some of my apartments."

Marguerite came into the kitchen with a triumphant look on her face. "It's all set. But I have to give them a cashier's check today, and that means I need to run to the bank and then get on the road." She looked at her watch and then over at Suzie. "Is that okay? I know I said I'd give you a ride back into the city. You could wait for me at the house or take the train."

"Let me give you a ride," Sam said to Suzie.

"No one has to give me a ride. I can take the train," Suzie said.

Sam shook his head, rattling the keys in his pocket. "I don't need Michael to bust on me for letting his pregnant wife take the train." He was half joking, but Suzie could tell from the look on his face that he didn't want Michael to think he was incapable of doing the right thing.

The minute they got in the car Suzie said to Sam, "I don't want this to sound the wrong way, but don't ask me about Bella."

Sam frowned at the road. Suzie stared at him for a minute and then looked down in her lap. Bella had told Suzie that she just couldn't deal with everything Sam had dumped on her right now. She said he'd called constantly and she refused to answer. She claimed it was self-preservation. Suzie thought she was just scared after everything that had happened with Ted.

"So what am I supposed to do?"

It took Suzie a moment to realize Sam was asking her for advice. "I think you have to leave her alone, Sam." She didn't want to betray Bella by saying anything more.

"Peter and Frankie have told me the same thing. I thought they just wanted to shut me up because they were tired of me crying into my beer. I asked Mindy and Ruthie too. But I guess you know their answer. You were my last hope." He frowned at the windshield. "What can I say? I'm desperate." He said the last thing without any pity in his voice.

Suzie's mouth twisted into a smile. She bit the inside of her cheek; she didn't want Sam to think she was laughing at him. "The restaurant looks good," she said.

"I've had stress dreams where I fuck everything up there in such a massive way that I take down the people who believe in me the most."

Suzie waved a hand in front of her face. "Oh, that's perfectly normal."

Sam laughed. "Normal? Now that's a word I didn't think doctors like you were allowed to use."

Suzie shook her head. "Tell me about the menu; start at the beginning."

As he drove Sam fell into a recitation of the meals, from appetizers to dessert. Suzie was hungry again, and she fell asleep with a hollow ache in her stomach at Sam's description of a warm orzo dish with fresh mozzarella, garlic, and spinach in a spicy butter sauce.

Her sleep was restless, uneasy, but she was still drowsy enough not to want to open her eyes and really wake up. Her cheek was pressed against the window, and while she knew Sam tried to drive smoothly, there was no way he could avoid the awkward shifts and change in speed that made her head jerk forward and her body brace against the seat belt. She searched for a comfortable position, adjusted the lap belt, and opened her eyes just as they hit the city. "Something's wrong," she said.

Sam took his eyes off the road quickly and glanced at her. "What?"

Suzie felt light-headed. She pressed her tongue hard against the roof of her mouth and counted to ten before she answered. "I think, I'm pretty sure, I'm bleeding." She said the last part in a whisper as she looked down at her lap. She touched her sweater where it was bunched between her thighs and quickly moved a hand to her puffy abdomen. She couldn't be sure of what she was feeling. There wasn't any cramping or lower back pain. At least she wasn't in labor, not yet anyway. "Can you get over to the hospital? Now?"

Sam nodded and jerked the car to the right. Suzie flinched as a taxi swerved around them. She fumbled with her cell phone, her top lip caught in her bottom teeth. She jabbed at the screen over and over, leaving messages first for Michael, then for her doctor, and then she clutched the phone in her hand until her knuckles turned white. A few minutes later it finally rang: the nurse told her she was in luck; her doctor was doing rounds at the hospital and had already been warned of her arrival.

Suzie ended the call and repeated the phrase: *I'm in luck*. The word *luck* was no comfort to someone who had lost so many pregnancies before this one.

Sam pulled up to the entrance as Suzie directed him to, the one that said no passenger drop-offs. She fumbled in her bag for her doctor's credentials. As soon as Sam slowed down, a burly guy in a security jacket stepped forward to tell him he couldn't be stopped at the curb. Suzie flashed her badge out the passenger's side window and he backed off.

Suzie opened the door before Sam had come to a complete stop. Over her shoulder from between gritted teeth she said, "I can get a wheelchair and a nurse at the desk. Find Michael, he's here somewhere." She hesitated before she tossed Sam her cell phone. She didn't know what was ahead of her. Sam would have a better chance of talking to Michael. Suzie walked away before Sam could even respond. She walked slowly, her coat doubled over and wrapped around her waist. She tried hard not to think about what was happening, even though she wanted to be prepared. A cold sweat broke out on the back of her neck as the sliding glass doors to the emergency room opened and Suzie walked inside.

It didn't take long for the ER docs to transfer her to the maternity ward. Her staff credentials and the presence of her OB sped up the process, and in under an hour they had a diagnosis.

Her placenta was detaching from the uterus. But the baby had a strong heartbeat. For the best chance of a full-term birth, Suzie would have to remain in bed most likely until the end of her pregnancy.

"If you're lucky," her doctor had said, "we'll get another eleven weeks at least."

Suzie had stared at him. There was that word again: *luck*. She knew the survival rate increased the longer they could keep the baby inside, but a term pregnancy couldn't really have anything to do with luck, could it? If you counted the previous miscarriages, wouldn't that make her the unluckiest mother-to-be in the world? Why should this time be any different?

Every time the door opened Suzie expected to see Michael. She had lost all track of time, had no idea how long she had been in the hospital, let alone the room. Had everyone disappeared? Not even Sam had shown up yet and she had given him strict instructions to find his brother. Suzie grabbed at a nurse who had just entered the room. "Has anyone seen my husband? Dr. Michael Turner? He's on cardiology—pediatrics."

"You have to relax," the nurse said as she removed the sheet to adjust the monitor. She frowned slightly at the belt and smoothed it out before she pulled the sheet back up. "I'll get the desk to page him, okay?"

Suzie nodded. She felt the tears that had been hovering at the corners of her eyes roll down her cheeks and into the creases under her chin. The nurse pulled a tissue from her pocket and dabbed at Suzie's face. "I promise. Don't get your pressure up. They'll make me stick you again." She gave her a half smile, half frown. She had a kind face, and Suzie searched it for an answer as to what her future would bring.

After the nurse left Suzie, she had nothing to do but listen to the heartbeats, hers and the baby's, along with the automatic whoosh of the blood pressure cuff. She shifted in the bed. The chux pads beneath her bare ass were bunched between her legs, and she attempted to straighten them out without moving too much. She placed her hands over her abdomen, careful not to disturb the monitor, and tried to tune out the noise from the other side of the door. She knew just down the hall babies were being delivered and she shut her eyes and imagined herself as one of those women. Eleven weeks. She would not accept the other option.

At the sound of the door Suzie opened her eyes. Michael. He took four long steps and bent over her bed and held her face cupped in the palms of his hands. He looked in her eyes and whispered everything she wanted to hear. They would be okay. Their baby would be okay. He wouldn't let anything happen to them. That was everything she needed.

By the time Marguerite and Hunt arrived at the hospital Suzie was propped against a tower of pillows in bed, attempting to eat and drink from a semi-prone position. Although she was tired and not really up for a late-night visit from all of them, she insisted Michael let them come in. Sam, who had been exiled to the waiting area hours earlier, had finally called his father in a panic, which was what had brought them to the hospital.

Right before they arrived, Sam had come into the room. That was the first time Suzie had seen Michael crack. He frowned at Sam and his face sort of melted into a shudder and by the time he was in front of him he was choking back tears. Sam opened his arms and Michael stepped into them, clinging to his brother. Overwhelmed by the ferocity of Michael's reaction and Sam's awkward attempt at comfort, Suzie had to look away.

Hunt took the chair next to the bed and reached for Suzie's hand, while Michael and Marguerite stood talking in low voices by the door. Sam had been playing with the channel changer and had been sucked into an episode of *Law & Order*. The sound offered a fill-in-the-blank purpose to the silence and now Sam was pressed up against the wall between the monitors and the bathroom, in an attempt to focus on the TV but not take up any more space.

Hunt patted her hand. "Don't worry, Elizabeth. You're going to be fine."

Suzie froze. "Suzie," she said gently. "Hunt, I'm Suzie."

"Of course," Hunt said, as if they were in on the same joke. "Of course you are, dear girl."

Suzie looked over at Sam, then Michael and Marguerite. Sam was engrossed in the TV and Michael and Marguerite were still bent together, deep in conversation. Suzie looked back at Hunt. "The baby is good, Hunt, see." She pointed to the monitor next to her shoulder. A tangle of electrodes and wires from beneath the sheets connected her to the screen, transmitting a constant stream of information.

Hunt relaxed back in the chair as he gazed at the screen. "That's the heart of a strong Turner baby if I ever saw one."

Suzie smiled, but she recalled several other lapses she had witnessed. At the time she had chalked them all up to Hunt's naturally scattered disposition. Always a million things going on at once, that was her father-in-law. She was relieved when Marguerite stepped forward and placed her hand on his shoulder. "We should go, Hunt. We want Suzie to rest."

Hunt nodded, totally agreeable. He did not look at Suzie again or say goodbye. Michael caught his father's arm as he passed and gave him a one-armed hug. "We'll talk tomorrow,"

Michael said, to which Hunt offered a singularly unusual grunt of acknowledgment.

As the door closed Sam looked at Michael. Suzie wasn't sure what, if anything, he had heard or noticed. Perhaps Hunt was simply tired, worried, or out of sorts. It was late, and he had been in a constant state of adjustment since his official retirement. Marguerite had been spending more time with Sam than with Hunt, consumed by the project of the restaurant. Hunt hadn't seemed to want a role other than a few routine legal issues that he took care of right away, and he had even delegated the work of budgeting and balance sheets to his accountant. Suzie ran a hand over her eyes and rubbed. It was nothing. It had to be nothing. It had been a long night.

"I should go too." Sam stood between the bed and his brother. Michael reached out a hand as if they were going to shake and then he pulled Sam to him quickly before they released.

"Would you call Mom?" Michael asked. "I just want her to know, and I'm not sure when I'll get a chance."

"Sure, I can do that."

"Thanks," Michael said softly.

Sam looked over at Suzie and joked, "You can thank me by naming my niece or nephew after me: Sam, Samantha, it works either way."

Suzie and Michael rewarded him with a laugh, and Michael said, "Is that all?"

"Oh," Suzie said, her brow wrinkling, "I'm going to miss your dinner next week!" She tried to hide a yawn, but her eyes were at half-mast.

"You can be my first takeout order." Sam waved a hand in her direction, then nudged Michael toward the chair as he opened the door to leave.

Suzie felt her limbs go limp. She felt the baby flutter-kick beneath her rib cage. Michael hunched over with his head resting near Suzie's stomach, and she picked up his hand and placed it on the right spot. The baby moved again and now there was a tight little knot there until its limbs repositioned. Suzie didn't realize she had been holding her breath until Michael spoke. "That's my boy."

"What?"

Michael shrugged and looked sheepish, his chin tucked to his chest, looking up at her from underneath heavy lids. "I was being a sexist prick. Our little girl could have that kick too." He smiled before he put his head back down on the mattress.

Suzie wound her fingers in Michael's hair. She sunk deep into the pillows and closed her eyes. She saw them as they were, united in love for each other and their unborn child. For this one moment they were protected, in a bubble. They had expected the worst and it hadn't happened. Not this time.

SEVENTEEN

One Crush Away
Bella—2011

The incessant buzzer caused Bella to sit straight up in bed, the blankets and sheets wound tightly around her limbs as if she'd been riding a bicycle in her sleep. For a minute, she had no idea where she was and her heart pounded in her ears until her eyes focused on the familiar shadows in the room. Home. She had been deeply asleep after nights of not sleeping at all. She was home. She peered at her alarm, afraid it was time to get up for work, but the clock confirmed that was hours away. This block and her building were usually quiet and she wondered if someone had been locked out and was randomly hitting buzzers. Except the consistency with which her buzzer was being hit would suggest it was more than coincidence.

She crawled from her bed and pressed the intercom. "Seriously?" she asked, her voice clogged with sleep. She hoped her anger transmitted through the ancient system and out the front stoop to the person with the excitable finger.

"Bella! Bella, it's me, Sam."

"Sam? What?"

"Sam Turner."

"Sam, I know who you are. Why are you here?"

"Can I—can we talk?"

Bella looked around the room as if someone, anyone, would tell her how bad an idea this really was. Sam probably had no idea that Ted was gone. Bella had been so embarrassed by her gigantic relationship fail that it had taken her forever to even tell Suzie, and then she begged her to keep it a secret. So for all he knew Ted could come bursting through the door. "It's almost two, do you know that?" Bella asked as she pressed the button to unlock the front door. She put her ear against the door and heard the front door open and shut and then the thud of feet on the stairs. She realized she was standing in her pajamas, and she grabbed at the first thing she saw, her mother's fur, which lived on a hook by the door.

Bella's apartment was on the top floor. She stepped out onto the landing. As Sam rounded the third floor he looked up the flight of stairs. Bella crossed and uncrossed her arms over her mother's old fur. She ruffled the tangles out of her hair with her fingers and touched the pillow crease in her cheek. Sam stopped short and just looked at her before he slowly walked up the next flight to where she was standing.

Bella rubbed at her eyes with a curled fist and blinked as he stopped on the step just below her. "Why are you here?"

"I was at the hospital with Suzie."

Her eyes widened, and she felt instantly awake. "Oh my God, no. What happened?"

"She was bleeding, and then they did something to make it stop. I think she has to be in bed for the rest of, well, you know." He hesitated. "I'm sorry, I didn't really think this out. I wanted to tell you but I guess I don't know the correct terms or—the thing is that she and the baby are okay."

"Way to bury the lede." Bella exhaled. "I'd like to kill the messenger now."

"I'm sorry. I was thinking all the way here what I was going to say and then I saw you." Sam shook his head. "I'm sorry," he said again.

"That still doesn't explain why you're here. You could have called me to tell me. Anyone could have called."

"I left my phone in the car." Sam hesitated. "Is that your mother's coat? I haven't seen that in—"

Bella stroked the fur and hugged herself harder. Of course: the night her mother died they had slept in her bed wrapped in this coat. "Sam," she said in a weary voice.

"Bella, I know I didn't have the right to say any of those things to you. I'm so sorry."

"Okay," she said slowly. "I think you already apologized."

"You wouldn't answer my calls."

"I couldn't, Sam."

"Bella—" Sam looked behind her to the open door of her apartment.

Suddenly, she understood his apprehension. "Are you here to challenge Ted to a duel? He's gone."

"What?"

"Ted. He's gone."

"When?"

"Since before Thanksgiving."

"He never came back from that writing thing?"

She sighed. "There wasn't a writing thing."

"But—" Sam hung his head as he figured out exactly what Bella was telling him. "I told you he was no good for you."

Bella's mouth twisted into a smirk. "He moved out before I came back after Thanksgiving. It was mutual." She shrugged. She hoped it appeared casual.

"Why didn't you tell me? At Thanksgiving, you should have told me."

"Why are you here, Sam?" She felt a flush start on her chest and rise up to her neck, past the fur collar.

"I never wanted to hurt you, Bella." Sam leaned against the doorframe. "I want another chance." He hesitated. "Can you give me—us—that?"

"Sam." Bella sighed. She felt an old ache in her gut. "Don't you see it was all too much? Ted had just left. You were telling me you loved me out of the blue. I just couldn't handle it." She looked at him. "You really pissed me off. Do you have any idea how long I waited to hear that from you? And it never came. So then I met Ted, only to totally give up myself in the process. I just needed some distance. From him. From you." She turned and walked back into her apartment. She needed something to do.

She heard Sam follow her in. He hesitated as he crossed over the threshold. She turned to look at him and saw that he was taking in all the packing boxes huddled against one wall. "You're moving?"

Bella gave a slight shrug. "I can't afford the rent alone."

"Talk to me," Sam said. "Please."

Bella stared at him long and hard. She shook her head. "Can you close the door?"

He did as she asked, turning the bolt.

"What happens now, Sam?" She was close enough for Sam to see she was trembling all over and she didn't care. Not anymore. He grabbed ahold of her fingers and tugged her hand, bringing her up next to him. She could smell the old fur coat mixed with the essence of Sam, his shampoo, his clothes, and his skin, his everything. She ran a tongue over her teeth, aware of her sleep breath. She placed her cheek against Sam's and said, "You're here, but what happens now?"

"I don't know," Sam whispered. "I don't know. But I miss you, Bella, all the time. I miss you so damn much." His hands were in her hair as he held her face away from his so he could look at her. "I've never felt anything for anyone like I feel for you. Not then. Not now. Not ever. Do you believe me?"

Bella wasn't moving but every molecule in her being was hurtling toward Sam. Attaching. Her lips moved against his throat, along his jawbone, and to his ear before they finally found his mouth. When Sam kissed her back it was like they were kids, fumbling, unsure of where to put their lips or tongue, of how much pressure to apply before teeth got in the way. When Sam pulled away Bella was scared that they had waited too long and that he would turn around and go. Instead Sam said, "I'm so nervous."

"Me too," she whispered.

Sam slipped his arms inside the fur coat and circled her waist. She rested her head on his shoulder. After a while they moved to her bed. The sheets and pillow were still warm from where she had been tangled in the blankets. Sam held Bella tightly and she pressed against him, relieved that she still fit. They talked in whispers even though no one could hear them. Sam told her about Suzie in the hospital bed, fiercely guarding that tiny life. He told her about Michael and how, in Sam's arms, Michael had needed him. He told her about his father, how he wondered if he was losing his mind.

As Bella told him she worried all the time how fucking fragile everything was, Sam ran his hands up the length of her body, finding his way inside the coat and under her T-shirt. Right away there was the familiar urgency between them. Bella shrugged out of the coat and sat up. Sam pulled the shirt over her head and took a nipple in his mouth as she tugged at his belt buckle and zipper. She pushed him back to climb on top of him. By then both of them were gasping for breath, neither of them able to slow down or make it last. Sam grabbed ahold of Bella's hips roughly, wanting her closer, matching her rhythm with his own.

"Look at me," she said, and so he did as both of them let go. Bella wasn't sure which of them laughed first or why, but soon they were laughing, clinging to each other, nearly crying. Both of them were breathing hard, as if they'd run a marathon. Bella pushed herself up and Sam reached to wipe the tears from her cheek. She caught his hand and held it as she tried to catch her breath.

The look Sam gave her was solemn. "I know," Sam said. "I know that I nearly blew it. I'm an idiot."

"Yup, you are." She leaned down and kissed him deeply and then pulled away. "But lucky for you I'm fond of your kind of idiot." Sam looked up at Bella. She saw him at fifteen, at sixteen, at seventeen. They had always been one crush away from each other, and yet this boy whom it felt like she had loved her entire life was now this man who was looking up at her as if she was his everything. Sam rolled her over onto her back and kissed her slowly. There were so many things Bella had to say, so many things she wanted to tell him. But not now. There would be time, much later in the quiet, there would be time.

Five weeks later Bella stood in the kitchen of Sam's restaurant wearing nothing more than an old T-shirt of his and smearing the last of the goat cheese on a slice of bread. Sam watched her as she scraped the remains of the cheese from the wrapper with her index finger and held it up by his lips. "Eat," she commanded. Sam licked the cheese from her finger.

Bella shook her head. His mother really had mastered this cheese. It was tart and creamy, flavored with a nice selection of herbs. "So good, right?" Bella took more bread and then went over to the walk-in. She bent over so that Sam could see the lacy strip of her underpants.

"Enough about the cheese!" Sam groaned. The Styrofoam cooler of goat cheese had arrived from his mother shortly after Sam had called to tell her about Suzie. It had arrived with no note, just the information sheet about the cheese and his mother's goats that was shipped with every order. It was crazy, Sam told Bella, to have any expectations where his mother was concerned; still, she confused him. Nevertheless, he and Bella had been steadily working their way through the cheese in the hours after closing each night.

Bella retrieved a platter of cold Greek chicken just as Sam slid his hands up her bare back and under the T-shirt. "Sorry, buddy, I found something else." Bella shimmied away from Sam's hands and turned around to put the chicken on the counter. She peeled back the plastic wrap and delicately picked a long strip of pepper and an olive off the top. When she saw Sam watching she dangled a piece of chicken in his face.

Sam took the chicken. Before he ate it he said, "You got a little something there." He pointed to her incisor as he popped the chicken in his mouth.

"When I get fat will you still want me?" Bella smiled and licked the lemony oil from her fingers at the same time. She took a swallow of water and felt the olive let go from her tooth.

"You have to ask?"

Bella shook her head. Every night they slept in

Bella curled with her back against his chest, as if making up for lost time.

Sam leaned across the prep table and took the chicken platter. They had become midnight food raiders since the restaurant officially opened a month ago. Bella never imagined how thrilling the routine of an ordinary day could be. Every night after closing Sam cleaned the kitchen and then prepped for the next day before crawling upstairs to their tiny room. Bella would wait for him in bed, the only real piece of furniture they had, among a fan of students' papers. As soon as she heard him on the stairs she collected the papers into a pile, removed her glasses, and placed them on an overturned box that served as a temporary nightstand. Sam would take three steps into the room before collapsing facedown next to her on the pillow, bringing with him the slight whiff of what he'd cooked that day along with the bleach he used to wipe down the surfaces of the kitchen.

Bella would climb on top of his back and knead her fingers into the deep tissue, softening the knots in his shoulders. While her hands worked she asked him about the day: what he cooked, what people had liked, and what he had eaten, which, despite the multitude of dishes he'd made, usually amounted to nothing more than tastes, and his stomach would always growl on cue. Somehow they managed to leave the bed and go down to the kitchen for a snack before going back upstairs, where sex took on the flavors of whatever they'd eaten that night.

They had almost lost each other—a fact Bella was reminded of twice a day when she saw her toothbrush next to his in a cup on the sink. It was still a miracle to both of them, she knew, that somehow she had found her way back. They had moved all of her uff from the apartment she had shared with Ted back to her er's house and into her old room because the space above the tavern was so small. Bella's father appeared to like Sam no better now than he had when Sam first broke his daughter's heart. But Bella believed her father would soften. In the last few weeks her father had popped into the restaurant after he got off the train, often sitting at the bar for a beer and whatever special Sam had made that day. Bella knew the small talk was minimal, but Sam claimed to have hope that they could work up to complete sentences soon.

Sam wanted Bella to have a place of her own, but he didn't want her to leave him, so he hauled an old door and a couple of sawhorses upstairs and made them into a desk jammed into the eave. When he told her the desk was for her writing she had cried. They slept twisted together on the hammock-like mattress every night, and Bella commuted to the city three times a week to teach her classes at Hunter. It was an arrangement that worked for now because they were making up for lost time. But Bella knew, eventually, they would have to live like grown ups and get a real place.

Bella replaced the plastic wrap on the chicken and put it back in the walk-in. Sam cleared the counter of the goat cheese wrappers and crumbs and met her by the light switch. He slipped an arm around her waist and turned off the lights before they started up the stairs. Bella felt a pressure in her chest when she looked at Sam, her heart slamming against her rib cage in anticipation of what would come next. A feeling she knew would never go away.

✦ ✦ ✦

Suzie stayed on bed rest for ten weeks before she delivered a healthy baby boy, Leo Samuel Turner, three weeks early, on her birthday. Bella and Sam went to visit them in the hospital when Leo was just a few hours old. Leo had a head of dark curly hair and, according to Sam, the features of Sam and Michael's grand-father, their father's father, who had lived to be one hundred and one years old. Bella insisted to Sam that he keep that bit to him-self. She told him all babies, no matter the gender, looked like little old men to everyone but their parents.

"Except ours," Sam said, surprising Bella. She remembered Ted's refusal to even entertain the thought of children. She hadn't even gone there yet—thinking about children that potentially belonged to Sam. But now that he put it out there it made the most perfect sense. Of course they would have children one day.

The elevator doors opened and Marguerite and Hunt joined them at the nursery window. "The doctor is in with Suzie, so I went and did some shopping downstairs," Marguerite an-nounced, waving a baby blue teddy bear. "It's so silly, I know." Her eyes were watery. She tugged on Hunt's sleeve. "Hunt, look at that precious boy."

"He is handsome," Hunt agreed.

Bella saw Sam glance over at his father. She wasn't sure if Hunt was looking at the right baby, although she supposed it didn't really matter at this stage.

Suddenly Hunt reached over and touched Bella on the top of the head. "The first time I met you, you were in your mother's arms." He screwed up his face as if he was thinking hard, and then he dropped his hand and relaxed into a soft smile. "Sam had been hit by a swing here." He touched the spot above his left eyebrow and Bella saw Sam mirror him, searching for the micro-scopic remains of a scar with his fingertips. "And you were crying because he was bloody and hysterical." He laughed. "Your mother handed me a towel. I think Sam's howling ended the picnic."

Sam shook his head and smirked. "I still have that ability."

"Elizabeth was so angry with me because I had taken Michael to look at the ducks when I was supposed to be keeping an eye on Sam at the swings." He turned to Sam. "I had no idea you saw me leave, and that you wanted to come with us and started to follow." He blinked hard several times before he turned back to Bella. "And Elizabeth said that was my problem. That I never paid enough attention to Sam."

Bella shuffled her feet and inched closer to Sam. Marguerite glanced quickly between the two of them, and then back at Leo. No one said anything for a long moment, and then Bella looked up and saw Michael walking down the hall. She nudged Sam with her hip. Michael had a couple of days' growth of beard, and his eyes were shiny with fatigue, but he was grinning as if it were Christmas morning. As he came toward them he tossed a tangerine back and forth in his hands.

"Here." He handed Sam the tangerine. "I'm going in to get Leo and bring him to Suzie. Everything's good. Everything's great." He bounced up and down on his feet.

"Sam?" Hunt said loudly, still waiting for an answer.

Michael's head jerked up as if it had been pulled by a string. He gave Sam a quick look that Bella couldn't interpret.

"Everything is good, Dad," Sam said reassuringly.

Marguerite said, "Michael is going to get Leo and bring him to Suzie now, Hunt."

"Leo?"

Michael cupped his father's elbow and turned him toward the window. He guided his father's hand so that it was pressed flat against the glass, hovering over the baby. "Here, Dad. Here's your grandson."

In that moment Bella knew that something was really wrong

with Hunt. That Michael had maybe known the details and that he was keeping it from Sam.

"Come here, Sammy," Michael said over his shoulder. He put Sam's hand over their father's on the glass. "Stay," he commanded as he pushed open the swinging doors to the nursery. None of them moved. Bella could feel nervous energy coming from Sam and Marguerite. When Michael reappeared he was wearing a smock and his hands were gloved and he was lifting his son from the plastic bassinet. Leo's head was covered by a blue cap and his body was mummified in blankets. Only his squishy pink grandpa face was visible. Michael held Leo aloft on the other side of the glass.

"Dad," Sam whispered, "there he is, there's Michael's son."

Michael looked at Sam and then to their father. When Bella saw the expression on Michael's face she wanted to run. Hunt was crying silently, the tears flowing freely down his cheeks. He didn't move to wipe them.

"Dad?" Sam prompted. "Dad?"

"You believe me, right?"

It took a second for Bella to realize that Hunt was still trapped in the earlier conversation. She had no idea whether Hunt even noticed Leo. Slowly she watched Sam release his father's hand from the glass as Michael put Leo back in the bassinet. They watched Michael adjust the tiny blue cap and tuck in the tails of the blankets. Bella thought of the thousands of nights Michael would spend tucking in his son before the boy wouldn't need him anymore. She remembered how Sam had told her that was one of his fondest memories from when he was still small enough to share a room with Michael: their father coming into their room carrying with him the exotic scents of the city, crouching down between their beds and asking them each to recall one good thing and one bad thing from their day.

"I believe you, Dad," Sam whispered.

Bella watched as Hunt's tears darkened his shirt collar. She saw Marguerite turn away quickly and fumble in her handbag.

"I believe you," Sam said again.

Bella held her breath, waiting for Hunt to acknowledge what Sam had said. Marguerite produced a tissue from her bag and stuffed it into Hunt's hand. "Hunt," Marguerite said. Her voice was loud and a little sharp. "Hunt."

Hunt turned to her and smiled. "Oh, what a day," he said. "What a day to remember."

Bella could see the relief in Sam's posture; his shoulders and spine relaxed.

"I'm hungry," Hunt announced.

Sam pulled Michael's tangerine from his pocket. He looked as if he was about to hand it to his father but then he began to peel the thick skin himself. The sharp tang of citrus filled the air. Bella watched Sam break apart the tangerine. He offered half the sections to his father. Hunt popped the entire thing in his mouth and began to chew. After he had swallowed Sam pulled apart the remaining sections one by one and fed them to his father. They all stood there for as long as it took, silent and waiting. There was nothing else to do.

EIGHTEEN

Fragile
Suzie—2011

When Suzie got out of the shower Leo had on his thinking face. He was staring wide-eyed, curled up on Michael's chest, his cotton-covered bottom perched up in the air. When he saw her he pursed his lips but he didn't protest, so she crossed the room and pulled on a pair of sweatpants and a T-shirt. She left off the bra. There was no need to be constantly fumbling with the hooks.

Michael's arms were wrapped firmly around the baby, keeping him in place, but his head was back against the wall, his eyes closed and his mouth slightly open. Residency and a fellowship, the life of a doctor, had trained him to sleep anywhere and at any time. Suzie had joked that a medical residency was the only thing that could possibly prepare you for the sleep deprivation an infant brought into your life.

Three months into this and Suzie finally was beginning to feel like a mother. She went over and lifted Leo off Michael's chest, holding him high against her shoulder. "Hey, little man, hey there," she murmured against his silky cap of hair. She felt him rooting around, his mouth open against her shoulder. He settled for gumming the skin with his sticky jaws.

She glanced back at Michael. He was awake now but he looked out of it, and no wonder, considering he had just worked a twelve-hour shift. An hour earlier, when he had walked in the door, she had been sitting in bed with Leo resting on the tent of her knees. You would never have known it by their son's sweet demeanor and spastic movements of joy, but he had been up for most of the night. Suzie calculated she had gotten roughly three hours of sleep in fifteen-minute increments. Her nipples were sore from nursing and she was pretty sure she smelled, since she couldn't remember the last time she'd showered. Michael had taken one look at her as he reached for Leo and urged her to take a shower. She knew he was exhausted but wanted to spend time with Leo.

Now Suzie said to Michael, "Go to bed."

Michael held out a hand. "I want you to come with me."

Suzie smiled. She would love to crawl back into the warm bed with Michael and sleep. Even if the sheets smelled musky and the bed was never made anymore. Last week she had found a dirty diaper under her pillow. Thankfully it was only pee and had been rewrapped securely with the sticky tabs. But still. A diaper in bed? Ugh.

She shook her head. "Little man is happy and I'm going to put him in that bouncy thing and try to make sense of our lives. Or at least take out the garbage."

Michael shook his head in protest and yawned.

"Go," Suzie said again, feeling energized by the shower and the smell of shampoo in her clean hair. "Go."

She watched as Michael hoisted himself from the couch. He undid the buttons of his shirt as he walked to the bedroom, tugging it from the waistband of his pants. At the corner of the bed

326 + ✦ Robin Antalek

he kicked off his shoes, unzipped his fly, let his pants drop to the floor, and then fell facedown onto the mattress. Suzie turned off the lights and shut the bedroom door.

Suzie looked at Leo. He was watching her, one corner of his mouth turned up in a half grin, his slick little baby-seal head wobbling only slightly on his strong neck. "Come on, buddy boy, let Daddy sleep. I'm going to teach you things in the kitchen that will make all the girls love you one day." She hoisted him on her hip, picked up the bouncy seat with her free hand, and set Leo up on the floor by her feet near the sink.

Several hours later the dishwasher was humming, the sink and surfaces were clear, the garbage was gone and with it all of the mysterious and moldy takeout containers from the refrigerator shelves. Suzie had stopped to feed Leo and put him back in the bouncy seat, and then she had dumped some pasta sauce into a saucepan and put water on to boil. It wasn't much, and she couldn't help but imagine what Sam would have to say about the choice of meal, but at least she and Michael would have a civilized lunch. She even went so far as to set two places at the table, reasoning that Leo, now dozing in the bouncy seat, would be good for at least another hour.

She was going through a pile of mail, paying bills, ripping up junk, when the bedroom door opened and Michael appeared in his boxers and a T-shirt. His face still had sleep creases and he stretched as he shuffled toward them. Suzie pointed to sleeping Leo and Michael's expression softened. He lifted his nose and sniffed the air. "Is this what heaven smells like?"

"Tomato sauce and disinfectant?"

Michael nodded and Suzie laughed. She got up to dump the pasta into the boiling water and poured Michael a cup of fresh coffee. He came up behind her, slipped his hands under the giant

T-shirt, and cupped her full breasts in his hands. "I love nursing," he said as he kissed the side of her head.

Suzie laughed. Her first instinct was to bat his hands away but she missed him, she missed this kind of touching. They had gone back to having sex when her doctor had cleared her at six weeks, but with their schedules it wasn't remotely a regular occurrence.

"How fast can you make this happen?" Suzie joked. But as she leaned into him she could feel that Michael's erection pressing into her lower back was serious.

Michael drew out her nipples with his fingers. Suzie gasped and felt them tingle, not unlike when Leo's mouth latched on and her breasts flooded with milk. Abruptly Michael dropped his hands and tugged on the corner of her shirt. Suzie reached to lower the flame under the pasta and followed Michael to the couch. He slid her sweatpants over her hips and down around her ankles as Suzie guided Michael inside of her. The sense of urgency was overwhelming and exciting. She closed her eyes and lifted her hips, meeting his thrusts with her own. She felt warmth spread in her lower belly, a delightful pressure that built quickly as they moved.

Within minutes Michael came hard, moaning deeply into the crook of her neck. Suzie laughed, shushing him, making him laugh as well, his shoulders and chest trembling against her. It felt like they were teenagers, rushing through sex for fear they'd be caught. Only now the person catching them was all of three months old.

Suzie held on to Michael tightly, her hands clasped against his lower back, enjoying the weight of him pressed against the length of her. "I'm sorry," he murmured into her hair. "I couldn't help myself."

Suzie ran a hand through his hair. He was still half inside her.

The space between her thighs felt wet and warm and she didn't want to get up, would have liked him to reach down and touch her until she came, but she smelled the sauce bubbling away and was sure the pasta was turning into a starchy mess and she didn't want to wake Leo. "I love you," she whispered into Michael's ear.

"I love you more, Suzie," Michael echoed as he slid a hand down her body, over her still puffy belly, and down between her legs until it was her turn to moan. "I love you more."

Later, Michael held Leo on his lap while they ate the pasta in front of the TV. A baseball game was on and Michael was explaining the rules to Leo, who was heavy-lidded. Suzie took advantage of the quiet and cleared the plates, cleaned the kitchen, and turned off the lights even though Michael protested her getting up to clean. There was a secret part of her that liked the fact that she was able to tackle so much in a day, conquer the Mount Everest of domesticity.

Michael got up and carried Leo to the crib in the corner of their bedroom. He looked over at Suzie and she nodded. It was time Leo got used to falling asleep there instead of in his parents' arms. Suzie held her breath as she watched Michael lean over the lowered bar and place Leo on his back in the center of the mattress. He draped a light cotton blanket around Leo's lower body.

Suzie glanced at their bed. Michael had made it up with fresh sheets and she couldn't wait to put her head on the pillow. He must have done it after he took a shower, while she was finishing up their meal. Her heart squeezed and her eyes filled with tears. Her hormones were still out of whack, but she was also crazy in love with her husband and her son. If someone had told her years ago that one day all this would be possible, she would have laughed in his face. She hadn't come from this; she had never known this as normal. She had imagined it was for other people, certainly not people like her.

The travesty of this all was that her mother, still sober and perfectly able, had seen Leo only once, while Hunt, who had been with Leo multiple times in his three months on earth, only sometimes knew who Leo was. It broke Suzie's heart to watch Hunt's slow degeneration. The moments she had seen the panic in Hunt's eyes haunted her.

Of all the kindnesses Hunt had shown her, the one Suzie would always remember was after the last miscarriage. They had been at Paradox Lake and he had asked her to go out in the canoe. Everyone had been tiptoeing around her, afraid to upset her even more, and while she understood why, she hated being pitied. The canoe ride was the last thing she had wanted to do, but she had gone because the alternative was being stuck in the cabin on one of the twin beds in the stifling attic, berating the state of her body and all that it rejected.

Hunt had offered to let her sit and not paddle; he said he would do all the work. But Suzie had refused to be idle. She took a paddle and fell in sync with Hunt as they traversed the length of the lake. When they reached a grove where papery river birch clustered in feathery clumps along the banks, Hunt guided them into the shallow water and presented Suzie with an old red plaid thermos that had been rolling around by his feet. Suzie took a large gulp and winced: the thermos was filled with Hunt's special summer mix of bourbon and sweet tea, and the liquor burned her throat.

They had sat in silence, watching the great blue heron on an island nest built for one. Suzie was aware of the ripples of fish beneath the surface of the water and the thick, velvety push of the waves as they rocked back and forth in the canoe, passing the thermos to each other. Eventually Hunt screwed the lid back on the thermos and lifted his paddle and they left the sanctuary of trees and headed back to the camp. Suzie had let something go that afternoon, and Hunt had given her the space to do it.

Michael turned to her now, a triumphant look on his face. He pointed to the bed and Suzie crawled gratefully up the length of the mattress until her head hit the pillow. Those three broken hours of sleep she'd had the night before had finally caught up to her and she knew her eyelids would not remain open for much longer. Michael settled in behind her, his familiar weight fitting against her curves, his arm tossed possessively over her hip, for a late-afternoon nap. Suzie drifted off to sleep listening to the sounds of her husband and son snuffling every so often in their sleep, and realized that if she could freeze a moment in time this would be it.

Suzie finally agreed to meet her father. Ignoring him was taking too much effort. The calls and the gifts that went unanswered and returned, the silence from her mother. She had told herself she was past caring, but then she looked at Leo. She wanted to be able to tell him one day that she allowed him to give her father a chance. That she didn't make that choice for him. She wasn't sure how far she would be able to take it, but, as she had told Michael, she was just going to commit to this one time. Michael had hugged her for a long time after she had told him that, and she knew without his saying anything that he was thinking of his own father.

She pushed Leo in his stroller, expertly navigating the lunch crowd perched on benches, swan necks bent over their cell phones, around to the boathouse in Central Park. At first she couldn't find him. It had been years; the last time in her mother's hospital room, and that time, like most times, anger and exhaustion had colored her impression of him. When she saw him standing by the water in a dark jacket he looked shorter and older, his full head of bushy hair now almost entirely silver. From the hunch of his shoulders he gave off an air of defeat. At one time that would have given Suzie a great deal of satisfaction, but now she just felt sad and tired.

Her father smiled as he walked toward them. When Suzie stopped he knelt down in front of the stroller and stared for a long time. Suzie pulled back the hood and fumbled with the blankets around Leo's sleeping face.

Her father stood slowly. "What a man. What a fine little man, Suzie. Mazel tov."

Suzie nodded, unable to say anything. Her father sounded like his father, a man who had died when Suzie was nine. Her grandfather's speech had been liberally sprinkled with Yiddish phrases, and to him she had always been his little bird, his *faigelah,* as he called her. From the few times she had visited his apartment in Brooklyn she recalled the peculiar odor of boiled eggs and fish—that and her father's disdain for her grandfather's refusal to give up his old world ways, which Suzie assumed now meant his religious traditions.

"Was there a bris?"

Suzie shook her head. "Circumcision in the hospital."

"Of course," her father said quickly as he shoved his hands in his pockets. Leo, waking up, made a little squawking noise, and Suzie's father said, "Would it be easier to walk?"

Grateful for something to do, Suzie pushed ahead without answering. Her father caught up to her left elbow. "How is Michael? His job must be challenging, especially with a new son at home."

"He's a wonderful father," Suzie snapped.

"I wouldn't expect any less, Suzie Q."

Suzie flinched at his use of her nickname. Her heart was racing. She needed to take a breath and calm down. "It's, you know, hard right now. We always feel tired and never feel like there's enough time. But we both know this will pass soon enough. I return to work next week."

"I see."

"Did you think I was going to give up being a doctor?"

"Not at all. I know how hard you worked."

"You do?"

"Your mother talks about you. And I know you, Suzie. You are my child. You have my work ethic."

"I do?"

Her father laughed. "Yes, you do." He paused. "Was that a serious question?"

Suzie shrugged. Her entire life he had always been *at work*, but she had never actually imagined him working, given everything else he was doing.

"I appreciate you seeing me, Suzie. I know you could have chosen not to."

"Well, with Leo," Suzie started. "I never wanted him to think I kept him from his grandfather."

"That sounds like you might be willing to try this again? Another meeting?"

Suzie stopped pushing the carriage and looked at her father. "I don't trust you. We don't have a relationship. But I don't want my child to grow up without a grandfather, so I'm here. Can that be enough for today?"

Her father stared at her and she stared back. There was a shadow of salt-and-pepper stubble on his jawline. "Absolutely, that can be enough. I'll do whatever you wish, Suzie."

Suzie nodded. "Can I tell you something? I hate tennis. I never played tennis. All those times I told you about matches I'd won? All those times I took your money for a new racket?" Suzie swallowed hard. Her ears felt hot. "I never set foot on a court. I wanted to see if you ever showed up at a match. I wanted you to catch me in the lie. I wanted you to care enough. But you never did."

Her father exhaled. He didn't seem to have anything to say in response. Suzie leaned on the bar and pushed the stroller hard so he had to work hard to catch up to her. By the time he did, she could hear his labored breathing. But he didn't complain and he didn't ask her to slow down. He matched her pace and they continued the loop out of the park in silence.

Bella's bright red coat was visible as soon as Suzie exited the hospital. She was already in line at the falafel stand across the street, holding a place for their dinner date. Whenever Bella was teaching late they tried to connect at least once a week. When Suzie had been on maternity leave that often meant Bella's keeping her company while she nursed. Slowly they'd progressed to coffee and walks with Leo in the stroller, and now that Suzie was back at work, a quick dinner. Suzie had been back at the hospital for a month now and she missed Leo and Michael even though they were both there at the hospital with her. At least Leo in the hospital day care and Michael on staff made it easier for her to steal moments with each of them during the day, something she wouldn't have if they had left Leo with a sitter at home.

She waved to Bella and crossed the street, breaking away from the chaos of the hospital entrance. Bella gave her an up-and-down appraisal as she handed her a falafel sandwich. "You are going to freeze, Suzie." Bella's cheeks were as red as her coat from the cold and most of her pale hair was stuffed under a bulky knitted cap.

Suzie glanced down at her lightweight cotton doctor's coat; underneath she wore black wool pants and a black turtleneck sweater. She had run from the hospital as soon as she could get away for dinner, afraid to go to the break-room for her coat in case anyone else stopped her to consult or chat. Michael and Leo had already left for the day. Suzie was on call that night and anticipated a long, restless night on the break-room couch. "I don't even feel it," she said, unwrapping the sandwich and taking a big bite. It was true that the stifling air in the hospital was overwhelming. Her sinuses were constantly clogged, her head stuffed with cotton. She worried that she was setting Leo up for a lifetime of colds by sticking him in the day care. She took a deep breath. The cold felt refreshing. She had to stop beating herself up.

Bella shook her head and said jokingly, "Doctors."

Suzie shrugged. They walked the half block down to a little park and took the only empty bench. To Suzie it looked like an outpost of the hospital: a mix of workers, maybe some families, everyone united in escaping the hospital air for a little while.

"How's my favorite baby?" Bella asked, licking hummus from her fingertips.

"Delicious," Suzie sighed. "He's the best little man ever. He smiles all the time and talks—well, you know, I think he's talking. We totally understand each other. He rolls over back to front, tries to get up on all fours and move."

Bella giggled. "How's the other man in your life? And you can leave out all the cute things he does like talking and rolling over."

Suzie laughed. "He's the best dad. He gets up with Leo if I've been on call, he changes diapers, he gives baths, he feeds him a bottle now that I don't nurse all the time. He does this cute thing where he gets very serious and has what he calls 'man talks' with Leo. Last one I overheard was about the importance of saying you're sorry." She frowned. "Sometimes I feel like I don't do enough for him. I wish I could take away the stress and the pressure of work, Hunt . . ."

Bella chewed and swallowed a bite of pita. "I don't know how much longer Marguerite is going to be able to keep this up. Keeping tabs on him is getting to be difficult. And I know we all try to pitch in, but he really prefers her. But the tricky thing is that Hunt's good days still outnumber the bad, so it's easy to get fooled into thinking everything is okay and then bam, it turns."

"That's typical," Suzie said slowly. "While the patient is cognizant he learns to compensate for the times he is less so." Suzie took the last bite of falafel and reached for the coffee on the bench to wash it down. "There's a drug trial. Michael asked Hunt's doctor and he thinks Hunt is too symptomatic to see any results, but he's willing to give it a shot, probably more for Michael than Hunt." She paused. "I know this is so irrational but when I think that my own father is perfectly fine when someone like Hunt . . ."

"What's happening there?"

"With my father?" Suzie shook her head hard and felt her ponytail loosen from the elastic. "We've seen each other twice." She hesitated, reaching up to secure the wad of thick curls at the base of her neck. "I'm trying." She shrugged and then admitted, "Not as hard as I should." She held her coffee cup up and allowed the steam to warm her face. "It's the age-old story, right? The doctor can heal everyone but herself. I spend all day talking to people about relationships, unraveling the threads, repairing, making amends. And I can't seem to get there."

Bella put her arm around Suzie's shoulders and squeezed.

"Life was so much simpler when we had nothing to do but hang out at the pool and check out the cute boys." She frowned. "You feel too skinny. You need more meat on your bones."

"You sound like Sam."

"What can I say? He's rubbing off on me. I'm going to get him to cook for you."

Suzie laughed. "Aren't we basically still checking out the same boys?" She glanced at her watch. "I've got to get back." She and Bella stood and gathered their trash. They hugged goodbye and Suzie ran back across the street, dodging a glut of taxis at the curb. At the sliding doors she stopped and looked back. Bella was still standing there watching her. They grinned and waved and then Suzie slipped inside the hospital.

✦ ✦ ✦

She could hear their voices as soon as she entered the restaurant. Michael had left Suzie and Leo with Marguerite and Hunt at the house and said he was going to see Sam. That was three hours ago and he wasn't answering his cell phone.

Suzie left Leo with Marguerite and decided to find out what was going on. She pretended to Marguerite that Michael had called and asked her to meet him at the restaurant. Suzie didn't know if she was very convincing, but she didn't want Marguerite to worry about anything else.

The brothers were surprised when she walked into the kitchen. Neither pretended to be happy, neither of them smiled. They were on either side of a stainless steel table. Michael was still wearing his coat, despite the kitchen's being overly warm, and his face and neck were flushed a deep red. Sam, in a T-shirt and apron, busied himself with chopping a pile of celery and onions into a fine dice. Michael looked down at the table and watched the blade of the knife move up and down.

"It's starting to snow," Suzie said. The heat in the kitchen hit her like a wall of fire. "What's going on?"

"I was telling Sam I supported Marguerite's idea of selling the house."

Sam's head came up sharply and he gave Michael a look that implied that was the very simple version of whatever had been going on between them. Suzie looked from one to the other of the brothers. "Did you have another idea, Sam?"

"No, no, I obviously will support whatever Marguerite wants to do. I just feel like taking Dad out of the last familiar place he knows, well, it's like we are saying this is the end."

Michael tapped the table with his index finger. His voice was scratchy and he sounded exhausted. "That's not going to make a difference. His doctor—"

"I'm tired of hearing the bullshit doctor excuse. Be his son, okay? I know what I see. I'm here more than you." Sam bit his lip. "I'm not willing to say this is it."

"Michael." Suzie jumped in, putting a hand on her husband's arm. "I know what Sam is saying and you do too. He sees Hunt's comfort level, and the familiar makes it easier." She stopped and then said, "But, Sam, you know, we all know, his disease is degenerative. With a schedule of its own unique genetic making. For all that we do know, we really know nothing."

"He's comfortable now as he goes in and out," Michael said. "But soon—"

"Comfortable?" Sam shook his head. "Let's wait until we get to 'soon' and then decide." Sam pointed his knife at Michael. "You have no idea how long. No one knows."

Michael hung his head. "You're right. But if we wait too late to start the process, it's going to be worse." He looked over at Suzie, then back at Sam. "I'm the last guy who wants to give up, Sammy," he added softly.

Suzie watched Sam's shoulders sag. She bit her lip. She didn't want to get between the brothers. They both had a point. They both were right. They both were stubborn. "Is Bella back yet?" she asked, hoping to change the subject.

Sam gave her a quick smile. "It's the night before break and she was going out for drinks, so probably not until later."

Michael turned to her and asked, "Is Leo okay?"

Suzie nodded. "When I left the house Marguerite was down on the floor chasing him and he was giggling."

Michael and Sam both broke into easy smiles at the mention of Leo.

"I'm starved," Suzie said. "Are we getting food from you?" she asked Sam.

"It's all ready to go." Sam pointed to the walk-in coolers.

"Aren't you coming to eat with us?" She looked over at Michael and widened her eyes.

"Dude," Michael said. "Come on, Sammy."

"You only love me for my food." Sam squinted at him; there was a slight smile on his lips. "I need some time to wrap it all up here."

Suzie turned to Michael. "Why don't you take Marguerite's car and I'll help Sam? Go spend some time with Hunt."

"Are you sure?"

Suzie nodded. She wanted to give the brothers space so they wouldn't walk into the house with the stale air of their argument. "We'll be there soon, go on."

Michael came close to give her a hug and Suzie could feel the heat rising off his body. He put a hand on her hip and she leaned into him as he pressed his lips against her forehead. He looked over at Sam and shrugged. "I don't mean to come off as a dick."

"You just are," Sam shot back with a grin. "Tell Marguerite to put the oven on three hundred and fifty degrees."

"Okay," Michael said. He headed for the door. When he was halfway out he said, over his shoulder, "Takes one to know one." As the door swung closed Suzie could hear him laughing.

Suzie smiled at Sam, who shook his head, but he was chuckling too. However differently Michael and Sam saw the world, now they seemed to find a way to come together in the end. Ever since Leo had been born, really ever since that day Sam had rushed her to the hospital, something had changed about the way the three of them saw one another. Suzie wasn't sure if Sam had ever forgiven her for what a brat she had been at fifteen, but at least it didn't feel as if it was always the only thing between them anymore.

"What can I do?" Suzie asked.

Sam scooped the onions and celery into a bowl and was fitting a film of plastic wrap over the top. He directed her to the walk-in, where she removed two pans of lasagna, one vegetable and one traditional. When she came back Sam had loaded bread and salad and squat plastic containers of oil and vinegar into a large basket lined with linen towels. They put it all in the back of Sam's dented Subaru.

It was really snowing now, and Suzie was glad she and Michael had left the city earlier than they originally had intended. Snow would only complicate the night-before-Thanksgiving crunch. Sam drove slowly, crouched over the wheel as if he were too tall for the car. The wipers were going at full speed, but even so the snow stuck to the windshield, making visibility difficult. It was probably less than four miles to the house, but they were crawling forward so slowly it felt as if they were moving backward. Suzie could hear the rumble of the salt trucks and the plows, but they were nowhere to be seen.

Suzie looked over at Sam. "Crazy, huh? How did this happen so fast?"

Sam squinted at the windshield and turned up the defroster. "Haven't you noticed that's how life is?" He shrugged. "All the good things happen fast."

Suzie nodded slowly and looked out the side window. She had left her cell phone in Marguerite's car and she knew that Sam didn't carry one. "Well, at least we won't starve."

Sam laughed. "Right."

Suzie shifted in her seat. "The last time you gave me a ride it was to the hospital."

"Seriously?"

"Sure, when are we ever alone together?" After she said it there was an awkward silence between them. Suzie hadn't meant anything by it, but now it was out there. She paused, searching for something to say. "Do you think Bella will make it home?"

"Of course, why not?" Sam frowned, still staring intently at the windshield. "This won't last forever."

"You are so calm."

"What?" Sam looked at her quickly before focusing his attention back on the road. "No, I'm just being logical: this can't last forever. Bella will come home. Tomorrow will be Thanksgiving, I'll bring the turkey, my dad will call me Michael."

"Really? Hunt calls you Michael?"

Sam rapped his fingertips on the steering wheel. "Some days are better than others. But there are times that no matter what I say or do, he insists I'm Michael and I know I have to just give up. He refuses to believe he has a son named Sam."

"He has a son named Sam. We all know that."

"Tell that to my father." Sam grinned. "I'm kidding."

"Can I ask you something?" Suzie paused. "What ever happened to those pictures?"

"What?"

Suzie cleared her throat. "The pictures of all the neighborhood moms. Michael told me once, a very long time ago, that you got rid of the pictures."

Sam opened his mouth and then closed it. He sighed. "I picked them up. My mother was calling my name and the last thing I wanted was for her to come out of the house and see the pictures. I didn't know yet. I didn't know she had decided that day to leave us and that she was getting the luggage out for herself, not for what I thought was some surprise vacation. So I ran down the steps off the porch and just started picking them up."

Suzie stared at him, openmouthed. It couldn't have been a coincidence that Sam and Michael's mother had left the same day Suzie and her family had. Had her father known that?

"I picked up the box from the road and I just ran from one to the other of the photos until I had them all. Don't ask me how I knew I did, but I guess it was because of all the times we had looked at them."

Suzie felt the shame of those afternoons in her old basement creep up. "I'm so sorry."

"We were kids," Sam said. "I don't blame you."

Floored by Sam's kindness, Suzie said nothing.

"Lucky for me, and for you, I suppose, all hell broke loose that afternoon when my mother put her suitcases in the car and told my father she was leaving. No one paid any attention to me for weeks. Believe me, the shoebox of photos was nothing. A few weeks later my father and I went up to Paradox and I took the box up there with me."

"Are they—?"

"No." The car lurched forward as Sam stepped on the gas. Suzie put a hand on the dashboard as the seat belt cut across her shoulder. The car in front of them had finally turned. The snow was getting lighter. Suzie could actually read the street signs: three more blocks to go.

"What did you do?"

"I forgot about them, as crazy it sounds, until a few weekends before high school graduation. Michael, my father, and I had gone up there for one last hurrah." He looked over at Suzie. "They had been stuck in the back of a drawer where I guess I had shoved them. I put them in the fire pit and lit a match." He made a gesture with his hand. "Poof."

They turned into the driveway. The way the snow had fallen it appeared as if the walks and roof were dusted in frosting. All the lights in the house were on. Suzie could see movement behind the curtains and she imagined Michael and Leo waiting for her. She looked at Sam. He was hunched over the steering wheel, peering up at the house. She imagined he was thinking about Hunt and Michael and maybe even Elizabeth, and about all the life they had lived inside those walls.

She saw them as they were that day. Fifteen and so unsure of everything and at the same time so cocky. She remembered what it had been like to cross the street and walk up those porch steps to hand him the envelope. Her knees had been shaky; she thought she might throw up. When he had hugged her she didn't want to let go. She wanted to hide. She wanted to run to Bella. She wanted to tell Sam everything as much as she wanted to destroy the evidence. She knew it wasn't going to work in Massachusetts. It wasn't going to work anywhere. Everything, all of it, had been some cruel joke.

"Hey," Sam said, touching her on the elbow. "It's all okay."

Suzie blinked. "It is?"

"Absolutely." He slipped the keys out of the ignition. "You ready?"

Suzie nodded. Her stomach rumbled. She wanted to hug her husband and her son. She reached over and touched Sam on the cheek. She said nothing because there was nothing left to say. They looked at each other for a minute and then Suzie dropped her hand and fumbled with the door handle. Sam got out his side, opened the trunk, and handed Suzie the pans of lasagna. He took the basket and she followed behind him, tracing his footsteps through the snowy walk up the porch steps and to the front door.

NINETEEN

Home
Sam—2012

Sam's mother and father were together on a bench in the backyard. For the longest time they had been sitting there quietly without moving or talking. His mother held his father's hand in her lap. Sam had no idea what they had to say to each other after all these years, or even if his father had any level of understanding. Perhaps this would be the one time in recent days and months when the pieces of his mind had reshuffled in his favor.

Above him Sam heard Marguerite's footsteps in the bedroom. The master suite was directly over the kitchen. It had been Marguerite who suggested they include Sam's mother in Leo's first birthday celebration. Sam wondered now if she was regretting that invitation.

From the living room Sam heard Bella making her best effort to entertain Tom. As fellow writers and teachers they seemed to be comparing notes in a genial manner.

Sam checked his time. On the large kitchen island he had placed the containers of food they had transported from the restaurant: orzo salad, beet salad, red potatoes in a lemon dill sauce, tomato jam, homemade spicy mayo, a sweet mustard, garlic pickles from Delancey, a selection of cheese, including Elizabeth's goat cheese, spiced nuts, and platters of fruit. In the refrigerator Sam had placed tequila-lime marinated chicken and a couple of dozen patties made from a blend of pork, veal, and beef, all from a farm in the Catskills. There were also brown paper sacks of cornmeal-dusted rolls that looked like miniature crowns; Sam had thought they would delight the birthday boy, who had just a few teeth and gums of steel.

Michael had called to say that they were running late. They were bringing Suzie's mother with them and Leo had taken a longer nap than expected. They wanted him happy for the party so they had let him sleep. Truthfully, Sam had never seen Leo unhappy. He was a little Buddha of a baby, as pleased to be passed to strangers as he was in his mother's arms. Even left on his own plopped on a blanket with a circle of toys, he greeted everyone and everything as if it had the capacity to bring him joy.

Everyone had wanted to do something for Leo and Suzie's shared birthday. Ruthie and Mindy were in charge of the birthday cake, while Peter Chang and Frankie Cole wanted to handle refreshments and decorations. Celia was planning on playing the guitar and singing a song, with words provided by Bella. Johnny was bringing some surprise guests that he promised would be leaving with him and wouldn't eat any of the food, whatever that meant. Sam checked the time again and hoped some of them would be arriving soon.

Sam picked up two large galvanized buckets and carried them out to the patio. He had brought several cases of the handmade sodas he ordered from a place in Williamsburg and used at the restaurant, and he filled one tub with the wavy glass bottles of sassafras, grapefruit, and mulberry fizz. He tried hard not to stare over at his parents, but his mother caught him looking and gave a small nod of acknowledgment. Sam ripped open the bags of ice and the contents crashed loudly into the tin, but neither of them looked over at him again. He rearranged the bottles and pulled the buckets under the awning and out of the sun before going back inside.

To keep busy Sam stacked plates and bowls on a wheeled cart, also tucking in a caddy of silverware. On the bottom shelf he added serving utensils, napkins, and a pile of platters. As he was readying to push it all outside he saw Peter Chang standing in the center of the backyard, holding a clutch of strings attached to helium balloons in a rainbow of colors.

Sam opened the glass door and Peter gave him a helpless look. "I can't let go," he said.

Sam laughed. "Yeah, so start tying them to anything."

"Didn't you hear me? I can't let go."

"Where's Frankie?"

"We had to take two cars. Have you ever driven with twenty-four balloons?"

"Why twenty-four?"

Peter shrugged. "Because they sold them in groups of six?" Classic Peter logic. Sam pictured Peter huddled over the steering wheel of his old Honda surrounded by balloons. He took a handful of the balloons and followed Peter around the backyard, freeing him to begin tying them to random chairs, the pool railing, and the fence.

From the driveway someone was lying on a horn. Peter said, "It's probably Mindy. She said they were going to need help with the cake."

Sam and Peter walked around the outside of the house to the

driveway. Mindy was standing at the back of Ruthie's car with the hatchback open. Ruthie was still behind the wheel, but on her phone. She waved to them and continued talking. Celia was in the backseat with a guitar in her lap, soundlessly mouthing words and strumming. She waved too but didn't move to get out. Mindy peered around the car and frowned. She looked pretty close to tears.

When they got to the open trunk Sam saw why Mindy looked upset. The cake was an enormous rectangle, larger than a carry-on suitcase, with a portrait of Suzie and Leo in fluorescent shades of frosting. Suzie's hair was the color of a bad clown wig and the frosting had been whipped and tufted so that it looked as if she had been caught in a windstorm. The top of Leo's head bore a line of frosting buttons in cobalt that gave the appearance of cornrows. The colors reminded Sam of the cake for Suzie's fifteenth birthday, the chunks that had ended up floating in her pool after the food fight that they had missed.

"Holy shit," Peter said. "What the hell is that?"

Mindy looked as if she was about to cry. "I gave them a picture. I said colorful. They said they knew exactly what I wanted. When we went to pick it up . . ." Her bottom lip trembled.

Peter pressed a hand against her lower back and rubbed. "Aw, come on, Mindy. Leo is too little to remember, and Suzie will laugh."

"But I didn't want a funny cake," Mindy wailed as Ruthie got out of the car and slammed the door.

"Okay, the best they will do is offer us some plain ten-inch rounds in exchange. But they want this cake returned." She looked down at the cake and winced as if she were seeing it for the first time. "For fuck's sake, was this done by a blind person?"

Mindy stifled a sob.

Sam said, "Come on, let's lift this out of the car and carry it into the house. It's too hot outside, the frosting will melt."

"That would only help," Peter said under his breath as they bent beneath the hatchback and slid the cake out. It was heavy, like raw cake batter and ten pounds of frosting heavy. They walked haltingly into the garage and through the side door into the kitchen.

Marguerite was standing by the sink when they came in. Her face barely registered a thing as they set the cake down on the table, and she walked over for a look. She had a fantastic poker face.

A quick look outside confirmed that Sam's parents were still on the bench, just as Bella came into the kitchen trailed by Tom. The girls hugged and went over to examine the cake with Bella. Whatever she said had them laughing. Tom leaned against the counter with his arms crossed, and Marguerite sighed. Sam opened the refrigerator and slid out the platters of meat to bring them to room temperature.

"Hey—beer's here," Peter said as he moved toward the glass doors. Sam looked up. Frankie had three cases of beer balanced against his chest. Peter went out and took the top case out of his arms and began breaking it apart and loading the beer into the cooler.

Sam decided to start the grill. Out back, Frankie handed him a beer, and Sam gestured inside. "Give one to Tom."

Marguerite poked her head out the door into the backyard. "Suzie called, said they'd be here in half an hour."

Sam looked over his shoulder at her and smiled. He wished she would come outside, but he knew she didn't want to interrupt his mother and Hunt. Sam had no idea if his father was even able to carry on a conversation. This morning he had decided again that Sam was Michael, even after Sam went upstairs to his room and retrieved the graduation photos off his dresser. Hunt had looked at Sam's photo as if he had never seen him before in his life.

Tom hovered behind Marguerite until Bella, Mindy, and Ruthie pushed past him into the backyard, forcing him to step onto the patio or be run over. From over the top of the opened grill Sam saw his mother raise her hand and gesture for Tom to come join them. When Tom reached them he extended his hand to Sam's father, who pumped it hard, smiling as if he were running for mayor.

"Here, do you need these?" Sam turned around. Marguerite was holding a pair of tongs and a long fork. She was whispering, as if afraid to be caught in her own backyard.

Sam took them and placed them on the table. "You okay?"

She nodded in response but her attention was obviously divided. "The other day I couldn't find him. For over an hour. I drove around the neighborhood and finally went into town. He's never done that before, just walked out of the house."

"Why didn't you call me?" Sam imagined looking out from the restaurant and seeing his father strolling by. He wondered if his father would recognize him then.

Marguerite picked up the tongs and held them up to the light before she set them down. "He was sitting at the bus stop bench on Main Street. He was wearing his slippers and the newspaper was tucked under his arm. When I pulled up he smiled at me and got into the car like he had been waiting for me all that time." She chewed at her lip. "I was so mad and relieved I was crying. I try not to do that in front of him, you know? And he didn't even notice. He told me it was hot and asked if we could stop and pick up some ice cream on the way home."

"Marguerite—"

"Ice cream?" Marguerite paused. "At breakfast he had been so, so clear. He talked about Paradox and going fishing. He wanted you boys to come, and Leo. He wanted to show Leo. A part of him must know, right? That he won't be here, mentally, anyway. But that morning, he was with me completely. I hate it. I hate it so much. I wish he would just lose his mind altogether and be done with it." Her hand flew to her mouth and covered it, as if she could take back what she'd said. "My God, what is wrong with me?"

Sam moved closer to her in an effort to shield her from everyone else. "Marguerite, let's go inside."

"I don't want to go inside, Sam." He backed off; she looked over his shoulder at his father and mother. "What do you think they are talking about?"

"It looks like my mother is doing most of the talking."

She shook her head; her face was red and her eyes watery. "I'm jealous. My God, I'm jealous."

"He loves you, Marguerite. He loves you more than—"

She held her hand up and shook her head. "Don't say that, Sam. Please, don't. He doesn't even know me anymore."

"Yes, he does," Sam said. "He does."

Her chin trembled. It didn't matter what Sam said to her and they both knew it.

"I don't know if we are going to be able to stay here much longer, Sam. I can't watch him all the time. The house suddenly feels so big." She took a deep breath, pressed her fingertips beneath her eyes, and backed away. "Oh my God, I need to get it together. Michael and Suzie are going to be here soon and I can't be like this."

"Go." Sam closed the lid of the grill. He glanced over at his friends lounging at the table by the pool. All around them were the balloons that Peter had tied to the chairs. They shimmered in the heat and floated above their heads.

Celia walked past Sam with her guitar slung across her back. In her arms was a tiny peach-colored kitten. Behind her, Johnny Ross carried an animal carrier and Sam thought he glimpsed the pale pink ears of a rabbit. These must be the extra guests Sam wouldn't have to feed.

Sam went over and stood behind Bella, massaging her shoulders. "You hungry?"

She leaned back in her chair and looked up at him. "Starved. You need help?"

Sam shook his head. The truth was that he just wanted to touch her, to feel her beneath his hands, to know she was there. That was all. That was everything.

Later that afternoon they sang "Happy Birthday" to Leo and Suzie, standing around the cake. Leo, from his perch on Suzie's hip, had already reached down and grabbed two handfuls of Suzie's frosting hair. He had smeared it across his cheeks in an attempt to get his fist into his mouth. Clumps had attached themselves to the tips of Suzie's curls and on each of Michael's shoulders like epaulets.

A watery line of DayGlo orange spittle fell from Leo's chin onto his bib as he squealed in chorus with their voices. Sam's mother stood to his right, clutching Tom's hand and singing loudly. Sarah Epstein stood beside Marguerite, who held the video camera with a shaky hand. Mr. Epstein, a surprise late arrival, stood by the hedges next to the back gate, unwilling to come any closer. There was a red tricycle at his feet with a blue bow attached to the handlebars. Everyone seemed to be aware that he was there, but only Sarah Epstein had raised a hand in greeting.

Frankie, Peter, and Mindy linked arms and kicked a chorus line, while Bella ended up singing their song when Celia forgot the words, and Johnny had to return the animals to their carriers because the cat and the rabbit had an uneasy relationship. Hunt clapped his hands out of time to their singing. He wiggled his fingers at Leo as if they had only just met.

Sam shared a look with Suzie that went on a moment longer than it should have. Sam was thinking about Leo, and maybe Suzie had been too. That if they had not been together on that day she never would have made it to the hospital. Or maybe she had been thinking about that other birthday of hers they had shared, the box of photos and a bed in her basement so many years ago. Would they ever have gotten here without being there first? Sam was doubtful.

They were here now, all of them. Relationships slightly re-arranged, but still together. That was more than any of them would have ever imagined years before. They had watched their parents stumble and vowed never to do the same, only to fail one another in entirely different ways. They experienced love, but they also caused disappointment and sorrow. They felt fear, and they knew loss. They ran away, only to return.

The house sold in two weeks and the new owners wanted a fast closing. The wife was pregnant with their first child, and she hoped to be settled before the baby came.

Marguerite and Sam's father had moved into the condo before the house went on the market. They had taken with them everything that mattered, forcing Marguerite to choose the items she hoped would jog some part of Hunt's brain.

The new place was part of a housing complex where, as Marguerite put it, they let them experience the last stages of life by moving them ahead one room at a time as they ailed, like a macabre board game. Right now, because Marguerite was fully able and living with Sam's father, they resided in a condo that had emergency call buttons in every room. They had day care for Hunt when Marguerite needed a break from trying to think for both of them. When Hunt became further incapacitated they could move to assisted living, with nursing care and meals included, or move just Hunt into a full-care nursing home, all there on the same grounds. Marguerite seemed too young for any of it, but she said there were a lot of women like her, and just a few men, willing to live out whatever days they had left with an incapacitated spouse.

Before the move, it had become painfully obvious that the more Hunt realized something was changing, the more agitated he became. There had been days where he accused Marguerite of leaving him, and others when he had unpacked boxes as fast as Marguerite packed them. He didn't know where he was going, only that he didn't want to go.

On one of the last days he was at the house, Sam's father followed him to the garage. All that morning he had been thumbing through the newspaper, although Michael and the doctors had said Hunt had lost the ability to comprehend written words. Still he sat frowning at the paper, maybe more from memory than anything else.

So it was a surprise when he followed Sam from the house into the garage. The garage was the last big clean-out before closing, and Sam had planned to do it with Michael later in the day. Hunt hadn't been a fix-it guy but he had puttered, a stress reliever after a week spent behind a desk. There hadn't been much from the rest of the house that had any emotional weight—most everything like that had been removed during the renovation—but Sam was somehow sure there were things there, of value to no one but him, that he might want to save.

Hunt stood in the center of the room, staring at the fishing poles that were lined up against the wall and shuffling his suede moccasins back and forth on the cement floor. Sam had already told Marguerite he was bringing the poles up to Paradox to store them at the camp, but he had not gotten around to taking them down yet. He had intended to do it then, but something in the way his father was looking at the poles stopped him.

"Do you fish?" Hunt asked Sam.

"I do. You taught me."

"I did?" Hunt looked pleased. "Of course I did." He put his hands on his hips and leaned over to take a closer look at the poles. "My father taught me."

"No, it was your mother."

Hunt grinned, exposing a flat expanse of puffy, fleshy gum. Michael had told Sam that with dementia, personal hygiene was one of the first things to go. And often Sam heard Marguerite asking Hunt, as if he were a child, if he needed help shaving or brushing his teeth. Now Hunt's eyes crinkled at the corners as he laughed. "That was a trick. I tricked you."

"You did?"

"Yes. I told you my father taught me. I guess you know me after all."

"I do."

"From where did you say?"

Sam swallowed and cleared his throat. "Here. We know each other from the neighborhood."

"I don't fish much anymore."

"I could take you. I know a great place up north."

"No, I don't think so. But you should take the poles. Get some use out of them."

"Are you sure?"

Hunt nodded, distracted, and glanced around the garage as if he was looking for something. "Of course I am." He walked with purpose toward the tool bench, a mess of junk from old Christmas tree stands to coils of extension cords, mouse traps and rusty saws, a broken birdhouse that Sam had built in Boy Scouts, and boxes and boxes of screws, nails, and assorted paraphernalia.

Sam watched his father. His clothes were too big; the khaki pants sagged in the ass despite a woven belt that cinched tight at his waist. He picked up random items from the bench and moved them from one place to another. When he was done he shoved his hands in his pockets and frowned down at the mess.

"Can I help you find something, Dad?"

Hunt spun around quickly, startled by Sam's question. "I thought you left."

"No, still here. Are you looking for anything in particular?"

His father ignored Sam's question, instead turning his back and opening the many drawers underneath the tool bench. They were old and overstuffed, the runners warped and swollen, and he tried but failed to close a drawer all the way before he moved on to the next. When he was done there he stepped back and scratched the top of his head before he lunged for the step stool folded against the wall. But he couldn't figure out how the lever worked and he fumbled around in frustration.

Sam walked over and flipped the lock that held the step stool closed and then set it on level ground. He held on to the handle while his father climbed up the three steps and reached for a box on the shelf above the table. Sam took the box from his father's hands and cleared a place for it on the table.

Hunt stepped down and rubbed his hands together before he flipped back the four corners. He lifted out an old tin box decorated with silver bells. Sam recognized it: his mother had once used it for storing cookies. Hunt wrestled with the rusted lid until it popped open with an exhale of air. Sam watched his father as he pawed through the contents and smiled to himself as he picked out a tangle of fishing lures. He held them out to Sam. "You are going to need these if you take the poles."

"I can have them?"

His father nodded vigorously, tufts of hair flapping against his scalp. "Of course. They go with the poles." He pushed the tin in Sam's direction.

Sam held it carefully in his hands and looked inside. Among the clump of lures was a Christmas ornament Sam had made in the shape of a fish. The word DAD had been spelled out on the body with elbow macaroni, but now only one piece of pasta remained, looking as if it was on its way to dust. Underneath the ornament was a smaller frame made out of Popsicle sticks. In the center Sam had glued a picture of him and Michael standing on top of the sledding hill, an old flexible flyer between them. Sam was no more than five and was making a goofy pose, one hand on his hip, the other flashing a peace sign behind Michael's head. For his part, Michael appeared to be suffering silently, a slight smile on his lips. The photograph had been in color, but now had cured to ocher. Sam actually remembered removing it from the avocado-colored refrigerator where his mother had Scotch-taped the photograph to the door. They had been making presents at school and he had dropped and broken the clay handprint that was to be his gift, so the teacher had suggested he bring a picture from home and she would help him make a substitute gift. How had something so minor lodged in the recesses of his brain?

Sam held the frame out to his father. Hunt took it in his hands, casually running a finger over the photograph. He studied it for a long time before he tried to hand it back to Sam.

Sam waved him away, but his father kept insisting, and now both of their hands were locked on the fragile frame. "You should keep this. I'll just take the lures."

"No, you." Sam's father pushed the frame at him but still didn't let go.

Sam pushed back and his father looked him in the eye. It was a searching look, and Sam hoped for a glimmer of recognition. He held his breath, every muscle and fiber wanting that one moment. His father's mouth was open, his face unshaven. Hair sprouted from his nostrils and ears. "Dad," Sam said gently, "one of us is going to have to let go."

His father tightened his grip on the frame and laughed, as if all along they had only been playing a game. "Dad," Sam ventured, slowly letting go of the frame. "Dad," he tried again, a little more forcefully even though Hunt was staring at the picture and not paying any attention to Sam.

Sam opened his mouth, afraid to let the moment pass without telling his father he loved him, that he wasn't going anywhere, but Hunt spoke first. "My boys," he said, gesturing with the frame toward Sam, "my boys."

Acknowledgments

I am forever indebted to Jeanette Perez, who introduced an early draft of this book to Katherine Nintzel at William Morrow. Kate, wise and wonderful editor, asked all the right questions to get that fledgling baby draft to become *The Grown Ups*. A mention here seems hardly adequate when it comes to my brilliant agent, Carrie Kania. Her unwavering, unquestionable belief in my ability to spin words into stories continues to sustain me. For Greg Olear, exquisite writer and friend, who read the original draft, and then some: I owe you big-time. For the ladies of Beth's Book Group: your support feels like a superpower. For everyone who so tirelessly promoted my last book: You changed my world. For Mom, Dad, Nick, and Holly, much, much love. Finally, for Hannah and Tessa, who make me want to be a better grown up, and for Frank, who still makes me feel like a kid.

Insights,
Interviews
& More . . .

Meet Robin Antalek

Photo by Jill Cowburn

ROBIN ANTALEK is the author of *The Summer We Fell Apart*, chosen as a Target Breakout Book. Her nonfiction work has been published at The Weeklings and The Nervous Breakdown, and collected in the following anthologies: *The Beautiful Anthology*; *Writing Off Script: Writers on the Influence of Cinema*; and *The Weeklings: Revolution #1, Selected Essays 2012–13*. Her short fiction has appeared in 52 Stories, Five Chapters, Sundog, *The Southeast Review*, and Literary Mama, among others. She has twice received honorable mentions in *Glimmer Train* magazine, as well as been a finalist for the Tobias Wolff Award for Fiction. *The Grown Ups* is her second novel. She lives in Saratoga Springs, New York.

You can visit her site at www.robinantalek .com ∾

Reading Group Guide

1. Robin Antalek introduces us to the summer of Suzie Epstein by writing, "It was the summer all the children in the neighborhood caught a virus." Why do you think she begins with this detail? How does the set piece of the virus add to the tension of the summer, and how does it foreshadow the themes of the novel?

2. Why do you think Suzie chose to hurt Sam? Even if she were to tell Sam about his mother and Mr. Epstein, why did she build a relationship with him first, and why did she wait until the day she left to show him the pictures?

3. Why do you think Marguerite and Hunt choose to renovate the family home? Does it go beyond the physical space? What are they trying to achieve?

4. Did you have a group of friends in your life similar to the one Sam had? Did you keep in touch? What pulls people together and pushes them apart over time?

5. On the surface, Sam and Michael are complete opposites. What do you think their most inherent difference is? Do they have anything in common? Who do you think ends up happier?

6. When Sam leaves Bella's apartment, Bella says, "Pretending was nice, wasn't it?" What do you think she's referring to? In their relationship, what is real and what is pretend?

7. When Suzie and Michael get engaged, Bella says that she is happy but that she doesn't "quite feel there." What does she mean by this?

8. Sam says that he is going to tell his father he is flunking out of school, but instead Sam goes to see his mother in Vermont. Why is it so important for him to see her at that moment in his life?

9. Of Suzie, Sam says, "I loved her only if love was all about getting to the next base." Do you think this is true? Is a fifteen-year-old capable of love, and is that what Sam felt? ▶

Reading Group Guide *(continued)*

10. Each of the characters experiences personal tragedy. How does their tragedy shape each of them?

11. The concept of being "grown up" is a recurring motif in the novel. How does each of the main characters define this differently?

Just for Fun: Playlists for *The Grown Ups*

WHEN I WRITE, if I'm really lucky, I'm really just transcribing this big movie in my head that unrolls and plays on a loop until I put it on paper. That's the only way I can describe what happens when I've really fallen into the story with a group of characters all clamoring to be heard. The songs I picked for Sam, Suzie, and Bella map out their emotional territory—and add to the their lives as only a great soundtrack can enhance a movie and sweep you right back into the moment.

Sam Turner

Lenny Bruce, the Historic 1962 Concert When
    Lenny Was Busted
West Side Story, Original Cast Soundtrack
Mr. Ed: Straight from the Horse's Mouth,
    Mike Stewart and The Stable Hands
At fifteen Sam's world is his friends and not much else. A lot of his free time is spent in the basement of his friend Peter Chang's house, where the boys hang to play video games, get drunk, and listen to a few albums belonging to Peter Chang's mother on an old-school stereo cabinet. The diversity of these albums is absurd, but that's half the fun.

"Your Body Is a Wonderland," John Mayer
Sam and Suzie Epstein do some exploring in her basement at fifteen, and later, Sam and Bella Spade begin a relationship while seniors in high school. Sam's desire for Bella combined with a refusal to define their relationship leaves them loosely attached through the next few years.

"My Father's House," Bruce Springsteen
Sam's father falls in love with Marguerite, and they embark on a massive renovation of Sam's childhood home. During this time Sam's father, Hunt, suffers a massive coronary and needs emergency surgery.

"You Can't Always Get What You Want,"
    The Rolling Stones
"You're Gonna Miss Me," 13th Floor Elevators
Sam's brother, Michael, is dating Suzie Epstein, Sam's first crush. It doesn't help that in Sam's eyes Michael always seems to get what he wants. These ▶

two songs encapsulate Sam's feelings from the time he finds out they are dating right up through their engagement and wedding.

"All Day and All of the Night," The Kinks
"Till the End of the Day," The Kinks
Drifting from job to job, in a perpetual state of dissatisfaction, Sam takes Peter Chang up on the offer of a week out on the Cape with their friends. To his dismay Bella arrives with her boyfriend, Ted. It's during this trip that Sam eventually concedes that Bella is his one true love. So he pines his way through the week. The pounding punk tunes of the Kinks seem just about right for the chaos that is the state of Sam's brain.

"The Weight," The Band
With its religious allusions to Nazareth, and the offer to "take a load off," this song seems just about right for Sam, who leaves yet another job, retreats to his childhood home again, adrift, tries to reconcile his less than stellar life so far to that of his cardiologist brother, only to discover that home is not what it used to be. His father is struggling. Sam's attempts to explain his feelings to Bella are rebuffed. Some serious soul-searching is going on here.

"Come As You Are," Nirvana
This message of acceptance should be Sam's anthem by the time he figures it all out. His opening of a restaurant coincides with the birth of Suzie and Michael's son, Leo.

"Feels Like the First Time," Foreigner
This is a fairly corny song, but it's one of those recognizable rock anthems that work. If you've traveled with Sam down his winding path to figuring it all out, this song makes a lot of sense by the end of the book.

Suzie Epstein

"Pictures of You," The Cure
Suzie's discovery of her father's shoebox of pictures is the catalyst that sets the summer of 1997 in motion and plays a role in linking this group of friends forever.

"Losing My Religion," R.E.M.
There are multiple layers of meaning here for Suzie. It's confessional, it's about pining for someone, and it's about losing that last tip of civility. Leaving her friends, moving with her family to "start over" even though the new beginning was doomed, losing her virginity, losing her identity. This song is all tied up in what was happening to Suzie Epstein in the years immediately following the discovery of those photographs.

"Wonderwall," Oasis
Suzie is as surprised as anyone when she falls in love with Sam's brother, Michael. She has been on her own for so long, taking care of it all for everyone, that it takes a while for her to understand that Michael is really there for her. It's not until she begins to trust him that she would ever allow herself the idea of being saved from herself.

"Just a Girl," No Doubt
This Gwen Stefani punk girl anthem seemed to embody the meaning of the burden of femininity that Suzie had pushed against for years. Giving Suzie this song when everything is right—med school, fiancé, friends, a generally fulfilled life—seems like less a fight song and more of a "look how far I've come" song.

"Back to Black," Amy Winehouse
Despite everything, Suzie struggles to have a relationship with her mother, Sarah. Ultimately, every interaction leads them in a circle.

"Cry Baby," Janis Joplin
Suzie is struggling to cope with her first miscarriage, a demanding medical residency, and her relationships with her husband, Bella, and her mother. That raw scrape of Janis Joplin's vocal chords as she wails *Cry baby, cry baby, cry* is the opposite of what Suzie allows herself, but what she desperately needs.

"The Drugs Don't Work," The Verve
After Suzie suffers several miscarriages in an eighteen-month period, her relationship with Michael nearly collapses.

"Happy Together," The Turtles
This song is a sweet retro kind of love song that perfectly captures the bliss Suzie feels when she and Michael finally have their baby boy, Leo.

Bella Spade

"Summertime," Billie Holiday
Nostalgia fuels Bella's early years—mostly because she has never known a time where her mother hasn't been sick. She pieces together the before from her mother's journals and photographs. She's also a dreamy kind of girl, expressing herself in writing that she isn't bold enough to share even though she longs for an intellectual and artistic life. The summer before she moves on to Vassar is life altering in many ways, and the languid mellow tones of Billie Holiday's "Summertime" capture this moment in Bella's life perfectly.

"Don't Forget Me," *"Pussy Cats" Starring the Walkmen*
Bella's mother dies during her junior year of college. Her best friend, Suzie Epstein, reappears in her life at her mother's funeral, and Sam leaves her without explanation. This song speaks to all of Bella's fears and so much more.

"Time After Time," Cyndi Lauper
Bella's gradual acceptance of Sam's disappearance is made easier somehow by Suzie's reappearance in her life. The catch is that Suzie is in a relationship with Michael, Sam's brother, and that makes forgetting Sam completely just a little bit harder.

"Bohemian Like You," The Dandy Warhols
Bella attends grad school at the prestigious Iowa City writers program, where she meets Ted, a fellow in poetry. They begin an intense affair and Bella, totally ▶

captivated, moves to a rustic cabin Ted has built in Montana without running water or electricity. With Ted by her side, Bella believes she has finally fulfilled her destiny of being a true artist unaffected by the material world. Unfortunately, she's not writing at all.

"Miss You," The Rolling Stones
Suzie and Michael get married. Bella attends with Ted. They are still living in Montana, but for Bella, economic necessity and maybe a lack of inspiration intrude, as well as the realization that she misses her friends and family and even running water. There is nothing romantic about outhouses. She takes a job back at the Iowa City workshop filling in for a teacher, and that job leads to an interview in New York City at Hunter College. Despite Ted's very vocal objection, he moves with her to New York.

"I Can't Make You Love Me," Bonnie Raitt
The relationship between Ted and Bella is cracking—despite everything—and after almost three years, they split up. Bella returns home for Thanksgiving with the story that Ted is on a writer's retreat.

"Sleeping Lessons," The Shins
Sam offers his heart to Bella over breakfast in the same diner where they spent a significant amount of time during high school. Still reeling from her breakup with Ted and Sam's sudden commitment to loving her, Bella rejects him and retreats.

"That Old Feeling," Frank Sinatra
Months after his confession, Sam arrives at Bella's doorstep in the middle of the night—and this lovely old song just *says it all* about how she feels about Sam.

Excerpt from *The Summer We Fell Apart*

THE SUMMER we took in a boarder my mother
started wearing headscarves. They were adorned
with elaborate patterns and colors as if a fistful of
crayons had melted on her head. Often she wore
more than one at a time twisted around each other
and tied low at the nape of her neck so a plume of
silk cascaded down her back. The scarves swayed
from side to side as she walked, like the dragons in
the New Year's Parade in Chinatown. They were so
odd an affectation that it prompted our boarder,
Miriam, to ask me if my mother was sick.

Miriam was from Switzerland and spoke
French, with only a minimum of English, so she
pronounced the word *sick* as *seeeck* and it took
me a few moments to understand what she was
asking. I was left to shrug and roll my eyes as if
to say: Parents? Who can explain them? Truth
was I had no explanation for the scarves, although
I guessed they were probably a result of my mother
getting home late from the theater with mussed
up, dirty hair. She was in a play in New York that
required her to wear a wig—some depressing
Bertolt Brecht thing. My mother was excited about
it because she thought it lent her credibility as an
actor. My brother George and I had used her comp
opening-night tickets not so much to see our
mother as to see the stage debut of a TV actor
George thought was hot.

So the weird headscarf affectation could be
explained like this: by the time the car she'd hired
brought her back from the city to our house in
Nyack it was close to dawn. My mother was vain
and, frankly, uninterested in the mundane lives
of her last teenage children—she was done—*fini*,
as the French say—but I didn't know how that
would translate, so I gave Miriam the universal
shrug. I could tell from the expression on her
face that she wanted more than I could give.

I'd caught Miriam more than once studying
the dusty family photos that lined the halls of
our house and ran up the steps like crooked teeth—
her face up so close to some of the old black-and-
whites that shreds of cobwebs clung to her chin
and nose. In pictures I can see we translate well
and so I understand her fascination. Our parents ▶

back then were often together, smiling wide, showing all their teeth, and holding cocktails or being hugged by someone famous (if only in their obscure theater circles). The rest of us—we are four in all—looking mildly amused or bored in all the pictures, even when we were babies.

Miriam had not met the rest of us yet since it was only George and me still at home. Miriam occupied Finn's old room with the crew paddles and lacrosse sticks hanging on the wall. Being the only female in the house besides my mother (who was most definitely not participating in the Miriam project), I was the one to get Miriam's room ready and I chose Finn's room because his has a little bathroom tucked under the attic stairs. When I was turning the mattress to freshen it, I found several *Penthouse* magazines and, tucked between the appropriately suggestive pages, love letters from an old girlfriend, Holly, along with an ancient crinkled condom pack.

I pocketed the condom (wishful thinking—I was going to college a virgin) and threw away the magazines, but I kept the love letters. I planned to surprise Finn with them when he came back from Europe at the end of the month.

Finn was off on a backpacking trip with our father and at some point they were supposed to meet up with my older sister, Kate, who lives in Florence and teaches English. Finn was the only sibling actually *invited* to join our father. George suspected Finn was asked because he is the true coward among us and will not question our father on why he has abandoned our family.

When George says things like that, I feel bad that Miriam seems to be idolizing us—at least the "us" in pictures. Our father is responsible for Miriam's presence in our house, which explains everything and nothing. All we know is that she is an exchange student for the year without a place to stay. She would be attending high school with me for senior year. I had no idea my father even knew such a thing as an exchange existed, let alone a single person in town who would even consider allowing my family to take someone in. I thought the whole concept of exchange involved another student participating in the exchange, but in Miriam's case that didn't seem to apply.

Miriam showed up on our doorstep the day our father's bags appeared in the front hallway. Their luggage commingled for a few hours while George (who frequently took our mother's side—because it seemed there was always a side to take) scowled at Miriam from the top landing, vowing to have nothing to do with her (lucky for Miriam his vows usually last all of five minutes), and I destroyed the French language in an attempt at conversation. Our father was, as usual, absent. Our mother was hiding on purpose in her room with the door bolted. I could smell the cigarette smoke from downstairs and I pictured her in her bed, the curtains against the early August heat. She would be smoking furiously, lighting the next cigarette off the last, all the while blinking and applying eyedrops (while she tried not to light her hair on fire) because her eyes watered from the gray cloud above her bed. The day would be no different from the others just because Miriam had arrived. My mother would only rise to shower and emerge from her room moments before the car came to take her into the city. This is why I know more about Miriam than anyone in the house. She puts double the amount of coffee and half the amount of water in the pot so the coffee is deep and thick and bitter. She prefers baths to showers—when she takes them—and she often wears the same skirt several days in a row, although she always changes her blouse. She eats bread and jam and cheese in her room or standing up at the kitchen sink. Sometimes she cuts the cheese with a knife and fork. She dislikes tomatoes and eggs. She carries an old-fashioned floral handkerchief in her pocket and adores television. I have found her several times sitting in the middle of the den transfixed by the small black-and-white my siblings have long derided because everyone we know has large color televisions where you can identify the actors without the aid of a magnifying glass. Miriam actually cleared off the accumulated detritus we'd neglected so that she could have an unobstructed view of the minuscule screen. Although I had no idea what to think about her viewing choices of the sitcoms—*Roseanne*, *Murphy Brown*, *Home Improvement*, and *Cheers*—it must have given her glimpses of American life that she wasn't experiencing by living with us. After several weeks at our house she surely must have figured out that no television show could accurately portray her existence in our world.

Since I was desperately searching for a way not to be me, studying Miriam became my secret hobby. As soon as I saw her leaning against the newel post in my front hall I'd wished I'd been born a mysterious European. I was tired of being the smart, creative, yet totally nondescript Amy. I was tired of those trite adjectives, period. The night before Miriam arrived, George and I held a bonfire fueled by the journals of my adolescent longings. I'd burned everything because I was sure this would be my last summer at home and I didn't want to take a chance that one of my siblings would take them and use them as fodder for yet another familial drama.

My guidance counselor had assured me I was smart enough to get into college and probably would get a scholarship to pay for some of it. I think he took pity on me—he had seen all of my siblings through this school, guided them all to college despite the apathy my parents displayed. I mean it was seriously all they could do to sign off on the applications. The guy deserved a medal. Before college I planned to spend my last summer traveling—even if I had to earn the money by working the arts-and-crafts table at the after-school camp for overindulged five-year-olds again all year long.

George fought with me over burning my journals—said one day I might want to write a book about our family. He was joking, I could tell. George was just a packrat. Burning the journals didn't bother me. If an occasion ever arose for me to pen my memoirs I was positive my childhood would never, ever leave me.

My summer job consisted of scooping ice cream and making milkshakes at the dairy shack late afternoons and evenings. Usually I spent the time before work sleeping, then fooling around with some fabric or paint, maybe a book (George and I had just gone to the library and the pile between us included: *American Psycho*, *Shampoo Planet*, *The Kitchen God's Wife*, and *How the Garcia Girls Lost Their Accent*), but this August was different. Now in the mornings I led Miriam to the swimming hole at the very back edge of our property. It was actually more than a hole, but that's how our father always referred to it back when he enjoyed playing the role of country dad. Going swimming meant a hike through waist-high weeds and prickly vines all the while swatting away mosquitoes and no-see-ums, but Miriam seemed to take it in stride. The yard and surrounding property, like the house and its inhabitants, were simply worn-out from years of neglect. I liked to imagine that when my parents had purchased this odd crooked house twenty-five years ago they had the best intentions for their young family—when in truth its purchase had been a recommendation from an accountant during a particularly flush period for my father. ▶

Excerpt from *The Summer We Fell Apart* (continued)

Once we got to the water, Miriam stripped down to her underwear and sunbathed topless. Her breasts were small although almost completely overtaken by large brown nipples. Under her arms were thick tufts of dark hair—at odds, it seemed, with her pale pink skin. On the middle toe of her left foot she wore a silver ring. I tried to look sophisticated in my one-piece black Speedo as I spread out on the blanket next to Miriam—but I failed miserably and ended up spending most of the time picking at the suit and redistributing the spandex around my midsection. All I could think was that facing my senior year of high school with Miriam, who was so comfortable in her skin, could only mean I had less of a chance with guys than I currently had.

On the days George joined us I expected Miriam to attempt to cover up, but she barely paid any attention to him except for when he dove into the water. George had been on the swim team all four years of high school. He was tall and thin with broad shoulders and a flat stomach and, with the exception of his time spent in the water, was extremely clumsy. Actually, much to the disdain of my parents, who had assumed their children, like them, would have a penchant for the arts (my collages and fabric creatures were not exactly the Great White Artistic Hope my parents might have dreamed about), all of my siblings excelled in one sport or another. Besides swimming for George, there was crew and lacrosse for Finn. Like my sister, Kate, I was a runner, although I only ran when I was feeling puffy and I exhibited no extraordinary athletic prowess and refused to join the track team as Kate had. I'd say my parents got exactly what they deserved by choosing to live in a small town that, despite its "artsy" reputation and access to New York City, was just like any other cookie-cutter suburb across the country.

When George climbed up to the highest ledge and performed an elegant swan dive—his body sluicing into the water like a knife, barely disturbing the surface—Miriam propped herself up on her elbows and nodded approvingly. "Beautiful," she whispered under her breath. "The boy can fly."

I nodded and was horrified to find water leaking from my eyes down onto my cheeks. George would be leaving for college in New Hampshire at the end of the month and I didn't know what I was going to do without him. There wasn't a moment of my life that I had ever been without George. As family lore goes, my first steps were not to my mother or father but to George. From the ages of three to five I slept curled against him in his twin bed because I was afraid of the monster in my closet. I would have stayed there forever had George not convinced me that he had erected a supersecret monster-detection system in my room that would keep me safe at all times. Miriam reached over and patted me on the thigh—an odd grandmotherly gesture—but she didn't say anything; she was still concentrating on watching George dive.

I closed my eyes and lifted my face to the sun; the dried tears left my skin with a tight feeling high across the cheekbones by the time George got out of the water and came over to us, shaking off like a wet dog.

With my eyes still closed, I lifted my leg to kick George away from me—the water in the pond was spring-fed and felt like pinpricks of ice. I always waited until the last minute to get wet; I had to be uncomfortably baked before I could be coaxed into the water. George laughed and then dropped down on the other side of Miriam. I knew this because she rolled closer to me to give him more room on the blanket. A few minutes passed in which I could only hear the sound of George's huff-like breathing and Miriam swatting away flies; then Miriam broke the silence.

"Teach me to do that, George?"

"Huh?" It sounded like more of an exhale than George actually answering.

"To dive," Miriam explained. "To fly."

So far I had seen Miriam venture into the water only twice, and each time she did that tiptoe wading-in thing people do when the water is too cold. With her stomach sucked in and her nipples hard and pointy, she patted at the water with flat palms. I can't even remember if she actually swam.

George seemed to be reading my mind because he said, "Do you swim?"

Miriam laughed. "Of course! Do you think I want to perish?" I was still mulling over her choice of the word *perish* for *die* when I heard George say, "Okay then— let's go."

Miriam hopped up. I opened my eyes and looked at George. He was scrutinizing Miriam and scratching his head. I could tell he knew I was looking at him and that he was purposely avoiding my glare. I never jumped off the ledge. When George first joined the diving team, I couldn't even look at him up there on the board. My palms went sweaty and I felt lightheaded. It had taken years for me to get used to watching George bouncing up and down on the edge of a thirty-foot-high rectangle. Now Miriam was diving? We—I—didn't even know the details of Miriam's exchange. Like who to call in case of an emergency. I only knew how she liked her coffee and what she ate.

She scrambled ahead of George to the rocks and then waited for him to catch up. Along the way he stubbed his toe and skipped around as he cursed in pain. Miriam made appropriate murmuring sounds, a little cluck in the back of her throat. She looked down at his foot when he made it over to her but he shook his head and brushed her off although I could tell he was pleased. George could be a drama queen.

George took the lead—only climbing to the lower ledge that was about four feet above the water. I couldn't even describe this as safer. Miriam stood beside him, peering down into the water as George pointed out the flat sheaf of shale rock to the right that she would want to avoid as she threw herself over the edge. That would be from experience. At one time or another that rock had sheared the skin off every one of my siblings, but not me. And that was not out of prowess—just avoidance. I never dove and in my seventeen years I have heard every word there is to describe my cowardice.

Miriam placed her arms over her head with her palms together, like a beginner ballet student, except her legs were together and her feet pointed out. Without waiting for George to correct her she toddled toward the edge and jumped off. I winced as she hit the water belly-first.

When she came up, she was laughing, although her chest and neck were red from either the cold or the impact or both. She looked at me and waved and I waved back, hoping the pain would dissuade her from any more diving. George stood with his hands on his slender hips—his bathing suit hung dangerously low—and shook his head from side to side.

She yelled up from the water, "Show me, George."

And George, as effortlessly as breathing, made a graceful arc into the water. Miriam waited for him to surface and when he did, she held up her arms in the victory position.

They continued like this for what must have been another hour because I dozed off and when I woke and checked my watch, I had less than thirty minutes to get ▶

to work. Before I left, Miriam insisted I watch her dive again. Her form had improved (or maybe *changed* was a better word) so that while she no longer looked like a demented ballerina, she now looked like someone with scoliosis.

George and Miriam's diving lessons continued for the rest of the week. The weather had turned oppressively hot, so much so that even the water felt tepid. When we weren't in the water and I wasn't working, we snuck into the movie theater in town. The back door faced an alley and a boy who had an unrequited crush on George propped open the door for us on the nights he worked. It didn't matter what was playing, because the theater had air-conditioning. We'd eat cheese sandwiches on thick sourdough bread, which Miriam made us, washed down with a huge Coke and some rum that George always provided. For dessert I contributed broken pieces of chocolate-dipped waffle cone that were free for the taking from work.

Sitting like that in the dark with George reminded me of all the hours we'd spent as kids in one theater after another while our parents rehearsed plays. Rehearsing really was a euphemism because in reality my parents spent more time fighting over lines, or fighting over actors or actresses that one accused the other of being attracted to. Not that we always understood it at the time—we only went to the theater when someone forgot to call the sitter and all of the older kids had plans.

By the time I was born my father's career had peaked. Years before he had written a play (about a large dysfunctional family, go figure) that had made it to Broadway and ran for nearly three years, winning several Tonys, including one for my dad, only to follow it up with four more plays that closed after five months, three months, six weeks, and the worst—opening night. That last, particularly painful failure happened the day of my fifth birthday. A day my father hasn't commemorated in twelve years unless you count him locking himself in his study to drink an entire bottle of Jack Daniel's.

After that, the offers were few and far between and so he took to the road, where obscure small towns filled with would-be theater-goers afraid to venture to the big city were more receptive to his work, and he reveled in their attentions, reluctant to relinquish the spotlight.

But an odd thing happened during that time. My mother's career mysteriously revived after she took a role as a crazy innkeeper in one of those stupid teen slasher movies that (surprise, surprise) made millions of dollars and my mother a "cult" actress. She wasn't quite in the John Waters league of quirky, but she was getting there. All of a sudden she was the one fielding offers and leaving for months at a time. And that was when my dad unexpectedly took a position as head of the theater department at Skidmore College in Saratoga Springs—about three hours north of where we lived. It meant he was gone, living in some rented room four, usually five, out of the seven days of the week. We were never invited to visit and we never asked. In terms of parental guidance, George and I may as well have been raised by wolves.

On Sunday evening, after we'd sat through a double creature feature of *Halloween* and *Nightmare on Elm Street*, it was close to midnight and still 95 degrees according to the digital time-and-temperature clock on the bank across the street from the theater on Main Street. George suggested swimming. Too lazy to go into the house, we cut through the now well-trodden path to the pond and stripped down to our underwear.

Well, I did, anyway. George and Miriam pranced like naked toddlers to the water while I, despite my rum buzz, felt like their maiden aunt standing in my bra and panties.

When George yelled, "Take it off, for Christ's sakes, Amy, and get in," I shivered but managed to undo my bra and toss it onto the ground along with my underpants as soon as they both disappeared underwater.

The water over my bare skin was . . . indescribable. How could a barrier of Lycra make such a difference in how it felt to swim unencumbered? This was nearly as delicious as the technique I'd perfected in the bath (with the door double-locked) involving the faucets turned on full blast. Almost.

I went under and opened my eyes. Through the cloudy haze of moonlight that spilled through the trees I could make out a flash of leg in front of me. I swam toward it only to have it disappear. When I popped up to the surface, it took me a moment to find George and Miriam. They were standing on the lower ledge, Miriam poised to dive first.

I was sober enough to think "be careful" but not enough to yell out to her. I'd noticed the raw skin and accumulation of deep scratches along her arms and legs from the rock. I'd insisted she put salve on some of the worst and then I had to help her apply it because she couldn't reach them. Her diving had not improved much in a week and so she hit the water with another grand belly flop. When she surfaced, she swam over to where I was treading water and we both turned to watch George dive.

"Goddamn! I haven't seen such a pathetic excuse for manhood in a long time!"

I spun around. The voice came from the bank and belonged to our brother, Finn. George flipped him the bird and laughed as I called out, "Finn?"

He didn't answer. Just stripped off his clothes and climbed up to meet George. They fake-tussled for a moment—their strong limbs and smooth torsos entangled and made paler than they were by the moonlight—before they fell into the water still holding on to each other.

I swam over to them and then was pulled underneath by a tug on my leg. I hadn't had time to take a breath and I fought harder than usual, kicking someone in the groin; with my toes I felt the curl of pubic hair and tuberous flesh and I instantly recoiled. Growing up with brothers was like living inside a boys' locker room and I was used to seeing (and smelling) a lot, but physical contact was another thing. It wasn't until I came up gagging, my throat and nose burning from inhaled water, that I realized what I'd done.

"Nice to see you too," Finn said, although through his scowl I could tell he wasn't that hurt.

"What the hell are you doing home?" George asked as he filled his mouth with water and spit it at Finn, barely missing his left ear. "It's not the end of August yet, is it?"

Finn shook his head and said without explanation, "I felt like cutting it short."

"Did Dad come with you?" I asked.

"Nope." Finn looked past me to Miriam.

I turned and motioned for her to join us. "Miriam, this is our brother Finn."

Miriam swam closer. "Finn," she said demurely, "hello."

I turned to Finn, "Finn, Miriam."

He flicked water at George before he said, "I know who she is." I looked at Finn and made a face like "don't be a rude shit," but he didn't get it. He oozed charm without trying, even when he was being a jerk. In that instant it struck me that Finn reminded me a lot of our father. He continued to ignore my pointed stare. Instead ▶

Excerpt from *The Summer We Fell Apart*
(*continued*)

he shouted to George, "Race you to the high ledge." And they were off.

"Weird," I said out loud more to myself than Miriam. I had never known Finn to miss an opportunity to impress a girl. Or maybe this was all part of his game. Who knew?

"Weed?" Miriam repeated incorrectly in an attempt to understand the word. She mispronounced it a few more times but I ignored her; I didn't feel like playing translator right now. She gave up and dipped her head back so her face was level with the water. Her hair fanned out around her like seaweed.

I was getting tired of treading water so I swam over to where I could stand on a rock. The water lapped over my breasts as they floated on top of the surface and I folded my arms in an attempt at modesty. Miriam didn't follow me. She was watching my brothers clown around on the high ledge, probably still pondering the meaning of the word *weird*. Let's see, what examples could I give her that she would understand? My life, her presence in our house, or my brothers up on that ledge? George hung back while Finn hot-dogged it, one set of toes curled around rock, his calf muscles taut, while he dangled the other leg over the side like he was going to fall. His arms made windmills while from his mouth came a *whoop-whoop-whooping* sound.

When Finn did finally dive, it was expert but not as elegant as George. I couldn't see the expression on Miriam's face but she clapped. Finn stayed in the water near Miriam and shouted insults to George until he jumped in—a major cannonball that drenched us all. I waited until the water cleared and George and Finn climbed back up on the ledge and then I said good-night to Miriam.

Her mouth turned down into a little pout but she didn't try and stop me from leaving. On the bank I skipped over my bra and underwear entirely and pulled on my T-shirt and shorts as fast as I could. I took a quick look back and felt a little guilty. Finn and George were ignoring Miriam, although either she didn't mind or didn't notice. I hesitated a second and then fatigue settled on me like King Kong himself and I dragged myself back to the house, dropped into bed in my wet clothes, and fell into a hard dreamless sleep. ∾

Discover great authors, exclusive offers, and more at hc.com.